Cinnamon Rolls & Villainy

Chanté A. Campbell

ISBN:

Paperback: 978-1-7353764-5-5

Hardback: 978-1-7353764-6-2

eBook: 978-1-7353764-9-3

Published by Fearless Lit

Interior design Chanté A. Campbell

Cover design by JV Arts / Title Art by Giulia_fw.arts

*Honestly, I wrote this one for **me**.*

But if you, like me, grew up wishing you could
***do** the rescuing instead of **being** rescued,*
always fell for the losing side of the love triangle,
*have been made the **villain** for standing up for what's right*
(mean gxrls of booktok, I see you)
or are a bit too queer, too neurodivergent,
*or too recklessly **YOU** to see yourself*
reflected in most characters in fantasy books
—well, dear reader, then
THIS BOOK IS FOR <u>YOU</u>, TOO.

AUTHOR'S NOTE

Fantasy can be an escape, sure, but that is not this book.

At times, this book is silly to the point of ridiculousness, but at others, it explores themes of religious trauma, misogyny, and the roles we personally play to enable injustice and oppression. It depicts queer, neurodivergent, and disabled characters who find joy within themselves and are celebrated for who they are by the people who love them, but also who face prejudice from people who refuse to accept them. It is my intention—as a queer, neurodivergent author who struggles with chronic pain—that this story ultimately make readers feel seen. However, please review the list of triggers included in this section carefully to determine if this book is right for you. There is no harm in putting this down and walking away. There are dozens of other books worthy of your time and attention. Protect your peace and your mental health; they are worth fighting for.

If you are a reader who likes to know the pronunciation of character names before you begin (same, friend), I have included that here as well. If you do better hearing instead of reading, a video of myself pronouncing these words can be found on my website under the 'Cinnamon Rolls and Villainy' heading. The website information can be found in the 'About the Author' section at the very end of this book.

Lastly, my early readers have told me it is necessary to include the following disclaimer:

WARNING: THIS BOOK MAY RESULT IN UGLY CRYING, THE DESIRE TO THROW THE BOOK/E-READER AGAINST THE WALL, NEEDING TO CALL YOUR THERAPIST, OR THE OVER-CONSUMPTION OF CINNAMON ROLLS OR OTHER DELICIOUS BAKED THINGS DEPICTED WITHIN THIS BOOK. THIS AUTHOR CAN'T BE HELD RESPONSIBLE FOR THE IMPACTS ON YOUR WALLET, YOUR EMOTIONAL WELL-BEING... OR YOUR WAISTLINE. (BUT YOU SHOULD TOTALLY EAT THAT CINNAMON ROLL).

TRIGGER/CONTENT WARNINGS:
(Warning: mild spoilers)

This book contains **depictions of Christain-esque religion,** including **abuse by religious leaders, discussions of religion** (both positive and negative) and **religious trauma.** Within this context there are instances of **transphobia** (including one incidence of dead-naming and forceful outing), **homophobia, misogyny, patriarchy, gender essentialism,** and **purity culture.** These ideas are mostly held by the villains of the story and blatantly challenged.

Throughout the story, there are depictions of the **mistreatment of women and children,** including forced arranged marriage, domestic violence, physical abuse (such as slapping), emotional neglect (emotional unavailable parents, absentee father), brief and mild childhood torture, childhood isolation/imprisonment, bullying, childhood trauma, and mentions of enslavement/child slavery. There is one very brief implication that a character may have been sexually assaulted.

The world is this book is rich with diversity and various races (human, fae, dwarves, etc). At times, certain hateful characters hold **prejudice** and **racist** ideas about these races. For example, humans may be seen as weaker or lesser than fae. These concepts do not go unchallenged.

Most of the main characters have various **disabilities** and **struggles with mental health**, including chronic pain, use of mobility aids, visual impairment, neurodivergence, mutism, anxiety, depression, panic attacks, and brief mentions of suicidal ideations. These are positive descriptions of characters who exist with these challenges; however, at times they do face **ableism** and **resource denial**. In addition, there are depictions of **physical illness**, including vomiting, seizures, body fluids, and scenes within a medical setting.

There are multiple scenes of **graphic violence**, including blood, battle scenes, hate crime, murder, scarring, near drowning, mass death, war, torture, and acts of cruelty.

The book contains **explicit scenes** of **consensual sex** (including penetrative sex, manual and oral stimulation, and knife play). There are multiple scenes of **alcohol use/consumption** and **drunkenness**.

This book underwent sensitivity reading, including by a diverse pool of beta readers and the hiring of a professional sensitivity reader. All efforts were taken to ensure this book is sensitive to the readers. However, if you believe this list is incomplete or if you believe anything within the books may be harmful to a vulnerable community, please email me. Contact information can be found in the 'About the Author' section.

PRONUNCIATION GUIDE

- Ayc - like "Ace"
- Loraphne - Lor-af-nee (rhymes with daphne)
- Xylie - Zi-lee (rhymes with Kylie)
- Bronwen - Brahn-when
- Peregrin - Pair-a- grin
- Tavish - Tav-ish
- Yris - I-ris
- Fennix - FIN-nix
- Onanna - Oh-nahn-nuh
- Marcellus - Mar-cell-us
- Hellevi - Hel-luh-vee
- Lahlis - Law-less

(For a more complete list of names and places, please see the video mentioned previously)

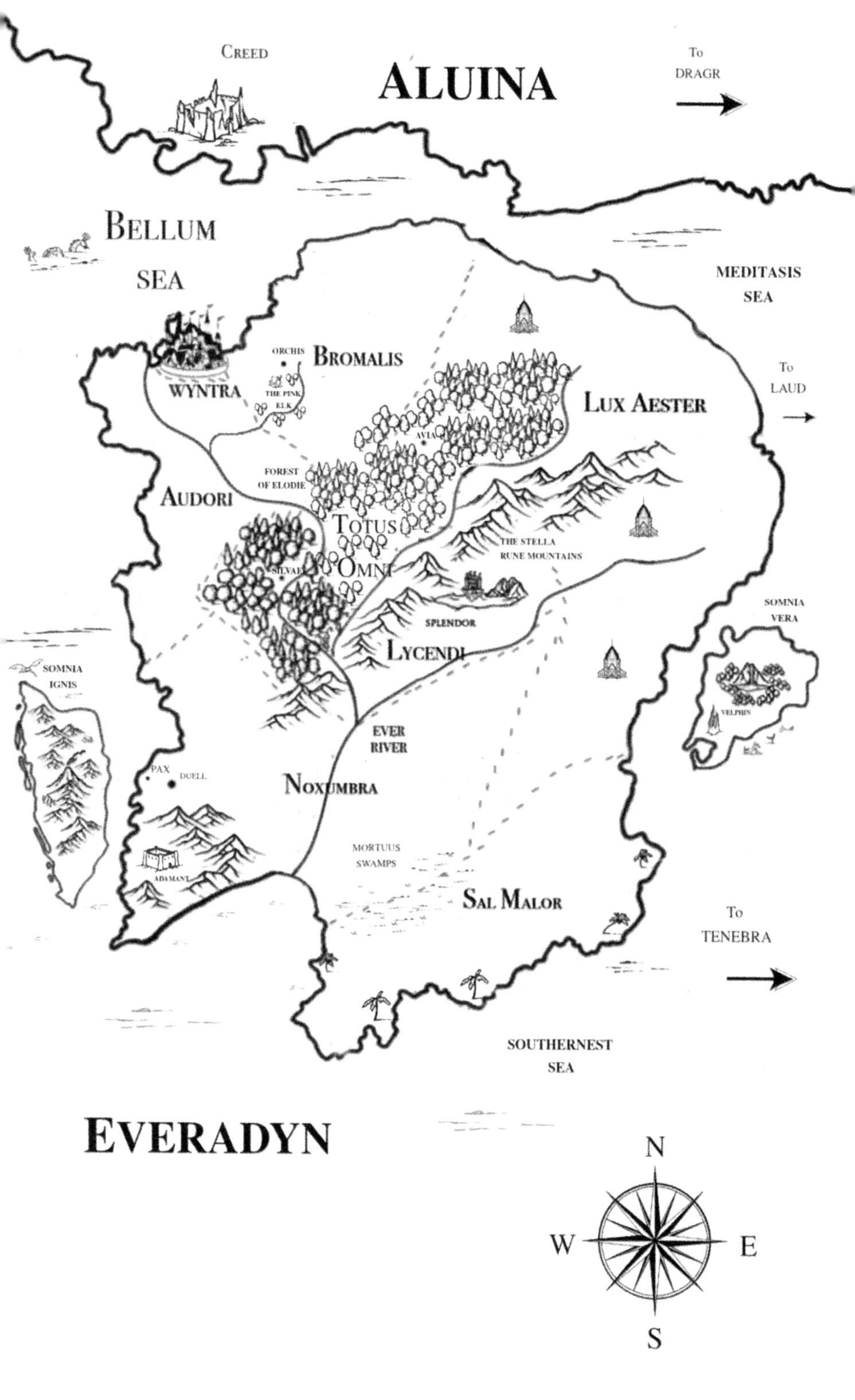

ALUINA

CREED

To DRAGR

BELLUM SEA

WYNTRA

ORCHIS
THE PINK ELK
BROMALIS

MEDITASIS SEA

To LAUD

LUX AESTER

AUDORI

FOREST OF ELODIE

AVIA

TOTUS OMNI

SILVAE

THE STELLA RUNE MOUNTAINS

SOMNIA VERA

SOMNIA IGNIS

SPLENDOR

LYCENDI

VELPHIN

EVER RIVER

PAX
DUELL

NOXUMBRA

ADAMANT

MORTUUS SWAMPS

SAL MALOR

To TENEBRA

SOUTHERNEST SEA

EVERADYN

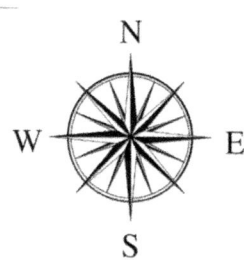

CHAPTER
ONE

I f Ayc Waylonder wasn't so damn good at making cinnamon rolls, he's certain the Sovereign of the Everadyn fae would have slit his throat a decade ago. Well, that, and she believes that killing a divina will curse all seven clans of her people with three generations of bad luck. But considering the magical gift the divine supposedly gave him seems rather useless, Ayc believes it's mostly just the cinnamon roll thing.

Even now, the Sovereign pins him with a look that declares that, if Ayc makes one wrong move, then curses and cinnamon rolls can be damned. She'll end him once and for all, right in front of the dozens gathered in Wyntra Castle's great hall.

"As I said," she begins. She's allowed her front canines to sharpen, a unique Everadyn fae ability. The points snap close to Ayc's ear as he slides the platter of freshly baked rolls beside her plate at the head table. "Give my people a good show and don't embarrass me."

The command lands like oil on fire beneath his skin. The aching blaze that lives there flares then fades back to a simmer.

"Do not set anything on fire again," the Sovereign hisses, "or I swear..."

The Sovereign's sharp fingernails dig into her throne's armrests. Her metallic red nail polish gleams against the dark metal of the throne, which is carved into the shape of a gryphon, its wings forming the high back. Ayc retreats a step, out of her reach. Her claws are just as deadly as the gryphon's. Ayc bears the faint white scars on his throat and chin as a testament. He's lucky. She's punished others with far worse scars.

"Yris," Fennix, her righthand man, the First of her Five, warns from his spot standing at her shoulder. Even with her sitting, Fennix, with his thick, blond beard and ruddy cheeks, only stands a head taller than Yris. More than once, Ayc has heard Fennix boast that his great-grandfather was a dwarf and credit this ancestry with shaping him to be a profoundly gifted warrior. Such statements were generally swiftly silenced by Yris's threats to remove him of his beard —and occasionally his tongue—if Fennix doesn't cease boring them.

Fennix is not unique in his heritage. Quite commonly, Everadyn fae have rich and blended ancestry. The crowd gathered around the tables behind Ayc are a rainbow of beauty with skin and hair in every imaginable shade, from the white of snow to the brown of the Elodie Forest to the black of midnight. A few are the rarer shades of pink, green or blue. They're all so vastly different, and it doesn't matter to most of them.

Everadyn is Everadyn, no matter how thin the blood. All of them are beautiful in their own way.

Ayc supposes, if he didn't consider Yris the villain of his own life story, he might have found her beautiful, too. She wears her hair, as she always does, pulled back in a severe updo that displays the golden circlet on her forehead. Her dark velvet gown contrasts her icy skin tone. She is, objectively, beautiful. The same way Ayc imagines sirens and dragons are beautiful, though he's never seen one outside of books. Ageless and breathtaking and, most importantly, deadly.

"Take a breath and smile, my lady," Fennix reminds the Sovereign. "Regent Amos is looking your way."

He nods discreetly at a male sitting at a nearby table. Pale as snow, the male uses the long sleeve of his sky-blue tunic to shine an already sparkling spoon—all so he can pretend he is *not* looking at the Sovereign.

Yris paints on a smile like a skilled artist, but her frigid tone doesn't change. "Do you understand me?"

Her eyes flash momentarily from green to silver. That silver gaze, the one all Everadyn fae's eyes shift to when they are angry, still sends a shiver down Ayc's spine even after all these years living in the fae court.

Ayc dons a broad smile, the one he's learned to shield himself with whenever he feels afraid. He sweeps a bow. "Of course, my lady. I *live* to make you happy." Reckless fool that he is, he barely hides the sarcasm in his voice. He swiftly straightens and whirls to face the great hall. "My wonderful fae!"

His booming voice echoes against the stone pillars and into the domed roof. High above his head, sunlight filters through stained-glass windows. Each window bears a symbol of an Everadyn clan: a sun for the Lux Aester, a moon for the Noxumbra, three stars for the Lycendi, a rose for Bromalis, an ocean wave for the Sal Maris, a flame for the Audori, and a tree for the Totus Omni. It casts the room into a multitude of colors, shining on the faces of the crowd as they turn toward Ayc.

The children and a few adults utter a cheer, knowing what's to come. Yris's court magician has come to give his show.

Ayc spreads his arms wide. "Happy Sovereign's Day!"

Ayc has dressed grandly for the occasion, trading his usual flour-dappled apron and batter-smeared shirt for a brown vest with a loose, long-sleeved white shirt beneath. A satin ribbon holds back his shoulder-length brown hair, and gold rings bedeck the lobes and helix of his ears. He has decorated every finger with rings and black fingernail paint. His leather bracelets are the only accessories that do not gleam. The inch-wide, braided leather is worn and the metal square at their buckles is long faded. He's worn them since childhood.

"I'm thrilled to see so many come to celebrate the fiftieth year of our Sovereign's reign," Ayc continues, as he saunters toward the crowd. "Though I think we all can agree she doesn't look a day past her fifth."

Laughter ripples through the crowd. Yris's gaze stabs at his back. Ayc doesn't dare look behind him. Instead, he searches the hall and finds what he's seeking for at the base of the nearest pillar where neither the candlelight nor the sunlight reaches. Shadow. All that Ayc needs to perform his best trick.

Ayc approaches it with wide, sweeping strides,

attempting to mimic the fae grace his tall human frame can't quite manage. Despite the pain tonic Ayc stole from Xylie's shelves and drank down this morning, the stiffness in his back reminds him of its presence with every step. Sometimes, the pain is a whisper, and sometimes, it's a scream, but it's never fully gone. Distractions, like this, help.

"Let's give the Sovereign a round of applause!" Ayc claps his hands together once. Golden sparks fly from his fingertips.

The children cheer, but the adults only applaud politely. For a people used to the wonders of magic, such a display is lackluster. Many divina are blessed with profound gifts. Telepathy. Shapeshifting. Dreaming of the future. Ayc's abilities are nothing of the sort. He long ago proved to Yris that his only use—besides his baking skills—is to entertain.

"Do you want to hear a joke?" Ayc asks, still moving through the crowd.

"Yes!" one brave child yells from a nearby table. He wears the traditional tunic of the Noxumbra, a material that flows like liquid night.

"Good!" Ayc calls back, as he discreetly undoes the clasps of his leather bracelets. "Because I'm going to tell you one, anyway. Why should you never insult a dragon?" He slips the bracelets into the pocket of his trousers, trading it for a pinch of the powder hidden within. "Because they get all fired up!"

Ayc snaps his fingers, and the powder ignites. Purple flames shoot from his palm. The Noxumbra child shrieks in delight. Someone at the table nearest Ayc whistles, and he turns toward them.

A pair of fae both gift him with flirtatious smiles, so alike that they must surely be twins. They both wear rouge across their sharp, pale cheekbones, blue crystals in their eyelashes, and a crown of flowers weaved within their hair. Their entire group at the table is dressed in the rich, flower-embroidered textiles of the Bromalis: tunics that blend pinks, reds, and oranges until it resembles a setting sun.

Ayc gives the twins a wink and swirls his hands to show the crowd his palms are empty. Then he closes his hand into a fist, stretches it forward, and opens his fingers once more. A white rose lies on his palm.

"For you, my love." Ayc offers the rose to the first fae, whose hair is shorn close to their head.

They blush as they accept the offer. Ayc repeats the gestures and offers a second rose to their twin, whose own hair cascades in ringlets of gold down their back. They meet Ayc's eyes boldly and reach for it, just as Ayc slides a foot backward into the shadow.

And he disappears.

The crowd sucks in a breath, including those who have seen the court magician perform before. This is the only truly astonishing part of Ayc's performances. Everyone searches the room, but even their fae eyesight can't see him.

"Now you see me," a voice says from above. The crowd tilts back their heads to find Ayc standing in the shadowed rafters far above. He winks at them. "And now you don't."

He vanishes again.

The crowd murmur and turn in their seats, until Ayc reappears again at the other side of the great hall, closer to the large, carved doors at the main entrance. They all applaud now, and Ayc grins triumphantly as the sound thunders through the hall.

Ayc fingers the powder in his hand, preparing for one last trick. "You have been a wonderful audience..."

The great hall door creaks open. And *she* enters.

Ayc's breath freezes on his lips. She has slipped in so quietly he doesn't think anyone else has noticed. The long, tight spirals of her thick hair look nearly violet as it descends her back, clipped back above her pointed ears— the way she's worn it for years. Dark, scale-like armor covers her black shirt and breeches that hug every inch of her wide, strong warrior's body, leaving little of her brown skin exposed. As she strides into the hall, her eyes search everything, before locking onto him. She stills. He can't see her eyes from here, but he has never forgotten them. He doesn't know what mystical creature runs far back in her blood, but he knows her eyes shift through dozens of shades, from brown to blue to green and back again.

Loraphne, the Sovereign's daughter, has returned.

How long has it been since he last saw her? It's been four years since she first left for the Adamant, the school for elite warriors. Four years since her presence stopped being an everyday torment. She's only been back a handful of times since, her visits as brief and wretched as a ghostly haunting.

"You're on fire," whispers a small child, sitting at a table close to Ayc.

Ayc jerks his attention back and flashes a smile. "Thank you!"

Then he feels the bite of heat against his wrist. A small flame nips at the edge of his sleeve.

Fuck, fuck, fuck, he thinks, as he waves his arm in overly-feigned panic, like he *meant* for this to happen. Laughter erupts as he seeks a way out. His throat tightens, like a hand has clamped around it. He was told not to set things on fire, and he knows the consequences of disobedience.

Some fae in the crowd begin to mutter, not buying his smile.

Someone rises from a nearby table, a pitcher in one hand and a cane in the other. They take two limping steps toward Ayc and then thrust the contents of the pitcher toward Ayc. The water splashes over his face and onto his sleeve. The flame extinguishes. The crowd hollers with laughter once more.

When Ayc's vision clears, he's met with a familiar scowl.

Peregrin's stormy gray eyes match the paleness of their ashen skin and the blond hair they wear shaved at the sides and only slightly longer on top. Dark green veins weave across their skin, snaking from the collar of their plain tunic and traveling up their neck. Like their cane, those veins are a reminder of the cursed blade they took in their leg two decades ago. Before that blade, Peregrin was a commander in Everadyn's aerial army, but now they are a fighting instructor at the Wyntra school who sometimes take pity on outcasts like Ayc.

"Thanks, Peregrin," Ayc mouths. The tautness on his neck eases, allowing him to breathe.

Peregrin only grunts and returns to their seat.

"See, all is well," Ayc says to the crowd, rolling back his scorched sleeve to show the unblemished flesh beneath. He pointedly doesn't look in the direction of the Sovereign or her daughter as he slips his hand into his pocket for more powder. "Thank you, and good day!"

He tosses the powder at his feet and disappears in a cloud of smoke and flames. When he reappears again, he's in the hallway outside the side entrance to the great hall, his heart hammering. He leans against the wall, slips his leather bracelets back on his wrists, and hopes, as he always does, that his performance is enough.

Ayc's divina gift is a talent that has spared his life for the last ten years. It's the only reason he's here, a baker and an entertainer who serves the fae Sovereign, and not dead or suffering like the rest of his people in his homeland of Aluina.

And if the Sovereign ever discovered it's all a lie, nothing and no one could save him.

✕

TEN YEARS AGO

It was the best batch of cinnamon rolls he'd ever made.

He remembers it clearly, even now: the artful swirl on the tops of the buns, the perfect shade of brown on the edge, and the way the smell of cinnamon permeated the air as he pulled the pan from the oven in Creed Castle's apothecary. He remembers thinking that his mother, who died only eighteen months prior, would have been proud. And he remembers how he nearly dropped the pan when a scream erupted from the hallway.

His entire body jerked, but he didn't have time to fully register the noise before the door to the apothecary slammed open and collided with the wall inside. Bottles of powders, elixirs, and dried plants trembled on the shelves. Ayc's hands, still in the oven mitts he'd pulled over his leather cuffs, clutched the pan of rolls tighter as a cloaked figure swept in.

The first thing he noticed were her eyes, burning bright like silver flame.

The second thing he noticed was that she was young, a girl no older than his own twelve years.

The third thing he noticed were the swords she carried in each hand, slender and slightly curved, their hilts a gleaming black. She extended one toward his chest.

"Is there anyone else here?" she growled, her lips drawing back to reveal canines far sharper than his own.

She was fae.

Ayc's heart stood still. His mother had always told him he had no reason to fear the fae—at least, most of the fae. The Everadyn fae, with their silver eyes and seven clans, who lived south across the Bellum Sea, were allies to Aluina. The Tenebra fae, with their glowing green eyes and their winged horses, happily shared their island in the warm Southernmost Sea with humans. It was only the third race of fae, the Drakr, who meant humans any harm, but they were kept out of Aluina by wards, powered by ancient magic.

But with this strange fae girl before Ayc and a sword pointed toward his chest, his mother's advice meant nothing. Ayc trembled so hard he couldn't remember how to move his mouth. He could only stare at the fae girl, taking in the dark curls peeking out of her hood, her brown cheeks, and the strong chin that lifted high as though she balanced a crown on her head.

Someone so dangerous shouldn't be so beautiful, he thought.

"Did you hear me?" she snapped. "Is anyone else in here?"

She kept the sword trained on his chest and glanced around. Behind her, a flood of cloaked figures rushed past the open door. More screams ripped through the air. Ayc trembled harder.

"Where's the master of this apothecary?" the girl asked.

Finally, he found words, though he couldn't make his voice louder than a whisper, "He... he went to deliver her majesty's medicine."

The silver faded from her eyes, revealing a royal blue that seemed just as unnatural. "Very well. Let's go."

Go? How was he supposed to convince his feet to move?

When he didn't budge, she sheathed one sword, seized his arm, and shoved him into the hallway with the pan of cinnamon rolls still in his hands. She pressed her sword toward his back, only a whisper away. With the smallest pressure, the slightest hesitation, it would pierce his clothes, his skin... his spinal cord.

Ayc stumbled down the hall of Creed Castle, passing by the exquisite tapestries and the handful of torches that cast dim light down the corridor. Around the corner, two familiar courtiers clung to each other, as two tall, cloaked fae barked at them to hurry.

"Follow them," the fae girl commanded.

His mind scrambled as he stumbled forward. Why were the fae here? What should he do? He needed to do... *something.*

"Do y-you, uh, like j-jokes?" he stammered, not quite sure why.

"What?" she snarled.

"J-jokes. Like, what happens if a witch has twins?"

She didn't answer.

"You can't tell which is witch."

The girl didn't laugh, didn't acknowledge he said anything at all. Ayc's mother used to laugh so hard at that joke that she'd have to wipe away a tear. His own eyes pricked with moisture at the memory. It'd been a while

11

since he cried over her, but at that moment, he missed his mother so much it felt like she'd died yesterday.

The women ahead of him started wailing; the fae shoved them around the corner, roaring at them to be quiet. At the end of the hall, a small staircase led to a massive red door Ayc immediately recognized. They were headed to the throne room.

"What—" Ayc tried again, desperately trying to distract from the pounding of his heart. "What about the one—"

"Shut up!" The girl shoved him up the stairs and through the door.

In the throne room, residents of the castle—all people whose faces Ayc knew, but whose names he didn't—were lined up in rows, paired off with cloaked figures who must have been more fae. Past them, he glimpsed the stage that held the throne... and the bodies.

A sword pierced the chest of Aluina's king and pinned him to his throne, his eyes wide and mouth agape, frozen in an eternal look of terror. His queen laid at the foot of her own throne, as though she'd been cut down as she attempted to run. Her blood cascaded down the steps of the thrones' dais, to where her son and his wife—the crown prince and princess—had fallen together. Their hands interlaced in a pool of crimson. A dozen bodies of guards, whose last act was a vain attempt to protect the royal family, sprawled across the floor of the throne room, some drenched in blood and some twisted in unnatural positions that could only be caused by sorcery.

Ayc's mouth opened in a silent scream. Despite living in the castle, he'd never met the king and queen, but the crown prince had spoken to Ayc a couple of times. The simple act always seemed far too kind, considering Ayc was nothing more than a simple, peasant boy from the northwest province of Aluina.

The fae girl shoved Ayc forward and steered him into line with the others. "Don't move."

Ayc couldn't if he'd wanted. It took all his will to remain upright and to hold on to the damn pan of cinnamon rolls. The steam still wafted off them. The smell of cinnamon burned in his nostrils, entwined with the metallic scent of blood.

Two fae marched before the line of prisoners. A short male with pallid skin and a thick beard held a paper and a quill. The other was a woman who reminded him of ice: pale and cold and eyes that froze him through as they glanced over him. Later, Ayc would learn that this was Sovereign Yris and her First, Fennix, but for now, he only instinctively knew he should fear them, the way a small child knew to fear the dark.

They spoke in the Everadyn language, not his own tongue of Aluinic like the fae girl had been speaking. But Ayc's mother had insisted he learn from the time he was little. Later, Evander, the master of the apothecary, continued Ayc's lessons to ensure he remained fluent.

"That should be all of them, my lady," Fennix said. "I counted twice."

Yris glanced over the line of whimpering, pleading humans. Her eyes flashed silver. "Very well."

Her head snapped toward Ayc. His knees nearly buckled, and only the girl's hand on his arm kept him upright.

"Loraphne," Yris said. It was only one word, heavy with command.

"Yes, Mother." The girl—Loraphne—turned to face Ayc. She lifted her wicked blade to his throat.

13

The human's whimpers grew into shrieks, but Ayc couldn't hear them as terror rippled through his every nerve.

The fae were going to kill him.

They were going to kill *all* of them.

"Please," Ayc begged the girl, his voice cracking. "Don't do this."

Loraphne's hand shook. Her eyes bled out into a dull grey, like she was trying to make them silver, to show her rage, but she couldn't quite manage it.

His pleading turned to sobs, his cheeks hot with tears. "P-please don't do this."

Her fingers readjusted on the hilt of her sword. Her eyes shimmered like diamonds with tears she didn't dare let fall.

"Stop!" the man beside Ayc yelled in the Everadyn language. "He's divina! *He's divina!*"

The girl jumped and pulled her blade back. Everything stopped. The sobbing. Ayc's trembling. Even the Sovereign froze.

In his fear, Ayc hadn't noticed that Evander, his master, stood next to him. The fae holding Evander captive clamped a gloved hand over his mouth.

"Let him speak," the Sovereign commanded.

The fae dropped his hand.

She moved toward Evander—toward Ayc—in a slow prowl. Ayc's tremble returned. "What did you say?" she demanded of Evander, switching to flawless Aluinic.

Evander did not flinch. The years had made his pale skin worn and his body bony and slender, but he seemed powerful as he dared to meet Yris's eyes. "The boy is divina. Touched by the divine. If you kill him, you will bring a curse upon your people."

Ayc's master had told him about the divina once. They weren't the sorcerers who were born with an innate ability to cast spells and shape magical forces to their will. Nor were divina the alchemists who used science to harness magic, or even the elementals who controlled a single element. Instead, divina were said to be touched by the divine the fae believed in, given a single unique gift.

But Ayc didn't understand why Evander said he was divina... because he was nothing more than an ordinary boy.

"How do you know those words?" the Sovereign asked Evander.

Evander lifted his chin proudly. "My great-grandfather was a Tenebra fae. He taught me well."

Yris shook her head. "Divina, like all magical affinity, is rare in humans."

Down the line, a woman whimpered. A nearby fae silenced her with a slap. Ayc winced at the sound of flesh against flesh, but Evander remained steady. "Rare, but no less powerful."

Yris stared at the apothecary, deadly still, for a moment that felt like an eternity. Then she turned her silver eyes upon Ayc. With a suddenness that took Ayc's breath way, she was before him. Loraphne stepped aside.

Yris's hand seized Ayc's chin, her sharp nails pricking at the tender flesh of his throat. A bead of blood raced toward the hollow of his throat. "Tell me, child, what is your ability?"

Ayc's mouth parted, but no words came out. Lie. He needed to lie, but what could he tell her? His heart pounded so hard he heard it like a scream in his ears.

"He has not demonstrated it yet," Evander said. "I knew his mother, and I took him in after she died. I have tried to teach to him, but he's young and a human. It may take time. But he has the mark." He nodded his chin toward Ayc. "On his arm. Show her, Ayc."

Cool sweat beaded on Ayc's back. Before he could make himself move, the Sovereign's claws yanked back his sleeve. He clutched his pan to keep from dropping it, not sure why, except he needed to grasp onto something. There, on his forearm just past his bracelet, was a single pink mark. His mother had told him it was an old burn he'd gotten from the oven rack when he was little. But it also looked like... a thumbprint.

Touched by the divine.

Yris's eyes flashed again. "Did you bake those?"

"W-what?" Ayc stammered.

Yris reached into his pan and tore off a chunk of cinnamon roll. She took a small bite, and her eyes fluttered closed for a moment. She turned away and walked back toward Fennix. Ayc could breathe again... if only a little.

"I know what you're thinking," Fennix said, loud enough that Ayc could hear, surely not thinking he understood the fae language. "But we can't let the boy live. Lahlis said everyone in this castle. That was the deal. The Drakr lord is not one to trifle with."

Ayc's knees nearly buckled, as though the ground had been ripped from beneath him. *No, it can't be.* Surely, he'd heard them wrong. The Everadyn couldn't be here because the Drakr fae asked them. The Everadyn were Aluina's allies; they protected them *from* the Drakr—the monsters who haunted Ayc's dreams with their glowing red eyes, and mouth full of fangs, and pale skin so hard, only a tungsten blade could pierce it. Centuries ago, the Drakr arrived from some distant land on ships and, according to legends, the backs of dragons. They attempted to conquer every land they saw. Despite years of bloody war, Everadyn and Tenebra gave not an inch of their land, but the Drakr stole what had once been the eastern coast of Aluina, everything past the Untamed Mountains. The only thing that stopped them from taking everything Aluina had was the Everadyn fae. Their sorcerers and alchemists helped Aluina build wards to keep out anyone who was not human or a friend to the humans.

But now... now, something had changed. The Drakr and Everadyn had made a deal. The death of everyone in the castle for... well, Ayc couldn't imagine what could be worth a price so high.

"Choose wisely," said a fae from the crowd, one completely cloaked, whose voice seemed to echo, like two voices overlaid. From the shadows of her hood, he glimpses only blood red lips and silver eyes. Ayc would later learn that this was the Sovereign's Second, Onanna, a powerful sorcerer. The rest of the Sovereign's Five were also in the crowd that day, too, but he wouldn't know that until much later. "The divine will repay the boy's death."

"But Lahlis—" Fennix began to protest, but Onanna interrupted.

"He did not choose his words as carefully as he should have."

Yris chewed thoughtfully on the cinnamon roll and licked her fingers clean. The entire room held its breath, no one daring to speak, though mercy was only available for Ayc.

"Everyone but the boy," Yris said at last.

Fennix nodded his head. "As you will it, my lady."

"Loraphne," Yris said, looking back to her daughter, "the

old man instead. And then watch the boy. If he flinches, make him bleed for it."

Loraphne nodded, adjusted her grip on the blade, and stepped toward Evander. The apothecary met Ayc's eyes as the girl lifted her blade to his throat. Her hand was a little steadier this time, but only a little. Her eyes were not silver, but gray.

Ayc wanted to scream, to beg, for the life of this man who was all he still had in the world, who had taken him in after his mother died, who had lied to spare his life. But he said nothing.

"Never forget where you come from, Ayc," Evander whispered.

"Loraphne, now!" Yris barked.

Loraphne jerked her arm. Ayc closed his eyes as warm drops splattered his face. Rain, he told himself. It was only rain. He had to believe it because he couldn't flinch.

Screams prompted him to open his eyes again, but all he could see was Loraphne's face, inches from his. As people around him begged for their lives, Ayc watched a single tear slip down Loraphne's cheek, forming a trail that turned to red when it met the blood coating her rich brown skin. It was a tear he would never admit he ever saw.

That day, Ayc learned that not all mothers are good mothers. His mother taught him to bake and to tell jokes and that heroes were kind first and brave second.

Loraphne's mother taught her to kill.

When Ayc looked away from Loraphne, it was done. Sticky blood coated the floor at his feet; the screams still echoed in his head. All these years later, and he still dreams about them. He remembers every moment of that day like it's etched into his very bones.

In the aftermath, Ayc was alone, the only human standing in a room full of fae and dead bodies, still holding a pan of fresh cinnamon rolls frosted in bright rubies of blood. His teeth chattering, he lifted his pan, because his mother always told him there wasn't much a good baked dessert couldn't solve. And today was the first day he realized she was lying.

"W-would... would anyone l-like a cinnamon roll?"

CHAPTER
TWO

NOW

A yc has just pushed through the door to his pastry kitchen when a voice pipes up, "How do you do it?"

Ayc squints into the sunlight shining from the single window in the corner. Through the particles of flour that always flutter through the air like pixie dust, he finds Xylie sitting on the long wooden counter at the center of the kitchen, her feet swaying back and forth. The pots and pans hanging from the iron rack above her head cast shadows on her face, which is fixed into an expression of all-knowing. If she shifts even an inch to her right, she'll crush a platter of his carefully crafted fruit tarts.

"Hello to you, too, Xylie," Ayc says with a grin as he adjusts the platter to add a few more inches between it and an impending disaster.

He examines the rest of his masterpieces that are laid out on the counter: cupcakes, biscuits, pastries, and, of course, little cups of his chocolate pudding that—other than cinnamon rolls—is his most raved about delicacy. It's all exactly the way he left it before he went to entertain at Yris's request. They look utterly perfect. One should never skimp on presentation.

Xylie scowls at him, narrowing her deep brown eyes. She means to look fierce, but her nose wrinkles. That, combined with her slight frame, makes her appear about as threatening as a bunny. Despite her turning eighteen last month, Ayc can't look at her without seeing the thin child who showed up at Wyntra seven years ago, looking as lost and confused as Ayc felt. She still wears her hair in dozens of braids, weaved with ribbons of turquoise, a color that stands out against her black hair and skin. Her knee-length coat—made of knitted blocks of swirling color pieced together with a deep blue border—has always seemed too chaotic and bright for her usual studious demeanor, but she wears it like a second skin, no matter the temperature.

"I know the fire trick is just powder," she says, pointing to the shelves in the corner of Ayc's kitchen, next to his massive stove. The glass vials line the shelves, filled with powders that have nothing to do with pastries. He stores them right above all the jars of ingredients she uses for her own alchemy.

When she accidentally started a fire in the castle dungeons, back when she first arrived from Lycendi lands, Yris banned her from doing alchemy, which was like trying to ban Xylie from breathing. Her father was an alchemist, and she inherited a gift that, even as the eleven-year-old she was then, far exceeded anyone Ayc has ever seen come through Wyntra. So, Ayc offered to share his little kitchen. Since Ayc also has an aptitude for setting things aflame, Yris had Onanna spell his kitchen to be fireproof. He didn't know seven years ago when he invited Xylie into his space that he'd never be rid of her again, that they would become inseparable. He's never regretted it, though. Not once.

Ayc's cheeky grin doesn't waver. "You've got it all wrong, Xy. I'm" — He swirls his hands through the air grandly — "touched by the divine." The burned cuff of his shirt catches his eye and he quickly rolls up both sleeves to his elbow, hiding it from view.

"Really?" she says flatly. "What's that on your hands?"

A few granules of purple powder dust his fingertips. Few would notice. But Xylie sees everything.

Ayc shrugs. "That's just sprinkles."

She leans closer, and with her sitting on the counter, she matches his tall height. She narrows her eyes, but doesn't fully meet his gaze, focusing instead on the center of his forehead, as she always does. "Then lick it off."

Ayc would have, except the powder would likely ignite in his mouth. Instead, he steps to the sink, turns on the pump of water, and washes his hands. "A good baker never licks their hands. It's unsanitary."

Xylie huffs. This is the game they play every single time he performs. He knows it's pointless to deny; she already knows the truth. He doesn't know if there's anything Xylie doesn't know. She could recite theories of alchemy and brew medicines from memory. She can explain the intricate workings of the inventions that blend sorcery and alchemy —the lights that turn on with a flick of a switch, the airships that sail above land, the indoor plumbing—which were new to him when he came to Everadyn. So, of course, she's seen right through Ayc's tricks from the beginning, but he's never been able to admit she's right.

And it's not that Ayc doesn't trust her. She's one of the few people in this castle he knows he *can* trust to keep his secret. But, sometimes, giving up the lies we cloak ourselves in is too uncomfortable a thought.

He never surrenders, but then, neither does she.

"What I can't figure out is the disappearing trick," Xylie says, changing tactics.

He turns off the tap, wipes his hands with a nearby towel, and leans his back against the sink, facing her. "How were you even watching me?"

She wouldn't have been in the crowded hall. Xylie doesn't just hate crowds; she becomes paralyzed by them.

"Through a crack in the side door," she snips back. "*Don't* try to change the subject."

"I'd *never*," he says.

"Then tell me how you do the invisibility trick."

Ayc grins again, big and bold and gleaming, and lies through his teeth. "There's no secret, Xylie, and there's no trick."

Xylie rolls her eyes. "What do you think I'm going to do? Tell my aunt?"

She snorts, but Ayc hesitates to laugh at her self-deprecating joke. Xylie's father was one of Yris's many half-siblings; apparently, Yris's father, who was Sovereign before her, was quite the philanderer. Despite having been taken in by Yris, Xylie can't utter a word in her presence. It isn't something unique to Yris. According to Xylie, she was six before she uttered a word, learning to speak the common sign language long before she ever felt able to utter a syllable. Her difficulty with speech returned when she was eleven, after she was the sole survivor of a Drakr attack on her Lycendi mountain village. She crammed herself in a cabinet which was hidden by a spell cast by her mother, a sorcerer. There, Xylie listened as her parents were slaughtered. She remained alone in the darkness until Everadyn warriors found her.

After, she didn't utter a sound, not for several years, and now, she speaks only to Ayc and her cousin, Loraphne. Before that, they learned to communicate through signs, something she returns to when anyone else is around.

Ayc wouldn't have blamed her if, after that trauma, she never spoke again. After Creed Castle, every word he uttered for a long time felt heavy and impossible. That kind of weight never fully goes away.

Perhaps that is what forged their friendship so swiftly and so strongly. Neither of them ever speaks of their past, but it mirrors each other just the same.

"Believe what you will." Ayc pushes himself off the sink. He picks up a tray of fruit tarts, drawing their familiar game to an end. "But right now, I have other jobs to attend to."

Baker. Magician. Server. All in a day's work.

"But—" Xylie begins to protest.

Ayc cuts her off. "Your cousin is here."

Xylie blinks. "Lora?" She snaps her fingers as a smile springs to life on her face. "Ha. I knew it."

Ayc arches an eyebrow. "You knew she was coming?"

"No, I knew there was a reason you caught yourself on fire."

Ayc snatches a tart off his tray. "I suppose she still strikes fear of my own mortality into me, after all these years." He pops the pastry into his mouth, knowing it'll likely be the only food he gets during the party. The acidic taste of strawberries explodes in his mouth and mixes with the sweetness of custard. The crust melts in his mouth, perfectly cooked but still soft in the center. Damn, he's good.

"Fear?" Xylie repeats skeptically. "With the way you always purposefully try to get under her skin? I'm not sure *fear* is the right word."

Ayc swallows and resist the urge to cram another dessert into his mouth. Though Xylie has always been close to her cousin, Ayc and Xylie have an unspoken, mutual agreement to not discuss Lora. He only broke that agreement in the hopes of distracting Xylie, but it's only gotten Xylie to latch onto something else.

"And what would you call it?" he asks, while backing toward the door. "Well-honed self-preservation instincts?"

"No." She runs a finger up and down her nose, the way she does when she's thinking. Then she says, with a nod of finality, "Unperceptive."

"I have no idea what you're talking about. And I'm leaving now." Ayc saunters toward the door. "Have one of the pudding cups, Xy. They're wonderful."

He leaves quickly, kicking the door closed behind him, but not quick enough to avoid Xylie's mutter of, "I'm only saying that, sometimes, I can't tell whether you actually hate her or just..."

Hate, Ayc thinks as he makes his way back to the great hall. *Definitely hate.*

It's a foundational truth so sturdy he could build palaces upon it. He hates Lora, and Lora unequivocally hates *him,* too. In the story of his life, if he's the hero, then he has *two* villains.

Yris.

And her daughter.

The Everadyn fae certainly know how to throw a party.

It's one of the many things Ayc has come to admire about them after all these years of living among them. As he serves tray after tray of his creations, a band plays their amplified instruments with such vigor the windows overhead rattle. Ayc weaves through the crowd, reciting jokes into pointed ears, and performing little magic tricks to appease the children. He lives for moments like this. Moments when he can forget everything. Moments when the thrill of being alive extinguishes the sting beneath his skin and eases the tension and pain in the muscles of his back. There is no past or future. No pain or memory. There is only music and laughter and joy.

He can survive on moments like these.

The crowd laughs and sings and dances. The clans all intermingle and befriend one another with only a few noticeable exceptions.

Yris and her Five do not join the fun.

Her daughter doesn't either. Ayc tries hard not to look at her, but he's aware of where she stands: in her usual dark corner, watching with a scowl on her face.

Then, of course, there are those visitors from the clan of Lux Aester. They sit, stiff as boards, declining to participate in such 'heathen' antics. Ayc reluctantly serves them. They take his sweets but turn up their noses at his jokes... or maybe it's at *him*. Ayc isn't sure what offends them most: his earrings, his long hair, or the nail polish on his fingernails.

He hopes all of it.

A girl who looks about seventeen is the only one who dares speak to Ayc. "I liked your performance," she says, but her words are so low Ayc barely catches them. She keeps her gaze fixed on her hands, folded primly against the blue skirts of the high-collared, long dress most Lux Aester women wear. In fact, she resembles most Lux Aester fae, who are not as free with their appearance—or their breeding—as the other clans. She is white and pale-haired and looks so uncomfortable in her own skin, Ayc winces for her.

Ayc is about to say thank you, when another voice rings out, "Sister Avabeth, what have I told you countless times?"

Oh, Ayc thinks, *fuck me up ways, sideways, and every way but here.*

Ayc knows that voice—knows it far too well.

Marcellus.

In the last few years, Yris has allowed Ayc to attend festivals around Everadyn, setting up a stall to sell his bakery creations. There, Ayc has heard Marcellus's voice magnified through the crowd, as though he's trying to drown out every note of happiness at the fair. Marcellus gives speeches that quickly turn into revivals, teaching people about the divine and the ancient texts that have been *"so disgracefully polluted through popular culture"*.

Hearing Marcellus's voice now, Ayc wonders if jumping out the nearby window would be an overreaction.

He's still considering it as Avabeth drops her head farther and murmurs, "A woman of the divine only speaks when spoken to."

On second thought, Ayc thinks that jumping out the window just got up-ranked to a *splendid idea*. Because it's a much better fate than what Yris will do to Ayc if he gives into his desire to punch Marcellus in his smug little face.

"Hello, Marcellus," Ayc says, hoisting his lips into a smile that's as heavy as an anvil.

Like most adult fae, Marcellus appears nearly ageless, but is probably at least a century old. He's so insidiously tangled in the roots of his clan that he must have been around for decades. And of course, he's far too handsome. Who would grant him the power he has if he wasn't? His blond hair doesn't fall past his ears, and he wears a smug expression that perhaps he means to look pious but comes across almost constipated. His expression becomes more pinched when he turns to Ayc. "It's *High Priest* Marcellus... as I've told you before."

Ayc shrugs. "I have a terrible memory."

Marcellus looks him over. "I *did* also enjoy your performance. It's a shame your talents are so wasted on entertainment. They're a gift from the divine, and therefore, should be devoted to his service. If you came to one of Lux Aester's temples, your gifts would be put to much better use."

I'd rather choke on my own dick, Ayc thinks.

"Oh, fuck no, that sounds awful," Ayc says instead, aware that it's only *slightly* better. "Thanks for the offer, though."

Marcellus shrugs. "The divine grants all men agency to choose."

"And the women just do as they're told? Your version of the divine sounds like an asshole."

Marcellus remains miraculously composed. Avabeth dares to peek through her curtain of hair but quickly drops her gaze when Marcellus's attention cuts back to her.

"This is why we must be careful of the company we

keep," Marcellus declares to her, and then to Ayc says, "I'll bid you farewell."

Marcellus bows his head in a note of respect and pauses a beat like he expects Ayc to do the same. When Ayc does not, Marcellus sniffs indignantly, turns, and walks away.

"Pious little shit," Ayc mutters.

Marcellus halts in place, his back tense.

A Lux Aester male sitting next to Avabeth bursts to his feet and roars, "What did you say?"

Avabeth squeaks and flings her hands in front of her face.

No one is allowed to bring weapons into the great hall. The highly-gifted royal guards cast a simple spell to ensure it before anyone enters. But the dinner knife the male clutches can certainly do enough damage. Ayc jumps back a step. The man *probably* won't kill him—given the whole divina and generations of bad luck thing—but damn, there's a lot Ayc can live through.

Marcellus turns around, but the expression of utter calm on his face tells Ayc he doesn't intend to assist. Ayc doesn't think anyone else at the Lux Aester table will either. Avabeth is still hiding her face in her hands.

Ayc smiles at the man and offers his tray. "Fruit tart?"

The man growls and advances a step, pulling back the knife.

"Stop!" hisses a voice so close to Ayc's ear that he jumps again.

It's another voice he knows all too well. It's one that shoots a vibration down his spine, that haunts all of his nightmares and, unfortunately, many of his dreams.

The Lux Aester fae stops. Marcellus holds up the palm of

his hand like he was the one to issue the order and not the woman who has appeared at Ayc's side.

"Loraphne," Marcellus addresses her.

And Ayc...

Well, as it turns out, Ayc really should have jumped out that window.

NINE YEARS AGO

The knife thudded into the wall right beside Ayc's head. Though Ayc had known it was coming, he didn't dare shield himself. He kept his hand flat on the wall as he was supposed to. Any closer and the blade would have severed his ear from skull. It wasn't luck, though. Peregrin had placed the knife exactly where they had intended.

Peregrin stood a few feet away, in the center of the Sovereign's office. The former elite warrior might as well have worn a helmet with a visor for how little feeling crossed their face as they gazed upon Ayc. Not a single emotion had played on their face over the last hour, as they threw knife after knife at Ayc. Not anger. Not interest. And certainly, not sympathy.

Behind Peregrin was Lora. Her long curls had been pulled back like she was trying to imitate her mother. Even her bored expression mimicked the look the Sovereign wore from her place sitting behind the desk.

"Come now, human," Yris said, barely glancing up from where she scratched a jet-black quill across a stack of papers. "Protect yourself."

Ayc shivered, unable to speak. This torture was the latest

of the Sovereign's attempts to convince his divine gift to present itself. It had been a year since the slaughter at Creed Castle, a year since he had been shoved onto a ship that crossed the Bellum Sea to Wyntra Castle. An entire year since the Sovereign had begun attempting to see what divine gift lurked within him.

At the beginning, her tactics seemed reasonable. Onanna, the sorcerer who was Yris's Second, had attempted to teach Ayc. Onanna forced him to read stacks of books, but he managed to focus only on a few pages, and those he read held knowledge that seemed to slip out of his head as soon as he forced it in. The sorcerer tried to teach him meditation, telling him to seek a magical thread that was supposedly within him, but he could never sit still longer than a few minutes. But when months went by with nothing to show, Onanna suggested a new tactic.

In her research, she had learned that, sometimes, a gift only presents itself after significant stress, like a survival instinct in a near-death experience. And so, Yris began attempting to *almost* kill Ayc.

First, she'd had him tied to the cliffs outside Wyntra that overlooked the Bellum Sea. Hour after hour, the tumultuous icy, gray water had crept up as the tide rolled in. Meanwhile, the fae children who lived at Wyntra jeered at him from above. Lora had stayed the longest.

"What's taking you so long?" she had demanded. "Hurry! Use your power! The water is rising."

Like he hadn't already known.

The water had been at his throat when she stormed away. It had been at his chin when Fennix finally came and cut him down.

Next, Yris had thrown Ayc into the pasture that served as

the gryphons nesting ground. It had been birthing season, and the only thing testier than the easily offended fledglings were their irritable new mothers. Ayc had tried to be respectful, tried to not wake any of the new fledglings as he waited. But he was always the restless sort. He couldn't help it, and his fidgeting made them agitated.

It had been Peregrin's own bonded gryphon, Tempest, that had been his salvation when the mothers had surrounded him, looking like they wanted to trample him beneath their sharp paws or at the very least peck out an eyeball. Perhaps, Tempest remembered all those times Ayc snuck food out of his window in the pastry kitchen. Carrot cake and raw salmon were her favorite.

When Peregrin had found him and their gryphon later, Ayc had been tucked beneath Tempest's wing as he slept.

Peregrin's intervention was perhaps why they were here, playing a role in Yris's game. By rights, Peregrin should be out in the courtyard, where they served as one of the many instructors of the Wyntra school.

In his time studying with Onanna, Ayc had learned that Everadyn had eight national schools—a school in each of the clans and Wyntra. Throughout their twelve years of formal training, each fae child would leave their local schools behind to spend a few weeks at a clan school, in order to learn the skill the clan was known for. Bromalis were known for their study of botany and herbology, and Totus Omni were artists, writers, and musicians. Audori were skilled in forging and metalwork, particularly the fae weapons, beautiful blades that blended tungsten, silver and iron. Lycendi were the healers, scholars and alchemists. Lux Aester were the irreplaceable farmers, masons and, of course, priests, while Noxumbra produced some of the greatest of fighters. Sal Maris were fishers, merchants, and sailors of ships of both sea and the sky. The time spent at each school would help pinpoint the children's interest and their talents.

But Wyntra was separate from it all. Every few weeks, children rotated in and out, and were tested and trained by the professors: the retired warriors and sorcerers and alchemists and priests, trying to identify the most elite of children. They would come every few years, starting from when they were young, to identify any child with innate gifts who might be sent to Velphin, the international school of sorcery. They returned a final time the summer after they turned eighteen, to identify the students' final placement. Based on their Final Testing, they would go to serve in the infantry or temples, the trades or the arts, on farms or in factories. The most elite students would be sent to one of three schools: Adamant, the school that trained the greatest warriors; Splendor, the school of alchemy and healers, or to continue training at Velphin, for sorcery.

Every Everadyn child's duty was to learn and be taught. But not Ayc. The only time he was allowed to leave his kitchen and closet-sized bedroom was to serve the desserts Yris requested or when Yris wanted to torture him like this.

"Are we almost—" Peregrin began, glancing toward Yris.

"Let Loraphne throw the next one," Yris said, without removing her eyes from her paper.

Peregrin stiffened almost imperceptibly. "My lady?"

Yris shifted her eyes upward and pinned them with her icy glare. "Peregrin, let her."

Peregrin hesitated, which was more defiance toward the Sovereign than Ayc had ever seen from anyone else. They glanced past Yris, to the fae who stood in the corner, a royal guard dressed in a silver cloak. Most of the guards pretended they saw nothing Yris did, little more than statues who could always be found in proximity to Yris. But this man, Irving, sometimes gave Ayc a sad, sympathetic smile that seemed genuine. The guard nodded at Peregrin.

Peregrin drew a short dagger from the dozens of sheaths lining their crossbody belt and handed it to Lora. The girl stared at it and then at Ayc. Something flickered over her face, a momentary lapse in the bored mask. Was it glee? Ayc certainly didn't hope for regret.

In the last year, he'd tried to befriend her, telling her jokes when he served her dessert. She gave him nothing in return other than blank stares or the occasional order to shut his mouth. The only thing he'd learned about her was that, though her mother called her Loraphne, almost everyone else called her Lora.

Lora tightened her grip on the knife. The sweat on Ayc's back had already drenched through his shirt, but he felt the panic everywhere now. On his neck, his forehead, and mostly, behind his sternum where his heart pounded.

"I'm not as skilled as Peregrin," Lora said. "I might hit him."

"Good," said Yris, meeting her eyes. "Hit him."

"My lady!" Peregrin snapped sharply.

"Don't question me, Peregrin! I will have you demoted."

Peregrin pressed their mouth taut, folding their hands together behind their back.

Lora still stared at the knife in her hand.

Ayc flattened his hands against the wood. *Please. If there are any gods listening, let me be magic. Please, give me a gift.*

He'd prayed the prayer many times. He'd prayed to the gods and goddesses the humans worshipped, even though his mother had told him they were nothing more than stories. He'd prayed to the divine the fae believed in. He'd even prayed to darker beings. No one ever answered.

Yris drummed her hand against the desk impatiently. "No more hesitating, Loraphne. Must I remind you *again?* Kindness is weakness."

Lora snapped to attention and turned. Adjusting her grip on the dagger, she looked at Ayc, her eyes darker than he'd ever seen.

"Remember, Lora," Peregrin began, but Lora had already pulled her wrist back and hurled the knife forward.

Fuck, it hurt. Years later, ayc can still remember the way it hurt as the knife sliced through the top of his ear. Blood flooded down the side of his face, and he bit down on his tongue to keep from crying out.

Yris clapped. "Well done, dear."

Lora only stared at Ayc, her expression cold and unfeeling.

This, he realized, was why all the other children called her villainess. From his window, he'd watched them play heroes and villains in the courtyard of the castle. The other children always made her play the villain, because she was so, so good at it.

And to think, he'd foolishly wanted to be her friend. Whatever mercy he thought he saw in her at Creed Castle, he was clearly mistaken. Those tears on her cheeks meant nothing. She was Yris's daughter, through and through.

Peregrin marched toward Ayc, each step punctuated by a limp. Sometimes, their gait was bad enough they had to use a cane, but today, they didn't have it. They yanked a handkerchief from their pocket and pressed it to the side of Ayc's head, to the bleeding ear. That hurt, too, so much that

35

a wave of dizziness nearly sent him to the floor, but Peregrin grabbed Ayc by the arm and kept him upright.

"I'm going to take him to the healer," they said.

Yris didn't protest as Peregrin dragged Ayc toward the door and out into the hallway. Peregrin stayed with Ayc, sitting on a nearby stool with arms crossed, as the castle healer laid Ayc on a bed and began to stitch. Ayc tried not to cry—he really did—but despite the numbing potion the healer smothered over the ear, he felt every stitch. He bunched the pillow around his face so Peregrin wouldn't see his tears.

After the healer was done, Peregrin escorted Ayc back into his room. Before Ayc could step into the pastry kitchen, Peregrin wrapped a fist around Ayc's collar and yanked him closer. They were hardly taller than Ayc was at thirteen, so the two were nose to nose.

"Listen to me, boy," Peregrin snapped. "If you don't figure out a way to prove useful to Yris, you're going to end up dead. She's going to figure out that man at Creed Castle lied, and there isn't a drop of magic in you. Is there?"

Ayc swallowed. He didn't nod, but he didn't deny it either, and that was just as good.

Peregrin released him. "You're smart. Figure something out. She's only going to let me keep saving your ass for so long."

Ayc nodded, mumbled something like thanks, and stepped into the pastry kitchen. Peregrin slammed the door shut. The lock on the outside of the door clicked.

Ayc slumped down on the floor, touching first the stitches that lined his ear, and then fiddling with the clasps on both of his leather bracelets. In the months he'd been here, he'd often dreamed someone might come to save him.

Perhaps, his mother might arise from the dead by some miracle and storm this place. Or maybe his father—who'd forgotten Ayc when his mother died—might remember he had a son and want to save him, too. Surely, anything was better than this.

But Peregrin was right. No one was coming to save Ayc. He needed to save himself.

He undid the buckle of one bracelet, but quickly fastened it again. No, his mother had said to never take them off, and he didn't want to disobey her now. There had to be another way. He looked around him, his eyes locking on the shelves full of powders—baking powders, ones Yris kept stocked to ensure she could demand desserts whenever she wanted.

Evander had taught Ayc a few tricks that could be done with the simplest of ingredients. Tricks that, if someone didn't know better, could almost look like magic.

CHAPTER
THREE

NOW

Lora stands beside Ayc, her back rigid as a spear. Her eyes flash momentarily silver—a threat— before turning back to the deepest of violets, so dark they are almost black. She's unarmed, but Ayc knows it makes little difference. She's been trained from birth to be a weapon.

The man holding the knife lowers the blade but doesn't drop it. He bares his teeth. "He insulted the high priest."

Lora releases a tight sigh. "I'm sure he did." Without looking at Ayc, she adds, "Apologize."

Ayc hesitates.

She snaps her head toward him. Her eyes flash silver again. "Apologize," she repeats, not lifting her voice from her normal cool, unemotional tone. So like her mother. "Or I will *let* him stab you."

"Sorry," Ayc mutters.

"Fucking *mean* it."

Ayc sweeps a deep bow. "My sincerest apologies for offending your sensibilities, High Priest Marcellus."

The Lux Aester male glances at Marcellus, who gives a nod. The fae who nearly separated Ayc from his liver flops down at the table.

"It's good to see you, Loraphne," Marcellus says.

Lora gives him what should be a smile but is merely a flash of teeth. "As always, Marcellus."

Marcellus doesn't question the cryptic reply but turns on his booted heel and saunters away. Ayc opens his mouth, not quite sure what he's about to say—but sure that it'll be really, really foolish—when Lora seizes his arm and drags him away.

"*Ow, ow, ow,*" protests Ayc, but she only tightens her hold. Not tight enough to stab his arm with the sharp points of her short nails. Just tight enough to show she might be considering it.

"Divine's sake," she grumbles, as she pulls him behind a pillar and releases him. "Nothing ever changes, does it? Four years I've been gone at Adamant, and it's still not possible for you to go one day without offending someone to the point of a justified stabbing."

She swings to face him, and her presence strikes him like lightning. No makeup softens her fierce expression, and she wears her armor like it is her very skin. She looks vicious... *and* beautiful. Perhaps, he has forgotten just how beautiful. Or if not forgotten that she *is* beautiful, forgotten how her beauty *feels*: like a punch in his stomach.

"Hello to you too, Lora." Ayc leans against the pillar and brushes off his sleeve to ease the wrinkles she created. He pretends he can brush off the effect of her just as easily. "Isn't there a corner you should be sulking in?"

She fixes him with a look that tells him—if he were a wise man—he would run. Ayc has been accused of being many things. Wise is fortunately not one of them. Instead, he returns her look with a grin.

"I think the words you are looking for, *cinnamon roll*," she says, "are: '*Thank you for saving my ignorant, insufferable ass*'."

"Oh, come on, *villainess*," he shoots back, as though no time has gone by at all, and they are still both teenagers, aiming shots at each other in the hopes one might kill. "All I did was call him a pious little shit. That's not an insult. It's a *fact*."

She opens her mouth but shuts it. Not even she can argue with that one. Then she opens her mouth again, because she can't stand to let him have the last word, can she? "Next time, I'll let them turn your ass into a pincushion."

"That would truly be a tragedy. My ass would be wasted as a pincushion. It's a fine specimen."

She snorts. "Only if we're judging asses by their resemblance to a smelly, barnyard animal."

A hand shoots between them, grabs one of the remaining fruit tarts on Ayc's tray and disappears again. Ayc and Lora turn as one.

"Oh, please don't stop on my behalf," says the pretty fae who has joined them, nibbling on the crust of the tart. Like Lora, they wear the scale-like armor of the Everadyn warriors, but the black makes their pale skin look almost translucent. An emerald green cloak, embroidered with elegant swirls on the edge—a sorcerer's cloak—drapes across their shoulders. Their long snow-white hair curls over their shoulder in a single braid. The only splash of makeup is the violet eyeliner painted into a tapered wing, bringing out the sapphire of their eyes.

"Who's the pious little shit?" they ask.

Lora closes her eyes briefly, as Ayc angles his body toward this newcomer.

"Marcellus," Ayc says.

They choke on the tart. "Marcellus? The High Priest?"

"Oh, you know him?"

"Unfortunately. I grew up in Lux Aester." They say it in the same tone as though they grew up in eternal torment.

"My condolences," Ayc replies.

"Appreciated. But you're right. He is a pious little shit."

Ayc gives Lora a look that clearly says *'Told you so'.*

In return, Lora gives him a look that says, *'On second thought, a stabbing is too good for you. Disembowelment would be preferred.'* He knows, because he's seen that same look as she's uttered those exact words before.

"Lora," the fae says, "who's your friend?"

"He is *not* my friend," Lora says through her teeth.

"Ouch," Ayc says sarcastically. "Honest as ever, Lora." He holds out his hand to the fae. "I'm Ayc Waylonder, court magician and baker extraordinaire. Pronouns he/him."

The fae's lips part slightly—a subtle 'oh' of recognition. Surely, they too know the tale of the human *divina* that the Sovereign keeps in her court. Of course, the story the Everadyn fae know about him is mostly untrue. Few who weren't at Creed Castle that day know his true story. Whatever reasons Yris had for the massacre, she wants no one to know about it.

And what has Yris told the people about Ayc, again? Something about rescuing him from Drakr who made their wealth selling human children into slavery. Yris, of course,

41

only saved Ayc after she saw his divina mark and knew what it meant. Certainly, not out of the goodness of her heart. Everyone knows that is a black, withered thing.

The fae presses their mouth closed and shakes Ayc's hand. "Bronwen. Pronouns she/her. I'm roommates with Lora at Adamant. It's wonderful to meet you. I saw you performing when I came in. Are your performances always so—" She giggles, but in a way that makes Ayc feel like she's laughing with him instead of at him. "—combustible?"

"Yes," Lora says flatly. "He might as well be made of paper, as easily as he goes up in flame."

Ayc shoves the tray toward Lora without taking his eyes off Bronwen. "Have a fruit tart, villainess."

Bronwen's gaze flicks from Lora to Ayc. "Before I felt like there was a story here, but now I'm starting to suspect there's a whole novel."

"It's nothing," Lora says, as Ayc simultaneously says, "Oh yes. Really funny story, too. She cut off my ear once. The healer was able to reattach it though, so no lasting harm was done, I suppose."

Lora folds her arms over her chest, wrapping her fingers around her upper arms. Unlike her mother's, her fingernails are painted a soft neutral color, and not a blood-red, and their points are far more subtle. But the talons are still there, a constant weapon. "I didn't mean to hit you."

"Do you mean to tell me that you had such poor aim you meant to *miss* me and didn't?"

She narrows the space between them in a single predatory step, so only the tray separates them. So close he can feel the crackle of fury and power that come from her. That he can see the silver tinge in her eyes. The hair on his arm stands on end, and the rest of the room disappears, his vision tunneling to the threat before him. Ayc knows he's in danger and he should run. He knows he shouldn't *like* the way he seems to get to her, the way he knows how to push her to see a little break in her normally cool, stony exterior. He knows a lot of things, but it all fades away when he looks at her.

"I'm a much better shot now," she promises. "Perhaps we should try again."

Bronwen steals another fruit tart from the tray, and the soft scrape of her green-tipped nails snaps the rest of reality back into place. A bemused smile flutters on her lips. "So, I was right. A whole novel, then?"

Lora takes a sudden step back and drops her arms to her side. "No, it's quite simple. He's an obnoxious, insufferable ass, and we loathe each other. We've hated each other for a decade. The end."

Bronwen shrugs and licks a dollop of custard off her finger. "Well, we almost killed each other our first year at Adamant. Now, we're the dearest of friends, so perhaps there's hope for you two yet."

Lora reels her head back as though appalled by the very idea, and Ayc laughs. He likes this one. She doesn't seem like most of Lora's friends of the past. They were all too cruel. Xylie excluded, of course.

"With that hilarity, I must be off," Ayc says, sweeping a bow in Bronwen's direction. "Lovely to meet you, Bronwen. Try not to let this one scowl in the corner too long. Her face is bound to get stuck like that one of these days. Oh, and Lora?"

He spins toward her, and even after all this time, she must recognize his tone, because she stiffens and gives a flat, "No."

"Did you hear the one about the two dragons who walk into a tavern?"

"Ayc, I swear to the divine—"

"You haven't? Fantastic! One says to the other, 'It's hot in here.'"

"—if you dare finish—"

"And the other one says, *'Shut your mouth.'*"

Bronwen giggles, which is kind of her. It's a horrible joke.

Lora rolls her eyes. "Two dragons would *never* fit into a tavern."

"It's a joke," Ayc says. "You're supposed to laugh."

But she won't. She never has, not in all these years. One of these days, he's determined to make her. Because it's a challenge, of course, and not at all because he wonders what her laugh might sound like.

Lora narrows her eyes, but they're the color of orchids not of steel. "You know what, cinnamon roll? Maybe *I* need a new pincush—"

The music cuts off mid-note. The effect is not a ripple, but a lightning strike. The dancers stop. The laughter in the hall ebbs. The servers stop milling about the crowd. Ayc's smile tumbles from his lips, and he snaps his gaze to the Sovereign. She's the only one with the power to cause the world to stand still.

Yris stands from her chair behind the table, saying nothing. The Five who sit at the table are watching her intensely. Jenesis, Yris's Third, a valiant gryphon rider, blinks rapidly, like she is trying not to cry.

Something is happening. Ayc's heart knows it, based on the way it's pounding a warning against his ribcage.

Yris's hands rise to touch the circlet on her head. Beside

him, Lora sucks in a breath so sharp it cuts straight through him. Her mouth moves, forms words he doesn't think she meant to say, so silent he shouldn't hear them.

"No, not yet."

Yris, the Sovereign, lifts the circlet from her head, the one she has worn for fifty years, and tosses it before the head table. It clatters on the ground, spinning and whirling and then finally growing still. No one dares move. No one dares even breathe.

Yris's words rise, echoing without the help of amplification, without anything other than the resonance of her own power. "The Sovereignty Trials begin at sunrise in three months' time. Clans, choose your victors wisely."

She sits back down.

Silence, silence, silence.

But in Ayc's head, it's so loud. He doesn't understand the weight of the Sovereign's words, but he can feel it in the tension in the room as though everything has changed in merely two sentences.

He barely manages to keep his voice a whisper. "What's happening? What does that mean?"

He looks at Lora, but she's...frozen. But not like stone. Like someone facing an oncoming stampede of horses with nowhere to run. If he didn't know her better, he would think she's terrified. Lora is never afraid.

It's Bronwen who answers, leaning close. "It means she's stepping down as Sovereign."

It clicks into place. In Everadyn, Sovereignty is not passed down through blood. In another country, Lora might be a princess, but there's no such thing here; she's not guaranteed a throne simply because of her birth. No, in Everadyn, a Sovereign isn't born or chosen. They prove themselves *worthy*. And once they have that power, it's theirs for a century or until they decide to give it up.

And Yris... Yris is giving it up.

"S-she won't be Sovereign anymore?" Ayc says, barely daring to breathe. Barely daring to hope.

Bronwen shakes her head.

There's another lightning strike, the third in a day. This one splits his life in two. A before and after. Everything changes in a single moment.

The tray slips from Ayc's fingers and collides with the floor. The clatter screams in the silence. His voice, unbidden, follows:

"Holy fucking shit!"

FOUR

A yc doesn't wait for the glare Yris fires at him before he picks up his tray and darts from the great hall. He lets the side door slam shut behind him but doesn't make it far before he catches himself on a stained glass window that lines the hallway. It's sweltering, and he throws open the glass and shoves his face past the enchantment that keeps the castle warm. Outside, night has fallen, and the cold of winter's dark nips at his cheeks. It's not the full bite of his childhood village. In Aluina, especially in his village of Hearth within the northwest province, winter came early and left late and roared like a beast the entire time. But the Wyntra air is enough to cool the burn of his cheeks.

He breathes slowly, the way Peregrin taught him, trying to ease away the anxiety—and the pain rising like a tide within him. The moon is nearly full in the sky, casting a silver glow over the courtyard. From here, Ayc can see past the castle walls. To the right, soft lights twinkle from windows in the town. To the left lies the barracks, dark by this hour, and past that, the cliffs which loom over the Bellum Sea. The smell of salt tinges his nose, familiar and comforting.

Slowly, his heart calms. Slowly, his brain stops spinning and focuses on a single thought.

Yris will no longer be Sovereign.

He can't quite make his brain accept it. He's watched her sink her nails into every fragment of her power and respond to any threat with only mercilessness. He's seen people punished for the smallest of infractions. He's heard of fingers removed when people question orders, tongues cut out to keep people silent, whole people who disappear and are never heard from again. Yris or her Five are all too willing to conduct violence, torture, or murder to keep Yris in power.

But here she is... stepping aside.

The elation of that is short-lived. Because who will have the power if she does not?

Ayc has heard of the Sovereignty Trials before. At festivals, there's always some bard who spins speculative tales of the heroic deeds Yris and her Five did as she proved herself worthy to lead all seven Everadyn clans. Everything in those stories was vague, careful not to give a future participant an unfair advantage.

The rules seem to be fairly simple. Each clan chooses someone who was born within their clan to campaign for Sovereignty. Those victors pick five people to go with them, the only five allowed to assist them on the quests they are given. Whichever victor is first to complete the quests becomes the next Sovereign, proven worthy to lead their people.

Seven clans. Seven victors. Seven people who might replace Yris.

Who will have power over me?

"I found you," says a voice Ayc doesn't recognize.

Ayc turns around, squinting in the dim light of the hallway. Only a few lanterns sway above their heads; a touch of moonlight drifts in through the window. In the mixture of fire and moon, the fae's hair appears molten. It takes a moment to place the fae as one of the twins from his earlier performance, the one he offered the flower before he disappeared.

Ayc puts a smile back on his face, like he wasn't having a panic attack moments before. He spins his empty tray in his hands casually. "It seems you *did* find me. How can I help you?"

The fae stops before him, close enough Ayc can see the crystals spark in their eyelashes with every blink. Despite being human, he's taller than an average fae, enough that the beautiful fae before him tilts their face up to look at him.

"You owe me a flower. It's quite rude to offer one and then not follow through." Their voice is as smooth as the rich cream he layers in between his cakes, laden with suggestion.

Oh.

Oh.

He likes where this is going.

He shoves thoughts of Yris far, far away. He's sure utter chaos is raining down in the great hall, but whatever happens tonight, or in the next three months, he has no power to control it. He's never had the luxury of many choices or chances, so when one presents itself so beautifully—one that has the promise to make him forget better than any tonic—he doesn't turn it away.

"You're right," Ayc says, laying a hand over his heart. "It was quite rude of me. My sincerest apologies, um... I'm sorry I didn't get your name."

"Wren," the fae says, stretching out their hand. "She and her pronouns."

He takes Wren's hand. It's as soft as the petals on the roses she still wears as a crown in her hair, and he catches the scent of lavender and vanilla. He imagines her hands have been carefully tended with the lotions and oils the Bromalis are so well known for. Ayc wonders if the rest of her is as soft, as smooth. How her hand might feel brushing down his chest. Lower. Wrapping around him.

Fuck, Ayc. Focus. He hasn't even given her his name yet.

"I'm Ayc. He and him, generally, but I'd answer to whatever if you're the one saying it."

She smiles, catching her lip between her teeth as she does so. It's a bashful gesture, but it doesn't match the look in her eyes. The way her brown irises nearly disappear entirely as her pupils widen. She knows exactly what she is doing, exactly what she wants from him. Heat awakens deep in his gut.

He breathes in. Out. Fiddles with his bracelets to ensure they are both secure.

"So," she says, "about that flower."

"I seem to have misplaced it back in my quarters." Ayc gestures with a thumb over his shoulder back toward his pastry kitchen. "If you would like to follow me there, I'd be happy to give it to you."

He offers her his arm, and she rests her hand in the crook of his elbow. When they reach the pastry kitchen, Ayc peeks in and thanks every god he doesn't actually believe in that Xylie is no longer sitting on the counter. He sets his tray down among the untouched desserts and leads Wren through the kitchen.

The remaining treats will never be delivered tonight, and he knows he will pay for it later. But for now, Yris can fuck off. She never actually said he had to serve at this party the whole time, and it isn't his fault if after all these years she doesn't know how to give commands he can't worm his way around.

At the back of the kitchen, he opens the door to his bedroom which is hardly larger than a pantry. It holds little, but he's done the best he can to fill it with things that make it feel like a sanctuary instead of a prison. A dozen blankets and pillows pile on his bed. A dresser, situated behind the door, is covered with rings and pots of nail polish and eyeliner. A bearskin rug, which he received in exchange for baking a wedding cake, lies on the floor, and a tapestry he avoids looking at now hangs on the wall his bed sits against. The scent of baked things—cinnamon and vanilla and flour—permeates over everything.

If Ayc has any doubt why Wren followed him back to this room, she dissolves it as soon as the door swings shut. She grabs him by the collar of his vest and yanks him toward her. Her mouth tastes like fae wine, rich and heady. His hands reach to tangle into her hair, and though it doesn't blaze like sunlight, it flows like silk through his fingers. He pulls gently, testing, and she rewards him by scraping her teeth along his lower lip.

And fuck, fuck yes.

He presses against her, pushing her back against the door, never losing contact with her mouth. She opens for him, and he claims her with his tongue, getting more of her taste. Her moan goes straight through him, making him harden until he aches, until he forgets everything else but how fucking good her body feels pressed to his.

He tugs the hem of her tunic, and she lifts her arms above her head. He tosses the fabric aside and takes her in. The golden ringlets trail past her collarbones, covering the fullness of her breasts. Such a pity to cover such a piece of art. He brushes the hair aside, uncovers her completely, and places his mouth where the hair was.

"Is this all right?" he asks.

"What a silly question." Her hands do swift, skilled work ridding him of his vest and shirt. Her hands traverse his torso, and they are every bit as soft as he imagined. He's not a proud man, and he considers begging for her to continue her path. But instead, she reverses her caresses back to his shoulders. "My twin, Sterling, was who you gave the first flower to. They were interested, too, so we cast stones. I'm really glad I won. Even better that you're interested. We weren't sure which one of us you'd favor."

I like them any way they come, Ayc thinks, but that isn't the right thing to say when you have a half-naked woman before you.

Instead, he breathes a hot breath against one taut nipple. "Tell me what you like," he says, before covering her breast with his mouth. He moves his tongue in a lazy circle. She gasps and tangles her fingers into his hair.

Looking down at him, her eyes flash silver.

The first time that happened in the heat of a moment, Ayc was only sixteen. He shrieked and stumbled away from the boy whose mouth was doing something incredibly fascinating only moments before. The boy had to explain that the Everadyn fae's eyes didn't only flash silver when they're angry, but also, when they're incredibly *aroused*. Ayc had kept his eyes shut through his entire first time, but now Ayc smiles at the effect he has on Wren and repeats his attentions to her other breast to make the silver shine brighter. He isn't used to feeling powerful, and there's power in being wanted.

"I like to be fucked," she says. "Hard and thoroughly."

He straightens and drags her closer, grinding his hips against hers so she can feel what those words do to him. She groans, and he wants to swallow that noise down. He aims for her mouth, but she presses a finger to his lips.

She adds, "And only for *one* night. Just so we are clear."

He nods. He didn't expect anything different. No one ever stays for long.

She giggles, a trilling sound. "I've never fucked a human before. Do you think you can manage?"

The word 'human' is a splash of ice to his veins, the reminder of why in a fae world, his finite life will only ever earn him the position of *one* night. He will always be too mortal, too weak, for more. And he wants more, someday. But impossible dreams are luxuries he can entertain a different time.

He shakes off the sting.

More to prove; always more to prove.

When he whispers into her ear, his voice is almost not his own. It growls from his throat as he slips the rings from his right hand. The soft thuds of metal hitting the floor punctuate his words. "I think it would be foolish"—*thunk*— "to underestimate what I'm capable of." *Thunk, thunk.*

"Prove it!" she snaps.

"And how would you like me to prove it?" He trails his

hand down the slope of her abdomen and slips past the waistband of her leggings. He watches her face as he glides his hand along her center, waiting for the flash of silver that tells him he's found the right place. When he does, he presses in. Circles slowly. Her breath starts and stops in tiny whimpers. The crystals in her eyelashes sparkle in the moonlight pouring from a window high above.

"There are so many options," Ayc teases. "Would you like my fingers?" He dips into her. Her head tumbles back against the door with a whine, and he pumps his finger in and out, just to hear that sound again. "Or maybe my tongue?"

She nods her head, her mouth parted.

"I can't hear you, Wren."

"Yes," she says. Almost a pleading, but not quite.

"Yes what, sweetheart?"

"Yes, *please*."

A minute later, he is on his knees before her, her leggings gone, one of her bare legs flung over his shoulder, and he is tasting her. Her hands slap against the door as he drags his tongue along her length, swirling around the spot he found with his finger. Her body bucks, and she rocks herself against his mouth. He seizes one of her hips and helps her to find her rhythm.

"That's right." He pauses long enough to coax. "Fuck my tongue like a good girl. Don't hold back."

Her eyes flash: two full moons in the dark. Her fingers latch into his hair as she does just that— riding his mouth as he exchanges broad sweeps of his tongue with fast flicks at her clit. He listens to her body, her little moans, studying her the way he studies a new recipe, adjusting to get it just right.

He slides two fingers into her tight warmth, and her movement freezes. She yanks so hard on his hair it hurts, and he loves it. Fucking loves it. Her muscles tighten on his fingers, and he pumps hard. He licks and nips, as her back arches off the door. Her legs shudder and threaten to buckle. She bites down on her own hand to muffle her moan.

When her convulsions slow, he tastes her, drinks her in one last time. She gasps, leaning heavily against the door. She is a piece of art, all spent and panting for him.

He pushes himself to his feet and cocks his head. "Did I prove myself?"

She grasps at his belt with frantic hands. He stumbles out of his boots and trousers, and she steps back to take a look at him. But his need is too great to contain now. He seizes her hips and turns her. He fists a hand into her hair and pushes her against the door. She yelps in surprise, and he freezes.

He begins to loosen his hold, but she says swiftly, "Don't. I like it. Just... are you on the monthly potion?"

The potion. The one that tastes like soured cream but protects from both infection and pregnancy. "Yes."

"Good. Me, too. Now, please, fuck me. Hard and fast."

Ayc slips out of the last layer of fabric and takes himself into his own hand, lining himself up with her entrance. He goes slow at first, listening to her body, waiting for her to relax around him. And yes, she feels every bit as wonderful as he imagined. She moans, and his restraint breaks. He thrusts the rest of the way into her. She cries out, first a "Fuck" and then a "Yes."

"Spread your feet wider for me," Ayc says. "You can take me deeper."

She does and arches her back for good measure. He

strokes one hand down the angle of her spine before fitting his palm to her hip, then wraps her golden strands around his other hand. When he has her just as he wants her, he drives deep, hard, like she asked for. She responds to him, rocking against him, and soon he finds a rhythm that has him seeing red.

She turns her head, biting into her forearm to remain silent.

"None of that. Don't cover that pretty mouth. I want to hear you."

He tugs on her hair until she arches against him, her bare back flesh against his chest. Each thrust drives her onto her toes and works a cry from her mouth. He buries his face in her neck, dragging first his lips and then his tongue in the soft place where her pulse thrums.

Beat. Beat. Beat.

That little vibration flickers through him. He revels in the way it speeds up with every thrust, the way it falls out of rhythm when he shifts her hip and finds the perfect angle. The way it almost stops completely when she throws her head back against his shoulder and cries out his name.

The heat in him is too much. It will all be over soon. So, he slips his hand between her legs. "Come for me again. Let me feel you."

She does, and the way she screams takes him over the edge with her. He grinds his teeth together to hold back the growl that forms as pleasure erupts down his spine. He slams his palm into the door, his vision going completely red behind his eyelids.

"All right," she pants, slack against his chest, her crown of flowers askew. His arm, still hooked around her waist, is the only thing keeping her upright. "I think you proved yourself, but I think I should stick around for an hour or so and try again. Just to be sure."

When she giggles, he laughs into her hair, trying not to inhale her lavender scent. Trying not to feel anything at all.

"Divine, that's so good," Wren says from behind her hand, and Ayc is only slightly disappointed that it is his *baking* talents that has made the whimpering noise come from her lips this time.

He sweeps his thumb across her chin to wipe up the chocolate mousse that has dripped there. He dips it into his mouth, the chocolate tasting salty from the contact with her skin.

"So, what do you think of the Sovereign's announcement?" Wren asks. "I take it by your reaction you were surprised."

His grin twists into something a little more sheepish. "I think the whole court now knows I was completely unaware."

She laughs softly, then presses the back of her hand over her lip to silence the musical noise. "I think all of us were thinking what you were brave enough to say. I assumed Yris would take every last day of the hundred years that law permits each Sovereign. It's strange that she's giving up her power."

Talking about Yris isn't something Ayc ever wants to do but talking about her *now*—when there's a naked person in his bed, draped in blond curls and moonlight—is especially distasteful. He has nothing to add, so he leans his back against the wall. The tapestry hanging there brushes against his spine. He tries not to think about *that* particular piece of art. He never should have bought it.

Wren searches his face as she nibbles at a lemon biscuit, selected from the plate of assorted baked goods he assembled for her. "Do you think you'll still be her personal baker and magician once she's no longer Sovereign?"

Ayc almost flinches. "I don't know." It's as honest as he can be. Long ago, he was bound to serve the Sovereign, and he suspects that oath will transfer to whoever succeeds her. The unknown causes a scream to build in his chest. He forces himself to take a calming breath. "Each clan picks their own victor, correct?"

"Yes." Wren plucks a chocolate-covered strawberry from the plate and sucks it between her lips. Ayc looks away before he loses his focus to more sinful thoughts.

"How are they chosen?" he asks.

"Different ways. I was only a little kid during the last Sovereignty Trials."

Ayc blinks, studying Wren's face. She doesn't look any older than him, and yet, she's lived over twice as many years.

"Noxumbra and Audori generally host a tournament," Wren continues. "Several of the clans, like Bromalis and the Totus Omni, have a meeting where there are nominations and votes."

Wren talks with her hands, big and bold and enthusiastically. A smile tugs on his lips, a little glow of warmth behind his breastbone. He likes that—her expressiveness.

Stop it. No getting attached.

He imagines dumping water on that little glow. Cold and frigid.

"Lux Aester will probably pray and ask the divine to appoint someone." Wren gasps. "Which means it'll be—"

"Marcellus," Ayc mutters.

"Marcellus," she agrees.

There's the frigid water he needed.

Please anyone but him. If there is anyone who might be worse than Yris, it'd be Marcellus. He would destroy everything good, every layer of diversity Ayc has come to love about the Everadyn people. If Yris is Ayc's villain, then Marcellus would be a nightmare, one with no hope of ever waking from.

Perhaps Ayc's distress shows on his face because Wren touches his arm gently. "He won't win. There's too many people likely to compete who are stronger than him."

"Who would *you* want to win?"

She answers quickly, like she's already thought about it. "I think Sterling, my twin, would make a great leader. They're kind and strong and wise. They have wonderful ideas about how to make Everadyn better, smooth relations between the clans, do something about the Lux Aester and the damn restrictive laws that they enforce within their clan. Maybe even—" She pauses, pursing her lips, as though trying to decide if she should say more, and then finishes, "Well, they have lots of brilliant ideas."

Ayc moves the plate of food out from between them so he can move closer. She sits with her knees pulled toward her chest and he spreads his legs on either side of her, so his chest nearly touches her calves. Not close enough, but it'll do. "Why not you?"

"Oh, no. Sterling is good all the way through, but me?" She lowers her voice to a whisper. "I have a wicked side."

Ayc wiggles his eyebrows and teases, "Do you?"

"Yes," she says with a wink that makes him sincerely doubt her answer.

"Are you a warrior, then?"

"Worse." She leans closer. "A herbalist."

Ayc throws back his head and laughs.

"Don't laugh," she says, but the sternness she aims for is broken by her own, barely restrained giggle. "I run the most popular herbal shop in Orchis. I've had people come from all over Everadyn to seek my advice, knowledge, and supplies. And besides, plants are no joking matter."

"Oh, I know," Ayc admits sincerely. There's not much difference between being an apothecary and being an herbalist. Before Evander died, he taught Ayc a lot.

She cocks her head curiously. "Oh? And what do you know of plants?"

Ayc fumbles with his smile. He's neared too close to his past. He quickly covers his error. "I'm a baker, remember? Got to know which plants will make something taste like eternal paradise and which will send you there."

Ayc trails his hand over her calf to distract her. It works, because she shivers and talks a little faster to hide it.

"As I was saying, the type of power that comes with being Sovereign is best left to those who are pure-hearted, like Sterling. But then, that's what worries me. No one survives the Sovereignty Trials without being a little vicious. The Trials are brutal, bound by very few rules. Almost anything goes in completing the quests, including violence between the victors and their teams. Generally, the one who wins is the one most willing to fight dirty. It's why I don't think Marcellus will win. He has too many rules to keep his version of the divine happy."

"I think that's giving him too much credit," Ayc says,

dipping his head to press a kiss to the inside of her knee. She lets out a little breath.

"What do you mean?"

"I don't trust that he loves the divine. I think he loves the power."

"Maybe." She studies Ayc thoughtfully. "Sterling will have to choose their Five well, to be more ruthless than they're capable of being. The competition will be fierce. Marcellus, maybe. Loraphne, certainly."

Ayc's hand freezes halfway down her thigh. "Loraphne?"

"Yes, the child of the reigning Sovereign almost always competes. Yris's father was the Sovereign before her. Loraphne is certainly going to compete. She could probably build a Five out of people who have graduated from Adamant or Velphin, and no one would stand a chance."

A cool sweat breaks out across Ayc's back. He drops his hand from Wren. He glances at the door as the familiar desire to run blazes through his legs. But he tried running once. It only ended in more chains.

Lora *can't* win. He cannot spend the rest of his life serving her, instead of her mother. He's watched Yris mold Lora in her own image for ten years. It will be another several decades of torment.

Soft fingertips touch the stubble at his jaw. "Hey, where'd you go?"

Wren hovers inches from his face, her eyes gleaming in the moonlight. They are filled with actual concern. For *him*. His heart contracts.

Stop that.

"Sorry," Ayc says, spinning a strand of her hair around his finger. "I just got in my own head for a second."

"Hm." She leans in, her lips close to his ear. "Bet I could

get you out of it." Her words turn to kisses on his jaw, down his neck. Her hand slips downward, over his chest, into his lap. A low growl involuntarily leaves his lips as her fingers wrap around him.

"I liked that noise," she giggles. "Let's see if I can make it better with my mouth."

Oh, yes, definitely. Do that.

She has dipped her head when a soft bell hanging from the ceiling in the corner chimes. Ayc stiffens and catches her wrist.

She straightens and whispers, "What is it?"

"It's charmed to ring whenever my kitchen door opens," Ayc says. "Someone is here."

Her eyes jerk to the door, flashing silver. She's already starting to move off the bed when Ayc tightens his hold on her wrist.

"No, stay. It's probably just a friend of mine. She doesn't do well with strangers." If it is Xylie, that is, but something in the way Ayc's hair stands on end, he doesn't think so.

Wren sinks back on the bed as he stands. "Do you have a wife?"

He opens his mouth in a soundless laugh. "No." He grabs his shirt and pants from the floor and slips into them. As he approaches the door, he removes his bracelets and tucks them into his pants' pockets. He opens the door only a crack, grabs the sword that leans against the wall nearby, and slips into the shadows.

The intruder has already made it to the icebox, where he placed his leftover pastries. In the icebox's light, Ayc can only make out a silhouette of wide hips and broad shoulders. And that's all he needs to place her.

He pauses a few feet away, out of the light where he

knows she can't see him. He watches as she selects a glass bowl of chocolate pudding from the fridge. She closes the door, and the darkness thickens. It isn't the first time she's come to raid the sweets from his kitchen. She's done it dozens of times. All the times before, he always simply watched until she snuck back out again. He doesn't know why this time is different, what compels him forward. Perhaps because it's been over four years since she's done it, or perhaps he's merely reckless. But this time, he steps closer.

He's just out of arm's reach when he wills himself out of the shadows. "If it isn't the great pudding thief..."

Mistake.

It's a stupid, fucking mistake.

She moves in a blur, honed from years of training, and in only a handful of seconds, it's over. She's kicked the sword from his hand and slammed him against the wall. He can't draw a breath, and he's not sure if it's because of the dagger she's pressing to his throat, the glow of silver in her eyes, or how she's managed to do all that without dropping the damn bowl of pudding.

He's lost count of the amount of times Lora has cut off his air supply. She does it so effortlessly. He resists the urge to shove her away, to end the unsettling feeling of her nearness. Instead, he relaxes against the wall and gives her his best, cheeky grin.

"Knife to see you too, villainess," Ayc says.

"You should know better than to sneak up on me, cinnamon roll." Her eyes fade back to a dark brown. She releases him, takes two steps back, and sheaths her dagger at her side.

Ayc rubs at his throat, soothing his molten skin with his

cool palm. "Says the person sneaking into my room in the middle of the night."

Lora lifts her chin and glares at him. She's dressed in the same skin-tight black clothes as earlier, but a loose, gray cardigan has replaced her armor. It drapes off one shoulder, its knitted pattern forming rows that sweep and twirl until they give the illusion of a never-ending forest.

"I was hungry," she says flatly.

"And there isn't a whole other kitchen you could raid? You had to come to mine?" Ayc turns on a nearby lamp mounted to the wall beside him, then steps to a nearby counter, opens a drawer, and pulls out a spoon. "You know, you could just admit that I make amazing pudding, and you were devastated you didn't get any at the party."

She gives him a look like she'd rather die.

He offers her the spoon. She eyes it like it's a weapon and doesn't take it, so he flicks it at her face. She snatches it from the air with such ease it might as well have been standing still.

"Enjoy your pudding," Ayc says. "Next time, just knock and ask instead of staging a robbery and nearly slaughtering me in my own home."

He walks around her, picks his sword off the floor and tosses it on the counter. He reaches into his pocket to pull out his bracelets and put them on. Lora hasn't moved toward the door; instead, she stares at the sword on the table.

"Why do you have that?" Lora asks.

"Protection."

Lora snorts. The dull blade bears more than a few chips and dents. It was an old training sword he found tossed aside as a teen and would do little against an actual intruder. "I guess it's a good thing it's not sharp, because you're more likely to stab yourself. I remember when Peregrin attempted to teach you. I would trust a toddler to run with a knife before I trusted you to fight."

Ayc shrugs and plants his hands on the table. He remembers, too, the way his arms shook as he held a sword for the first time. He was only fourteen then, knowing Yris watched him closely. By then, she knew about his ability to turn invisible, and Ayc feared what she might make him become if he showed a talent with a blade.

Anything she wanted. The very darkest of weapons.

Fortunately, he proved to be what she suspected: a weak human, good to entertain and bake and nothing more. Invisibility might have been a useful ability for her—if someone other than silly, pathetic Ayc was blessed with the talent.

Lora stabs the spoon into the pudding, then stirs it much more gently. He almost tells her to stop; the consistency is already extra whipped, the way she likes it. For her, the texture is more important than the taste. Instead, he watches her, the same way he imagines people watch a dragon who has entered their home unexpectedly. She finally lifts the spoon to her mouth and, afterward, licks her lips.

"Did you know?" Ayc asks, looking pointedly away from her mouth. "That your mother was about to call the Trials?"

Her hand holding the spoon twitches. Ayc doesn't actually expect her to answer, but at last, she murmurs, "My mother only tells her plans to those she trusts the most."

"Which excludes you?"

Something flickers over her face; Ayc can't place it before it's gone. Her voice remains monotone. "I suspected something when she summoned me from Adamant two weeks from graduation."

And, of course, Lora came running. Ayc and Lora both stand at attention when Yris snaps her fingers. But Ayc does it because he ran out of choices long ago, and Lora does it out of loyalty. They couldn't be more different.

She takes another bite, and Ayc dares to ask, "Do you want to be Sovereign?"

"Of course I plan to compete." Her answer is quick—too quick—punctuated by her eyes transforming from a steely, tired gray to a sharper onyx black. "It's what I've been raised to do since the moment I was born."

Ayc releases a tight sigh. He doesn't point out that her words fail to answer his question.

"Ayc."

Wren stands in the small opening in his doorway, looking utterly divine in only her sunset-hued tunic.

Lora stiffens with the spoon near her lips. Her gaze flicks between Ayc and Wren, before she drops the spoon. It plunks into the pudding.

"I didn't realize you had company," Lora says, her words turning into a hiss, her eyes narrowing as she fixes on Wren. "Especially such poor taste in company."

Wren only smiles graciously, leaning against the doorframe. "It's lovely to see you, too, Lora. It's been a long time. Seven years, right?"

Tension crackles from Lora, like a lightning storm approaching, and her fingers twitch toward the dagger at her side. Ayc swiftly maneuvers himself between the two women. Clearly some bad blood exists between the two, and he very much does not want a knife imbedded in Wren's throat.

"Wren, sorry," Ayc says. "Loraphne was just taking her pudding and leaving." He gives her a pointed look and gestures to the door with a swirl of his wrist.

She narrows her eyes further, until they are dark slits, but her hand doesn't move closer to the dagger. Instead, she turns on her heel and marches in the... opposite direction of the door, toward the icebox. She whips it open, balances a plate of fruit tarts on the pudding bowl, and then grabs a pan of cinnamon rolls, which glisten with spirals of icing. She kicks the icebox closed and sends Ayc a glare that dares him to protest. He doesn't.

"Have they not been feeding you in that warrior school of yours?" Ayc asks instead.

"Some of it is for Bronwen," she says as she makes her way to the door.

"Good. I hope you both enjoy it. Oh, and you should go see your cousin."

Lora pauses, and the set of her shoulders softens at the mention of Xylie. "It's the middle of the night."

"And you think Xylie is sleeping? It's like you don't know her at all. She's not here brewing, so if she's not in her room, I'd check in—"

"The library," Lora finishes for him. "I know." She reaches for the doorknob with her elbow.

"And Lora..."

She glances at him over her shoulder. He makes a face, crossing his eyes, sticking out his tongue. She rolls her eyes, a fracture in her stony demeanor. He'll take it.

"Good luck with the Trials," he says, but he's never meant anything less.

When Lora is gone, Ayc returns to Wren's side. Without hesitation, she pulls him back to the bed, undressing him, burying her fingers into his hair as she presses her body to his.

"I didn't realize," she says, teeth grazing his ear, "that you and Loraphne were so close."

He laughs hard, because nothing has ever been funnier. The noise cuts off as her legs wrap around his waist, yanking him close to her center. She grinds against him, and it takes a moment of pained cursing before he can make himself respond. "You know what they say about friends and enemies."

"Keep your enemies closer? I thought that was only so you could more easily slide a knife between their ribs."

"Exactly." That sums up his relationship with Lora perfectly. Knives hidden behind verbal jabs and chocolate pudding and poorly timed jokes.

The ache in his back isn't quiet at the moment, so Ayc grasps Wren's hips and flips their positions, so she rises above him. She strips her tunic from her body and tosses it to the side. He positions his hands behind his head and grins up at her. She is all gold and silver in the moonlight. He desires to think of nothing else.

"Should I be jealous?" she asks.

"Why would you be jealous? As you said, this is only for the night."

"Then let's not waste it."

They do not. Not a single second.

CHAPTER
FIVE

In the two months that follow, life at Wyntra wraps itself around the upcoming Trials. It's all the cooks and maids whisper about when they gather in the kitchen to eat leftovers and gossip. They beg Ayc to tell them what he knows. So, he listens closely while he serves dessert to Yris and her Five, as the names of the victors are declared.

"Mienna from Audori," Fennix says over winterberry pie, a stain streaking from the corner of his lip. "She's a fire elementist. She'll be a strong competitor."

"Marcellus from Lux Aester," Jenesis sighs over an apple and cinnamon crumble. "But of course."

"Sterling from Bromalis," says Onanna over chocolate cake covered in molten sauce that she does not touch. In all these years, Ayc has never seen her eat, just like he's never seen her face past the hood of her dark cloak. He's only ever glimpsed her blood red lips and eyes that always glow silver.

"They don't stand a chance," murmur the twins, Kol and Krane, Yris's Fourth and Fifth. They, too, are sorcerers and share an eerie ability to speak in unison.

From his place in the corner, Ayc thinks that underestimating the people around Sterling might be their undoing. Then he thinks about naked skin and soft screams and yellow hair turned gold in the moonlight until Yris snaps, "Human, stop smiling like a fool and go do something useful."

Noxumbra hosts a tournament to decide their victor. Yris has the reports and rosters brought to her every day but doesn't attend the tournament she must have won fifty years ago. She is Noxumbra, like her father and mother before her, and when she won her Trials, she did so as Noxumbra's victor. Now, she watches through reports as her own daughter competes. Each day, Lora's name rises and rises, until there are only two names on the top. Loraphne and Wylder.

Ah, Wylder. Ayc remembers that asshole well. How could he forget the cocky son of a bitch who thought being the son of the Noxumbra regent meant he was destined to be the greatest fighter of his generation? And perhaps he would have been, if Lora wasn't better than him, which was proved every time Wylder visited Wyntra, which was frequently, coming either for school or when his father came for business.

During Wylder's visits, Ayc unfortunately got to know him far too well. Wylder attached himself to Lora's side, and when he wasn't with her, he was eagerly joining in on Yris's game of tormenting Ayc. He was particularly skilled. Somehow, Wylder saw pieces of Ayc no one else did and aimed a metaphorical knife right at his most tender places.

Ayc would like to forget all that. He would especially like to forget about the time when he was eighteen, and he found Wylder and Lora together in some dark corner of the stables, his mouth at her throat, her skirts raised around her waist, his hips thrusting into hers with the same violence with which he wielded a sword. Ayc hurried away before Lora's eyes—wide open and fixed high above her—could turn to Ayc. Try as he might, that dreadful image is permanently branded in his brain. He can't shake it, just like he can't quite rid himself of wondering if, in the four years they trained together at Adamant, they continued their sloppy lovemaking.

He doesn't know why it even interests him. They deserve each other: the villainess and her dark knight. And now they're in a tournament, battling against each other for something they both want. How awkward for them.

Ayc is certain Lora will win.

When the paper comes the next day, only one name is on top.

"Wylder for the Noxumbra," Yris says flatly, but she crushes the paper into her hands, and Ayc senses danger coming from her in waves. He slinks out of the room, leaving the pan of cinnamon rolls for them to serve themselves.

As winter begins to wind down, each day brings less icy sea breezes and a little more promise of spring. More victors are named, and Ayc begins to hope Lora won't be his next ruler, after all.

Hason from Sal Maris, a high-ranking captain in the navy.

Ruatha from Lycendi, a woman skilled in both sorcery and alchemy.

It leaves only Totus Omni. Ayc knows little of Lora's father but knows that he belonged to the Totus Omni. Meaning Lora has one more chance to be elected as victor.

"She'll have limited choices in her Five if she wins their

vote," Fennix says, sucking on a caramelized apricot. "The Totus Omni's Council of the *People* always gives guidance the victors have little choice but to follow."

A bit of disdain rings through his voice. Most of the clans have an elected council, whose purpose is to represent the wishes and desires of their people to the clan regent. The other clans refer to this as the Council of Elders, as strict age limits are enforced on who can be elected into the position. But the Totus Omni refer to it as the Council of the People, because they are the only clan who intentionally ensure that the council seats are equally shared by both the experience of the elders and the vision of the youth.

"If it isn't Noxumbra," Yris says, barely looking up from her plate, "she needn't bother. There's never been a Totus Omni winner. They're all weak and pathet— *For divine's sake, human!*"

"I beg your forgiveness, my lady," Ayc gushes, as he grabs a napkin to mop up the lukewarm pitcher of tea he has 'accidentally' knocked over into her lap. She snatches the napkin away and wipes furiously, growling at him to get out. He does.

The word comes on a late winter morning which threatens that spring—and the beginning of the Trials—is all too near.

Loraphne has been chosen by Totus Omni.

She is the seventh and final victor.

Ayc thinks long and hard about running, but he already knows, he has no where to run.

EIGHT YEARS AGO

Ayc couldn't breathe.

No matter how much he fought he couldn't lift his head above the water. His lungs burned. Screamed. Begged. Perhaps, this was how he would die.

The hand tangled in his hair ripped his head above the surface of the fountain. He gasped for air, his vision blurred by the water pouring into his eyes. Peals of laughter rang out around him from the group of fae children who gathered to participate in his torment. He recognized them as children who lived here in Wyntra. They were his most frequent tormentors, always finding new ways to terrorize him: cornering him, shoving him into manure carts, and now, nearly drowning him in the fountain.

Ayc had refused to learn their names, least they tormented his dreams, too.

"Should we dunk the cinnamon roll again?" asked the leader of the group. Despite his scrawny build, the grip he had on Ayc's hair was too strong for Ayc to escape.

Cinnamon roll. It was the nickname they tormented him with, not just for the treats he baked, but for how pathetic they found him. Soft. Doughy. Weak.

"I think he's sufficiently drowned," said a voice Ayc knew all too well.

He couldn't see past the four children who stood at the edge of the fountain, but he knew Lora watched everything from a few feet away. She *always* watched his tormentors, ever the villainess with her minions. If she wanted, she could stop it. The children admired Lora, perhaps because she was the Sovereign's daughter or perhaps because of her unyielding strength and talent with the blade. If she told them to stop, they would. But she never did.

The children uttered a collective moan of

disappointment. And Lora adds, "But you can do it one more time, just to be sure."

The hand shoved Ayc under once more. Something deep within roared at him to fight back, but Ayc couldn't bring himself to do it. If he clawed and flared and lashed out, someone might get hurt in the process. Probably himself, to be honest.

He was on the verge of his lungs bursting once more when the hand released him. He surged upward and grasped for the fountain's edge. The children were already walking away, laughing and shoving each other. Only Lora remained, a few feet further into the courtyard garden, leaning against the statue of a full-figured, beautiful fae warrior who Ayc didn't recognize.

Ayc scrambled from the fountain and tumbled onto the ground in a pile of awkward, lanky limbs. Two pristinely polished boots appeared in his vision.

"For divine's sake," Lora said, "why can't you ever just try to defend yourself?"

Ayc shoved himself upright and sprinted out of her reach. He kept going, past the hedges, into the area of the large courtyard set up for training. His own boots squawked at him with each step, the worn, patched things logged with water. Lora's footsteps crunched on the gravel as she pursued him. She didn't run, but merely strolled comfortably behind, knowing she'd eventually catch him.

He knew he made a pathetic sight. A tall, gangly boy being chased by a girl a head shorter, but he didn't care. Because his pounding heart and crawling nerves reminded him he knew exactly what that girl was capable of, and gods, hadn't he been tormented enough for one day?

He made it to one of the exits in the Wyntra Castle,

stepping into the darkness of the arched walkway before realizing his mistake. At the other end, two fae guards stood motionless. Beyond, the homes and barracks of the aerial armies pressed together, clustered around streets wide enough to hold a gryphon.

"Ayc, stop!" Lora called from behind him, but Ayc had already halted.

He couldn't go any further. Yris might have allowed his door to remain unlocked during the day, but only because she had more than enough eyes in this castle to ensure he never made past the courtyard. All she had done was widen his prison. And Lora, of course, was his most dedicated prison guard.

Ayc swung around to face Lora, right as she lunged. Ayc's back slammed against the stone wall of the passageway. He didn't see Lora draw the knife, but its point was pressed against Ayc's throat within a blink. Every nerve in his body focused in on that millimeter of flesh where the metal hovered, close enough to touch but not enough to break skin.

He was taller than Lora now, and he looked down the slope of the blade, into her cool eyes currently the color of earth after a spring rain. They watched each other for a long moment in silence, breathing in and out in unison. This was all, by now, a familiar pattern: the children's torment, her blade at his throat. And he was so sick of this song and dance. So sick of being afraid, of everyone always having so much power over him, of everyone finding so much delight in his fear.

And so Ayc took a breath and forced himself to smile. Not a wobbly smile, but one that was easy. Light-hearted. Unaffected.

"Hey, Lora," he said, in the tone he often used when he'd whisper a joke to her at mealtime—one she never laughed at.

She responded predictably, with a low growl. "Do not."

With the small act of defiance that was his smile, Ayc found his usual terror fading. She hadn't killed him yet, and if today was the day, well, at least he would be done with all the games. His smile was a lie, but it at least gave him a little power.

"Did you hear the one about the beehive without an exit?" Ayc said. "It was un-*bee*-liev-able."

She wrapped her hand around his shirt collar and yanked it tight around his neck. "I think I'm really going to stab you this time."

He only forced his smile to be bigger. "If you stab me, do you think your mother would still make me bake her apple crisp for the third time this week? I'm so sick of peeling apples. A stabbing would be preferable."

The muscles in her cheeks spasmed, like she was barely withholding some emotion. "She would probably still make you."

"Damn." Ayc sighed. "You're right."

Lora released him with a thrust and sheathed her blade in a smooth motion. Ayc took his first full breath in several minutes.

She planted her hands on her hips and huffed out a breath, her chest rising and falling. Ayc fixed his gaze on her nose, so his traitorous eyes wouldn't follow the movement of her body. He needed to keep pretending that he hadn't noticed that his own body wasn't the only one that had changed over this summer. If he thought about the changes in Lora, it made the already humid air feel downright suffocating. He should feel nothing other than fear and hatred toward her, and he didn't appreciate whatever nonsense went through his head when she was near. He didn't even like noticing that she'd begun wearing her hair differently since she returned from visiting her father this summer. Gone was the updo that resembled her mother's. Now, her curls spilled around her shoulders, their tight spirals held back only by clips on each side of her head. He liked it so much better, and he hated himself for it. He had no business liking *anything* about her.

"Why won't you ever just try to defend yourself?" she snapped, repeating the same words from earlier. "Can't you just use your power?"

He moved away from the wall, backing toward the courtyard, so he was positioned toward an escape route. "I've used my power."

She arched a single eyebrow. "The little sparks in your hands? Pathetic."

Ayc had practiced for weeks before he dared show Yris the trick he'd been working on, so he was sure she wouldn't notice the powder. She hadn't, but she wasn't impressed, either. She and Fennix and Onanna didn't stop coaching and pressuring him for more. Bigger flames. Brighter flames. Shoot it farther and make it take shape the way elementals could. None of those things he could deliver.

Ayc shrugged. "I guess the divine didn't bless me with much."

Lora took a step toward him. Her hands didn't fall on the hilt of her dagger again. Still, his heart pounded with something that wasn't fear, exactly, but wasn't exactly *not* fear either. "You have to start doing *something*. Onanna thinks you're hiding your true gift. My mother disagrees. She thinks that man at Creed Castle lied, and you don't have magic at all. She's got a plan to make you reveal the truth once and for all."

A shiver ran down Ayc's spine.

"What plan?" Ayc demanded.

Lora shook her head. He couldn't read the emotions on her face. Was it amusement? Surely, she was amused that their game was about to be over.

"Dammit! What plan, Lora?"

The fierceness in Ayc's voice startled even him, as did the step he'd involuntarily taken toward her. She slid her feet apart, into a fighter's stance, her hand back on her blade. He drew himself short.

Lora's other hand fluttered at her side. Anxious? No, of course not, because when she spoke, her voice was cold as ice. As cold as her mother's. "I don't know. But I hope you haven't been lying. Because my mother *will* find out the truth, and if she finds out you've been lying this whole time, she's going to make me kill you." She paused and released her dagger. "I really don't want to have to kill you, Ayc."

Something within Ayc broke in that moment. It wasn't the sudden shattering of a window by a thrown rock. Instead, it was the rupturing of ice that had long been splintering and needed only a snowflake to lead to complete ruin.

"Don't pretend to care!" he growled, his voice echoing against the stone. It didn't sound like his own voice; it sounded more like a monster. "You're a cold, heartless bitch, just like your mother."

She took another step back, her eyes wide. For a second, it almost seemed like his words hurt. Then she shook her head, and her face was stone once more.

"Fine. I won't pretend." She marched up to him, yanked

herself to her full height, and put her nose within an inch of his. "I wish she would have let me slit your throat two years ago. Then I wouldn't have had to listen to your awful jokes this entire time."

Her hot breath brushed his chin, and his traitorous eyes dropped to her lips and his stupid head wondered—not for the first time—what it would be like to kiss her. And he *hated* himself for it. What kind of person did that make him? That he wanted to kiss someone so heartless. Someone who treated him like he was nothing. Someone who wanted to kill him.

He whipped around and stormed away. She hurled words after him. "Figure it out, cinnamon roll! You don't have much time left."

Back in his kitchen, Ayc admitted Lora was right.

Ayc's time was running out.

Later that night, he stood at the window in his kitchen, the one that looked out into the courtyard, which was now bathed in the deep violet of dusk. He watched Peregrin walking away from the training rings in the courtyard, the last of their students gone to wherever they went at the end of the night. Just as she did every night, Tempest came to meet Peregrin and walked with them on their way back home. As though sensing she had an audience, Tempest cocked her head to the side so one silver eye shone back at Ayc. She lifted a wing, as though to wave. Ayc waved back, and she added a little prance to her step.

When the warrior and their steed disappeared from view, Ayc let his head fall onto the window. Dampness clung to the glass from the humidity in the air. How many days did he have left? Surely, it was two years more than he should have had; by rights, he should have died in the massacre of Creed. But he was only fourteen. He wanted *more*.

He fiddled with the buckles on his bracelets, the ones he'd promised his mother never to take off. Just like he'd promised to stop doing those little tricks he was so, so good at as a child—disappearing and not being found if he didn't want to be. She warned him of all the things that might happen if he continued. But now, the little trick might be his only shot at escaping this place.

Where would he go if he left? Out there was a land he didn't know. He couldn't return to Aluina. No one in Wyntra would speak to him about Aluina's fate, but he gathered enough from whispers to know the Drakr ruled over Aluina now. There was no home left to return to. Surely, that's why Yris didn't bother to have this window locked. Even if he could slip out the window without someone seeing him, she knew he had no where to go.

And what would happen if he tried to run and Yris caught him? He shuddered at the thought.

But he couldn't stay here either. His time to convince her had run out. Yris would call his bluff and kill him. Maybe, in a month. Maybe, tomorrow. He could stay and die, or he could take a chance and live.

Considering it that way, Ayc didn't have much of a choice.

He slipped off his bracelets and laid them on the window sill. Darkness had completely fallen by then, and the world outside was black enough his own reflection could be seen in the glass.

The shadows brushed over him, like fingers touching his skin, and he willed it to cover him, to surround him. To *become* him. He found it as easy and natural as taking a breath. Like it was a part of him. And that terrified him.

When he looked back in the window, his reflection was gone. He took a breath. Let it go. His face returned.

He could do this.

Two hours later, he was ready, a bag packed with food from his kitchen. He always kept spare, preserved food, in case Yris got annoyed with him and dismissed him before he ate his share of food at mealtime. A spare change of clothes was also in the bag, as well as a little bit of the money from the scant wages Yris paid him.

Then he took off his cuffs, slipped out the window into the shadows, and *ran*.

CHAPTER
SIX

NOW

The first day of spring decides to be defiantly cold and rainy, as early spring days often are along the coast. So Ayc, defiantly, decides to get drunk.

"Xylie, we're getting drunk!" he proclaims when she walks into the pastry kitchen, dressed in her usual multi-colored cardigan over a plain tunic and breeches. He lifts his goblet toward her, sloshing red fae wine down the side, and almost dripping on the edible flower he has been carefully constructing. He saves it by swinging wildly to the left just in time.

She folds her arms over her chest and squints at him. "You're already drunk."

"Am not. This is only my fir—" He holds up one finger and then adds another. "My *second* glass of wine."

"And that's all it takes."

"Why are you so mean to me?" he says, but she's right. His skin is already flushed with heat from the fae wine, but at least it drowns out the sting of pain almost as well as Xylie's tonics.

Xylie studies him. She takes in the single-tier cake before him, piped with a delicate design and half covered in gold and silver edible blooms. She stares longest at the flour-dusted letter sitting beside it.

Xylie shrugs. "Very well, but I pick the music this time." She heads to a small table, where a series of statues sit beneath a window. It's the same window Ayc slipped out of eight years ago, when he attempted to escape. Instead, he only succeeded in locking himself in more chains.

Fuck, there's a depressing thought. I'm not nearly drunk enough.

Ayc tips up his goblet, sucking it down as Xylie hovers her fingers over the hand-sized statues. She picks up one shaped like a gryphon with its beak open in a roar. She taps its side three times, and a steady-but-rapid beat pours from the mouth. Xylie always craves the ones with this particular tempo; Ayc prefers them, too. These songs don't only sound good to his ears, but they *feel* good to his head, like a balm for his ever-chaotic mind.

Ayc cheers and gets up to grab another goblet from a cupboard. He fills it half full for Xylie—it's all she'll drink anyway—and fills his own all the way to the brim. She takes her glass and hops onto the counter, swinging her heels to the rhythm of the music. Ayc slides barefoot across the flour-dusted floor.

The magic that can only be cast by alcohol, good music, and a great friend descends on Ayc. Every note soothes across his skin, easing the sting there. His heart soars through his chest. Laughter teases his lips. Xylie and Ayc drink their goblets of wine. She cheers and provides backup vocals as he belts the lyrics—loudly and off-key—into a wooden spoon. Sometimes, he simply dances, occasionally coaxing Xylie off her counter to spin under his arm. Only once does he try to sit down to make another edible flower.

"It's lopsided," Xylie critiques.

"*You're* lopsided," Ayc fires back. Then he squints at the flower with one eye. "Oh, fuck, you're right."

He decides that he's done decorating for tonight, and since he is far too drunk to try to safely move the cake to the icebox, he jumps up for another dance. He's in the middle of a tight spin when the door opens. He tips to the side and puts a hand out to catch himself on the wall.

"We're dancing!" he says, once he's recovered enough to slide across the floor toward the newcomers. "If you come in here, you have to dance."

It takes a moment to focus his eyes, to see the two who have entered. He comes to an abrupt halt. "Oh fuck, Xylie. Don't let me drink anymore. I think I'm hallucinating."

Xylie says nothing. When he glances back at her, she's staring down at the floor. If Lora was alone, Xylie wouldn't have gotten suddenly silent, but Bronwen is by her side. Ayc supposes they aren't a hallucination, then.

Today, the two women are not dressed like warriors. Bronwen is adorned in her emerald sorcerer's cloak, a long-sleeved dress that matches, and a gracious smile. Lora wears a knee-length white tunic, dark breeches, her gray loose sweater, and her normal devoid-of-emotion expression. They both look fuzzy around the edges, but Ayc thinks that's probably just the fae wine.

"Ladies, I didn't know you were back at Wyntra. Welcome! To what do I owe the pleasure?" Ayc props his arm on the closest wall, trying to make it look cool and casual and *not* like the wall is the only thing holding him upright.

"Oh," Lora says, looking him up and down. "You're drunk."

"Pfft." Ayc waves a hand through the air. "No."

Bronwen arches an eyebrow, and Lora snorts. Clearly, he's not fooling anyone. With his apron untied and hanging loose, the ribbon in his hair barely clinging to a few strands, and enough flour dusted on his skin to make him look like a ghost, he's sure he looks like quite a sight.

"Very well." Ayc shrugs. "A little. Yeah."

Bronwen's smile falters, and she glances at Lora. "Maybe, we should come back in the morning."

Lora cocks her head slightly, a strand of dark curls tumbling over her nose. Her eyes are a hazy green that reminds him distinctly of the summer light playing on forest leaves. Beautiful.

He nearly gags at the thought. He needs to tell Xylie to remind him to never drink this much again.

"I need to get this over with," Lora says at last.

Behind him, soft feet plop on the floor. Xylie slides past Ayc and pauses long enough to sign something to Lora. Somewhere in his muddled, sloppy brain, Ayc knows he understands the common sign language Xylie uses. But right now, he's seeing too many hands and fingers and Xylies to make sense of it. Then Xylie is gone, and Ayc is alone with Lora and Bronwen, two graduated Adamant warriors. And Ayc isn't so drunk that he thinks that this is going to be anything short of disastrous.

Bronwen searches around the room, locates the recorder on the table, and makes a gesture. One murmured word and a pulse of power causes silence to fall over the room. Ayc's head is still loud, filled with a mix of music and the start of a slow hammer at his temples.

"Oh, my divine." Bronwen gasps. "That cake is beautiful." She sweeps toward it, but halts before she reaches the table like it's a precious artifact she doesn't dare breathe on. Bronwen's eyes are bright as she takes in the details of the cake, the flowers, the layers of white frosting, the delicate pearls he's beaded across the side. "Ayc, you did this?"

Ayc nods. He takes a step toward her. The room is an asshole and tips sideways. He sits down hard on the stool at Bronwen's elbow. "I've got a bit of a side business. I'm a baker, didyaknow?"

"Yes," she says, giggling beneath her breath, though he's not sure what he said that was so funny.

"I make cakes for special events and festivals and... and... Well, I mean I do but only when it doesn't interfere with my other duties, of course." He loses his train of thought for a second and has to seek it out again. "What was I saying? Ah yes, my other duties. And don't worry, Lora. I pay for the ingredients out of my own wages. Don't tell your mother I'm stealing from the castle. I like my balls exactly where they are."

Lora releases a tight breath. Her feet pad on the floor away from him. A cabinet opens and shuts. Water runs and shuts off at Ayc's sink. He glances over his shoulder to see her pausing in front of his and Xylie's shelves of ingredients. Lora selects a jar from its row. Ayc squints but can't make out what it is.

Bronwen's voice draws his attention back. "It almost makes me want to get married one day, just to have a gorgeous cake."

"Not the type marrying?" Ayc coughs and sets his full goblet down on the counter next to the nearly empty bottle. He's had quite enough. "I mean, marrying type?"

In Aluina, the culture of picking one person to swear forever to was nearly universally accepted. But in Everadyn, the ideas and beliefs vary from clan to clan. Like Aluina, some marriages are political and strategic. Some are a show of love, but life partners are just as commonly united only on their own words and desires, and not a formal ceremony.

"I'm not sure I'm even the *relationship* type," Bronwen says.

"Ah, well, who says you need a wedding to have cake? You can throw a 'I'm an amazing, powerful sorcerer' party, and I'll bake you the cake of your dreams." He perches his chin in his hand. "Tell me do you like passion fruit or do you prefer chocolate?"

Bronwen is still laughing when Lora returns to Bronwen's side. She sets a cup on the table before Ayc, one of his own cups, filled with water and speckles of purple, green, and yellow—some crushed, dried herbs and powder. "Drink," she commands.

He frowns up at her. "Is it poisoned?"

"Poison is a coward's way," Lora says, ice crackling beneath the words. Her eyes seem distant as she runs the pad of her thumb over the tips of her other fingers. Each nail has a fresh paint of taupe. "It's ginger, milk thistle, and some plant Xylie marked 'For when Ayc is too drunk to remember his own name'."

Fuck, Ayc knows that mixture. "You're trying to sober me up?" he accuses with a gasp, giving Lora his best scandalized expression.

"I'd rather you be a little more clear-headed for this conversation."

"But I'm feeling quite *fabulous*," Ayc whines. "Any chance I can get you to come back tomorrow?"

She fixes him with a deadly glare. "Just drink it."

Ayc could argue, but then he knows how useless it would be. There's a remedy for his drunkenness, but there's absolutely no cure for Lora's stubbornness. Ayc shrugs and drinks the water down.

"Who's getting married?" Bronwen asks, bringing his attention back to the cake once more.

"A Lux Aester girl," Ayc replies, setting down the cup. He can already feel the effects of the concoction working, the haziness in his head fading, his words coming more smoothly, the warmth disappearing. Fucking wretched. "And I do mean *girl*. She's seventeen. Marrying a man who's probably nine thousand years older than her." Ayc picks up the letter on the table and waves it, shaking off a cloud of flour. "Her name is Avabeth. I met her briefly at your mother's fiftieth anniversary celebration. She wrote me a letter afterward and asked if I would make her a cake."

Two pairs of eyes turn to look at him—Bronwen's wide, Lora's unreadable. Ayc swallows against the bitter taste in his mouth. Like Aluina, marriage is common with the Lux Aester, but it's more than tradition. They see it as a sacred duty to fulfill. And for the females unlucky enough to be born to the clan, it happens young and with little choice.

"Her parents agreed to pay for it?" Bronwen asks, surprised. "Generally, a random relative or woman in the village makes a cake. The fae of Lux Aester don't waste money on such things. The cost to ship this, alone, will be pricy."

Ayc tosses the letter back down. "No one is paying anything. She deserves to have a beautiful wedding cake, so she's getting a fucking beautiful wedding cake."

It comes out harsher than he meant. Bronwen blinks rapidly, her eyes briefly glistening with a different kind of silver. Lora taps two fingers to Bronwen's elbow in a tender gesture of comfort. Ayc feels like he's forgetting an important detail, something that Bronwen told him before. It takes him a moment to find it in his still slightly befuddled brain, but ah, yes, Bronwen was born in Lux Aester. He wonders how she got here, an Adamant warrior and sorcerer, but he's never been one to pry into someone's past. He hates it when people sniff too closely to his own.

"So..." Ayc drums his fingers on the countertop, the rings on his fingers *thunk*ing against the wood. "Why're you here, Lora? I'm sure it's not for the pleasure of my company."

Lora's face draws tight, her eyes momentarily falling closed as though she's in pain. "Can I sit?" she asks, pointing to the stool on the other side of the counter. She doesn't wait for his response but settles upon it and positions herself to face him. Bronwen remains at his side, almost as though one of them wants to be close in case he decides to run.

Oh, shit.

The happy warmth beneath his skin fully dissipates, and ice takes its place. A crackle of pain weaves through his spine.

"I've come to ask you something," Lora begins.

"No, I will not fill the fountain in the courtyard with chocolate pudding. I've done the mathematics, and it's simply not feasible. Besides, can you imagine the flies?"

89

The attempt at humor wins a half-smile from Bronwen and a glare from Lora.

"This is serious, Ayc," Lora says. "I know it's difficult for you, but can you please try to be serious for five minutes?"

"Fine, fine, fine. Sorry. Continue."

Lora takes another deep breath and looks to Bronwen. There's something in her expression that strikes Ayc as pleading. Bronwen gives a firm nod.

"I've been working to assemble my Five," Lora says, looking back in Ayc's direction, but not meeting his eyes. "Bronwen is my First. Xylie is my Second."

"Really? You asked Xylie?" Ayc assumed Lora would fill her Five with elite warriors and the strongest of magic wielders, like Yris did. Xylie's knowledge and intellect will make her invaluable. She's a brilliant choice. He's simply surprised that Lora saw that, too, even if the cousins have always been close. "That's a... a really good choice."

"I know," Lora says. "Peregrin is also in my Five."

Ayc raises both eyebrows. Another surprising... but strong choice. Yris underestimates Peregrin. She gave the order to pull them from commander of the aerial armies and put them in the school the moment they had a lasting injury. It was a mistake. Anyone who knows Peregrin knows they're a good teacher, but a great warrior, whatever challenges they're forced to overcome.

"I think that's great," Ayc says, rocking his weight side to side on the stool. "But why are you telling me any of this? I told you before, I wish you luck, but I thought there's supposed to be some rule that you didn't discuss matters of your team outside your Five before the Trials actually begin. Or..."

Ayc trails off. A shadow flickers over Lora's face, her eyes darkening into a deep forest green. A suspicion forms in Ayc's stomach, like a knife wound.

Oh no... oh no... ohnononono...

"I want you to be one of my Five," Lora says. "My Fifth."

A shrill sound screams in Ayc's head. His heart slams against his sternum as though begging for escape.

And then he laughs. So loudly he presses a fist over his lips to quiet himself. "That's a good one," he says when he can breathe through the laughter. "You had me for a second. I thought you were serious."

He stands up, but Bronwen's hand claps down on his shoulder and shoves him back. It's the first sign that behind all her polite smiles and soft femininity is a fierce warrior.

"She *is* serious, Ayc."

Ayc snaps his head between Bronwen and Lora. They have to be joking. But their expressions are nothing but earnest.

"Are you fucking kidding me?" His voice goes so high it cracks. He's feeling suddenly far too sober. The concoction has never worked quite this fast before. "I'm human; not Everadyn. I can't be one of your Five."

"You've lived in Everadyn for more than five years," Lora explains, like she's Xylie quoting directly from a book. "You can be, if I choose you to be."

"But why in every fucking star in this divine-forsaken universe would you ever want me to be one of your Five? You *hate* me."

Lora doesn't try to deny it. The muscle near her jaw spasms as she grinds her teeth. "I have my... reasons."

"They're bad ones," he states desperately. "According to some people, I'm an utter fool, less trust-worthy with a sword than a toddler, and only slightly more useful than barnyard shit."

"Divine." Bronwen's eyes widen. "Who told you that?"

Ayc looks pointedly at Lora, who uses that moment to stare at a flower on his cake like she, too, thinks it's lopsided. Bronwen follows the path of Ayc's vision and sighs.

Lora snaps her gaze back to her friend. "In my defense, barnyard shit can fertilize crops. It's actually *highly* useful."

Ayc might have thought she was joking, but he's quite sober now and knows better.

"The point remains," Ayc says, "that by your own admission, I have nothing to offer you as one of your Five."

"Invisibility is not nothing," Bronwen says.

"Lora could buy an enchanted cloak. It would talk far less than me."

"A trait I would greatly admire," Lora says beneath her breath.

"Lora," Bronwen warns, pressing fingers to her temple like a hammer is pounding there. Ayc knows the feeling.

"See!" Ayc throws up his hand to emphasize the word. "Problem solved. I'm sure your mother would front the bill for the cloak. And speaking of your mother!" There it is. He should have thought of it sooner. Yris is his best hope. She will hate the idea of Ayc being one of Lora's Five. She won't stand for him having even an ounce of power. And Lora has always tried to please her mother. "Does your mother know about this? Surely, she won't want me to–"

Lora holds up a hand to cut him off. "She knows."

The two words are heavy and say so much that Lora doesn't. Yris knows. Maybe, she even wanted this.

His stomach plummets all the way to his feet. He feels a

door slam, a key lock, quite like the one to this very kitchen used to on the outside of the door.

Fuck... oh, fuck...

What game is Yris playing here? Because it is *always* a game with her. What hand of cards is she holding? It doesn't matter, because if she wants this, saying no is futile. Yris will simply march in here and give an order he can't escape from.

"You're allowed to say no, Ayc," Lora says, her voice a touch softer. "You have a choice."

Ayc glares at her for a long time, because surely she knows that's a lie. Surely, she knows what Yris has done, and that he doesn't have choices. He hasn't had choices in eight fucking years.

Then he grabs his goblet and drinks it all down. Every last drop. When he lowers his wine, he gives Lora his best smile. It's one of the biggest lies he's ever told.

"Then, in that case, it'll be my pleasure."

CHAPTER
SEVEN

Ayc is far too hung over to be facing off with a perturbed gryphon especially this early. The sun has barely made it past the horizon. But after last night, he supposes this is simply the way his life is going now.

"It's not my fault, Tempest," Ayc tells the gryphon, whose silver eyes, narrowed in displeasure, are level with Ayc's own. She angles her sharp beak toward the ground, but it looks particularly lethal this morning. Her mighty body stands between Ayc and the door to Peregrin's home.

"Xylie" —Ayc points a finger at the fae at his side— "didn't tell me we were coming to see you when she dragged me out of bed this morning."

Xylie huffs. Even at this early hour, soldiers march up and down the streets of the barracks where Peregrin's home is located. Shadows briefly block out the sun as gryphons, bearing their riders, fly overhead. They cut through the fierce wind and sweep low above the rooftops, practicing flight maneuvers and drills. So instead of speaking, Xylie signs furiously, "*Well, if you wouldn't break the rules and sneak the gryphon treats, she wouldn't expect it from you.*"

He gives only one sign in return, and it's crude enough Xylie signs back. "*I'm leaving you here to die.*"

She steps around Tempest, who doesn't take her eyes off Ayc, and slips into the door of Peregrin's home.

"I'll make it up to you," Ayc promises Tempest. "I'll bake you a dozen of those apple and carrot cakes you love."

Tempest growls deep in her throat.

"*And* a dozen of the raw salmon muffins, even though they are truly disgusting and make my kitchen smell like a fish market for a week."

Tempest glares for one moment more, and Ayc is sure he's about to lose an eye. Then she bobs her head in approval and turns her neck expectantly. Ayc grins and scratches the spot he knows Tempest loves, right in the place where black feathers give way to gray fur. She makes a sound that's a mixture of a bird's hum and a cat's purr.

The door behind Tempest jerks open. "Boy, how many times do I have to tell you not to pet my gryphon like she's a damn dog?"

Peregrin stands in the doorway. One hand holds their cane and another a steaming mug. Still, they appear perfectly militant and composed for this ungodly hour. Their pressed uniform has no wrinkles. The sides of their head are freshly shaved, and the blond hair on top is carefully slicked back so not a hair is out of place. But the green veins that run over their ashen skin stand out more prominently today. Ayc already knows keenly that one can seem perfectly fine and not be well at all.

"Good morning to you, too, Peregrin," Ayc says, not bothering to stop his petting.

"Get your ass in here."

Ayc steps around Tempest, who narrows her eyes once more as though to say, *Don't forget your promise.* Ayc struggles with each step to the doorway. On top of his headache, every muscle in his back is coiled into a tight knot. He tries to keep his steps light, tries not to let it show.

As Ayc steps past Peregrin into the threshold of Peregrin's home, Tempest turns to face her rider. She lifts a wing expectantly. It blocks out the faint sunlight and casts them in darkness. Her wings are a work of art, an entire spectrum of dark and light, spreading from the deepest black on the ridge to the purest white on her flight feathers.

Ayc has heard that riders and gryphons communicate within their heads, talking in words only each other can hear. According to other gryphon riders Ayc has overheard, Tempest should have remained in the aerial army when Peregrin was dismissed. There, she was meant to bond with a different rider. But Peregrin and Tempest's bond is too strong. Tempest follows Peregrin everywhere not like a faithful pet, but like the truest of friends. Even now, Tempest knows Peregrin's need.

Peregrin sighs in gratitude and reaches into Tempest's wing to carefully select a small gray feather, no bigger than the tip of Ayc's ring finger, one not critical for flight. Ayc looks away, feeling as though he's intruding on a private moment. Soon, the feather will be in Peregrin's tea. Gryphon feathers possess healing properties, ones that can ease pain, but more importantly, keep the poison that still lives in Peregrin's veins at bay. It's the only thing that has kept Peregrin alive.

Peregrin closes the door with their elbow. Though Ayc can hear voices, Peregrin's small sitting room is empty as they enter. Plush couches, embroidered pillows and pressed flowers framed on the wall preach of Zinnia's touch, but the fossilized skull of an infant dragon that sits on the mantle is all Irving. The toys scattered across the floor belong to Ember. The only thing that speaks of Peregrin is the belt of knives hung high above the front door, far out of Ember's reach, next to Zinnia's apron and Irving's silver, royal guard cloak. But that itself befits Peregrin—testifies to how their partners and their child are their whole heart.

"Come along," Peregrin says and starts toward the door on the far wall, where the voices are coming from.

Ayc catches Peregrin's elbow. "Why am I here, Peregrin? Why did Lora choose me?"

Peregrin hesitates, studying the door to ensure it remains closed before they turn toward Ayc and lower their voice. "I don't know. I know that the Totus Omni's Council of the People gives guidance on who the victor should choose for their Five. Following their advice is supposed to mean blessings from the divine. It's cryptic and open to interpretation, but I suspect you fit their advice. However..." Peregrin trails off and studies the content of their mug, a tea nearly as dark as coffee.

"What?" Ayc presses.

Peregrin sips on their tea as though needing it for strength. "I suspect Lora didn't choose you. Yris did. And I am sure Yris was not happy with most of Lora's choices, so Lora relented on this one."

"Why would Yris do that?"

Peregrin looks at him pointedly. "What has Yris always wanted?"

Ayc's lungs suddenly feel as though they don't have

enough air. He inhales through his teeth as a spasm rakes at his back.

"I don't understand," Ayc says. "How would *this* get her any closer?"

Peregrin shakes their head. "I don't know. Just... be careful."

It is *entirely* unhelpful advice, but Ayc has barely opened his mouth before Peregrin turns and walks toward the door. Ayc heaves a sigh and follows.

Peregrin's dining room and kitchen is cramped in the best of circumstances. One wall holds a deep fireplace, a kettle hung within it. The other holds a sink, an icebox and a small counter. A long wooden table stretches in between, nearly butting against a dish-filled shelf which sits along the wall. Ayc has been invited to numerous dinners around this table with Peregrin, their partners, and their child. Now, the room is filled with Loraphne and her Five.

Bronwen sits with her legs tucked beneath her on the bench closest to Ayc, leaning forward to talk to Irving who sits on the other side. Irving wears the brown with black-trimmed leather armor Ayc is used to seeing on the royal guards who stalk around the castle or trail behind Yris at a distant, but today, he also wears a broad smile, so wide a dimple flashes on his dark brown cheeks—something he never exhibits in Yris's presence.

A fae Ayc doesn't recognize sits beside Bronwen. Their back faces Ayc, revealing only a head of dark, tight ringlets. The fae's hand wraps around a braided leash that fits to the ornate collar of a large dog with wavy, brown and white hair. The dog turns its head to peer at Ayc with one brown and one blue eye for a long steady moment, before turning back around. Behind the collar, the dog wears a harness with an extended piece of metal that forms a handle, one that Ayc has seen on guide dogs for the blind.

Xylie has avoided the table altogether, of course, and sits on the kitchen counter, swinging her feet. Loraphne watches everything from a chair at the end near the fireplace. She holds a little leather book on the table in front of her. Ayc knows she almost always carries two books with her, tucked into a pocket. One for reading and one for writing. Based on the flowing script on the pages, this one is for writing. She taps a quill on the corner of the page.

Behind her, Zinnia takes a kettle off the fire. Beside her, Ayc glimpses the shape of a small boy just before that boy turns into a blur of motion.

"AYC!" Ember shrieks a moment before he flings himself at Ayc.

Ayc barely catches him. The shriek of his name slams around in his already pounding head, but he can't ever hold it against Ember. The boy has Zinnia's sea-green eyes and Irving's brown skin, but Peregrin's take-no-shit attitude.

"Hey, little fae," Ayc says, jostling him playfully. "Are you giving your parents trouble for me?"

Ember smiles wider, flashing the dimples that he also inherited from Irving. "Always."

Peregrin rolls their eyes, but it's Zinnia who scolds Ayc as she approaches with a steaming mug in her hands. "Must you always encourage him?"

"You know I must," Ayc says.

She presses the mug into Ayc's hand. He inhales the bitter scent of coffee. She has served it in the mug that Zinnia always sets aside for Ayc. He used it the first time Peregrin invited Ayc here, eight years ago. Zinnia wrapped a blanket around his trembling frame and pressed this cup into his hand. He dropped it immediately, chipping the rim of it.

When he apologized profusely, she simply shrugged and said, "Well, it just means it's yours now. And you can come use it whenever you like."

It wasn't the first time Zinnia showed him kindness. She has showed it since he arrived in Wyntra. As a cook in the kitchen, she would deliver ingredients Ayc needed for the desserts that Yris requested, and she always included something extra, knowing Yris sometimes forgot his basic needs—like food that wasn't a pastry. This mug and Zinnia's kindness still mean more than Ayc can say.

Ayc stoops to leave a quick kiss on Zinnia's cheek. "Bless you, woman. I don't deserve you. Neither do Peregrin or Irving."

"Oh, they know," Zinnia says.

"Aye, we do," Peregrin agrees, and gives Zinnia one of their rare smiles.

Zinnia opens her arms to Ember. "All right, little one. Time to leave the people to their meeting."

Ember sticks out his bottom lip. "Must I?"

"Consider yourself lucky, friend," Ayc tells him. "This meeting is bound to be unbelievably boring. I'd trade places with you if I could."

Ember taps a little finger against his chin as though considering this. "I guess." He pouts a moment more, then the smile bursts back on his face. He slaps his hands down on Ayc's cheeks. "But can we go down to the shore afterward to look for sea monster fossils? It's been *for-ev-er* since you took me."

Copying the boy's excitement, Ayc turns to Zinnia and Peregrin with wide eyes. "Can we?" Yris has, after all, excused him from all his normal duties today. Surely, this meeting won't last all day.

Zinnia glances at Peregrin, unspoken words seeming to pass between them. Ayc's chest constricts, as it always does seeing Peregrin and their partners. The love between the three of them is so real it's nearly touchable, a physical force no one can deny. They already know that Irving is the least strict parent, so there's no need to include him in the unspoken discussion. He would say yes without hesitation.

"Very well," Zinnia says, holding out her arms. Ember squeals in delight and jumps into his mother's arms.

Peregrin lifts their cane toward Ayc. "But stay out of the caves down there. If I have to rescue you both from a half-flooded cave again—"

"It was *one* time," Ayc protests.

"One time too many," Zinnia says, before leaving.

Irving jumps up from the table and follows Zinnia out. He pauses to kiss Peregrin's cheek and squeeze Ayc's shoulder.

When Ayc turns back to the table, he finds Lora looking at him, in a way that tells him she's been watching the entire interaction. He sticks out his tongue and crosses his eyes. She turns away swiftly, shaking her head.

Well, Ayc supposes he's stalled long enough. He takes a step forward to claim a spot at the table, but Peregrin's cane taps Ayc's foot in a signal to wait. They wave a hand over his mug. When they pull back, a second feather has disappeared into Ayc's coffee.

They whisper, "Tempest said to tell you that you look like utter shit."

A gryphon feather isn't something Ayc would ever request. It's too intimate a gift, but Tempest has always been able to sense when he's having the worst of his days and given it freely. Ayc takes a sip, and the effect is nothing short of magical. His muscles loosen; the headache dulls; the blaze beneath his skin turns to only sparks.

"I don't deserve any of you," Ayc whispers back in a glib tone. But he's not joking. Not really. No, not at all.

Peregrin waves their cane dismissively. "Just sit down, boy."

Ayc sits down in the chair Irving has abandoned, facing Bronwen. Peregrin settles in the chair beside him. Ayc looks across the table to the one person he has yet to meet. Blue brushes the deep black skin at the fae's cheekbones, their arms, and their collarbones that peek out of the deep V of their vest. A chain with a single pink-hued pearl sits in the hollow of their throat, which they run between their finger and thumb, no longer holding the leash.

"Hello, there," Ayc greets. "Ayc Waylonder. You can refer to me by he and him."

Ayc stretches out his hand, but the fae doesn't take it. Instead, he looks past Ayc's shoulder with a soft, kind smile.

"Name's Tavish," they reply. "I go by he and him. And this boy here is Saga." Tavish scratches the dog's head which peeks over the table.

"Hello to you too, Saga," Ayc greets.

The guide dog cocks his head, like he's studying him with those two-colored, intelligent eyes.

Glancing around the table, Ayc feels like he's missing something. Anyone who didn't know Xylie and Peregrin wouldn't understand why they are brilliant choices. Anyone who *did* know Ayc would question Lora as a leader. But inviting a fae who is blind into a brutal and vicious game is a move that some people might find beyond reckless.

Whoever this Tavish is, Ayc suspects he has a fascinating story.

A chair screeches as it slides against the floor, and Lora stands. "Now that we are all here, we should get started. Peregrin, thank you for giving us use of your home. I must remind everyone that we can't hold meetings within Wyntra Castle. It's meant to be neutral territory. We only have a week until the Trials begin, and we need to strategize."

Her voice resonates through the room. Strong. Sharp. Commanding. Right now, she sounds almost exactly like her mother. Ayc drags deeply on his coffee, scalding his tongue. His headache taps at his temple once more.

"There's not a lot we can do without knowing what the quests are, which we won't know until the first day of the Trials," Lora continues, sitting back down and eyeing the book before her, as though reading from her notes. "But we can make sure we are as prepared as possible for whatever scenarios arise. Xylie." She shifts her attention to her cousin sitting on the counter. "I need you to dig through the library and read anything and everything you can find on the last several Trials. What is recorded is limited to keep it secret, but I'm sure you'll agree that the more knowledge we have the better."

Xylie nods eagerly. Nothing excites Xylie like homework.

Lora makes a tick on one of the lines in her book. "Tavish."

Saga turns his head first, locking those different toned eyes on Lora. Tavish picks up the leash he's left draped in his lap and his gaze follows. "Yes, my lady?"

Ayc cringes. Ugh. My lady? Is he going to have to call her *'my lady'* now?

Lora's shoulders tighten. "You don't have to call me that."

Thank fuck for that.

"Sorry," Tavish says. "But what about when you're Sovereign?"

"I'm not—" She begins, then stops. Her hand holding the quill flutters, before she tightens her hold. "We will worry about that later. For now, Lora is still fine."

Ayc studies her hand. The shudder was so small he shouldn't have noticed, but he did. It's... odd. Like the idea of actually being Sovereign makes her nervous.

"All right, Lora," Tavish corrects.

Lora takes a breath and gets back on track. "If I get you maps of Everadyn, can you put your gift to use?"

Tavish forms a fist around his necklace, fiddling with the pearl with his thumb once more. "It'll be difficult without knowing the quests or having something to seek, but I'll see what I can sense."

Ayc trails a finger around the rim of his coffee, hesitates, and then dares to ask, "And what exactly is your gift?"

It happens again. The dog looks at Ayc, and then Tavish follows. "I'm a navigator."

Ayc is grateful that Tavish can't see him, because his eyebrows rise halfway up his brow.

"I know what you're thinking," Tavish says with a smile. "A navigator who can't see."

"I wasn't..."

"It's fine. It's a logical thought. I'm divina." He turns his wrist to show Ayc. A hypopigmented mark, like a thumbprint, lies at the hollow of his wrist.

Ayc slips a finger under one of his cuffs and touches his own mark, the one an oven, and not a supposedly divine

104

being, branded into his skin. Peregrin studies him over their mug, narrows their eyes slightly. The warning that they've given Ayc many times rings in his head.

Control your emotions. Bury your lies.

"Lora told me you are, too," Tavish adds. "Invisibility, right?"

Ayc's skin grows too tight, but he forces himself not to hesitate. "Yes."

Out of the corner of his eye, he sees Xylie wave to him. When she has his full attention, she signs quickly. At her movement, Saga looks to Xylie, sitting on the counter, and then Tavish is able to look right at her. Which is even odder, because Xylie hadn't spoken, so there was no sound to follow.

Xylie frowns. She runs a finger up and down her nose. She's noticed the oddness too, then. Some connection between this fae and the guide dog exists that goes beyond the usual bond.

"What?" Tavish asks.

"She wants you to explain how you navigate," Lora translates for Xylie, when Ayc doesn't, too distracted by his thoughts to remember Xylie asked.

"Ah." Tavish hesitates and then takes a breath. He speaks in a rush, his words slightly tumbling over each other, like he'd very much like to have them all out and done. "I was born blind. But I've always had a gift of *knowing* which direction to go. It's hard to explain, but I simply know. For example, Ayc, when you go to the shore with the boy later—sorry, I couldn't help but overhear—I know you should look for what you seek in a southeast direction, where rocks have newly moved. I don't know what that means, or even how I know it. I just do. It doesn't always help me. I still need my cane and Saga to keep me from walking into a ditch most days."

"That's brilliant," Ayc says. He has to admit that the team Lora has assembled is... unconventional, but brilliant. *Except for me.* He's the one choice he still doesn't understand.

Xylie jumps off the counter, pads forward, and kneels before Saga. She lifts a hand to let him sniff her fingers; she doesn't touch him but peers at something on his neck. The collar. Her eyes fly wide, and she signs above her head so Ayc can see her.

"It's enchanted. I can sense it," she says. Her hands speed up in excitement, flying so quickly Ayc struggles to read her words.

"She's asking if it's—" Ayc hesitates. "What kind of collar?"

Xylie rolls her eyes but spells it out again, slowly this time.

"A Kindred collar?" Ayc says, a little uncertainly.

"Um, y-yes." Tavish brushes his hand against the leash. "How did you know?"

Xylie only shrugs.

"Xylie knows everything," Ayc explains, ignoring the glare Xylie fires at him like an arrow. "What's a Kindred collar?"

It's Bronwen who answers, placing her elbows on the table and leaning closer. She holds a cup with a small spoon, which slowly spins in a circle without being touched, undoubtedly commanded by some spell. "It's an enchanted collar that forges a connection of senses between the dog and their companion, but only when a bond already exists. What it does depends on the bond between them, but I hoped it would allow Tavish to see through Saga's eyes. Which it does, so long as he's holding the leash."

Ayc's mouth parts in surprise. He's never heard of such a thing, but that isn't too uncommon. Despite all the time he's spent in Everadyn, he still doesn't know all the ways magic presents itself. The fae themselves don't know. Magic, as he understands it, is a force, quite like nature— chaotic and ruled only by itself. Those who are able to tap into the force are always finding new ways to shape it. Sorcerers conjure new spells, and alchemists invent new methods of harnessing the force. It never ceases to amaze him.

A grin spreads over his face. "I fucking love magic."

"It has its perks," Peregrin grunts into their tea.

Ayc knows what they don't say. *And its curses.* After all, the blade that left them in so much pain was also magic, and Ayc has certainly experienced his own downsides of magic.

"I never imagined it possible." Another smile graces Tavish's face, this time growing and spreading until it lights up his entire face, as he strokes his dog's ears. Saga lays his head on the fae's lap. "Saga has been my eyes in many ways since he was a pup. Ever since I found him on the docks of Anaca in Tenebra and snuck him aboard the *Maiden's Tears.*" The name of the ship strikes a memory, but before Ayc can ask, Tavish continues, "But Bronwen gave me this collar a year ago. It has been truly life-changing... though, at times, a little overstimulating. I only wish everyone had the resources to experience it."

Xylie pushes to her feet and signs, this time looking to Lora to translate. Lora pulls her sweater tighter around her body. A line between her brow hints that she's frustrated by the derailment of this meeting, but she obliges her cousin.

"She wants to know where you got the collar. They are incredibly rare."

"I know a friend who's quite gifted in the finding and procuring of enchanted objects," Bronwen replies. "Met him during my years at Velphin. I ran into him on break from Adamant last year. He mentioned he had it, and I 'sweet-talked' him—" She wiggles her eyebrows, and Ayc chuckles. "—to giving me a reduced price. It wasn't just me, though. I never could have afforded it without Lora's help."

"Lora?" Ayc blurts before he can stop himself.

Lora glares at him. "Is there something you'd like to say, cinnamon roll?"

I didn't know you could be kind.

He bites the inside of his cheek to hold in the words and looks down at his coffee mug. It's not entirely true. Lora is capable of kindness, but she very rarely chooses it. Or maybe... maybe he's wrong about that.

For the first time, he considers the weight of it. All these people, including Xylie and Peregrin, two of his favorite people in the world, have chosen to put their support behind Lora. Perhaps Xylie might be blinded by her personal connection with Lora, but Peregrin wouldn't be at this table if they didn't believe Lora was worthy of being Sovereign.

But why? What do they see in her that Ayc cannot?

It's an unsettling question, so Ayc simply shakes his head.

"Thank you again. Both of you," Tavish says. He turns his head in Bronwen and Lora's general direction. Saga still has his head resting in Tavish's lap, eyes closed, content in a way only a beloved dog can be. "I can't repay—"

Lora holds up a hand. "You're here. That is more than enough."

Ayc snaps his fingers, as a thought jumps into his head. "Tavish, did you say the *Maiden's Tears?* Like the pirate ship?"

"Err..." Tavish rubs the back of his neck, looking like he might like to crawl out of his own skin. "Uh, yes."

Ayc has exactly three thousand questions he needs to ask, because whoever this fae before him is, he's certainly *not* a pirate.

But Lora interrupts: "Could we get back to the purpose of this meeting?"

"Yes, of course." Tavish nods. "Sorry."

"Not sorry," Ayc says, but he flicks his wrist, "but, sure, continue. What were we even talking about, anyway?"

"Maps," Lora says with a tight sigh.

Bronwen takes her elbows off the table and wipes the bemused smile off her face. Xylie returns to her counter.

"I think we shouldn't limit the maps to Everadyn," Bronwen says. "We should probably include maps across all of the continents."

"Tavish?" Lora asks.

"Yes, all the continents," Tavish replies.

Lora makes another check in her book and moves on. "Peregrin, from a military and battle perspective, how should we prepare?"

Peregrin squares their shoulders and sits up straighter like a soldier called to attention. "The Trials are brutal. Anything and everything is allowed. Other than the people in this room, you can trust no one, certainly not the other victors and their Five. No matter who they were to you before this."

Peregrin emphasizes the words with a nod in Lora's direction. Lora's eyes shift away. Clearly, Wylder and Lora's relationship isn't in the past if Peregrin feels the need to bring it up. Peregrin *hates* discussing relationships. Ayc gulps down his now luke-warm coffee to ease the bitter taste in his mouth.

"Alliances may be advantageous at first," Peregrin continues, "but they should only be formed knowing that the ally will ultimately, by the end, be another enemy to be defeated. Form alliances wisely, or don't form them at all, and always know that at any moment they may betray you. Or that you'll eventually have to betray them."

Lora scratches her quill in the page's corner, scribbling a jagged line hard enough it nearly digs through the paper. "I understand."

"The opening day of the Trials is a bloodbath. It generally turns into an all-out brawl getting over the bridge out of the city. I was there at the last Trials, and two of the victors and all of their Five died, then and there."

Blood drains from Ayc's face. Bronwen squares her shoulders as though preparing for a fight; Tavish grabs his necklace so tightly his knuckles blanch. Ayc looks sharply at Xylie.

It hits Ayc like cold water to his face. There's so much at stake. Not just who will become Sovereign and control his destiny, but all their lives. Xylie's life. She can fight, as almost every Everadyn child is trained to do. She's a good shot with a bow, but she's not a warrior. By rights, she should be doing Final Testing at Wyntra this summer. She's guaranteed a spot at Splendor, Lycendi's university. That's where she should be in fall, if she chooses to go. Instead, she could be dead.

Over my rotten fucking corpse.

He has loved the girl like a little sister since the moment

she arrived at Wyntra, looking every bit as scared and sad as he felt inside. He'll be damned if he lets a single hair on her head be harmed.

Peregrin's voice sounds like a distant echo, but still clangs like a warning from above. "We should all be prepared for the fight of our lives—"

"Do we have to cross the bridge?" Ayc interjects. "There are other ways out of Wyntra."

Peregrin, Lora, and Bronwen's attention snaps to him.

"It's tradition," Lora says. "A parade of victors march out of the city. It's how it's always been done."

"But is it *required*?" Ayc presses.

"Ayc has a point," Bronwen says. "If it isn't an actual rule, we could go a different way. It would be safer for everyone."

Lora is silent for a long moment, unnecessarily straightening the sleeves of her cardigan. Ayc expects her to ignore his logic. To tell him it's the way it always has been, and she will do what's expected of her. Then she asks, "Is it required, Peregrin?"

Peregrin lifts their hands in a shrug. "I don't know. It'll be frowned upon if you don't, but I don't know that it's an actual rule."

Lora's dark eyes travel from Xylie, to Tavish, and linger longest on Ayc. He studies the last remnants of his coffee, blackened at the bottom of his mug.

"Xylie, see if you can find anything on it in your studies," Lora says at last. "If it's a rule, we have no choice. If it's not, we'll find another way out of the city."

Something unhitches in Ayc's chest. He's both surprised and relieved.

"But Peregrin is right either way." Lora folds her hands

together and rests them on the table, strangling them tightly. A slight pause hovers between her words, as though she's choosing each one of them with care. "This will be a fight of a lifetime. It's an incredibly huge risk for all of you, and I don't take that risk lightly. If you didn't understand that until this moment, I understand if you would like to back out now."

Ayc doesn't look at her. Yes, he wants out of this, but he has little choice. And at least this way, he can watch out for Xylie.

"We are aware of the risks," Bronwen says. "We are with you, Lora." She presses a palm over her chest, fingers spread apart over the space where her heart beats.

Xylie, Tavish, and Peregrin all nod. Ayc forces himself to do the same and drinks down the last bitter, cold swig of coffee. The magic of the gryphon feather has quieted his pain from a roar to background noise. But it remains, a reminder of the villains in his story.

"We will have to make sure all of us are properly armed. If you don't have a weapon, let me know your preference and I'll obtain it for you." Lora turns to a new blank page in her book and slides it to Peregrin along with the pen. "Add whatever else you think is necessary."

Ayc learns that Bronwen prefers her staff, which is leaning beside her on the table even now. The hand-carved wood is painted with a brilliant jewel-toned rainbow, from green to blue to purple. The sharp blade that tips the wood makes the weapon taller than Bronwen. Tavish asks for a cutlass, as a last resort, and Peregrin, of course, will use their dozens of small knives. Xylie signs for a bow and arrows. Peregrin then looks at Ayc.

"Um, shit—" He's spent the last ten years trying to keep

himself out of fights, not walking into them. "A longsword, I guess."

Lora scoffs. "Peregrin, are you sure he can handle that large a weapon without cutting off his own head?"

Ayc rolls his eyes, but says nothing. What is he supposed to say that won't chip away at the secrets he wraps himself in?

Peregrin doesn't look up from the list where they carefully write 'longsword' after Ayc's name. "He's adequate."

"Adequate?" Lora repeats. "I've seen him fight, and in my experience..."

"I'm not sure judging him by how he chose to handle teenage bullies is a fair assessment of his ability. It's been four years since you left for Adamant. You have both grown considerably."

Peregrin's voice is calm but pointed as a blade. They've never hesitated to give a student blunt and honest feedback, the type that feels like the broadside of a sword slapped against the cheek.

Lora opens her mouth to argue, but whatever enters Peregrin's expression is enough to make her mouth snap shut.

"And I would be very careful not to mistake his kindness for weakness," Peregrin says. "A kindness—need I remind you—that you would be dead without."

Tension surges in the air, so heavy surely everyone in the room perceives the weight. Ayc wants to tell a joke, anything to crack the heaviness in the air, but for once, not a single one enters his mind. Lora doesn't look at him. And perhaps just like him, she feels like she's back on the bank of a river eight years ago. He can still feel the water and blood pouring down his chin.

"I feel like I'm missing something," Tavish whispers to Bronwen, loud enough that everyone hears.

"Me too," Bronwen replies, looking from Ayc to Peregrin to Lora. "A whole fucking novel."

Lora allots each person homework before closing the meeting. Ayc is to get a list of food he believes they'll need and to bake anything that would pack well and not spoil during a long travel. They spend the last hour discussing the victors, or at least, Lora, Bronwen, and Peregrin do. The other three merely listen.

Lora, being the Sovereign's daughter, knows most of the victors. She's able to discuss weaknesses and strengths, reading off diagrams and notes she's sketched in her little book. Ayc does his best to focus, to sit still, but their words turn into droning, and he downs a second and then a third cup of coffee in an effort to stay awake. He refocuses only when they bring up Sterling. Lora doesn't say much, other than that they shouldn't be underestimated. Apparently, there are rumors that they have surrounded themselves with an impressive Five.

Ayc hides his smile behind his empty coffee mug. He knows who he'll be secretly rooting for.

When the meeting finally ends, Ayc says a quick goodbye and sticks his head in Ember's bedroom, where the boy is playing with figurines of gryphons and dragons. "Ready?" Ayc asks, but Ember is already halfway out the door.

Ayc and Ember race down the path that leads from the cliffs onto the shoreline, far faster than the steep and narrow path should allow for, but they've taken this path since Ember was a toddler. The Bellum Sea is a violent beast, icy cold and frothing, crashing into the shore with a roar as loud as lightning. The shrill wind screeches as it comes off the waves and lashes at Ayc's loose hair. The water turns into a gray, foggy haze as it meets the horizon.

Sometimes, Ayc can almost forget that his true home lies across these waters, but today, he wonders if Creed Castle still sits in ruins. Did the Drakr rebuild it for their own use or leave it as burned-out rubble? Ayc can still remember the sight of the castle engulfed in flames as Fennix yanked him, hands bound, onto the ship that would carry him to Everadyn. Ayc's eyes sting with more than just sea spray when he looks too long, so he turns away. Ember has waited patiently at his side, kicking up clouds of sand with his little feet.

"Where should we look first?" Ember asks.

Remembering Tavish's message, Ayc leads the boy away from the tide and toward the base of the cliffs. He searches the places where the rocks have slid down from yesterday's rain. Ember has brought little shovels, a bucket, and a sifting tool. They sift sand and study every rock like it might be gold, their laughter lost beneath the howl of the wind.

It doesn't take them long to find it. The jagged tooth is as large as Ayc's outstretched palm and still wickedly sharp.

"What do you think it is?" Ayc asks from where he kneels. He brushes off the sand before handing it to the boy.

The boy has to hold the tooth in both hands. He studies it with a smile too wide for his face. "That's a leviathan tooth. They're extinct, now, but Dad says they were the most fearsome and most glorious beasts on sea or land. This is probably a baby tooth because fully grown, they could swallow an entire battleship in one gulp. Most people think they were really mean, but some stories say they would actually guide lost ships back to shore. They died so long ago we'll never know, though."

His smile plummets from his face, and he suddenly looks too solemn for his young age. He grabs Ayc's hand and sets the tooth back into his palm. "Keep it. Mama says that you and Perry are about to go on a really important journey soon. They won't tell me, but I know it's gonna be dangerous. It'll keep you safe."

"We're going to be fine," Ayc says swiftly.

He tries to hand the tooth back, but Ember fists his little hands and refuses to take it.

Ayc swallows to rid the tightness in his throat and forces his voice to be light. "Tell you what. I'll keep it safe for you." He tucks it into the deepest of his vest pockets; it fills it completely, as firm as a knife. "But when we get back, I'll give it back to you."

Ember nods and then throws his arms around Ayc, holding him so tightly that Ayc can't draw a breath. He pats the boy's back and doesn't allow himself to believe that he's made a promise he won't be able to keep.

Her gaze is a physical weight on him, and Ayc looks up. High above the shoreline, on a piece of cliff that cuts through the beach and juts into the sea, Lora stands. From this distance, Ayc can barely make out her face and the hood of her cardigan hides her hair, but he instinctively knows it's her, watching him.

She swiftly turns back to the sea.

Ayc wonders if she ever thinks about it, too. That distant

castle she helped ruin. The blood she shed. The child she was before that day. The people she and Ayc would have become if that day never happened.

Hoping is foolish, but he hopes that she does. He hopes he's wrong about her. She has convinced people he loves and trusts to follow her, to support her. He hopes they're right.

He hopes she is the type of person who looks at the sea and regrets.

EIGHT YEARS AGO

Dogs.

Of all the things destined to be Ayc's downfall, why did it have to be dogs? Ayc loved dogs. Dogs generally loved Ayc, but as he ran through the Elodie forest, the bray of the bloodhounds grew increasingly louder. He didn't bother attempting to remain invisible, because the Sovereign's dogs could smell him regardless.

It had been a week since he fled. Seven days of running until he threw up and then running some more, only sleeping for a few hours in the shadows before waking again. A few days ago, when he'd reached the forest of Elodie, the sacred woods that were home to the Totus Omni, he'd dared to hope that this would work. That maybe he could hide in the shadows of the woods indefinitely, or at least until he could find a way back to Aluina. He didn't know what he would find there now. Ruin, surely. But it was home.

But now Ayc would be lucky to make it another day.

He'd heard the dogs braying this morning and had been running ever since. Their brays and barks, mixed with the calls of their owners, grew steadily closer. And to make matters worse, Ayc now feared he was running in circles. The tree trunks here were all broad as a house, but he was certain he'd run past the one with the gnarled base at least once before. If he was right, then soon there would be a break in the trees where the Ever River flowed through the heart of the forest. He thought he might hear water, but he couldn't be sure over the pounding of his heart.

He broke through the trees and found he was right. The turquoise waters of the Ever River stretched before him. In some areas of Everadyn, the Ever River was wide enough to allow a battleship to pass through, but here it was only the width of Wyntra's great hall. The mighty trees rose above it and cast their branches across, tangling with branches of trees on the other side. The water flowed steadily, parting around rocks and beneath fallen tree trunks. He'd grown up swimming in the lake near his childhood village and then in the riotous ocean shore around Creed. He could probably swim across. But perhaps it was too great a risk.

He turned northward and raced along the bank. He'd made it only a few steps, before a voice rang out, "Stop!"

A cloaked figure darted from behind a tree, holding twin short swords. In the shadows of the hood, Ayc barely made out her face. Lora.

No, no, no. Ayc reeled back several steps and almost fell over his own feet, before catching his balance.

"Ayc, stop and listen to me!" she snapped. "If you keep running along the bank, they will catch you. Go across the river. It's too deep here for the dogs to get across. It'll buy you time."

What... What was she saying?

Was she actually... helping him?

She pointed upwards with one of her short swords, at the nearest tree whose branches stretched across the river. "Climb, Ayc. Go!"

Ayc stared at her. He couldn't trust her, could he? A dog howled, followed by a chorus of others. So close now. He didn't have any longer to question it.

Ayc rushed to the tree. Its nearest branch stretched high above his head, but the mighty roots rose in arches from the ground. He scrambled onto the first root and then clambered to the next. If he jumped from here, he could catch the lowest branch. But if he missed, he would end up in the river.

I won't miss, he told himself. He sucked in a breath and jumped. His belly hit the branch; his palms slapped down on the bark and slipped off. Lora's sharp cry echoed from the ground beneath him, before his arms tightened around the branch. His shoulders ached from the days of carrying his pack, but he refused to release. He swung his leg over, straddling the branch.

He glanced down, but Lora still stood on the bank.

She waved her sword and yelled, "Go!"

He pushed to his feet and found his balance on the thick branch. Spreading his arms wide, he walked across the branch as quickly as he could without tumbling off the side and into the water below. He'd reached the point where the branch intersected with a branch of a tree on the opposite bank when chaos erupted on the ground beneath him. The dogs burst from the woods, the search party called to one another, and an icy voice pierced above all of it, "Loraphne!"

Panic descended Ayc's spine.

Yris.

Don't look back.

Ayc stepped carefully onto the next branch. It dropped beneath his weight, and he stumbled to his knees. He seized the wood with both hands only moments before he was dumped in the river. Remaining on his hands and knees, he scrambled across this branch.

"Loraphne, don't just stand there!" Yris commanded. "Go after him."

Of course, Yris would demand it be Lora who followed him. Ayc held his breath, hoping Lora would refuse. But Lora sheathed her swords and made her way to the tree. Beyond her, a small army of royal guards and infantry gathered. Dogs sniffed at the tree roots and brayed an alert but were signaled back by handlers. Yris stationed herself at the water's edge, Fennix and Onanna at her sides.

Onanna had enough power to stop Ayc, but she didn't move, didn't interfere in Yris's game.

"Hurry, girl!" Yris snarled at Lora, who had paused to judge the jump from the root to the branch. "What's wrong with you? I've raised you to be stronger than this. Move!"

Lora leaped for the branch, grabbed it, and let the momentum vault her around. She landed in a crouch on the branch, as smoothly as acrobats Ayc once saw perform at Creed Castle. Ayc swallowed his remaining fear and pushed himself forward. By the time Ayc reached the trunk on the other side, Lora walked on the branch like it was solid earth. Ayc slipped and almost fell his way down the trunk to the ground, landing on the opposite riverbank.

"Boy!" Yris roared with so much force that Ayc spun around to face her, half expecting her a foot away and not still across the river. "If you run any farther, then the divine better have mercy on you when I catch you, because I certainly will not."

He hesitated for only a moment, his nervous fingers falling instinctively to his wrists. But his bracelets weren't there to fiddle with. He remembered his ability, stepped backward into the shadows of the trees, and disappeared.

"Did you see that?" Fennix asked.

Even from the distance, Ayc could make out Yris's smile. "Yes, I did."

A crack split the air, followed by a scream so loud Ayc felt it ricochet through his bones. Lora tumbled from above. Ayc's heart plummeted with her. He bit down on his tongue to keep from screaming her name.

Water exploded in all directions as she impacted the river and disappeared beneath the surface. Calls of alarm rippled through the dog handlers and guards as they hurried toward the water's edge. Fennix himself rushed forward, but Yris caught his shoulder.

"No one move," Yris commanded. "Loraphne can manage on her own."

And so, of course, no one moved. Not Fennix or Onanna. Not the royal guards. And not the rippling surface of the water.

Ayc counted his heartbeats, loud in his ear. One. Two. Three.

But Lora did not rise to the surface.

She would come back up, Ayc told himself. *She would.* And right now, he needed to run before someone else decided to follow him. But his feet had grown roots, his gaze still fixed on the water.

Please, Lora, come up.

But she didn't.

How long had it been? Seconds? Minutes? Surely, far longer than it should have been.

Fennix's voice sounded out, "My lady, we should—"

"She's fine," Yris said, sounding almost bored. "She's strong enough to do this on her own."

"She could be hur—"

"You will not intervene." Yris didn't spare her First's frantic, disbelieving expression a glance. Instead, she continued to search for Ayc across the river, her eyes roaming over him without seeing him.

The reality trembled through Ayc's spine.

Lora was *drowning.*

And no one, not even her own mother, was going to save her.

Which meant there was only Ayc. And if he saved her, he forfeited every chance of escaping. Feeling as though he couldn't draw a breath, he looked at the water one last time, at Yris, and over his shoulder at the darkness of the deep forest. There was decision here, but it didn't feel like a choice. Not at all.

Ayc hurled his pack from his shoulders, charged into the light, and flung himself into the river.

Silence. It was so silent beneath the river. The water stung his eyes as he forced them to open. He tried to make sense of the shapes before him. Rocks and the limbs of old fallen trees and—*there!* Lora floated as though still straining toward the surface, but branches along the riverbed had snagged her cloak, holding her in place. Blood pooled around her head, the water stained red. And she was still, a type of unnatural stillness he knew too well, that drained every ounce of warmth from his body.

Ayc kicked his legs frantically to close the distance. He yanked at the cloak's clasp in order to free her, then grabbed her, hugged her body close, and kicked toward the surface. The dead weight of her body threatened to drag them both back down again. The river's current pulled against him, but Ayc fought. He fought harder than he'd ever fought before and slowly propelled them upward.

"Help!" he screamed as his head broke the surface. He tried to maneuver Lora's face above the water, to let her breathe air, but he managed only one more breath before they sank beneath.

Lungs burning, Ayc tried in vain to reach the surface again, but they sank lower, toward the riverbed.

We're going to drown, he thought. *We.* Because it didn't once cross his mind to let her go.

Arms wrapped around Lora from above. Ayc glimpsed Fennix's face and released Lora into his grasp. Fennix surged upward, and Ayc followed. As soon as he reached the surface, arms seized him and dragged him toward the water's edge. Ayc didn't fight the guard but kept his entire focus on Lora as Fennix gently laid her upon the rocky bank. When solid ground appeared beneath Ayc's feet, his legs buckled. He gasped for air, but he couldn't breathe—because Lora wasn't breathing!

He tried to crawl toward her, but the guard grabbed the back of his shirt and held him in place. "I'm so sorry, Ayc," the guard whispered into his ear. Later, Ayc would remember that this was Irving. Ayc would realize that his restraining hands had been kind and his apology sincere. But in that moment, all Ayc could see was Lora.

She was far too still, her face a shade of gray it should never have been. She was fire and fury. Vicious and unbreakable. She could not *die*!

Ayc sucked in enough air to yell, "Is she all right?" It was a cry, a scream, a roar of fury, all in one. He wanted to sob, to tear everyone here apart. "*Is she all right?*"

Suddenly, she gasped, coughed, cried out—then rolled to her side and began vomiting. River water flowed past her lips. She was breathing, ragged and gasping, but *breathing*. The panic in his chest surrendered, leaving only rage.

He snapped his head to Yris, who hadn't rushed to her daughter's side. Who only stood, still staring at Ayc.

"How could you?" he roared. Water dripped down his face, but he could barely feel it. He could feel nothing but the heat of rage. "How could you just stand there? She's your daughter. *Your fucking daughter!*"

Red flames impaired his vision; his voice deepened. Somewhere in his head, he heard an old warning, a voice that was now only a memory.

Be calm, sweet boy. No one likes who they become when they're angry.

Ayc pressed his eyes closed. Breathed in and out slowly. He bent over, curling into a ball to hide his movements. He reached into the pocket of his trousers, relieved to find his bracelets still there, and slipped them both back on his wrists. He secured them a moment before hands with sharp nails seized his arms and yanked him to his feet.

Yris grabbed his chin in her hands. Her smile was more wicked than he'd ever seen it. "Invisibility, huh, human? I knew there was something you were hiding from me. I bet there's still more, and soon, you'll show it all to me."

"I'll never give you what you want, bitch," he snarled.

Her blood-red fingernails dug in harder, sharp as a monster's talons, creating scars he wears to this day. Blood joined the river water on his face and poured down his jaw. "We'll see about that."

CHAPTER
EIGHT

NOW

The day before the Trials start, the castle of Wyntra hosts yet another party. The night holds the first true warmth of spring, so the event fills the courtyard instead of the great hall. The training equipment has been tucked into storage to make room, and the gardeners have trimmed the hedges back into orderly rows. The tall pots, which have been empty all winter, now display flowers imported from the Bromalis greenhouses. A band of string and brass instruments performs on a makeshift stage, amplified so they can be heard over the wind that always breezes through Wyntra. Their tune might be a little too lively, considering that half the party guests might slaughter each other tomorrow. And the other half have come to cheer on their favorite victor in that slaughtering.

Ayc, for once, is invited to be a guest at the party, not to serve at it. But still, he carries a tray of layered cakes, fruit tarts, and bite-sized cinnamon rolls, as he traverses the crowd. He learned long ago that the best way to overhear the most tantalizing gossip at a party is not to attend it, but to serve at it. No one ever sees the staff.

He mills around the crowd, tucking little pieces of information away in his mental pocket. He notes little details, people whispering, snippets of conversations, bets placed and money exchanged. Wylder—fucking Wylder—is the favorite to win, even in clans outside Noxumbra. Ayc hopes many people will be losing a lot of money, and then tosses that information out of his head as soon as he hears it. There are far more important things to learn.

After a week of getting to know the rest of Lora's Five better, he's now even more certain he brings little to the table, but at least, he can do this.

Later, he finds Bronwen and Tavish standing near one of the fountains on the outskirts of the crowd. Tavish presses so close to one of the roaring gryphon statues carved into the fountain's tall basin, he might actually be trying to hide behind it. He grips his cane with one hand and the other coils around Saga's guide handle. The leash of the Kindred collar is also wrapped carefully around the handle, but Tavish is careful not to touch it. Saga pants happily, weaving his head this way and that to take in the dancing, thriving crowd. Tavish wears a long, silver coat over his vest, but he looks as uncomfortable and unnatural as a boy playing dress up in his father's clothes.

Bronwen leans against the side of the fountain, dressed as she did for the last party: in the form fitting armor and green sorcerer's cloak. Her makeup is done with artful precision, the wings of her violet eyeliner so sharp they might be lethal.

In the last few days, Ayc has learned more about Bronwen and Tavish. Bronwen's story unraveled piece by piece, while Tavish blurted his own on a single afternoon.

Bronwen attended two renowned schools. She was born in Lux Aester to parents she stated she'd scarcely seen since the age of nine, when she demonstrated affinity for sorcery and was sent to Velphin, School of Sorcery. When she tested at Wyntra in her eighteenth year, she tested into both Adamant and further instruction at the School of Sorcery. She chose Adamant and became both a warrior and a sorcerer.

It's impressive how much she's managed to accomplish in her relatively few years, particularly because she's a female born in Lux Aester. Frequently, girls from Lux Aester are prevented from participating in the formal schooling process. Most are married before their Final Testing at Wyntra would take place, and Lux Aester certainly doesn't usually send their girls to learn sorcery or to become warriors. The Lux Aester's brand of religion teaches that those gifts are best left in the hands of males. That females are too volatile.

More likely, Ayc thinks, Lux Aester knows that educated women are impossible to control.

Tavish has an even more unlikely story. He told Xylie and Ayc one afternoon after they left another meeting at Peregrin's house. As they all walked along the shore, Tavish retraced his life, almost all twenty years of it. He stumbled with his words, but once spoken, they hung in the air, joining the forceful sea breeze that whipped at their skin.

His mother was a successful Sal Maris merchant who had a brief, but loving affair with a sea nymph. Tavish was born and lived on the sea until it became clear he was blind.

He spent a few years on land because his mother was too terrified he'd slip overboard and be lost to the ocean. But when his divina gift began to manifest, he begged his mother to take him back to sea. She assembled a crew, and they became treasure hunters, searching the seas for downed ships or finding pearls like the one that Tavish still wears on his neck.

"The sea wasn't something I could see then," Tavish explained. "But it was something I could hear and smell. More importantly, it was something I could feel." He touched his sternum, right over his heart, with the hand wrapped in Saga's leash. As they walked, the dog looked frequently out to the crashing, gray waves. Ayc has noticed that Tavish mostly relies on his cane and the guide handle on Saga's harness, as though perhaps looking through Saga's eyes can be too much. But Tavish didn't seem to mind it then, walking beside the sea.

"Only now," Tavish continued, "I can see it through Saga's eyes. Somehow, it's so much better than I imagined it."

Tavish had a wonderful life, until he was ten, and his mother's ship was overtaken by pirates. The only thing that saved Tavish was his divina gift. His mother's last act was to explain to the pirate captain exactly what the boy could do, and the pirate captain—a Tenebra fae known as Zephen—saw it for the advantage it was. He spared the boy and had everyone else tossed to the sea.

It was a story that felt all too familiar to Ayc—like the same knife had given them both equally brutal wounds. Ayc kept his gaze fixed on the ocean, not glancing at Xylie even when she stepped closer, brushing her shoulder against his. Luckily, Tavish didn't notice and continued his story.

Tavish spent years trapped in a life he didn't want, navigating pirates to lost treasure, to merchant ships, to get-rich-quick-schemes, and away from oncoming storms. He told Xylie and Ayc about finding Saga and sneaking him aboard. When Zephen inevitably found the pup, he nearly tossed him into the sea, but Tavish made a deal: Saga's life in exchange for leading Zephen to his biggest payload yet. Tavish could feel the value of it, though he didn't know what they would find until they came upon it.

On Tavish's guidance, the pirates overtook a ship of Drakr by surprise. The element of surprise was perhaps the only reason the pirates were able to overcome the Drakr. One skilled Drakr could outmatch all but the most highly trained fae. To Tavish's dismay, the Drakr didn't have treasure in their holds; they had *children*. Children who were being transported from Tenebra to Drakr—for slavery. And it was, indeed, lucrative for the pirates when Zephen sold the children himself.

Tavish was quiet for quite some time after that, watching the sea. The tide rolled in, hissing along the sand. But slowly, stroking Saga's head, he told the rest.

After that, Tavish never knew whether his gift was leading the pirates to a treasure of goods or people.

"I thought about jumping into the sea so many times," Tavish admitted. At this point in the story, the three had stopped to sit in the sand, watching the waves. They'd all removed their shoes and ground their toes in the cool sand. "So, Zephen couldn't use me anymore. But Saga..."

That, too, felt all too familiar to Ayc.

"It wasn't your fault, Tavish," Ayc told him. The words felt hollow, even to him.

Tavish shrugged. "It was Bronwen and Lora who saved me."

Ayc leaned forward, propping his elbows on his knees and chin in his hand. "Tell me *everything*."

Tavish explained that, apparently, Adamant puts their first-year students through 'survival training'—which involves throwing eighteen-year-olds into hazardous conditions and seeing if they survive. During theirs, Bronwen and Lora were abandoned on a driftwood in the middle of the Southernmost Sea. And who would have come upon the thirsty, slightly delirious, beautiful fae but Captain Zephen?

The captain believed he'd discovered a magnificent treasure. How could he have ever guessed that he'd brought aboard the most dangerous creature at sea?

Leviathans have nothing on Loraphne.

"Well," Tavish said, fiddling with the pearl at his neck, "the *Maiden's Tears* had a hull and deck full of children in cages. Bronwen and Lora took one look at those kids... and everything turned to chaos. I think Bronwen would have let a few of the pirates live or dumped them overboard. But Lora... Lora slaughtered every single one of them."

A chill swept over Ayc's arms. He could imagine it clearly: the way Lora's eyes would have sparked to silver rage when she saw the children. The way it looked like dancing when she fought with her twin blades. And there must be something, deeply, profoundly wrong with him, because there were only two words that came to Ayc's mind. And one was *vicious*, yes. But the other was *beautiful*.

"I think Lora might have killed me, too." Tavish laughed nervously. "She had her knife to my throat when Bronwen reasoned that I clearly wasn't one of them. They let me explain, and I told them about my gift. Told them, I could navigate them back home... and the kids, too. And so that's what we did. We made sure all the kids made it home."

In the three years since, Tavish had been living in self-imposed isolation in the Forest of Elodie, among the Totus Omni. He enjoyed a quiet life walking the woods with Saga by his side, always missing the sea. Lora and Bronwen wrote to him, sent him gifts, but they hadn't visited until Lora returned to place her name for consideration as victor of the Totus Omni. And once she was elected as victor, she showed up at Tavish's little house, built into the side of a tree, and asked him to be her Fourth.

"And here you are," Ayc said.

"And here I am," Tavish agreed.

Now, a few days later at the party, Ayc offers his new friends his tray. "Cake?"

Bronwen lays a hand over her stomach. "I don't know that I can. I've had three already."

"I mean, we all might die tomorrow," Ayc encourages.

Tavish makes a noise that sounds like the squeak of a mouse.

Bronwen purses her lips and hums softly as she considers. "You're not wrong." She takes another cake. "Learn anything interesting?"

"It depends," Ayc says. "Do we care that Ruatha and Mienna were each other's first lovers when they were teens orienting at Bromalis?"

Bronwen raises her eyebrows. "Are they still fucking?"

"Per Mienna's Third, it was a brief affair that turned into ruin in the span of two weeks. As such things generally go between the young. And now, it appears they are completely apathetic towards one another."

"Pity. I suppose it's not much use then. Anything else?"

Ayc hesitates. In truth, he saw Hason, the Sal Maris victor, and Mienna whispering behind a hedge. Ayc crept close and overheard a plan that's imperative for Lora and her Five to know or else the Trials may be over for them almost as soon as it begins. But right now, too many people might overhear Ayc and know exactly whose throat to slit.

"Yes, but let's not discuss it here. Later, in private."

Bronwen nods and takes the last cinnamon roll off the plate.

"One more cake left, Tavish. Tray is just in front of you, chest height." Ayc positions the tray accordingly. "Sorry, none for you, Saga. Chocolate will make you sick, but I'm sure Tavish has been sneaking you plenty of jerky and cheese from the table."

"I have." Tavish lifts a hand until he brushes the edge of the tray and then takes the cake quickly. He only holds it awkwardly in his hand. Sweat beads on his upper lip.

"Why are you hiding over here, anyway?" Ayc asks.

Bronwen eyes Tavish. The lines that form around her lips spell worry, confirming Ayc's suspicion that she hasn't wanted to leave her friend's side.

Ayc sets the tray down on the edge of the fountain and clasps a hand on Tavish's shoulder. "What do you say, Tavish? Why don't we go have some fun? It's your last chance to flirt with some beautiful people, whatever your preference."

Tavish's eyes fly wide. "I... well I can't— I don't think. Oh divine! Surely I—"

Ayc looks at Bronwen, alarmed. "Did I break him?"

Tavish presses the fist that holds the cake to his mouth, biting a knuckle. Bronwen bumps him gently with her shoulder. "I think Lora and I have let you stay holed up in the woods too long."

"Have you never been to a party before?" Ayc asks kindly. "The Totus Omni have some wonderful parties."

At least, judging by the parties he has attended, when he's been in Elodie for festivals. Despite also being deeply spiritual in their connection to the divine, the Totus Omni couldn't be more unlike the Lux Aester. Their parties are always filled with laughter and good food and people who accept one another just as they are. He always returned to Wyntra reluctantly. If Ayc had choices, he would call the Totus Omni lands his home.

Tavish drops his hand and shakes his head. "I'm not really a party person. I haven't been to one before... at least one that didn't involve pirates. Which I tried my best to stay far away from, because it generally ended in someone being stabbed." He nearly crushes the little cake. "Oh no, someone's going to get stabbed, aren't they?"

"No." Bronwen lays a soothing hand on his shoulder. "Victors would be disqualified if they or their Five harmed anyone before the Trials officially begin tomorrow."

"Speaking of which, where is Lora?" Ayc asks.

He spotted Peregrin sitting on a set of stairs that leads onto the wall surrounding the courtyard. Their stormy eyes have been studying everything all night. Ayc is sure Xylie is inside, avoiding the crowd, but Ayc hasn't seen their victor since the party began.

"She's inside," Bronwen replies, the lines reappearing on the corner of her lips. "With Xylie."

"Why?" Ayc asks.

"I think she's trying to give moral support."

"Moral support? For what?"

An edge Ayc has never heard before enters Bronwen's voice, as razor sharp as the dagger on her belt. "Yris is insisting Xylie must come out for the formal introductions. Lora tried to argue her on it, but Yris threatened that she won't let Xylie participate in the Trials if she doesn't."

Anger flickers beneath Ayc's skin like flames and makes the sore muscles in his back tighten. He snuck a pain tonic from Xylie's stores before the party, but nothing can flare his pain like strong emotion. Anger can feel so much like pain.

"Can Yris do that?" Ayc asks through his teeth.

Bronwen tosses up her hands. "I don't know. Lora didn't know. Xylie researched, but she hadn't found an answer yet. Yris didn't exactly give us much time." Bronwen growls. "Fuck. Every time I think Lora has managed to find the courage to get out of her mother's claws, Yris finds a way to stab them back in."

"Yris's claws go deep," Ayc says, his fingers touching his chin, where little white crescent scars still exist from the day beside the water. From a dozen other days too. He certainly has never found a way out of her claws, and Lora? He's always known Yris's claws embed themselves in both his and Lora's spine. But he never thought Lora to be unwilling.

How much can change in four years? Surely, not that.

"Maybe, I should go—" Ayc begins, but the music dies out.

The musicians scurry off the stage, and Yris sweeps onto

135

it, wearing a deep red gown that's the exact shade of dried blood.

Fuck. Too late to save Xylie now.

"My good Everadyn fae," Yris announces, her voice carrying through the courtyard. Ayc swears he sees some of the potted flowers shrivel in response. "Are you ready to meet your victors?"

The crowd cheers.

"From Bromalis," Yris says, "I give you Sterling and their chosen Five."

Enthusiastic clapping breaks out among the crowd. Ayc joins in until Bronwen frowns at him and arches an eyebrow in a silent question. He swiftly drops his hands. Sterling takes their place center stage, followed closely by their Five —who are a set of fierce looking fae, most of who are dressed in chainmail that shimmers like a rainbow in the torchlight that illuminates the courtyard. There, on Sterling's right, in her rightful place as their First, is Wren.

Ayc has somehow not crossed paths with her all night, though he certainly has looked for her—the fool he is. Instead of armor, a pink and orange gauzy dress drapes over Wren's body, making her appear as though she's wearing the sunset, an outfit that compliments her twin's tunic. It dips low on her chest, hinting at her full breasts, before it stops below her sternum.

Every nerve in Ayc's body stands at attention. As though sensing his gaze, Wren turns her head toward him. Their eyes connect. The feeling is heady, like drinking fae wine too fast. He knows better than to hope, but a smile curls on her face, just for him, and fuck, he *hopes*.

"A friend of yours?" Bronwen whispers in Ayc's ear.

Sterling and their Five make their way from the stage.

Ayc doesn't say anything before he springs forward, pushing through the crowd, and to his relief, Wren heads straight toward him.

They meet in the center of the crowd. Bodies press around him, but all his senses focus on her. The slow, silky smile she gives him feels like a gift he doesn't deserve. "Hello, Ayc."

Something tightens in his spine at the sound of his name on her lips. "Hello, Wren."

Wren leans close so she can whisper in his ear. She smells like lavender, and it conjures the memory of her taste. He shivers. "So I was thinking—"

"For Totus Omni!" Yris calls on the stage. "We introduce Loraphne and her chosen Five."

"Shit!" Ayc holds up a finger. "Hold that thought."

When he turns toward the stage, Loraphne is already standing at the center, her chin held high and her face cool as stone. She's accented her dark armor with a cape that flows to her ankles like a tapestry. A tree embroiders the rich, dark velvet. The spiraling, entwining branches bear vibrant shades of leaves: red, yellow, and orange until the cape perfectly captures the beauty of autumn in the forest.

Bronwen stops at Lora's right side, and Xylie stands on her left. Ayc can see ornate hoops dangling around the tops of Xylie's pointed ears—ones that Ayc found at a fair and bought for her. They're enchanted to dull noise, but they've never been enough to help her join a party before. She looks like she might vomit, her eyes pressed closed, her head bowed. Beside her, Tavish forces a smile, Saga sitting at his feet. Peregrin stands as straight as the army leader they once were.

Ayc rushes forward a step, but Wren catches his hand. "Wait."

"I have to go," he says apologetically, pulling away.

"Ayc, what—" She begins to protest again, but he rushes to the stage stairs and takes them two at a time.

A few cheers soar through the courtyard at the sight of the Sovereign's daughter, not only from the few Totus Omni present, but scattered through all the clans, some polite, some enthusiastic. And then Ayc comes to a halt beside Tavish and stands to face the crowd, Lora's Fifth, and the cheers slow and then stop.

Fuck.

Ayc sees the expressions change through the crowd: many curious, some confused, and some—like Marcellus and his Lux Aester crew—furious. In the center of the crowd, Wren's face flashes through a variety of emotions, first confusion, then disbelief, and finally, horror.

"She can't choose him," a Lux Aester fae says, not even trying to whisper. "He's human."

"That's good," says someone closer to the back—Hason, the navy captain. "It means he'll be easy to kill."

Laughs scatter through the crowd, loudest from someone close to the stage. Him, Ayc recognizes all too well. He hasn't changed much in four years. He's still all dark hair, pale, chiseled cheekbones, and narrow dark eyes. The kind of handsome the world pauses to notice.

Wylder.

Fuck, fuck, fuck.

Is this Yris's plan? A way to get rid of Ayc, once and for all. Someone will kill him and take the curse upon themselves and their clan, instead of on all of Everadyn.

Ayc's vision tunnels. He barely sees Xylie turning to him,

her eyes wide, or Peregrin stepping in his direction. The laughter of the few rattles through his ears, but it pales in volume to the silence of the majority. They don't join, but they say nothing to those who do. Then a growl cuts through it all, one fierce and loud enough to silence the laughter.

Ayc's vision widens and snaps toward the center of the stage, where Lora stands. Her eyes glow silver as she locks on to Hason; her lips draw back, revealing sharpened canines. Her voice is more vicious than he's ever heard it, not like her mother's, but entirely her own. Utterly cold, utterly lethal, utterly sincere. "If you touch him, I will rip out your heart and shove it down your throat before it stops beating. He's *mine!*"

Silence.

The crowd doesn't utter a sound. Even the wind quiets. But Ayc's head has never been so loud. It feels as though a lightning bolt has struck his chest. *Explosive. Electric.* Lora turns to look at him, her eyes still glowing silver, and she is glorious. *Fierce. Breathtaking.* His skin vibrates in the wake of her words, and he ignites, every part of him set ablaze—not in pain, but in something far more consuming. Something he doesn't dare name.

But it's just a flash. The lightning fades, and the realization of the true meaning of her words sinks in. His own personal villain just told the entire court Ayc belongs to her.

And the fire—still all-consuming—turns to rage.

No, to *hate*.

"Enough," Yris snarls, breaking the tension in the air. "Must I remind you all there will be no bloodshed here until the trumpets sound tomorrow? Anyone who tries will be disqualified from competing in the Trials." Her eyes flick to Lora, silver momentarily flashing. "Thank you, victor. You may leave."

Ayc doesn't wait another moment. He throws himself toward the stage stairs. The only one who is faster is Xylie, who darts past him and toward the safety of inside the castle. But the thought of being inside is too hot and stifling to Ayc. He would like very much to plunge himself into the icy waters of the Bellum Sea. Anything to stop this fire within him.

He's only made it to the exit of the courtyard that leads to the barracks and the Bellum, when a hand catches his wrist. He whips away, already knowing who he'll find. He supposes Lora is using restraint not to just pin him to the wall with a knife at his throat, like she did when they were kids. Behind her, Bronwen races after them, Saga guides Tavish toward them, and Peregrin's limp grows more pronounced with every step as they hurry to catch up.

"Ayc," Lora says, "there's no reason to be afraid. I won't—"

"I. Am. Not. Afraid." Ayc snarls each word through his teeth. "Why would you say that? '*He's mine?*' What the fuck, Lora?"

She casts her gaze away from him, toward the wall, and lingers there, as though counting stones to avoid looking at him. Both Bronwen and Tavish are standing a few feet away by the time Lora inhales through her nose and speaks, "Because I couldn't let myself or my Five seem vulnerable. But more importantly, I'm trying to *protect* you."

Ayc snorts. "No, you're trying to let people know I'm *your* pet now, instead of your mother's."

"*What?*" Lora snaps, and the word is both shocked and

angry. She steps forward this time and draws herself to her full height. He doesn't cower back. He lets her put her face inches from his, so when she speaks again, he can feel the force of her words against his neck. "What the fuck are you talking about?"

"You know exactly what I'm talking about."

From somewhere, Ayc hears Bronwen hiss, "I think we need to calm down" while Tavish curses, "Damn, I knew someone was gonna get stabbed." Distantly, Ayc is aware of cheering back in the courtyard, of Yris's voice echoing. But Ayc's entire existence has narrowed down to only this woman before him. The stubborn set of her jaw, the angry rise and fall of her chest, her eyes transforming from a deep violet all the way to black. All that exists is the way he feels like he is on fucking fire with her this close, with her words still pounding in his head. He hates that she still impacts him like this. He wants to tear off his skin if it means he'll just stop feeling *this*.

"As I said," Lora says through her teeth, the sharpened canines contrasting against the darkness of the tunnel, "I was trying to protect you."

Ayc cracks a smile, but he's sure it looks mean instead of carefree. "That's real cute. You're trying to protect me *now*? You've never wanted to before."

"Are you serious?" Lora seethes. "All I've ever tried to do is protect you, you unbelievably obtuse asshole!"

He laughs—humorless and cold. It may be the best joke he's ever heard, if it wasn't so cruel.

"Shut up, both of you!" Peregrin snaps, shoving a hand between them. "Stop acting like fucking children. You can't do this here. Not where people can see."

"Fine." Ayc flings himself around and marches away.

"Wait, Ayc." The heat in Lora's tone fractures, and in its place, her voice is almost colored in panic. "Will you be here in the morning?"

He doesn't turn back. "Of course I will!"

Not that he has a fucking choice.

CHAPTER
NINE

The water drips into Ayc's eyes as he makes his way back to his kitchen in Wyntra Castle. Whatever warmth the night held has surrendered again to a winter's chill, but it's far, far better than the heat he felt long after he stripped down and dove naked into the icy waves of the Bellum.

The party has dissipated from the courtyard by the time he makes his way through. He shivers and pushes back the hair clinging to his face. His damp clothes paste themselves to his skin. At least, no one is waiting for him. Not Peregrin to yell at him, or Xylie to check on him, or Lora to fight with him more. Good. He wants only to be alone.

But when he reenters the castle and turns the corner that leads to his room, he freezes in place. A figure steps from the shadows by his door. Ayc curses himself for being relieved too soon. He would have preferred Lora. Fuck, he would have preferred a Drakr hiding in the darkness to Yris.

"Have a good swim, human?" the Sovereign asks, as she draws herself to a halt still ten feet from him.

Only a few moonbeams make their way through the windows; all the lanterns were turned off hours ago. In the darkness, Yris's nearly white hair and pale skin make her look like a wraith about to devour him whole. He searches the darkness behind Yris, but if she's chosen to have a guard with her, their cloak's hood is up and the enchantment renders them invisible. Either way, no one will intervene between Ayc and Yris.

Ayc doesn't draw any closer. He bows his head and pastes on a smile. "Good evening, my lady. Isn't it a bit past your usual bedtime? Shall I fetch you a cup of tea and some leftover cake?"

"No." She takes a few more steps. Only five feet between them now. "I've been waiting to speak with you. It will only take a moment."

Unease drags at Ayc's smile. Keeping it in place feels painful, as if he hammered nails into the corners. "Of course, my lady."

Another two steps. Only three feet now. "You caused quite a scene today, yelling at my daughter the way you did. I would never have suggested you to fulfill the Totus Omni's silly little prompt if I thought you would be so disrespectful."

"*Why* did you suggest me?" Ayc dares to ask.

"I have my reasons."

One more step, until he's within reach of her pointed talons. He doesn't retreat. He refuses to let her know that he still fears her, even if he does. Even if he knows people would be foolish not to fear her.

"But I want to make it very clear, human. She will be your Sovereign one day, and I'm sure you know the oath you took will bind you to her. Until then, you will obey Loraphne as you obey the Sovereign."

The words land so forcefully he stumbles back.

No, she can't...

"Do you understand me?" Yris snaps, her eyes flashing silver. "Her commands will be my commands. The consequences of disobedience will be the same. That is my will."

The order yanks at his throat like his collar pulling taut. He nearly chokes, nearly sputters. His pain buzzes like a thousand hornets writhing. A scream builds in the back of his throat. A smile spreads on Yris's face, telling him she knows exactly what she's done, the chains she has added to his neck.

And his worst fears are realized. Lora has always had power over him.

Now, it is limitless.

"It seems like you understand." She reaches her hand with her sharpened nails to pat his cheek. It's all he can do not to flinch. "Keep her safe."

She walks away, leaving Ayc fighting for breath in the hallway. When she's gone, Ayc stumbles the dozen feet to his door and launches himself inside. The door slams behind him with such force it shakes in the frame. Only the light of the moon illuminates the room, and he wishes he could rip off his bracelets, slip into the darkness, never to be seen again. But running away stopped being a possibility a long time ago.

He presses his fists to his temple, taking gulping breaths, trying to fight the panic rising.

This can't happen.

This can't—

Hands slip from behind him, covering his eyes. "Surprise."

Before he can recognize the voice, Ayc moves instinctively. He grabs the wrists, spins, and shoves her toward the door, pinning her arms above her head. She gasps in surprise, and he freezes, forcing air between his teeth. But he doesn't release her, because Wren looks so pretty, pressed against his door, her arms stretched above her head. He draws in another deep breath. His senses flood with lavender, and that feeling returns—the one like drinking fae wine much too quickly—blurring his panic, his racing thoughts, his pain. Fuck, she couldn't have come at a better time. He needs this.

"I wasn't expecting that," Wren says, a slow grin curling up her glitter-dusted cheeks. "You're full of surprises."

"You startled me," he explains, curling his fingers between hers and bringing her hands down beside her head.

"Not as startled as I was to learn you're one of Loraphne's Five." She blinks, the gemstones in her eyelashes catching the moonlight. "Whatever happened to being enemies?"

Ayc hovers his lips near hers but doesn't let them touch. "I suppose we're keeping each other closer than normal."

"Yes, her comment made it seem like you two are *very* close."

Wren pulls her lip between her teeth, then releases it. Is she actually jealous? The thought thrills Ayc. Maybe, he actually got under her skin. The idea that someone might not be entirely unaffected by him is intoxicating.

"She couldn't let any of her team look like an easy target." It's the same explanation that Lora gave him, the one Ayc still doesn't quite believe.

Wren raises an eyebrow. "It seemed that, last time we spoke, you were appalled by the very idea of her being Sovereign. And now you're helping her?"

Ayc really wishes they were talking about anything else. "It's complicated." Hoping to distract her from further questions, he tilts his head and hovers his lips over her jawline, but doesn't touch her. Her breath quickens, her breasts rising and falling so heavily it brushes against his chest. He revels at the effect he has on her. It makes the need rise swiftly in him. It takes all his restraint not to strip her bare.

"Why?" Her word turns into a gasp as he presses a kiss to the curve of her neck. Her arms squirm, but he tightens his hold, keeping them in place. "What power does she have over you?"

Ayc pretends not to hear the question, least it stokes the panic. He needs this too desperately: needs to forget the pain and this night. And most importantly, he needs to forget Lora and the fire she causes and how it still simmers within him. He calls it hate, because that's the easiest, safest thing to call this feeling, the one that refuses to be shaken no matter how he tries.

"Is this what you came here for?" Ayc asks. "To interrogate me about Lora and her Five?" He grazes his teeth against her neck next, followed by his tongue. "Or did you come here for something else?"

His hips surge forward, eliminating the distance between them, showing her what he's prepared to give her. The thin fabric of her dress leaves little to the imagination. She makes that moaning noise deep in her throat, the one he would be willing to do *very bad things* for.

The moan turns into words, "Fuck me, Ayc. Please."

He leans back so he can study her eyes. "Did you come here to be fucked? Or did you come here to be fucked *by me*?" He needs to be clear for the sake of his own sanity.

This time, when she pulls away, he releases her. She slides her hands on either side of his face in a touch far more tender than he expects. It makes something dangerous constrict in his chest. Her eyes blaze silver. "Ayc, I want *you* to fuck me."

She hauls his mouth to hers, and the last of his restraint shatters like porcelain against cement. He growls into her mouth and yanks at her skirt, not stopping when he hears the seams protest. She attacks him with the same veracity and desperation. His trousers are only at his knees and her skirts around her waist, when he lifts her up, and she wraps her legs around him and—*yes, fuck, yes*. She is already bare for him, and he slides inside her.

"So fucking good," he snarls into her ear. "You feel even better than I remember."

She slips her fingers into his hair, matching every thrust of his hips with a tug at his roots or a nip at his neck. It drives him harder, faster. More. Fucking more.

"Have you thought about our night together since then?" she asks between gasping breaths.

He's too lost in her to deny it. "Yes. All the time."

"Me too," she breathes, her tongue trailing over his ear. "All the time."

It shatters something in him, and one hand releases her ass to yank at her bodice. The deep V dips to the side, threads whining in protest, but soon one of her breasts is free—full and taut in the dim moonlight. He pulls it into his mouth and matches his administration with the movement of his hips. He alternates sucking and broad, circular strokes of his tongue.

Her hands tighten in his hair, holding him close. "Ayc," she whimpers. "*Ayc!*"

His name transforms into a scream on the final note. Her legs tremble as her body surrenders to the pleasure. The feel of her release almost drives him over the edge, but not yet.

Before her body has subsided, he maneuvers them to the floor, nearly tripping as he does so. He kicks his legs free of his pants and slides down her body to put his tongue where he was just buried.

"Again," he encourages. "I want you to scream my name as you come again."

And she does. Again. And again. And again.

"Where did you get these?" Wren asks, pointing to the bracelet on his wrist which lays lightly on his chest, only an inch from where her head rests on his shoulder.

They have since moved from the kitchen floor to his bed, their clothes discarded somewhere in between. They've crawled beneath the blankets, his arm wrapped around her. Every breath he inhales is lavender. It's dangerous how much he likes it; he could get used to this.

She traces a finger over his bracelet. The smooth brown leather. The braided edges. The metal plate in the center embossed with the silhouette of a bear. "You always wear them."

It's not the first time he's been asked about the bracelets, but other than a handful of exceptions, he's always deflected the question. He answers honestly now.

"My mother gave them to me when I was little." He lifts his wrist and turns it so she can see the extra little holes they had to poke into the leather to fit his small wrists.

She trails her fingertips down his arm. "According to the stories, your parents sold you to the Drakr, and Yris saved you and took you in."

She says it like she's skeptical of the story's truth. She peers up at him through the jewels in her lashes. He considers telling the true story, if only to make Yris angry. She certainly doesn't want anyone knowing the part she played in Aluina's ruin. He still doesn't understand her motivations for doing it, but he knows it's a secret she's buried. She's reminded him frequently that the fewer people who know who he truly is, the less likely the Drakr will know someone from Creed survived and come finish the job Yris started. He knows that's the least of her fears, but it's always been enough to keep him silent.

He's never told anyone, and he's not truly ready to tell Wren either. It would feel too much like stripping himself bare, all the way down to his soul.

Instead, he says, "My mother was long gone before Yris needed to save me."

"Your mother was good to you, then?"

"The best."

Ayc was only ten when she died; his memories of her feel like recalling dreams. Some are hazy and sweet, and some shine bright and vivid. He can remember her brilliant smile and her easy, quick laugh. He can still feel the wooden stool beneath his bare feet as she taught him to bake. He can hear her humming as she tended to the counter of her little bakery in their small, sleepy village.

"How'd she die?" Wren asks.

He releases a deep breath. "The way humans so often do. There was a sickness in the village. Lots of people died, and so did she."

"I'm sorry." She lays a gentle kiss on his breastbone, as though she thinks it might soothe the pain she knows lies beneath. "It's a special kind of pain, losing your parents. I lost mine, too. My father died in the last Trials. He was the Bromalis victor."

Ayc winces. "No wonder these Trials mean so much to you and your sibling."

Wren nods and continues, "My mom died seven years ago. She was a warrior in the aerial armies. After Aluina fell to the Drakr, she was a part of a movement that wanted to help human rebel fighters reclaim their homeland."

Ayc adjusts to see her face, afraid she might be teasing him. But her tone, and her face, is deeply serious. "I never knew about a rebellion in Aluina... or that anyone in Everadyn wanted to help."

Wren sets her head on her hand and looks down upon him. "Everadyn fae were allies to Aluina for centuries. It's why they were the only fully human-controlled territory left in the continents. They were able to withstand against an invasion from the Drakr because Everadyn fae had helped them ward their boundaries against their entry, so only humans and their allies could enter. We had trade agreements: enchanted weapons and army support in exchange for lumber from their forests and iron from their mines. Sorry... you probably know this."

Ayc certainly knows about the former allyship and the wards, though little good the wards did. Before the Drakr took Aluina, Ayc suspected the wards were nowhere near as strong as people thought. When Ayc woke from nightmares about the Drakr, his mother always assured him it was fine, but then he would see her sitting up the rest of the night, a crossbow sitting on her lap. There were rumors of lapses in the ward, of gryphon riders who flew to human aid when Drakr's attacked border villages near the mountains. Peregrin was even one of them until a Drakr drove a magical blade into their leg. After Creed Castle, when Aluina fell completely under Drakr control, he always assumed the wards were never that strong to begin with.

But he's never heard it from the side of an Everadyn fae. Ayc suspects Yris has forbidden anyone in Wyntra from discussing it with Ayc.

"Please, go on," Ayc says. "I don't know as much as you would think. I certainly don't understand how the Everadyn and Drakr became allies."

"No one really does, just that it began when Yris became Sovereign. It happened subtly. Trade agreements with Drakr for resources and a slow decline of conflicts, though nothing that contradicted our existing allyship with Aluina. Well, except how Yris slowly relocated our soldiers stationed in Aluina back to Everadyn." Wren shakes her head. "Looking back, I don't see how we missed it. Perhaps we just didn't pay attention, until it was too late. Until the massacre at Creed Castle."

Ayc fights not to flinch, like the words don't come with images of blood and the sound of screams that still make him want to wretch. Mercifully, she doesn't seem to notice and goes on.

"When Yris refused to send aid to stop the Drakr onslaught and ordered the rest of the Everadyn soldiers back, so many people were angry. *I* was angry. I'm still angry."

A rumble of that rage echoes in her voice, and Ayc draws her back to his chest. Whatever connection he senses between them tugs at his heart. It feels like a balm against an old wound, knowing that she cares so deeply about the fate of his people. She settles her head back upon him, so he can feel the vibration of her words as she continues, "My mother was so furious she joined a group who were giving aid to Aluina. They fought for a couple of years, rescuing humans and bringing them here or to Tenebra, out of Drakr reach. They even set fire to a Drakr army base, but then the Drakr retaliated and burned down a village. Well, one village in every single clan. So many people died."

Ayc's shoulders tense. "How long ago was that?"

"Seven years ago."

Ayc's eyes flutter shut as the timeline settles into place. Xylie's village. That's why the Drakr's attacked, when there were no attacks in the years before or in the years since. Her village and her parents were revenge for an act of rebellion.

"Yris was furious," Wren continues, "and in order to restore peace with the Drakr, she rounded up a dozen fae who helped with the rebellion. All the other fae were banished, but my mother—" Wren's voice tremors, and she cuts off. Ayc soothes a hand up and down her spine as she takes a few shuddering breaths to gather her strength. "Yris thought my mother was the leader. She wasn't, and Yris had no proof. But that didn't matter. Yris had her executed anyway. She made Sterling and I watch."

"Fuck, Wren," Ayc says, unsure what else to say. "That's awful."

"It really was," Wren agrees.

Ayc sees a spark of a tear on her cheek and reaches to caress it away.

He thinks he remembers that day, seven years ago. The Wyntra students murmured about an execution, and Ayc stared in horror as a stage was built with a single block on it. People gathered in the courtyard. The air hung heavy and thick as when a storm blows in from the sea. Loraphne cornered him and said she was in a particularly bad mood, and if she saw him in the courtyard that day, she was going to stab him. He went down to the beach, but he knew the moment it happened, because a gryphon's scream shook the sky, far louder than the crashing waves.

Surely, that was the day Wren's mother died.

He doesn't burden Wren with his recollection; she has enough memories of that day.

Wren sniffs and moves on. "I want you to know that assholes like Hason are loud, but most people in Everadyn—Lux Aester excluded—don't hate humans or think of them as inferior."

"I know," Ayc says softly.

For every loud asshole kid at Wyntra, there were just as many who were content to leave him be or even be friendly. He never could tell which would be which, so with the exception of a few brief flings, he never trusted anyone enough to build any friendships. His presence has always been welcomed at festivals, and he's met many dozens of humans who have made Everadyn their home, found sanctuary here after escaping Aluina. Mostly, the Everadyn are kind. Mostly.

"What happened to the rebels after that?" Ayc asks.

"I don't know. I think the movement disbanded, but I think a lot of people would want to help Aluina if they weren't so scared of Yris and the people loyal to her. It's one of the things Sterling and I want to change. We've sat by and let Aluina suffer for too long. Things are going to change after these Trials." Wren sits up and gazes down upon him. The moonlight frames her from behind, a soft, alluring glow. "And you could help us."

"What do you mean?"

"I know you feel trapped. You must if you've agreed to be one of Lora's Five. You don't have to tell me why, though I wish you would." She fans a hand over his sternum and waits. When Ayc says nothing, she sighs and moves on. "But you don't have to help Loraphne, Ayc. You said so yourself; you keep your enemies close. That close, you could make it —" She pauses, as though choosing her next words delicately. "You could make it... *difficult* for her to win."

"What? Like, sabotage her?"

"Exactly."

Ayc laughs. Surely, she can't be serious. But Wren doesn't join in, and the laugh suffocates in his throat. He sits up.

"You're serious, aren't you?"

Wren pulls the blanket around her shoulders and closes it over her naked chest. "I wouldn't joke about something like this. I want my sibling to win. They will be a far better Sovereign than Loraphne would ever be."

"Maybe, but..."

"But, what?"

And that's the question, isn't it? But *what?*

Ayc doesn't want Lora to be Sovereign and condemn himself to obeying her for the rest of his life. And here he is, uniquely in a position to prevent her from winning. All he would have to do is say nothing and let tomorrow take its course, let the plan he overheard Mienna and Hason discuss play out. Yris gave him an order to protect Lora. *Keep her safe.*

But she was foolish enough not to say Loraphne's name. Little details like that are easy to exploit.

The idea cements itself on his chest, heavy, but attractive. For once, he could seize a little power. For once, he could perform a little villainy of his own.

But would he be able to live with himself if something happened to Lora when he could have prevented it? What kind of monster would that make him if he let her die?

Wren gently pushes the hair from his face, drawing him out of his thoughts. "Just promise me you'll think about it."

Ayc catches her wrist and lays a kiss on her palm. "I promise."

The worry on her face doesn't ease. "I hope you do. I hate to think of us going into the Trials on different sides, of us being put in a position where we could be forced to kill each other."

Ayc laughs at the absurd thought. "Kill each other? I'd never kill you."

Wren doesn't join his laughter, and he swallows down the merriment. "That's what the Five are meant to do," she says.

"Fuck that. I don't plan to kill anyone, least of all you. That's not the kind of man I am. And you'd never hurt me."

She gives him a wistful smile and runs a finger across his collarbone, sweet and light. "You're a good man, Ayc. You've got a kindness in you I wasn't sure existed anymore, besides Sterling. I'm glad I met you."

"Thank you." He hesitates, then adds, "And don't go across the bridge tomorrow."

She blinks. "I thought that was a requirement. Everyone has always gone over the bridge."

"And it turns into a bloodbath. There's no actual rule.

Xylie did research, and it's merely a tradition. Leave the city a different way. Fight another day."

Her eyes flick across his face, and then she smiles, a full, relieved grin. "Thank you, Ayc." She frames his face in her hands and kisses him. It's not a kiss like they've shared before. Instead of lust, there's tenderness and affection that makes it feel like candlelight during an otherwise long, dark night.

When she leans back, she asks, "Who's Xylie?"

Ayc grins and settles back against the wall, happy to move on to less complicated topics. "She's Loraphne's Second and her cousin. She's also my best friend. She's lived in Wyntra almost as long as I have."

"She's Yris's niece?"

Ayc nods.

Wren lets the blanket fall and turns so she can relax her back against his chest. He wraps his arms around her, reveling in the feel of her skin against his.

"That's odd," Wren says. "I've come to many parties at Wyntra, and I've never met Xylie."

"You wouldn't have." Ayc nuzzles Wren's neck, and she curls her head to the side to give him more access. His fingers stroke slowly across her belly. "Her brain works differently than most people. It makes her the smartest person I know, able to notice things people miss and remember every detail she's ever read in a book. But I think that can also make everything else feel like... too much sometimes. She can't speak around most people, except for me and Lora. She was only there tonight because Yris forced her to be."

"I suppose that explains why she looked like she was going to be sick," Wren says sympathetically.

When Ayc's fingers trail down to her hip, she lets her knees fall open and leans her head back against his shoulder. Her breaths are already speeding up in the way that's quickly become one of his favorite rhythms.

"What about the man beside her?" she asks. "He looked like he might be... well, blind."

"Tavish? He's our navigator."

"Navigator?" Ayc isn't sure if her gasp is one of surprise or because his fingers are now on the inside of her thigh. "How is that possible?"

"I'm not going to tell you that."

"Why not?"

"Not my story to tell. Besides. I think I'm done talking for a bit."

She makes a strangled noise, as he's finally, finally found her center. "All right, but then I really have to leave. It's late, and tomorrow—oh, fuck, don't stop. Tomorrow is—*fuck, Ayc*. No, you're right. We should definitely stop talking."

After, she kisses him again like before, slowly, tenderly. It feels like the beginning of something new. "Promise me you'll be careful, Ayc. I'm afraid I'm starting to find myself hopelessly attached to you."

"It's my baking skills, isn't it?" he teases.

She laughs. "That's part of it. But only a part. And now I have to go." She groans and wiggles from his grasp. He makes himself let her go.

She steps into the kitchen but returns wearing her dress. It lays crookedly on her chest now, and he grins at his work, not sorry. She isn't looking at him, though, but rather at the tapestry that hangs on the wall beside his bed. She cocks her head. "I didn't notice it before. It's a beautiful tapestry."

It is. Breathtaking, in fact. The fabric is made so artfully that it almost doesn't look like fabric. The first time he saw the tapestry, it felt so real that for a moment, he was a kid again, lying on the floor of the forest around his village—trees and flowers rising above his head, fireflies lighting the air. The branches high above frame a full moon and a whole universe of stars.

Wren reaches out to run her hand over it. "It's so soft. Like liquid." She glances at him. "Who's the artist?"

Ayc shrugs. "I don't remember. Saw it at a festival a couple years ago. Bought it on a whim."

"I see." She frowns at the tapestry once more, before returning to him. She grants him a kiss that's far too brief. "Promise me you'll think about what I said. And be safe."

He swallows. "I promise."

When she's gone, Ayc collapses onto his pillow where her glitter still lies, grinning a smile he's sure looks absolutely ridiculous. Hope is a dangerous thing, but it's too big to contain, so he lets it fill his whole chest.

A couple hours later, he awakes to pounding at his door. He rolls out of bed, half-asleep, and collides with the floor. He fights with the blankets that have tangled around his waist, manages to get to his knees and jerks the door open.

"Oh my divine!" Xylie shrieks and then flings herself around. "You're naked! *Why are you naked?* And why are you still in bed? The opening ceremony is starting *in fifteen minutes.*"

"Oh, fuck me," Ayc swears.

This time, Lora really is going to stab him.

TEN

"I'm here; I'm here," Ayc says between gasps as he comes to a stop where Lora and the rest of the Five have gathered in the tunnel between the courtyard and the barracks.

The gray predawn light cloaks all of them in shadow. He leans a palm lightly against the stone wall. He smiles, so it'll seem casual, when really his back is spasming hard enough it threatens to double him over.

In less than a minute, he dressed, buckled his new longsword at his side, and slung his cloak and pack over his shoulder. Then he ran to the courtyard with Xylie at his side. Alongside the weapon, Peregrin procured him simple leather armor. It buckles tight at his sides and rises in a high collar to protect his neck. He hates the way it constricts against his chest. It's a reminder that someone might aim a blade for his heart in less than an hour.

Xylie wears her own new armor, with her usual coat pulled over it and the noise-dulling ear cuffs. Tavish's armor is similar to Ayc's, but he wears cuffs that extend from wrist to elbow. Even Saga is wearing a leather vest, the harness and guide handle now fitted over it. It looks—Ayc thinks with a smile—ridiculously adorable. Peregrin appears every bit of the warrior they are, dressed in a lighter version of the Adamant armor, theirs a color that reminds Ayc of a cool, gray dawn instead of black.

Each of Lora's Five wears a pin on their chest, a tree with branches spiraling toward the sky. The symbol of the Totus Omni.

"Late night?" Bronwen asks with a hint of a smile. Her staff leans casually against her armored shoulder, the blade at the end gleaming in a nearby torch's light.

He ignores the question and glances to Lora, trying to gauge how angry she is. It's difficult, because she continues to stare into the courtyard. There, everyone gathers in clusters made of the victors, their Five, and the ones who have come to cheer for them. The stage before the crowd is empty.

"I thought you weren't coming," Lora states without emotion, adjusting one of the dozen leather straps that cross over her chest, though it already fits perfectly against her scalelike armor. "I'm going to hurt you."

Ayc gives her a cheeky smile, though she's not looking at him. "Let me guess: peeling off my fingernails one by one?"

"Castration with a dull knife."

"Shit." Definitely pissed at him, then.

He considers apologizing, but when she swings her steel-colored eyes upon him, the idea dies a rapid death. "Were you with Wren?"

Ayc straightens. His smile falls. "I don't think that's any of your business."

Her eyes darken. "It *is* my business. According to the

rules of the Trials, after the trumpet sounds today, she could slit your throat in your sleep."

"She's not going to—"

"Loraphne," calls an unfortunately familiar voice.

Ayc bites back an audible groan as Marcellus strides toward them. He wears no armor, still dressed in the holy blue tunic and a white cape like he thinks the divine himself can protect him. Beside him is who Ayc can only assume is his First: a pale, sour-faced male roughly the size of a small hut that Ayc has frequently seen beside Marcellus at festivals. He's dressed similarly, but instead of a single broadsword like Marcellus wears, he's armed heavily—a war ax over one shoulder, a sword over the other, and multiple throwing axes and knives at his hips.

Marcellus's approach has a visible impact on the Five. Color drains from Bronwen's face, and Xylie moves to halfway hide behind Ayc's back. Peregrin subtly unlatches one of their knives from their belt. Saga stands at attention, laying back his ears, and Tavish picks up the leash of the Kindred collar. Lora marches forward to intercept Marcellus as though aiming to keep some distance between Marcellus and her Five.

"Can I help you, Marcellus?" Lora asks, not attempting warmth in her tone.

He spreads his hands in a peace-making gesture. "I and my First, Brother Erech, wanted to wish you the best in the Trials, before it all officially begins. We all know you have a long legacy to follow."

"Thank you," Lora says. She doesn't wish him luck in return.

The slight doesn't go unnoticed. Erech's face turns more sour, and Marcellus's eyes tinge silver around the very edges, coming and fading in a blink. He glances past Lora and surveys the people behind her. Ayc pastes on a smile and resists the immature urge to send Marcellus a vulgar gesture.

"It's quite a party you've assembled here, Loraphne. Quite unexpected, and just..." He hums thoughtfully. "Just so full of irony."

"What do you mean?" Lora asks, her words cold as ice.

Marcellus smiles and, as he speaks, his gaze moves from Peregrin, to Xylie, to Tavish and finally to Ayc. "I mean, you have a warrior who can't walk. An academic who can't talk. A navigator who can't see. A human who's barely even useful. And..." Marcellus settles heavily on Bronwen, and his smile turns dark. "A sorceress who isn't a woman at all. Isn't that right, Brother Eliaki?"

The words are meant to be a blade, and they aim true. It slices across every one of the Five. Xylie presses her forehead in Ayc's back, Peregrin curses, Tavish sucks in a breath, and Bronwen, for her part, only lifts her chin in self-assured pride.

The anger sweeps over Ayc—swift and complete. Red flashes across his vision, and his hand curls around the hilt of his sword before he knows what he's doing. He strides forward but makes it only two steps before Peregrin seizes Ayc's wrist and casts him a heavy look. Ayc remembers himself, just in time.

A hiss of metal echoes as Lora draws one of her twin blades a few inches from her scabbard. Her tone matches the ominous noise, "*Her* name is Bronwen, you son of a bitch!"

Bronwen steps forward and lays a hand on Lora's shoulder. "It's fine, Lora. His words hold no power over me." She meets Marcellus's gaze, unflinching. "Not anymore."

Marcellus's confident smile flickers like a candle threatening to go out before a strong wind. He looks away from Bronwen to Lora once more. "I am only pointing out the irony, Lady Loraphne."

"Just like you," Ayc says, grinning at him. "You're a man who's clearly a giant dick. Only in personality and not in actuality, though, I'm sure. Very ironic."

Bronwen laughs, before pressing her fingers to her mouth to silence it. Lora shoots Ayc a glare, but the way Marcellus's smile disappears completely from his face tastes too sweet.

"Watch your tongue, human," Marcellus growls, his eyes turning fully silver this time. "Or one of these days, I'll cut it out."

Xylie's fingers curl around the back of Ayc's sleeve, but Ayc only rolls his eyes.

Lora takes another step forward. "Do not threaten my people, Marcellus, or I'll—"

"You'll what?" Marcellus scoffs. "Rip my heart out? You allow your weaknesses to be too transparent. It'll make you far too easy to defeat."

A voice booms out through the courtyard. "All victors join me on the stage."

The reigning Sovereign stands at the center of the dais, dressed in the same armor her daughter wears. Ayc hasn't seen her in it since the day at Creed Castle. The air loses all its warmth.

It's time.

Lora's eyes shift to her mother. She steps toward the stage, but Marcellus grabs her arm and yanks her a step closer to him. Fury explodes once more within Ayc's chest, and his vision tunnels to Marcellus's hand wrapped around Lora's arm. And Ayc, fuck—

Ayc wants to break *every single one* of his fingers.

It takes every last shred of Ayc's will to resist. He presses his eyes closed against the heat of rage.

"When I am Sovereign," Marcellus says, "and mark my words, I *will* be Sovereign. The divine has willed it." Lora barks out a mocking laugh, and Marcellus's words become a snarl, "When that day comes, I will take great pleasure in having you bow before me."

Ayc snaps his eyes open in enough time to see Lora shove Marcellus back with a hand on his chest. "I will be *dead* before I bow to you."

Marcellus draws himself up and smirks again. "So be it, Loraphne."

The air grows even colder. Marcellus turns and marches toward the stage, Erech following after. Lora glances back at Bronwen, who nods and lays a hand over her heart.

Lora raises her chin as though wearing a crown and marches toward the stage and her destiny.

So be it, Loraphne.

Marcellus's words echo in Ayc's head, and he remembers all at once. The words he heard last night, what Wren asked Ayc to consider, the decision he didn't quite make. All he has to do is nothing. Say nothing. Do nothing. Let fate take its course. And maybe, unwarned, Lora survives. Or maybe all of this ends before it has barely begun.

And Lora ends up dead.

It should be the easiest thing in the world to let Lora walk to her fate, after all she has done to Ayc. But watching her walk through the crowd toward the stage, he feels like that fourteen-year-old boy again, on the banks of the Ever River, staring at Lora's blue face, unable to breathe until she did.

Like that day, saving her doesn't feel like a choice.

Ayc sprints toward her, ignoring Peregrin and Bronwen's protest. He catches Lora's arm right before she steps on the stairs and yanks her to the side. Hason nearly collides with them and glares before ascending to the stage.

"Ayc, what are you doing?" Lora hisses.

Ayc pulls her a few more feet from the steps and leans in closer than he normally lets himself dare. He whispers, "The other victors are going to try to kill you, as soon as the trumpets sound."

She stiffens. "What?"

"I overhead something last night. Hason and Mienna were talking. They see you as the biggest threat, and there's a plan amongst all the victors to take care of you as soon as the trumpets sound. And I realize I should have told you sooner, and I'm sorry, but just—you have to be careful."

"I'm Yris's daughter. I already know I have a target on my back." She pauses and then adds, "But... thank you."

Ayc searches her eyes, her face. But as usual, it's as emotionless as it is beautiful. He doesn't know if she's taking his words seriously.

"Lora..."

"You have to let me go now, Ayc," she says softly.

He hasn't noticed that his hand still lingers on her bicep, on the smooth material under the shoulder armor. He can feel the warmth of her skin beneath it. The fire of last night is still there, sparking in the ashes.

Something tugs at his throat, and he recognizes the

order he has been given. He yanks his hand away as though it burns.

She slips away from him and up the stairs, her autumn-colored cape flowing behind her. She takes her place with the six other victors. At least, she is the last one on the stage, closest to the stairs.

When he turns back around, he finds Wren standing in the crowd, staring at him, a frown on her face. He forces a smile for her. Wren only nods and turns her attention back to the stage. Ayc lets the coolness reflect off his skin. There are far too many emotions this morning to take it personally.

Ayc starts back toward the others. Tavish and Xylie have lingered in the tunnel, but Bronwen and Peregrin have approached. They position themselves at the side of the crowd, only ten feet from the stage.

"What was that about?" Peregrin demands when Ayc rejoins them and Bronwen.

"I think the other victors are going to turn on her as soon as the trumpet sounds," Ayc tells them both lowly. "Based on something I heard last night."

Bronwen and Peregrin exchange a look. Peregrin's eyes narrow, but they don't appear surprised.

"Even Wylder?" Bronwen asks, glancing to the other end of the stage where the tall fae towers.

Ayc shrugs. "They said *all* the victors."

Bronwen scowls as she fixes her eyes on Lora. A pulse of power releases from her skin, like a gust of wind. "They can try."

Bronwen adjusts her hold on her staff, and Peregrin slides one small dagger from their belt. Ayc drops his own hand to the sword that hangs on his hip, an unfamiliar weight. The blade Lora acquired for him is exquisitely made, obviously crafted by an Audori sword-smith, a blend of tungsten, iron, and silver, the very best Everadyn has to offer. The leather-wrapped hilt fits his hand like it was made for it, and when he pulled from is sheath when Peregrin first gave it to him, Ayc found it perfectly balanced.

On the stage, Yris stands before the seven of them. The first rays of dawn stretch over the parapet, bathing everything in a pink glow. "My good fae, I give you your victors."

The crowd cheers loudly.

Beneath the noise, Ayc hears Bronwen sigh. "Well," she says, not taking her eyes off the stage, "I guess you all know now."

"Know what?" Ayc asks, though he knows she's referring to what Marcellus said. "That you're a strong, powerful woman who overcame a lot to get to where you are? I already knew that."

Bronwen grants him a smile, before shifting her focus back to the stage.

Yris makes a beckoning gesture. Fennix approaches her, carrying a satin-covered tray holding seven metal bracelets. A rainbow of gemstones decorate the silver circumference of the bracelets. Yris takes one, undoes its clasp, and approaches Wylder. He extends his wrist, and Yris snaps the bracelet on.

As she speaks, Yris makes her way down the line, giving a bracelet to each victor. "These are chroniclers. They will guide you through the quests. As you accomplish each one, a gemstone will light up. If you wish to forfeit your claim to sovereignty, you may remove the bracelet from your wrist. Only you will be able to remove the bracelet. When a victor completes all seven quests, the chroniclers will send out a message. All victors who remain alive at that time will return here to pledge allegiance and witness the crowning of the new Sovereign."

Yris stops last at Lora. She extends her wrist and tries to meet her mother's gaze. Yris barely looks at her as she slides the chronicler into place and then backs away. Lora looks down at her arm. She yanks her sleeve back, baring her forearm. Her lips part. The same surprise echoes over many of the victors' faces as they stare at their own arms.

At the top of her voice, Yris declares, "May the Trials begin!"

From on top of the wall, the sound of trumpets roar, so loud the stone trembles.

Lora jerks her head up. Ayc's hand tightens on his sword. And before the trumpets have fallen silent, Hason, the victor from Sal Maris, who stands beside Lora, draws his cutlass and aims it straight for Lora's neck.

CHAPTER
ELEVEN

The blade cuts through the air toward Lora's neck. Her name rips through Ayc's throat. "*Lora!*"

Bronwen throws up her hand, and a wall of power blasts from her palm. It slams into Lora, and she flies backward off the stage. Hason's sword passes through empty air. And then blood sprays from his neck as Peregrin's knife embeds within. Someone in the crowd shrieks. Someone else bellows in fury. The screech of metal, as numerous weapons are drawn, is a third, ominous scream within the crowd.

A fae with a badge bearing a wave on their chest, surely one of Hason's Five, flings themselves at Bronwen, a cutlass raised. Bronwen swats the sword away with the blade of her staff and then slams the blunt end into their face.

"Bronwen, look out!" Ayc calls out as another Sal Maris Five charges at Bronwen from the side. But the fae crumples before reaching her, a knife in the side of their neck.

Peregrin rushes forward to yank their knife free, as Bronwen impales her opponent with the other side of her staff. Around them, skirmishes break out. People from the opposing teams launch themselves at each other. The bystanders scramble toward the castle for cover, knowing it is against the rules to assist any team now that the Trials have begun. The bloodbath of the Trials first day isn't waiting for the bridge. It's happening now, right here.

"We have to get out of here," Peregrin snaps. "Ayc, get back with Xylie and Tavish."

From the corner of his eye, Ayc sees a blur of scarlet as Mienna, the Audori victor, leaps from the back of the stage —toward where Lora has fallen. Ayc spares one glance to where Xylie and Tavish stand in the shadows of the tunnel. No one has noticed the two, and Peregrin and Bronwen have positioned themselves between them and the crowd, even as they engage in yet another battle. Xylie and Tavish are fine.

But Lora...

It's not a decision nor even a thought. Ayc flings himself forward—not toward Xylie and Tavish, but toward where Lora has fallen. Peregrin curses him, but Ayc slows only long enough to pull his new sword from its scabbard. Running with the blade feels awkward, and his muscles protest. He drives his legs harder, until muscle memory kicks. Finally, he sees the benefit to all those years Peregrin made him run the shoreline—where Yris did not often go—with a sword in his hand. Ayc smooths out his gait and shackles his pain behind his mental wall.

Behind the stage, Ayc finds Lora with her twin blades crossed above her head, blocking Mienna's single short sword. A bright yellow flame hovers over Mienna's other hand. She heaves the fireball toward Lora, who spins away. The fire narrowly avoids Lora's hair and lands instead in one of the carefully trimmed hedges behind her. It ignites in a burst of light.

"We have had enough of your family's rule," Mienna seethes and hurls a rapid barrage of fireballs.

Lora dodges and ducks, a graceful blur of motion. Behind Lora, more hedges and a few of the precious Bromalis blooms in the tall pots explode and wither instantly. The flames come too swiftly for Lora to form a counterattack. Mienna marches forward, drawing back her blade.

An idea leaps into Ayc's mind, and he knows it is a foolish one. He does it, anyway.

Pulse hammering in his neck, he hoists his sword and charges forward. "Hey, fire-wielding bitch!"

He swings his sword at Mienna's back. She pivots toward him and knocks his strike away. He leaps back and lifts his blade to shield himself as she drives her sword toward his heart. Metal clashes with enough force to rattle his teeth. He pushes his weight against their entangled weapons; she bares her teeth but doesn't budge. He doesn't stand a chance against her, but he just needs her focus completely on him for a second. A second is all Lora needs.

One swift stroke of Lora's short sword cleaves Mienna's head from her neck. Blood showers Ayc's face. Hot, broiling nausea races up his throat, and he swallows hard against it. He has not witnessed death since he was twelve-years-old. It is not any easier to stomach.

When Mienna's body crumples, Lora glares at him, her own face painted in red. Her dark hair cascades behind, free except for the place she's pinned it on either side of her head. She looks as fierce as the flames blazing in the hedges behind her. Wiser men would have cowered at her sight; Ayc revels in it.

Vicious, beautiful villain.

He shakes his head to clear it of his own foolishness.

"I had it!" she snarls.

Ayc clucks his tongue. "That's a really peculiar way of saying *'Thank you'.*"

"Just go!" She points her sword toward the tunnel.

Ayc sprints in that direction; Lora follows close behind. The air whizzes as an arrow slices by his head, close enough that he feels the heat. An archer stands within a dozen feet, already notching another arrow. Ayc quickens his pace. Only ten yards separate him from the tunnel, but the archer is already releasing the arrow. It soars straight for Ayc's face.

It freezes in the air, hovering only inches from his nose. Bronwen appears at Ayc's side, seizes the arrow, and heaves it back the way it came. The magical force propelling the arrow matches the speed of any bow and slams into the Audori symbol on the archer's chest with enough power to send him spinning.

"Where's Peregrin?" Ayc demands. He dares to glance back toward the courtyard but can only make out a mass of bodies ensnared in combat.

"Waiting on the other side of the tunnel," Bronwen says. "Hurry!"

"Loraphne!" barks a voice.

Three fae have broken from the crowd and charge toward them. Ayc doesn't try to identify whose team they belong to before he launches himself into the tunnel; Bronwen and Lora's feet pound on the stone behind him. Only when Ayc joins Tavish, Peregrin, and Xylie on the other side of tunnel does he look back. The three pursuers chase just behind Lora. Peregrin adjusts his grip on a knife, Tavish clutches Saga's leash tighter, and Xylie raises a bottle of bright green liquid.

As soon as Lora and Bronwen are clear of the tunnel, Lora yells, "Now, Xylie!"

Xylie hurls the bottle, then seizes Ayc's hand and yanks him with her behind the wood pile in front of a nearby home, where Peregrin has already steered Tavish and Saga. The bottle sails over Lora's head, collides with the tunnel's wall, and shatters. The courtyard wall explodes in green fire. Lora and Bronwen dive to the ground as stones fly above their heads. The earth trembles, and the wall buckles. When the dust and flames settle, the courtyard's exit no longer exists; the three pursuers are gone with it. Whatever Xylie lined the tunnel with last night certainly worked exactly as they all planned.

Ayc climbs to his feet, pulling Xylie up with him. His gaze snaps to Lora—and Bronwen—but they're already jumping to the feet and headed toward them, unharmed, brushing dust from their armor. Sounds of battle—metal clashing, people screaming—carries over the ruin, but it's no longer their concern. There are other ways to get to the barracks, but they're difficult to reach. Xylie has bought them all precious time. Ayc's heart rate slows, but the nausea lingers like the stickiness of blood on his face.

He hopes Wren is fine, that she and Sterling and their group ran as soon as the trumpets flared. He has no way of knowing.

"Let's go," Lora orders.

They rush down the path they previously decided upon, Saga leading the way. He trots like a pup on a luxurious stroll, his tongue drooping from the side of his mouth, through the silent barracks and to the cliff side. They weave down the narrow path to find the last member of their party, Tempest, waiting for them in the sand.

She flaps her wings and clacks her beak in displeasure.

"We're fine, Tempest," Peregrin says, limping toward her side. "Just got slightly delayed."

She clacks again, unconvinced.

"We don't have time to argue," Peregrin responds, to whatever the gryphon said in their mind. "Are you still willing to carry them?"

Tempest demonstrates her assent by stretching her front legs forward like a cat. She holds the position in a bow, the way Ayc has seen when she has allowed Peregrin to mount. There's another pathway off this beach, but it's miles down and a steep, treacherous climb. Tempest, however, agreed to fly them out and land them all in a place a mile from Wyntra. Still, she can only carry two at a time.

Peregrin nods to Lora. "You first."

"No," Lora says. "I'll go *last*."

"Lora," Bronwen begins, "you're the future Sovereign."

Lora lifts her chin again, like she already wears a crown. "Tavish and Xylie first. Then you and Ayc. Peregrin and I go last."

Peregrin and Bronwen both open their mouths, but Lora snaps, "You either trust me to lead or you don't. Xylie and Tavish, hurry!"

Xylie clammers on first. Even though Saga is half Tavish's size, Tavish manages to gather the dog in his arms and climb behind Xylie. The dog rests squished between Xylie and Tavish, already whining in concern.

"Hold on tight," Peregrin says as Tempest straightens.

Xylie clings to Tempest's neck feathers, and Tavish

buries his face in Saga's fur. Tempest rocks back on her hind legs and then launches herself into the air. Xylie screams, and Tavish lets out a shriek that he tries to pass off as a laugh.

As they become a distant dot in the sky, Ayc studies Lora as she turns a slow circle, watching out for any approaching threat. She has left herself on this beach, vulnerable to whoever might pursue her, choosing to send the others out instead. It's a choice Ayc knows Yris wouldn't have made.

"Why are you staring at me?" Lora demands.

Ayc flicks his gaze back toward the sky. "I wasn't."

Tempest returns a few minutes later without Tavish and Xylie. Ayc hopes that means they're safely waiting at the landing spot and not splattered on the rocks. Tempest repeats her low bow.

"You go first," Bronwen says to Ayc, her cheeks slightly flushed.

Ayc can't help the grin as he jogs to Tempest's side. He's wanted to ride this gryphon since the first time he saw her. He mounts and slides his hands into her feathers. Tempest looks back at him, and Ayc swears the gryphon winks a silver eye. After climbing aboard, Bronwen steadies herself on his waist, her staff now strapped to her back.

Ayc can't help the cheeky grin he tosses her over his shoulder. "You can feel free to hold on as tightly as you need."

Bronwen grins good-naturedly, but Lora calls over the wind. "Do not flirt with her!"

Ayc begins to roll his eyes, but a sting flares beneath his skin. That was an order. "I'm only being a gentle—"

His word turns into a holler of surprise as Tempest launches herself into the sky. He grabs fistfuls of feathers and tightens his legs on her side. The earth falls away, Lora and Peregrin shrinking into toy figures in the sand. The wind howls, and Tempest's wings beat against the air like thunderclaps. On Ayc's left, the ocean stretches to the horizon, and on his right, the buildings and stone castle of Wyntra fade away swiftly, giving into rippling grass, browned from winter. Miles in the distance, Ayc can make out the tilled fields, orchards, and clusters of houses from distant Bromalis' villages.

Ayc laughs at the exhilaration. He could do this every day and never tire of it, but Bronwen flings her arms around him, holding as tight as she can with his pack between them. He almost cracks another joke and remembers himself.

As though sensing his thoughts, Bronwen says, "Don't worry about the flirting." She has to yell so Ayc can hear her over the wind. "I, unlike Lora, know you're only teasing. And besides, for the record, you're not my type."

"Oh?" Ayc calls back with a smile. He likes Bronwen; she's gorgeous and strong, but she's also Lora's best friend, so he never entertained the idea of anything more than friendship. Besides that, there's Wren, who has occupied most of his recent thoughts. "And what *is* your type?"

Tempest dips to one side, twisting into an extreme angle Ayc is almost certain isn't actually necessary and just the beast showing off. Bronwen clutches at Ayc's waist, and only when Tempest levels off does she respond.

"I like most anyone, except for two exceptions, and you happen to be one of them. One is Lux Aester men."

Ayc doesn't know whether to wince or chuckle, so he does a bit of both. "Fair. I like men, but Lux Aester ones are also, definitely, not my type either. What's the other?"

She pauses for a moment. "People who look at my best friend the way you look at Lora."

Ayc laughs. It's the most absurd thing he's ever heard. "Like what? Like I might like to kill her?"

Bronwen laughs too, loud enough he can hear it over the wind. "No, like you haven't decided whether you're going to kill her or kill *for* her."

When Tempest lands for the final time, Lora dismounts gracefully from Tempest's back, but Peregrin remains sitting. They stand in an open field, facing east where the Bromalis lands stretch out in rippling grasslands.

"We should keep moving," Lora says, marching past them to lead the way. "I made arrangements to stay at an inn about three miles from here."

"Do you still think that's safe?" Peregrin asks. "Given what just happened?"

They say it without emotion, though Lora and Ayc still wear Mienna's blood on their faces. Ayc scrubs at it with his sleeve. The nausea gnaws at this stomach.

Lora doesn't pause. "I know and trust the innkeeper. And I paid him well enough to ensure we are the only ones there for the night. We need time to plan."

"Plan?" Tavish repeats. "How can we plan? Yris didn't even tell you the quests."

"But she did." Lora stops, extends her arm, the one now wearing the chronicler, and rolls back her sleeve. On the underside of her arm, words are scrawled like tattoos. She holds it up to allow everyone else to see, then crouches at Saga's eye level to show Tavish when he touches the leash.

Unearth a priceless treasure.

Forge a new path.

Reveal a long-concealed lie.

Face your worst fear.

Make a great sacrifice.

Undo an unforgivable wrong.

Upturn the hands of fate.

All Five of them blink at the seven quests in silence, and Ayc wonders if they are thinking the exact thing he is: It's the most cryptic bullshit he's ever read.

"Great!" Ayc says, clapping his hands. "Super easy. We should knock that out by midnight and all be home tomorrow morning in time for cinnamon rolls."

Four hands lift upward and flip him off.

TWELVE

The innkeeper of the Pink Elk Inn introduces himself as Vidar, pronouns he and him. He's a stout human with ruddy skin and biceps the size of tree trunks, who proudly wears both a bushy red beard and a floral pale green dress covered in a cream apron. He has a thundering brogue that tells Ayc he's originally from the northeast province of Aluina. Ayc likes *him* immediately.

His cooking? Not so much.

The amount of salt in the porridge makes Ayc's eyes water, but Vidar has lingered at the table. He levels a fierce expression on Ayc, his eyes almost disappearing behind bushy eyebrows.

Ayc swallows. "It's good," he lies.

It must be convincing, because Vidar moves away from the cluster of tables Lora and her Five pushed together. Maps now cover the surface, Tavish leaning over them, his finger brushing over Saga's leash. His dog sits in a chair next to him and stares down at the paper. Bowls rest near everyone, but neither Lora and Bronwen have lifted their spoons. Xylie and Peregrin must have noticed, because they don't attempt to consume their own porridge.

"You could have warned me," Ayc hisses across at Lora, who scribbles in her notebook, line after line of notes.

Her pen pauses, and her focus shifts toward him. "And miss the look on your face?" she asks, her mouth a taut line. She returns to her book.

Ayc grabs his mug of coffee to wash the salty taste from his mouth and to keep his hands from throwing her some offensive sign language he knows she'll understand.

"Vidar is not known for his breakfast," Bronwen says with a snicker. In her hands, she cradles a teacup that Vidar brought her, the hand-painted cup almost completely swallowed in the palm of his massive hand. Bronwen dumped the contents of a small package into the tea, and Ayc suspects it's the blend of herbs that make her body adhere more closely to her true gender.

"Lunch and dinner are...passable, though," she adds. "As long as you throw your porridge out the window behind you as soon as he isn't looking."

Ayc glances to where Vidar now stands behind the front counter, which is painted an eye-watering pink. A fierce-looking falcon perches on a stand on the counter's edge. Ayc almost thought it was stuffed when he first arrived, but every so often, it flaps its wings indignantly and glares at Ayc in a way that makes him believe the bird might be considering pecking out his eyeballs just for sport.

"How did you all become such good friends with an innkeeper?" Ayc asks.

The inn isn't close to any major village. Instead, it's situated off a road that passes through several Bromalis farms and an impressively large nursery that fills the air in the tavern with the smell of a dozen types of flowers. But the inside of the inn speaks more of Aluina than of Everadyn: the great stone fireplace and the wood-paneled walls and the busts of long-dead animals. On the mantle, there's a statue of a woman holding a coin and a four-leaf clover, with a fox curled at her feet. Ayc can't remember the name of the deity but recognizes the image as the goddess of good fortune and mischief. It's the type of irony he saw in most of Aluina's gods and goddesses, a contradiction of powers that made them useless at best and untrustworthy at worst.

This place strikes him with a deep longing for a place he hasn't seen for ten years. It's tampered, however, by the pink fabric and jewels that drape from antlers of the mounted elk heads and cross through the ceiling beams. Those elements do not resemble Aluina and speak entirely of Vidar's own personality.

Bronwen looks to Lora, who sets her quill down and looks around the table.

"Any thoughts on the quests?" Lora asks.

And subject changed, Ayc thinks and adds it to the mental note of all the questions Lora has avoided lately.

Everyone remains silent.

"Come on," Lora presses. "Any ideas at all?"

"Well, they're all a little..." Tavish pauses, cocking his head as he considers the right word.

"Vague as fuck," Ayc supplies for him.

"Thank you for that, Ayc," Lora says flatly. "Elegant and well-spoken, as always."

"I'm not wrong, though."

She doesn't argue, which is a mistake, because Ayc definitely takes it as a victory.

"I mean," Bronwen says, "he isn't." She holds out her

hand toward Lora, and Lora sets her wrist in her First's palm. Bronwen runs the finger of her other hand along the gems on the bracelet. Delight lights up her face. "The magic in this, it feels old. Maybe the oldest magic I've felt. It almost feels..." She hums as though trying to find the right word. "Well, it feels *alive*."

Lora withdraws her arm and eyes the bracelet quite like a snake has coiled onto her wrist. "Does anyone know how the quests are chosen? Does the reigning Sovereign play a role or does the magic decide for itself?"

Xylie signs an answer, and Ayc translates, "No one knows for certain. But what I found in the Archives suggests it's a bit of both."

"Interesting," Bronwen murmurs.

Xylie goes on, *"Some of the wording sounds odd. Like 'Reveal a long-concealed lie'. You would think it would say 'Reveal a long-hidden truth'. But it doesn't."*

Ayc fumbles over the last few syllables of the translation. A shiver crawls down his spine. He glances at Peregrin only to find their focus already boring into him. But no, surely, Yris wouldn't have willed ancient magic to make a quest just to set up Ayc, would she?

He tries to push the unease away, but it lingers, burying itself beneath his skin.

Lora makes a note of what Xylie said in her journal. Ayc glimpses a big 'Lie' and a flourishing question mark, before she looks back up. She taps her pen on the page, leaving flecks of black ink on the parchment. "Maybe we should focus on the first quest. It's the clearest. *'Unearth a priceless treasure'.*"

Tavish rubs a hand over the back of his neck. "Damn. I was afraid you'd say that."

Lora straightens. "Why? Have you thought of something?"

"Yes, but you won't like it."

"Show me," Lora insists.

Tavish fumbles through the papers, almost knocking over a few bowls of porridge. Peregrin catches them and begins dumping them out the window beside the table, glancing to make sure Vidar is still in the kitchen. Outside the window, Tempest bends their head to sniff at the now-dumped contents of the bowl and then raises her head to glare accusingly at Peregrin.

Tavish pulls out a map of Everadyn and lays it at the top. A single X has been drawn on it, and Tavish taps it with a finger. Ayc can't see exactly where it is on the map from his place at the table. "I sense something here. I have for a long time, as far back as when I sailed with the *Maiden's Tears*."

Lora stiffens as she stares down at the map.

Bronwen's face drains of the little color it possesses. "Somnia Ignis?"

Ayc splutters on the coffee he's sipping. Peregrin nearly drops another bowl of porridge out the window. Xylie maneuvers onto her knees to lean across the table and get a better look.

"The Isle of Nightmares?" Ayc says. "Are you seriously suggesting we go to the Isle of Nightmares?"

The island off the western coast of Everadyn is a place no one desires to go. Horror stories whispered at night tell of endless, deep caves where dragons make their nests and old, dark magic that turns nightmares into realities. Many people who dare to go there never return.

Tavish shakes his head quickly. "I'm not suggesting *anything*."

Lora spins the map around to face her. Ayc doesn't like the way she traces her finger from where the Pink Elk would be on the map to where the X is marked. "But you feel something there? Something that could be a priceless treasure?"

Tavish nods.

Xylie taps Ayc's shoulder to gain his attention. *"Translate for me,"* she says. And then her hands are spinning in the air so quickly Ayc struggles to watch them and talk at the same time.

"Xylie says there are legends about a great treasure on Somnia Ignis. Some say it's— *What? Slow down, please. Don't speak to me in that tone of sign. All right, all right*—Some say it's an artifact to communicate with the dead. Other sources say it's a jewel the size of an adult skull. But to get it requires facing the worst things imaginable." Ayc lets out a low whistle and fakes exuberance, "Well, that sounds fantastic! When do we leave?"

Xylie's eyes narrow, and she exaggerates her next signs.

"Go fuck yourself," Ayc translates, then winces. He clears his throat. "Actually, I think that was just for me."

Tavish snickers beneath his breath, his head still bent over the map.

Ayc squints down at the paper, then reaches across to press his finger to a spot on the opposite coast of Everadyn. "What about Somnia Vera? The Island of Dreams? That sounds much better."

The island east of Everadyn is the mirror to Somnia Ignis. Instead of fog and mountains, Somnia Vera bares lush forests and tropical plants and waterfalls that flow into sapphire pools. He's heard it called a paradise on earth. "No dragons," he adds, with a wistful sigh. "Just merfolk and fauns and—"

"The oldest and deadliest sorcerers that have ever lived," Bronwen says over the lip of her teacup. There's a contradiction in her voice, a tone both wistful and bitter.

Ayc lifts his finger to see the sketch of a castle with twisted, spiraling towers set on the island. Velphin, School of Sorcery, the map reads. "Didn't enjoy your experience there?"

Bronwen shrugs. "On the contrary, it probably saved my life. And also almost ended it on at least thirteen separate occasions. Many of the master sorcerers at Velphin are determined to turn prospective sorcerers into the most powerful of beings, or to kill them trying."

"Like Adamant," Lora says. "But with children."

Warmth drains from Ayc's face. No sorcerers he's met have ever discussed their experience at Velphin, but he's heard a few drunk elite warriors report what Adamant is like. Only the very best survive to graduate. But no one goes to Adamant until they are eighteen. The first testing at Wyntra, which searches for those with an affinity to magic, occurs at only seven years old. Ayc can picture all the kids he's seen through the years from his kitchen window. They're all so very tiny.

"Fuck," Ayc says, with a whistle that serves to release the horror building in his chest. "Maybe they should rename it the Island of Nightmares, the Sequel."

"Oh, shut up, Ayc," Lora says without emotion, but Ayc's jaw snaps shut.

Fuck.

"Can I see your arm again?" Bronwen asks, holding her hand out to Lora. Lora extends her arm. "Perhaps it could take out two quests at once. Forge a new path. If no one has been on the specific path to the treasure, maybe it'll work for both."

Xylie signs. Ayc doesn't translate, Lora's order lingering. He's having a bad enough day without adding anymore discomfort. Xylie gives him a pointed look and signs again. Ayc shakes his head.

"Except for whoever put it there," Lora translates, a line forming between her eyebrows as she looks between Ayc and Xylie. "You're right, Xylie. And there have been many books written about the dragons on Somnia Ignis. That path wouldn't be new."

"But that's the question, isn't it?" Peregrin says, dumping the last bowl of porridge and setting it back in front of Ayc. "Does the path need to be new for anyone? Or only new for *you*? Many of those quests are vague. We can't assume even the ones that seem obvious are as straight foreword as they seem. I imagine it's designed that way. Seven victors with seven quests and a multitude of ways to complete them."

"Nothing can ever be simple." Lora grits her teeth, the frustration standing out sharply for a second before she schools it into place. "Is there anything else you are sensing, Tavish? Any other great treasures we can try for instead?"

"Maybe," Tavish says, smoothing a hand over the map, no longer touching the leash. Saga cocks his head toward the window, distracted by something outside. But once again, Tavish's hand stills over the Isle of Nightmares. "But nothing feels as strong or as right as this."

Lora stares at the map for a long moment. At last, she says, "Then that's where we should go. If you are all in agreement."

Bronwen and Peregrin nod without much hesitation, Xylie following right after. Tavish turns ashen, but mumbles, "Yes."

"Ayc?" Lora prompts.

Ayc blinks at her and says nothing. He thinks about signing to her, but signing is talking and he thinks it might violate the order. Peregrin's gaze shifts to Ayc's face, their eyebrows knitting together.

"What's wrong with you?" Lora demands. "Is this because I told you to shut up? For divine's sake, you can talk."

Oh, thank fuck.

"Sure? Why not?" Ayc says sarcastically. "What's the worst that can happen?"

"We all get eaten by dragons," Tavish mutters.

"We're not going to be eaten by dragons," Bronwen says, good-naturedly.

Xylie's eyes sparkle, and she smiles much too brightly for this situation. Her hands move in broad, frantic motions. *"Did you know that, when dragons consume prey, they like to keep them warm and alive for as long as possible. They start with their nonessential parts like the arms and lower legs before moving on to more essential places. The process can take hours before the prey bleeds to death or loses something vital enough to kill them."*

Ayc is suddenly very, *very* glad that his stomach is empty. "For fuck's sake, Xylie. I didn't need to know that."

"What did she say?" Tavish asks, his eyes wide. Saga's attention is still focused on the window, ears perked.

"I'll tell you if you really want," Lora replies with a grimace of her own, "but trust me. You really don't want to know."

188

Saga growls, startling them all. His ears lay back against his head, and Tavish picks the leash back up from the table. "We're about to have company."

Bronwen and Xylie rush to flip over the maps. Peregrin draws a dagger and hides it beneath the table. Lora's hand drops to her own sword. Ayc is still deciding what he should do, when the door to the inn flies open and a tall, cloaked figure barges in.

The clang of the bell hanging above the door summons Vidar from where he disappeared into the kitchen. He's drying a pint on his apron and scowls at the figure. The falcon now perches on his shoulder.

"I need a room," says a deep, resonating voice. And fuck, Ayc has a suspicion on whom it belongs to.

Lora confirms his suspicion. Her hands arise from her sword hilt and strangle together on top of the overturned map. Peregrin doesn't sheathe their blade.

Wylder.

"No vacancies," Vidar says.

"It's not even noon, and there's barely anyone here." Wylder searches the room and freezes as he takes in the group at the back. He's dressed in the same dark armor that Bronwen and Lora wear. Splatters of blood mar his face. His dark eyes lock on Lora, who stares down at her hands, pointedly not looking at him. He lingers far too long, before he looks back to the innkeeper.

Vidar slams the pink mug down on the counter, his face turning redder. His rage suggests he doesn't know that the male he's talking to could turn him inside out at a second's notice. "I said no vacancies! The lady paid me well for the use of the establishment. If you would like to stay, take it up with her, or you can fuck off."

His falcon flaps its wings and emits a series of calls that demonstrate its solidarity with its owner.

Wylder's hands curl into fists at his side. But after hesitating, he flings himself around and saunters toward them.

Saunters, Ayc thinks. *Like a fucking peacock.*

Wylder stops beside the table and grants Lora a smile as if it were a gift. "Hello, Lora."

Her hands tighten together, and she doesn't return the greeting nor look at him.

Wylder moves his smile on to Bronwen, as though hoping for a warmer greeting. "Bronwen, good to see you."

Bronwen brings her teacup to her lips, but it's her middle finger she delicately lifts instead of her pinky.

Wylder's smile flicks off like a light. He searches over the others, his eyes narrowing as he notices Ayc at the other end of the table. A muscle in his jaw spasms as he draws his attention back to Lora. "Lora—"

Lora finally snaps her head toward him. Ice is warmer than her gaze. "No," Lora says, and the word echoes with heavy command. "You cannot stay here."

Wylder sets his hands on the table and leans closer, lowering his voice. "Is this how it's going to be between us now? Are you going to bear hard feelings for the tournament forever?"

If possible, the tension in Lora's shoulder tightens. Ayc catches Xylie's eye and lifts a single eyebrow in question.

She signs, "*He played dirty.*"

Ayc rolls his eyes. Of course he did. Wylder, as son of the Noxumbra regent, couldn't afford to lose.

Lora returns his question with a harsh one of her own.

"Did you know the other victors were going to attempt to kill me on that stage?"

Wylder scoffs. "Of course n—"

"Don't insult me by lying to me. You're bad at it."

Wylder draws a long breath between his teeth and ducks his head, his hair sliding forward to cover his eyes. "I knew, but I didn't play a hand in it."

"Your silence was helpful enough," Lora hisses, lightning crackling under her tone, the first emotion she's allowed in her voice.

Asshole. Ayc swallows down the word with some coffee. Ayc hates himself a little, that his silence almost assisted them, too. But he, at least, hasn't been—presumably—sharing Lora's bed for the last four years.

Lora's bed.

Heat rises up Ayc's neck, and he drowns that too with the rest of the coffee, wishing it was something stronger.

Around the table, no one else speaks, but all wear a slightly murderous expression.

Wylder removes his hand from the table and straightens to his full height. "This is a game, Lora. I thought we'd agreed to put our feelings aside and play it."

"I suppose I didn't realize that you could put your feelings far enough to the side to simply watch me die. But thank you. I understand the game-board far better now." She nods toward the door. "You can leave." She snatches her pen from the table and resumes scratching in her book.

Ayc nearly smiles. Fuck, he could live for a century off the pink-tinged rage on Wylder's face.

"Dammit, Lora," Wylder curses. "Ryker was hurt getting out of Wyntra. I need a place to put him, so I can find a healer."

Lora's pen halts.

"Ryker?" Bronwen repeats, her eyes widening.

The name rings like a bell in Ayc's mind, but he doesn't quite know why.

"I know you're furious with me," Wylder continues, "but surely, you won't hold it against *him*."

Lora's eyes shutter closed. Bronwen presses two fingers to the back of her elbow, a silent signal.

"Fine," Lora spits. "You can stay. For your *brother's* sake. Not yours."

Brother. That's right. Ayc forgot Wylder has a brother. Unlike Wylder who frequently visited Wyntra with his father, Ayc only met Ryker during his Final Testing, two years ago. Ayc nearly called him a liar when he said Wylder was his brother. His personality was light to his brother's dark: all blond hair, polite manners, and a flirtatious smile. Still, Ayc kept his distance, not wanting to be too close to Wylder, even by association.

Lora snaps her book closed and adds, "Your weapons and the rest of your Five stay outside. I'm sure Vidar has room in the stable."

Wylder grunts. "You're being ridiculous."

"Those are my terms. You can abide by them, or you can fuck off. I frankly don't care which."

Wylder opens his mouth and then snaps it shut. He storms to the door, growling something unintelligible under his breath. He pauses only long enough to talk to Vidar, who gives him a key.

A heavy silence lingers. Lora's sigh should have been silent, too, but in the stillness, it echoes so loudly Ayc feels it in his bones. Something passes over her face, a crack in the stone, there and then gone so quickly he can almost pretend he didn't see it.

Pain. Wylder hurt her.

Bronwen glances at Lora, her face twisting in sympathy. As though knowing Lora wouldn't want the attention, she says nothing. Doesn't reach out a comforting hand. Ayc finds himself longing to reach out too, but he's quite attached to his hand.

Instead, he swallows down a lump in his throat, leans over the table, and grins. "Hey, Lo-*ra*." He practically sings the last note, so she'll know what's coming.

She snaps her head in his direction. "Must you?" she says in a low warning tone.

"I must, and this one is good."

"They're *never* good."

"What did the ocean say to the shore?"

"That's ridiculous. The ocean can't talk."

"Exactly. It just waved."

Lora glares at him, but Tavish laughs loudly. Peregrin rolls their eyes.

"I'm going to kill him," Lora whispers to Bronwen, strangling the pen in her hand. "I swear I'm going to kill him this time."

Bronwen pats her cheek sympathetically. "I know, honey."

Ayc only lifts his coffee to his lips to hide a triumphant smile. The villainess is murderous once more. All is right again.

The door to the inn flings open again. Wylder reenters with a fae's arm slung over his shoulder. His brother's feet stumble with each step, barely holding him upright. Blood mats his hair and face, pouring from a jagged wound that gapes from his temple to his scalp. He, too, wears dark armor: an Adamant warrior, like his brother.

Bronwen springs up and hurries to Ryker's other side.

Through the mask of blood, Ryker grins at Bronwen. Unlike his brother, it lights up his face. "Well met, Bronwen," he says, his words hitched at the edges, like it hurts to speak. "I've missed you. Adamant isn't the same now that you're gone."

"Always the charmer," Bronwen says. "Let's get you in a bed before you fall down."

They move toward the stairs. Xylie grabs her pack and rifles through it. She grabs two bottles with tonics and shoves them into Ayc's hands. One is carefully labeled *Pain Tonic*. The other is labeled *Wound Cleansing & Healing*.

She nods toward where they are ascending the stairs. "*Give them to him. And tell them to hurry with the healer. If his wound isn't healing yet, that blade had to be tipped with something.*"

Ayc could name thirteen things he would rather do than follow Wylder up those stairs, including being mauled by a dragon for three days before succumbing to blood loss. But if Ayc doesn't agree, she'll ask Lora, who will do it and have to spend more time with the man who betrayed her. Ayc reluctantly shoves to his feet.

By the time he catches up, they're in a room upstairs—what Ayc suspects is the smallest room at the establishment. He lives in a modified pantry, and this room is smaller, barely leaving room for the bed that Bronwen and Wylder are helping Ryker into. The blood from Ryker's head stains the white of the pillow.

Wylder swings toward Ayc as soon as he enters, and his face twists into *that face*. The one like Wylder has smelled

194

something foul. A look of profound hatred. Some students who came through Wyntra disliked Ayc because he was human, some because of Yris's game. But for Wylder, it was more personal.

"What are you doing here?" Wylder demands.

Ayc holds out both hands, a bottle in each. "Xylie sent these. One's for pain. The other is for wound healing."

When Wylder hesitates, eyeing the bottles wearily, Bronwen takes them from Ayc. She sets the one for the wound on the small stool beside the bed and uncorks the pain reliever. She hands it to Ryker. It seems to take all his strength to prop himself up on his elbows and drink it down.

Ryker slumps back onto the pillow with a sigh. Ayc knows that feeling of relief well. "I don't know who Xylie is, but they're my new favorite person. Tell them thank you for me."

"I'll tell her," Ayc says, heading toward the door.

"And thank *you*, Ayc," Ryker calls after him.

Ayc halts and turns back, surprised Ryker remembers his name.

"I hope you've been well," Ryker says, and he's grinning again, a dimple flashing. In that moment, he looks far younger than his twenty years. Younger and more innocent than anyone related to Wylder has a right, and Ayc almost wishes he hadn't written Ryker off as soon as he met him.

Ayc grants him a smile in return and teases, "Could be worse. I could look like you do at the moment."

Wylder shoots him a glare, but Ryker snorts a snippet of a laugh. "False. I'm handsome even looking half dead. Bronwen, tell him I'm handsome."

From where she kneels beside his bed, she pats his arm.

"Yes, yes, you're quite splendid." Bronwen cuts a sharp glance at Ayc and Wylder. "Now, if you two would stop standing there and be useful. Ayc, ask Vidar to send up some clean water so I can wash this wound out. Wylder, time to haul ass to get a healer."

Wylder doesn't budge. "Bronwen..."

The mistrust hangs thick in the air. Bronwen draws herself upright and squares up with him, nearly matching him in height. Silver crackles in her eyes. She looks so fierce and vicious, that even Ayc takes a step back. "I may be furious enough at you that I want to curse your asshole to always be itchy, but you know I'd never harm Ryker. My loyalties don't disappear as easily as yours."

"You don't understand—"

"You poisoned Lora before your final match, Wylder. *Nothing* could make me understand that."

"You what?" The two words echo through the small room, first from Ayc and then from Ryker.

If looks could wield knives, Wylder would have embedded one in Bronwen's gut. She doesn't even flinch.

Ayc can imagine it clearly: Lora and Wylder toasting each other before the match, a tradition they would have learned during their testing at Wyntra. Lora feeling the effects, growing weaker, getting sicker, but stepping into the ring anyway—because she'd never back down. Lora, being defeated, perhaps in an embarrassingly easy way. Did she know how her mother would react to the news? Did she think about that as she yielded?

Ayc forces his jaw to unlock and releases the anger threatening to crack open his chest with a low, mocking whistle. "Fuck, Wylder, I used to think you couldn't be a bigger bastard, and here I am, proven wrong."

"I didn't ask your opinion, cinnamon roll," Wylder snaps.

Ryker lets out a deep sigh. "I know it's difficult, Wylder, but try not to be an ass and just go get me a fucking healer, all right?"

Wylder hesitates, looking from Bronwen to Ayc and then at last to his brother. He curses under his breath and spins on his heel. "I'll be back soon." On his way out the door, he shoves Ayc in the shoulder. "You don't need to be here. Out."

Ayc doesn't argue. They step out into the hallway, where garlands of pink lights drape across the top of the walls. Their rosy glow is too merry for the otherwise dim hall. Ayc hurries for the stairs, Wylder right at his back. Maybe if he can get out of here fast enough, Wylder won't have time to do anything to piss Ayc off more.

"Why do you have a sword, anyway?" Wylder asks. "What are you going to do with it? Stir some frosting?"

Damn. Not fast enough.

Ayc shrugs. "I'd say I'd shove it up your ass, but it's much too tight for that."

Wylder seizes Ayc's arm and whips him around. He fixes him with a murderous look that four years ago would have made Ayc run away. But Ayc isn't that boy anymore. He stopped being afraid long ago.

"Listen here, you waste of air," he hisses, hushed enough that his voice won't carry past Ayc's ears. "Insult me again, and I promise you—"

"Wylder," Ayc interrupts, in that voice he so rarely uses, the one that comes from a place deep within him. A dark place. His voice growls like a monster. "Take your fucking hand off me."

Wylder yanks his hand back, his eyes widening in shock. Ayc turns and descends the stairs two at a time.

He finds Lora waiting for him at the bottom. She's rocking her weight from her toes to her heels, like she's anxiously doing some form of exercise. She stills as soon as she hears his footsteps.

"Everything good?" she asks.

Ayc is just about to respond when Wylder pounds down the stairs, shoves past them, and slams the inn door on his way out. Ayc nods, then slips around Lora and approaches Vidar at the counter to relay Bronwen's request for fresh water.

"I'll take it to them," Vidar says and heads into the kitchen. Still perched on Vidar's shoulder, the falcon swivels its head to Ayc and lifts one foot in what Ayc swears is an attempt at a vulgar gesture. Its talons, Ayc notes, are painted pink. Then the door swings shut and blocks the bird from view.

From behind Ayc, Lora blurts, "I need your help with something."

Ayc turns around slowly. "*You* need *my* help?"

She nods stiffly, like the motion hurts.

Ayc leans against the counter. "And what do you need help with?"

She pauses again. At the table, Tavish tosses a ball to Saga, and the dog woofs happily as it jumps down from the chair to get it. Xylie squints at a scroll. Peregrin rests their head on the wall beside the open window, their eyes shut, but Ayc knows better than to assume the warrior isn't aware of everything that's happening.

"I'll tell you when we get there," Lora says at last.

"There?" Ayc repeats, looking back to Lora. "Shit, you're really going to murder me, aren't you?"

"Yes," she says, without hesitation.

She is still stone, and Ayc doesn't know if she's joking or not. "Can I at least know *how*?"

"A slow, flesh-eating bacteria implanted in your tooth that slowly spreads to the rest of your body and kills you by consuming you from the inside out."

One side of her mouth tilts upward. It's not a smile, but it's something close to it. Ayc is too mesmerized by that little motion to think of a comeback. So he only says, "Fantastic. Let's go, then."

CHAPTER
THIRTEEN

They don't speak as they walk, which is all right by Ayc, though it doesn't help the lingering doubt that Lora might actually murder him. Still, it gives him time to dig out a semi-squished muffin from his pack, which Lora insisted he grab before they left. He savors every bite as Lora leads him through the orchards in a southeast direction from the Pink Elk. If he's going to die, there's no sense in dying hungry.

She walks briskly a few feet in front of him, her cape snapping behind her. Occasionally, she glances back at him, locking onto the muffin in his hand.

"You know, if you want one, you can just say please," Ayc says.

She looks away swiftly. Says nothing. Then a minute later, "Well, do you have more?"

"Yes."

"Then I would take one."

Ayc ducks carefully under a branch. The trees here have only begun budding leaves, not even close to their destinies of bearing fruit. "We really have to work on your pronunciation. That sounds nothing like please."

She stops and turns toward him, her eyes narrowing into dark slits that makes his blood thrum a warning at the pulse point in his throat. "Please," she growls.

He swings his pack off his shoulder, digs inside, and pulls out the muffin. "Savor it. It's all unleavened breads after that."

She snatches it from his hand and turns back around. He can't see her face, but he can hear her soft 'Mm' of pleasure. Raspberry muffins with white chocolate morsels are a particular favorite of his, and he smiles in satisfaction.

She's still silent when they exit the lines of purposefully planted trees and enter a line of cedar and pines. The late morning sunlight forms lattice work on the forest floor as it passes through the evergreen leaves above. Old pine needles crunch softly beneath their feet, the only sound for several yards until it's joined by the bubbling of running water.

The trees yield to riverbank. A steep, short rocky slope dives into the turquoise water of the Ever River. The sun gleams off the water and fractures into fragments of shimmering light, looking like an ever-spinning sapphire.

Lora pauses where grass turns to rock. He steps beside her. She's finished her muffin, devoured it though he still has some of his own remaining. She shifts her weight once more, from her toes and back to her heels. She *is* nervous.

"Are you going to tell me why we're at the river?" Ayc asks.

She stills but doesn't look at him. She shakes her hands out at her sides, as though trying to be rid of the tension. "I need you to, uh, teach me to swim."

Ayc blinks. "You don't know how to swim."

"No, I do. Well, I did. My father taught me when I was a kid, but—"

She stops. Lora rarely mentions her father. At some point, Ayc began assuming he doesn't exist. That Lora is some kind of miracle conception, or that perhaps, Yris performed some mating ritual like a preying mantis and bit off the head of her lover during the deed. Ayc really doesn't like to think about it. He knows only that Lora's father is from Totus Omni. When Ayc first came to Everadyn, Lora used to leave Wyntra for a few weeks in the summer and always returned in a fouler mood than when she left. He guessed she was visiting her father, but he knew little else.

"But," she says after a long pause, the word sounding almost painful. "I haven't swam in... in eight years."

Ayc's last bite of muffin goes down like a stone. "Oh."

He knows exactly what happened eight years ago. If he closes his eyes, he can see her blue lips.

"So, you're afraid of being in the water?" Ayc asks.

"I'm not afr—" Lora starts, and then she abruptly stops. She glares at the earth at her feet. "Yes."

Some dark part of him is tempted to tease her. She has shown a crack in her impenetrable armor, and he could so easily use it against her. But she's swaying her weight once more, this time from side to side, still unable to look at him. This is what she looks like when she's vulnerable, Ayc realizes. It's disconcerting to see such an invincible force appear... uncertain. He doesn't like it. At all.

So instead, he fills the silence with a question, "Tavish said that you met him because Adamant dropped you in the middle of the ocean on nothing but driftwood, right?"

She winces. "Yes. Adamant likes to find out the recruits' greatest fears and try to break them of it through immersion therapy. Bronwen and I were also dropped down a pit of snakes. Bronwen is terrified of snakes."

"Fuck." Ayc shudders. "I think most people would be, rightfully, terrified about being in a pit of snakes... or being dropped in the middle of the ocean, for that matter."

"It... wasn't pleasant," she admits, her voice tight. "And it did little to actually break our fears. Bronwen still hates snakes, and I still can't fucking bring myself to get in the water. I know it's ridiculous. I can sail on a ship, as long as there's something between me and water, but as soon as I think about swimming in it—" She cuts off and shakes her head, baring her teeth. Her canines grow to points, but this time, Ayc knows her agitation is focused on herself.

"I wouldn't call it ridiculous," Ayc says. "I mean, this river nearly killed you once. I think most people fear things that can kill them."

"That's the point." She touches the chronicler on her wrist. "Face your worst fear."

Ah, so she came to complete a quest.

"But why did you ask for *my* help?" Ayc asks. "Why not ask Bronwen? Or Peregrin?"

She looks at him at last, but her face remains as unreadable as a blank page. She studies him for so long, he's tempted to scrub a hand over his face, concerned crumbs have lingered somewhere.

"Because I didn't want them..." She curls her hands together at her sides, as though resisting the urge to flutter them again. "Seeing me so vulnerable."

Ayc's mind fills in what she didn't say. She doesn't want *them* seeing her vulnerable and thinking less of her. But not *him*. She doesn't put enough value in his opinion to care.

"All right." Ayc drops his pack onto the shore and begins

to undo the ties of his leather armor. "I suggest we get to it then, if we want to make sure we're back in time for Vidar's lunch."

He wrestles out of the leather armor and shirt and reaches for his pants. Lora utters a squawk like a startled bird.

"What are you *doing?*" she demands.

"Obviously, I'm undressing, so I can get into the water."

Her eyes widen so far he's quite concerned they might fall from their sockets. "And your *pants*, too?"

Ayc would not have taken Lora to be so modest. But she looks completely undone at the sight of just his chest. Yris has wrung her up tighter than Ayc thought.

"I'm wearing underpants," he assures her. "Modest ones, thankfully."

She yanks her gaze away from him and fixes it on the river. "Well, what do you normally wear when you swim in the Bellum at Wyntra?"

"Nothing."

Her voice raises an entire octave. "You swim *naked?*"

"For fuck's sake, Lora! You didn't tell me to pack swimming clothes, and I'm assuming you don't have any either. Do you intend on swimming in your armor?"

She tightens her hands into fists, like she's grabbing hold of her control and yanking tight. "Well... no, that would be unpractical. I just didn't think—"

"You can turn around if it makes you more comfortable, but the water isn't going to hide much."

She peeks at him from the corner of her eye, but doesn't turn. Ayc shrugs, undoes his belt, and lets it go. The weight of his sword drags his trousers to his ankles. She spins fully around, putting her back to him. Luckily, he's chosen to wear dark underclothes that hug his hips but stretch almost to mid-thigh. He's seen swimming clothes for males far more revealing than this.

"Your turn," Ayc prompts.

"Get in the water first," Lora commands. "And don't turn around until I come in."

Before Ayc can feel the pull of the order, he wades into the water. He bites back a yelp at the shock of cold. Soft silt parts beneath his toes. It's less deep here than in the Forest of Elodie, and he wades several feet before the water reaches his shoulders. And it feels... good. It makes his teeth instantly chatter, but the chill washes over his muscles like a balm. Sometimes, the pain becomes so much a part of his existence he can almost forget it at times, until it ramps up to a point he can no longer ignore it. Or in times like this, times when he finds relief, and he's reminded what it's like to be without pain, or at least for the pain not to be so strong.

On the shore, he hears the rustle of metal, the soft thump of it hitting the ground. He remains turned toward the opposite bank. He hums, an obnoxious tune he knows she hates. It keeps him from thinking about the fact that Lora is undressing a few feet away.

Finally, there's two splashes behind him as feet enter the water. His head instinctively turns, but a stab of pain between his eyebrows stops him. Another splash, and then a long moment passes with nothing. He hums some more, counts to ten in his head, but still there's nothing.

"Lora?" he calls. "Are you coming in?"

"I-I'm..." Her teeth sound like they're chattering too, but then she must grind them together because the next words are a growl. "I'm trying."

"You're frozen in fear right now, aren't you?"

"No," she snaps. "I simply find myself... unable to go any further."

"I'm turning around now."

"No!"

Ayc throws up his hands. "Come on, Lora. This is ridiculous. Just let me turn around so I can help you."

It takes what feels like a small eternity before she lets out the smallest sigh. "All right."

He turns back to the bank and freezes.

My gods.

She stands, eyes closed, in ankle-deep water, dressed only in her undergarments. The dark fabric of the bustier slips over her shoulders and ends just below her ribcage, baring her soft, wide stomach. The underpants are modest like his own, extending down her thigh, and yet, there is more of her on display than he's ever seen... ever dreamed he would see.

For one moment, all rational thought dumps from his head and into the river. His eyes trace her broad curves: the width of her shoulders, the rise of her chest, the hill of her stomach, the fullness of her hips, the honed muscles of her legs. Every part of her screams of warrior and strength and a feminity that isn't soft like a violet, but fierce like a fire.

The impact on her body strikes like lightning, reminding him too much of when he stood on stage and she called him *mine*. It's strong enough to shock him back into reality. And no. Absolutely *not*. He's not allowed to feel desire for her. He is not a hormonal teenage boy anymore.

Get your shit together, Ayc.

He forces himself to think of anything unpleasant and unattractive—burned cakes, dead frogs, the smell of

Xylie's potions as they brew, Wylder's twisted up face. Still, he's entirely grateful he's standing in cold water and briefly considers dunking his head underneath to banish the heat.

She snaps her eyes open. She lifts a foot, but instead of stepping forward, she slams it back into place. She growls in frustration. "This is so ridiculous. So illogical. I know that I can't drown in this little water, and yet, my body refuses to acknowledge what my head knows. You'd think I was facing a fucking dragon."

Ayc seizes control of himself at last and splashes toward her. "You can't rationalize your way out of everything." He stretches out a hand. "Come on."

She stares at his hand like she's never seen such a thing.

"I promise I don't bite." He grins cheekily and winks. "Unless someone asks me first, of course."

Silver edges her dark pupils. Anger. That emotion is something he's much more used to reading in her face.

She bares her teeth, canines flashing. "You're vile."

But she takes his hand.

He steps backward, and her hand tightens on his— lightly at first, but when he gently guides her forward, she clutches it so hard it hurts. He says nothing; he probably should at least tease her for it. He probably *shouldn't* like the weight of her hand in his. But his head and his body have both betrayed him today.

She focuses hard on his face, not quite meeting his eyes but locked on. Intense. His chest feels too tight, but he forces himself not to look away.

Her body stiffens once more; she halts in place. "Please tell me you also have embarrassing fears."

"Oh, I fear many things. Being buried alive. People who

207

sneeze on me. Those hideous mole rats Wyntra was infested with one winter."

She narrows her eyes but lets him pull her forward another step. "You mock me."

"I would *never*. Also, I don't like eating certain types of fish because I'm quite certain I'll choke on one of their little bones and die. Oh, and *you*. I'm terrified of you."

Perhaps, he shouldn't admit it. Now that he has a little glimpse at her vulnerability, maybe he should hold onto the slight shift in power. But it doesn't feel like much of a sacrifice. She needs it, and so he gives it, almost without meaning to.

I'm such a fucking fool.

Lora snorts. "Now, I know for sure you're tormenting me."

"Villainess, you're the most fearsome creature I know." He tugs her hand. She steps again, almost too focused on him to notice. "And look at that. You've taken three steps."

She glances down at the water, now up above her knees. Her grip tightens on his hand even further, and she jumps a step forward, not to be deeper in the water, but to be closer to him. Her other hand seizes his shoulder like it's a lifeline. Instinctively, his other arm wants to come forward, to wrap around her waist and draw her in, but he halts himself.

"This isn't working." He considers his options and comes up with a horribly bad idea. "Fuck it. Don't stab me for this."

"Wha—" she begins, but the word cuts off into a cry, as in one swift movement, he releases her hand, sweeps her legs out from beneath her and pulls her into his arms. One arm rests behind her back, the other beneath her knees, and before she can manage much more than *"Fuck you!"*, he carries her into deeper water.

"You *fucking* asshole," she snarls. The cold water rises over her body, and she yelps. He tells himself it's only pure survival instinct that sends her arms around his neck. When she buries her face into his neck, he tells himself that, too, is only an instinct.

Ayc doesn't go as deep into the water this time, stopping where he's sure she'll be able to comfortably touch the bottom.

"If you ever tell anyone about this," she hisses, her warm breath teasing the skin of his neck, "I'll murder you. I'll take every curse and damn my own soul, but I swear to fuck, I'll murder you."

He tells himself it's instinct that flares his body with heat; a survival mechanism against the numbing cold of the water. "I won't say a word. Seventeen hungry dragons couldn't torture it from me."

"Good."

She shivers in his arms, teeth chattering. He suspects it's more than just the cold raking through her. He gathers her closer to the warmth of his body. The touch of her skin against his chest turns the embers beneath his skin to an inferno in an explosive burst. He almost drops her in surprise. If he could shut off his emotions right now, that would be fantastic.

"Can I set you down now?" Ayc asks.

She doesn't say anything. She exhales slowly, her breath tingling the skin of his neck, making his pulse do erratic things. The effect on his *entire* body is difficult to ignore, but he closes his eyes and wills himself to think of other things. *Naked mole rats. Dry cake. And Wren.*

He pictures her flowing hair, the feel of her skin against him. *Wren, Wren, Wren.*

At last, Lora nods. He loosens his grip, and she stands. But her hands stay on his shoulders as she studies the lines of his chest. Her stony mask has been fitted back into place, and he can't begin to guess the meaning behind her analysis.

"What's that?" she asks, still staring at his chest.

"What?" Ayc looks down his front, and she brushes her fingers on the hand-sized tooth hanging on a leather cord around his neck.

"A leviathan tooth." Before Ayc left, Irving sealed the fossil in a protective coating and wrapped a strong black cord around the top so Ayc could wear it. "Ember and I found it on Bellum shore. Legend says they were the most fearsome and most glorious creatures on sea or land. Ember wanted me to keep it. For good luck."

"Ember is a sweet child," she says, almost distractedly. Finally, she uncurls her other hand from Ayc's shoulder and retreats a step. Ayc inhales, and it's the first time in minutes he can fully breathe.

"I'm in the river," Lora says.

"That you are."

She inspects her chronicler. None of the gems have lit up. "I'm facing my greatest fear. Shouldn't it be glowing?"

"Maybe you need to actually swim? Or go under the water?" Her eyes widen, and Ayc adds, "I won't let you drown."

"I know." She says it without hesitation. "You're the only one who came into the water that day. I never asked you why you saved me." She looks up a him. "Why didn't you just keep running?"

Ayc's eyes shutter closed, not sure what she will see reflected in his gaze. He has asked himself that question every day for years. Perhaps, if he ran, nothing that came after that day would have happened. But maybe it would have. Yris never intended to let him go. Despite the disappointment he's proven to be, she still doesn't intend to free him. It would be admitting defeat.

"Because you would have died," he says at last. "And I couldn't let you die."

He silently begs that she doesn't ask him why. It's not a question he's ever wanted to answer, not even to himself.

She doesn't ask him. Instead, there's a soft splash. He opens his eyes to see her head under the water. She's beneath for only seconds before she shoots upright. Water beads on top of her hair like morning dew on rose petals and slides down her rich brown skin.

She wipes the water from her eyes, gasping. "I really hated that."

Nothing has changed on the chronicler, so they try a few more things. With Ayc close, she floats on her back and warms up to doing a few overhead strokes. Between every two, she stops to catch her breath and grab a strangle hold on her fear, but she makes it several yards. The gems on the chronicler remain dark.

Finally, she roars "Fuck!" and storms from the water. "Why isn't it working? I don't have time for it not to work."

"Hey, it's all right," Ayc says, as he follows after her. "It's only day one."

On the shore, she plants her hands on her hips. Whatever modesty she felt before seems to have given way to rage, because she doesn't scramble to put on her clothes.

"My mother won her Trials in three days. *Three.*" Her teeth are chattering, and she doesn't seem to notice.

Ayc kneels beside her pack. He undoes the blanket rolled at the top. "But that's a rarity, right? Xylie told me that normally the Trials take weeks to months to complete. Your grandfather's took a year, right?" He stands and unfurls the blanket. He hesitates, then closes the distance and drapes her blanket over her shoulders.

She nods, a grateful gesture, and pulls the blanket tighter around her. "That was prior to airships being invented. Travel across Everadyn is a lot swifter now."

Her voice is calmer now, the chattering of her teeth slowing, but she continues to glare at the rocks beneath her feet. The instinct to comfort her remains, so he offers, "Maybe you're wrong. Maybe the water isn't your worst fear. None of those silly things I listed are my worst fear. Most of the things that truly frighten us are more... insidious than that. People's worst fears are the things they don't dare admit, sometimes even to themselves. Like losing the people they love."

She searches him up and down, and he avoids the intensity of her scrutiny by stooping to grab his own blanket. "Is that your worst fear?"

He wraps the blanket around his own shoulders. Now that he's out of the water, his body is reminding him of how cold he has become. He shivers. "No."

"You don't fear losing the people you love?"

"I already have."

The truth tumbles from his mouth before he can stop it. A stricken look passes over her face, and though she schools her expression quickly, he knows he saw it. And somehow, that look makes the truth continue to pour out.

"Losing the people you love is the worst type of pain, but I've lost before, and as much as I have no desire to face it again—as much as I'd do anything to keep Xylie and Peregrin safe—I know how to survive it."

Her breath hitches, but she swiftly exhales. "What is your worst fear then?"

No, he's been transparent enough for one day. He isn't telling her that.

"It's silly," he says, though it isn't. Not to him.

"Come on. Tell me."

There it is. A direct order. Ayc grits his teeth. Does she know? That he cannot refuse her? Surely, Yris told her.

He tries to resist, but this time the pain comes like a searing brand against his chest. It takes only a few seconds to want to make it stop.

"I'm afraid I'll become a monster," he admits, glaring at his feet. "That everything good in me will disappear, and I'll become a villain."

In the long silence that follows, the river is so loud it sounds like a wail. He drags his toe through the soft earth, not looking up.

"But... that's ridiculous," she says at last.

His teeth lock together. "Thank you very much." He tosses his blanket aside and snatches his pants from the ground, nearly tumbling to the side in his rush to pull them on.

She holds up a hand. "No, that came out wrong. I only mean that could never happen. You don't have it in you to be a monster. You're a cinnamon roll. You're far too kind and sweet and soft."

Ayc isn't quite sure whether or not she means it as a strange compliment, but there's something about the way

213

she's looking at him that suggests it might be. Perhaps, *cinnamon roll*, for once, isn't an insult.

FOURTEEN

"Rise and shine, everyone!" Ayc cheers brightly, sometime in the unholy middle of the night hours. "Are you ready to go to eternal torment?"

The pillow Lora chucks at his head lands with enough force to send him backward into the pallet of blankets on the inn room floor. He considers himself lucky it's not the knife she apparently stores under her pillow as she sleeps.

Wylder and his injured brother remain on the opposite side of the hall, not cleared by the healer to travel, and the rest of Wylder's Five are still in the stable. Their nearness made Lora insist the Five all share a room, and one person be awake to guard during the few hours they were able to sleep.

Sharing a room with them all has taught Ayc a few things: Peregrin snores, Tavish buries his face in Saga's fur, Bronwen mutters what sounds like spells, Xylie wraps her many braids in a scarf, and Lora sleeps with her legs curled all the way to her chest and the blanket pulled up to her nose. He might have called it cute, but he likes his head attached to his body far too much for that.

After Lora and Ayc returned from the river, she sent Peregrin on Tempest to the nearest town with an air dock to determine when the next airship would be headed south, while Lora and Bronwen disappeared into the inn's room for an hour. When Peregrin returned with news that the airship did not leave until early the next day, they decided to remain at the Pink Elk. They plotted, tossed around ideas that might solve the quests, ate Vidar's tolerable lunch and dinner, and then were ordered to bed by Lora. It's why the sun isn't close to rising yet when Ayc ends his own watch by waking all of them as he was directed.

They all dress quickly, shuffling back into their armor and boots, and roll up the bedrolls. Ayc swallows down a tonic when he's sure no one is looking, hoping it will ease the tightness that extends from his lower back all the way to his knees, like a bowstring that will snap if it pulls any tighter.

"We have rations we can eat on the road," Lora says, when they're all ready. She opens the door a slit and studies the hallway outside, before she slides out. "Let's go."

"No more salt masquerading as porridge?" Ayc asks, as he follows the group, tying his loose hair back with a ribbon. "Damn."

Lora ignores him. She pauses briefly at the top of the stairs to glance at the door at the end of the hall, where Wylder is, and then descends the stairs with a force that makes the steps sound like drums. Ayc pretends he doesn't notice.

Despite the late hour, Vidar looms behind the counter, a fluffy dressing robe with lace cuffs pulled over his broad chest. Lora breaks from the group and makes her way over to him. She reaches into a pouch at her side and then presses a handful of coins into his palm. Ayc has to strain to hear the words, she's talking so lowly.

"There should be another shipment coming in a few days."

Vidar grunts. "I'll keep it safe, and when it's ready to move on, I'll make sure it gets to the next location."

"Thank you, Vidar."

"Are you dealing in opium?" Ayc asks, when she makes her way back to where they are now waiting at the door.

"Yes," she says flatly. "It's quite lucrative."

"You're being sarcastic, right?"

Lora shakes her head, pushes past him, and jerks the front door open.

Ayc arches an eyebrow at Bronwen. She grins at him, but there's so much mischief dancing in her eyes he has no idea if it's a confirmation of Lora's sarcasm... or a nefarious confession. Bronwen quickly follows Lora out into the darkness of the night. He'll get no answers from either of them.

Outside, the moon exists as only a sliver. Bronwen holds her hands together. A sphere of light builds between her fingers. She tosses her hand upward, and the light soars to three feet above their heads. It lights up the darkness as they leave the Pink Elk behind and tread northward, further into Bromalis territory.

It's several miles yet to Orchis, the largest city in Bromalis territory, where there's an air dock. After a bit of prowling beside them, Tempest bows and allows Peregrin to climb aboard. Ayc digs through his pack for the unleavened bread wrapped in cloth and serves it with preserves he packed in a small, unbreakable jar.

They walk and eat in silence. Ayc almost starts cracking lame jokes, almost starts performing magic tricks, almost starts doing anything that will take away this nervous energy vibrating within him. *Anything* to forget that they are on their way to catch a ship which will carry them toward an island full of dragons and skeletons and an untold number of other dark things.

Like he said. Eternal torment.

Here the fuck we go.

The airship looks precisely like any ship which traverses the water would, except the hull is twice the size and stuffed full of passenger cabins. It rests in its dock—a casing of wood on all sides—with its three, deep blue sails still furled. At its front, its mast is carved into the shape of a roaring gryphon, claws extended and wings spread wide.

Ayc hands one of the crew his ticket and steps on board. From the deck, he can see two people standing at the helm: the sorcerer and the captain. One keeps the ship afloat with the magic that runs within them and one steers the ship and commands the sailors who are scurrying around the deck to prepare for launching. Other crew members attend to passengers: escorting them to cabins and handling luggage.

One immediately rushes over to them and holds out a hand to Lora. "Can I take your pack, my lady?"

"No, thank you."

"Then might I see you to your cabin?"

Lora nods, and they follow the attendant toward the

door that leads down to the cabins. Xylie presses close to Ayc's back, but when he peeks over his shoulder, she's simultaneously fiddling with the earcuffs and taking in everything that's happening on deck. Saga woofs softly as though excited to be back on a ship. Tavish smiles.

The attendant has just opened the door to the hull, when a voice bellows out. "Loraphne!"

Ayc's nerves spark to attention, and he knows who he'll find before he turns. Wren stands near the entrance ramp, wearing rainbow-hued chainmail, her hair yanked back in a braid. A look of rage fixes itself on her face, as her narrowed eyes lock on Lora, who shoves her way to the front of the Five, putting herself in front of Ayc.

A chain reaction sparks, like when he combines two powders to make a small explosion. Wren draws a curved, slender blade from her side, and just as quickly, Lora's own twin blades are in her hands. The rest of Sterling's Five rush from the ramp, past the astonished ticket attendant, and draw their assortment of weapons. A knife is already in Peregrin's hand, and a pulse of power hovers before Bronwen's lifted hand. Xylie snatches a potion from the bag at her side. Saga growls, and Tavish wraps the hand not holding Saga's leash around his cutlass. Crew members scramble out from between the two groups. The attendant descends the stairs and pulls the door closed behind him.

Bloodshed. That's the only way this will end.

Ayc lunges forward without thinking, putting himself in front of Lora, facing her. He holds his hands up as one of her swords comes within millimeters of his throat. "Easy, easy. Let's, maybe, think this through, before it all ends in mutually assured destruction."

"It won't be *mutual*," Wren snarls. A viciousness vibrates

in her voice, and Ayc stiffens at it. It seems quite unlike the fae whose body he's spent nights learning.

"Get out of my way, Ayc," Lora commands.

When Ayc's feet remain planted, the pain claps like thunder through his head, but he fights through it. His words are tight, but he gets them past his teeth.

"And let everyone die? I don't think so."

"Move, Ayc." This time the command comes from Wren. "We outmatch you and your Five, Loraphne. We'd win this fight."

"Wren," Sterling warns, finally making their way onto the deck, "stop this. All of you, stop this."

"I don't care what skill level you all think you have," Ayc snaps. "This ends with Xylie throwing the potion she's holding and setting the whole damn ship on fire."

"I can assure you," says a new, rugged voice, "that this actually ends with you all being kicked off my ship."

The handsome, male fae who stands to Ayc's right is dressed in a broad captain's hat and bright blue coat that contrasts their brown skin. The ship's sorcerer—a stout male with pale skin and horns peeking through curls above his pointed ears—has joined him as well. Power pulses from him, warning that he's capable of far more than floating a ship.

"I understand you two are in the middle of a rather intense game," the captain continues. "But you both have purchased safe passage on my ship, and it's my duty to ensure your safe arrival. If anyone prevents me from fulfilling my duty, I'll see them thrown off my ship. And I won't bother landing first. Do you understand?"

Lora glares at Wren—who holds her blade so tightly her hand shakes—and then at Sterling—who never drew their blade. Her gaze fixates on Sterling's hand, and Ayc notices what holds her attention. One of the gems on Sterling's chronicler is lit.

"I swear on the divine," Sterling says levelly, "neither myself or any of my Five will attempt to harm you or your party while you are still on this ship."

"Where are you departing?" Lora asks.

"The Audori dock."

A stop before them, then. They can guarantee they part ways without immediate battle when they depart the ship.

Lora nods and sheaths her blade. "Very well. I swear we will not start any battle." She sends a cold, dark glare to Wren. "I *will* finish one, though."

The words must be enough, because Sterling looks at the others. "Put away your weapons."

The Five do as they're told, Wren doing so last of all and with a look of fury. Bronwen drops her hand, Peregrin puts away their dagger, Xylie tucks away the potion and flaps her hands near her face. Ayc steps to Lora's side, and the pain subsides.

"Fantastic!" The captain claps and gives a broad, handsome smile. "We will be launching in five minutes. I suggest you find your cabins before then. No one is allowed on deck except for crew until we're at a safe altitude."

He marches away. Ayc draws in a steadying breath and offers Wren a smile. She does not return it. Instead, she gives him a look that, briefly, looks a little like hate.

Tavish, Ayc, and Peregrin make their way back onto the deck as soon as there's a knock on the door from an attendant, letting them know they are free to exit their cabins. They leave behind a napping Bronwen, Xylie studying another scroll, and Lora knitting. Her needles clink together dangerously fast considering she's also reading what—based on the carved, untitled black cover—looks like a classical novel, the second of the books she always carries with her.

As they ascend the steps from below, Ayc inhales. The air smells damp and crisp, like after a fresh rain, as they float through misty clouds. The captain and sorcerer still stand at the wheel, while crew follow the captain's barked commands. They pull on ropes to furl and unfurl sails as directed.

Ayc approaches the side of the ship and leans onto the railing. More clouds snake below. Past them, rolling fields form patchwork quilts, and colorful villages appear like scattered gemstones. With an eagle's cry, Tempest breaks from one cloud, curls her legs beneath her and completely twirls in the air, before gliding and disappearing into the next cloud.

"Show off," Peregrin mutters.

Ayc smiles. He loves it—the smell, the wind in his hair, the skitter of his heart. This is his second time flying in two days, and the exhilaration radiates through him. "If I was lucky enough to be a gryphon rider, I don't know that'd I'd ever step foot on the ground again."

"There's nothing quite like flying," Peregrin agrees.

"I don't know," Tavish says, patting Saga's head. Beside him, Saga's paws rest on the railing, his tongue lolling out, the breeze shuffling his fur. He looks the kind of happy only a dog can be. Tavish, however, doesn't hold the leash, avoiding the sight below. "I think I much prefer the ocean. At least if you fall overboard, it's a much gentler landing."

"The ocean and five dozen sea monsters," Ayc says. He grabs the leviathan tooth around his neck and gives a playful growl.

Peregrin smacks him in the gut lightly with their cane.

Tavish laughs. "I'll take the creatures in the sea over gravity. The creatures never frightened me much, anyway. If a shark or kraken attack you, they're just hungry and doing as nature intends. If a person attacks you, who knows their motivation? That's the only kind of monsters I fear."

He has said it in a tone far more lighthearted than the seriousness of the statement demands. Peregrin grunts, but Ayc can only blink at him, unsure what to say. Even Saga cocks his head, like he's silently asking, *"You all right, friend?"* That almost makes Ayc laugh.

At the silence, Tavish's eyes fling wide. "Oh divine, that was really dark, wasn't it?"

"A little, yes." Ayc laughs.

From behind him, he hears his name, and the hair on his arms rise as he turns his head to find Wren a few feet away. Over the wind and the sailors shouts, he never heard her approach.

"Can we talk?" Wren asks, her voice softer than before. "In private?"

Before all this, Ayc would have made bold assumptions about what her invitation means. But the cold way she looked at him earlier gives him pause. He searches her face, but it's guarded, like she wants to give nothing away.

Still, he says, "Of course."

"Be careful with that one, boy," Peregrin says before Ayc can take a step.

Wren folds her arms over her chest. "And what does that mean, Peregrin? I thought we were friends."

"*Allies* is perhaps a better word." Peregrin's gaze locks with Wren's like two blades clashing. "Which means I understand too well how hard you fight for your goals. But currently, we are fighting for distinctly different causes, are we not?"

She narrows her eyes. "I suppose we are."

"Am I missing something?" Ayc asks, looking between the two.

They break the battle of eye contact.

"It's nothing," Wren says, offering Ayc a sweet smile he doesn't believe. He feels as though he's missing—how had Bronwen put it—a whole novel? Ayc glances at Tavish, but his back is to them, scratching Saga's ears like he's trying to pretend this isn't happening.

"Be careful," Peregrin repeats to Ayc, firmly.

When Wren heads toward the stairs that lead to the hull of the ship, Ayc follows her. Even in the armor, she moves gracefully, her hips swaying enticingly. He forces his attention to the back of her head and reminds himself he doesn't know the reason she sought him out. She leads him past the cabins on the first level and stops at a door right before another set of stairs descends deeper into the hull.

"I don't have a private room, but this will do." She pulls open the door to reveal a room crammed with crates, mops, and buckets. "After you."

He steps into the cramped space and finds the one spot where he can stand without tripping over something. He glances back to find Wren paused in the hallway, silhouetted in light. She closes a pouch hanging on her belt, steps inside, and shuts the door.

His body tightens at her nearness, every part of him aching to close those last inches, but he refrains. Though it's dark, he can make out every line of her face, but her expression still offers no hint to where they stand, here, now, in the middle of this game. Then her hands launch into his hair, and her mouth presses to his. Her tongue pleads for admittance against his lips—urgent, desperate. He opens for her, tangles his tongue with hers. She tastes... different. A heady sweetness of honey mixed with the sharp tinge of something more savory, like dill. The overwhelming taste fades after a moment and leaves behind only sweetness and warmth. His greedy hands seize her hips and pull her forward, flesh against him. She sighs with reluctance when she pulls back.

"That's a welcome surprise," Ayc says with a huff—something between a laugh and a sigh.

Her smile is brilliant in the darkness. "Why is it surprising that I'd kiss you?"

"Earlier you looked like you might want to kill me."

"Oh, that." She flicks a wrist in the air. "It's a game, Ayc. Try not to take it too personally."

Ayc frowns. That sounds much too similar to what Wylder told Lora. But then Wren presses a kiss to his jaw, and he forgets that unpleasant thought.

"I will admit." Her voice is nearly a purr. "I am quite frustrated with you."

"Why?"

"I think you warned Loraphne about the plot against her yesterday morning. Didn't you?"

"Yes." The answer comes without hesitation. He can't think of a reason to lie, but it comes too quickly. Something within him still warns him to be careful.

"Why?" she asks, nuzzling her nose against his neck, her hands sweeping down his chest. "I didn't think you wanted her to win."

"I don't."

"Then why not just say nothing and let the plan play out?"

Again, the words slip out without consideration. "I couldn't let her die."

Her lips pause against the collar of his leather armor. "Why not?"

"Because that's not who I am. I told you, I don't mean to kill anyone, and if I hadn't told Lora, it would have been as good as if I killed her myself."

She leans back and cocks her head. "Is that the truth?"

Part of it. Ayc grinds his teeth against the words and manages to nod.

She shrugs and then tugs at the ties of his armor, loosening them from his body, even as she returns her lips to his jaw. "Where are you headed?"

The desire to tell her is overwhelming, but he would be betraying Lora... and by extension, Peregrin and Xylie, too. "I shouldn't tell you that."

"True. At least tell me what quest you're working on?"

He wishes to stop talking, strip her from her armor, and ease the ache building within him with the warmth of her body. More importantly, he desires to stop the nagging voice that sounds far too much like Lora, warning him that Wren shouldn't be asking so many questions. Lora has no business being in his head right now.

"Maybe we should talk about something else," Ayc suggests.

"Or perhaps we shouldn't talk at all." Her hands slip

beneath his armor and slide up the bare skin of his chest. Her eyes soften as she studies his face. She stands on her toes and kisses him—not with lust, but with a tenderness that makes hope shimmer within him. He's not sure what he's hoping for. A chance, maybe. An opportunity to be something *more* to someone. A chance to be seen as something worthy.

"You have taken up far too many of my thoughts these last two days," she admits, as she pulls back.

"Have I?" he asks with a cheeky grin. "How problematic for you. You have other things to be thinking about. Like crushing your many enemies."

"Indeed."

Her hands fall to his belt, and at the tug of leather and clink of metal, his cock springs to life. She shoves his pants and underclothes down. His sword thuds upon the ground, a sound that gets lost in his groan as she takes him in her hand. He lets his forehead fall forward onto hers.

"Should I show you what I've been thinking about?" Wren asks.

"Please do."

She pushes him. He trips over his trousers and lands on the crate behind him. She falls to her knees and wraps her mouth around him. He tangles her braid around his fist, desperate to hold her there. Everything else fades away until he can think of nothing but her tongue and her hands and her glowing silver eyes and the sweet, little noises she makes as he thrusts his hips to fuck her mouth. Her noises grow louder when she slips out of her armor and climbs on top of him and chases her own pleasure with a violent abandon. He clamps his hand over her lips so the cries don't echo through the entire floor of cabins.

They are both still breathless when they reluctantly disentangle and reach for the few clothes they scrambled out of. They haven't been gone long enough for Ayc's liking, but they've certainly been gone long enough to be missed by their separate parties.

She smiles at him sadly as she adjusts her chainmail over her trousers. "Promise you'll be safe, Ayc, wherever you're going."

Ayc laughs and shrugs off the concern, though it's nice that she's worried about him. "I promise." He hops on one leg as he pulls on his trousers. "I'll do my best not to get eaten by a dragon."

Wren freezes, stooped halfway to the ground where she reaches for her belt and sword. Ayc realizes his mistake immediately. She's much too smart not to understand the hint.

"Dragon?" She snatches her belongings from the ground and jerks upright. "Are you going to Somnia Ignis?"

No, is what he means to say, but what comes out is "Yes." He snaps his teeth together with enough force the click rattles through his head. What is wrong with him? Is he so high off sex that he's lost all common sense?

Her braid, messy from his hand, whips behind her as she shakes her head. "Does Loraphne have a death wish?"

Ayc sighs, not looking at her as he does up his belt. It's too late to take back the confession now. "Maybe she does."

She stares hard at the floor, replacing her belt with shaky hands.

"It's going to be fine, Wren," he says gently.

"It won't," she snaps. "You'll die there."

It stings, that she thinks him so weak, but he brushes it aside. "I'll be fine." He searches the floor for the ribbon that fell from his hair. When he finds it, he slips the circle onto his wrist. "Maybe, the dragons will befriend me. They're pretty cute, if you think about it."

"This isn't funny, Ayc! Instances of dragons befriending a person are rare, and I've never heard it happening with someone who isn't a Drakr fae. What are you even going to do on that island? What quest could you possibly need to complete?"

Again, his tongue rebels against his desires. "Unearth a great treasure."

Shit. What the fuck is wrong with me?

"Oh." She shrugs. "We already solved that one."

"How?" Ayc asks. It's only fair. Information for information, and to his relief, she grants it.

"There's a plant called golden root that grows only once a decade. Once harvested, it can be made into a potion that can cure almost any ailment. Luckily, one of the Five's father discovered it recently and was waiting for it to bloom. Which it did. Last night. We harvested it. But in case any other victor wants to go get more, I wouldn't bother. We harvested all we could, then I burned the rest."

Ayc jerks back, her words landing like a shock of cold water. "You...what?"

She smiles proudly. "I made sure no one else could get their hands on it. Don't tell, Sterling. They don't know."

Ayc presses his mouth shut when he realizes it has dropped open. Golden root is more powerful than any other plant, capable of healing nearly any ailment. Terminal diseases. Crippling pain. Life-altering injuries. It can even bring people back from the brink of death. And as Wren said, it only blooms every decade and yields so little a lottery is held to determine the few dozen people who will get the powerful healing potion. A priceless treasure, indeed. And now it's gone.

"You destroyed a priceless plant that could save lives because you didn't want anyone else to have it?" Ayc repeats, his jaw taut, hoping she'll deny it.

She frowns but nods.

"That just seems..." He stops and tries to disentangle the various emotions that are knotting together. Anger that she did it, confusion that she's capable of such a thing and, mostly, the feeling of his heart slowly sinking into his gut.

"It seems *what*, Ayc?" she demands with the viciousness he heard earlier edging her voice.

Heartless.

He means to swallow down that word, to pick something more gentle, but it seems he's only capable of the truth today. "Cruel, Wren. It seems unbelievably cruel."

Truth is a sword, and he expects Wren to run from the cutting blade, but she only scoffs. "Cruel? You have no idea how incredibly long a hundred years is. What if Loraphne wins? What if Marcellus wins? Can you imagine the cruelty they will wrought on Everadyn?"

Ayc can imagine it. If Marcellus won, Everadyn would become like Lux Aester, forced to conform to their narrow ideas of gender and love and what it means to obey the divine. He'll rule over them with an iron fist and a lack of mercy that will make the monster that Yris is seem like a puppy dog. Everadyn and its people will either be destroyed or they'll rebel and go to war against a tyrant. Either way, the things he has come to love about the Everadyn people—their diversity, their love of life—will be over.

If Lora won... well, that, for some reason, Ayc can't draw a clear picture of.

Maybe, Ayc simply doesn't know Lora as well as he thought. It's become clear in the last few minutes that, no matter what he and Wren have whispered to each other in the night, he doesn't know her well, either.

"Sterling has to win," Wren adds, taking a step closer. "Surely, you can see they are the best option."

"Marcellus can't win," Ayc says in way of agreement.

"And I'll do anything to stop that from happening. If a small act of cruelty prevents years of torment for the Everadyn people, I'll do it. And you can hate me if you—"

"I don't hate you," Ayc says. But he doesn't know what he feels. The hope he had when he walked into this closet has dimmed, turning to one tiny candle that flickers in the wind. He tries to understand her rationale, and perhaps he does a little. But the knowledge of the lives it'll cost is something he can't reconcile. And he wonders if, put in Wren's shoes, Lora would have burned the plant.

Wren's sigh teases a few strands of hair that have fallen before her face. "That's a relief." She steps forward, so only centimeters separate them once more. Her voice is soft as rosebuds, as her pink-hued lips. "Then will you do something for me?"

She reaches up and brushes her fingertips across his jawline, across the scars that other fingertips have left on his skin. He doesn't know whether he longs to lean in, or if he desperately needs to flinch away. So, he stands utterly still.

"What?"

"Don't go to Somnia Ignis."

"I don't exactly have a choice."

"But you do." She reaches into the pouch at her side and removes a smaller leather pouch. "Sprinkle a little of this herb into Loraphne's water before you set off for the island."

She holds the pouch out to him, but he only stares at it. Warning clangs in his head like a bell tolling out the eleventh hour. "Will it kill her?"

"It will *weaken* her. It will buy Sterling time, or at the very least, it'll keep you from ever stepping foot on the Isle of Nightmares." She takes an urgent step forward. "If you won't do it for yourself, do it for Everadyn. Or, at the very least, do it for *me*. I don't like the idea of something happening to you. Please, Ayc."

His head feels like he's gone to war. He doesn't want to touch the pouch, but the concern in her voice reminds him that she actually cares about him. Which is something he can say for only a few people. He stretches out his hand. She presses the leather into his palm and folds his fingers around it. She lays a kiss upon his knuckles. "Thank you."

Ayc nods, not trusting his voice. It's betrayed him too much already.

"I'll leave first," she says. "I'd rather not give the rest of the Five any reason to doubt my loyalties to my own sibling." She grants him a goodbye kiss so quickly that he's spared the decision of whether or not to kiss her in return. Then she's gone.

When the door closes, he stares at the pouch like it's the last shred of hope. Hope that the kindness within Wren, the will to do what is best for her people, outweighs the ruthlessness she warned him of. He takes a breath, opens the pouch and stares hard at the contents. The deep purple flowers within grow on leaves so dark green they are nearly black. He recognizes it immediately. Evander, master of the apothecary, was a fantastic teacher. He seemed to understand the chaos in Ayc's head, and instead of books, he would spend hours showing Ayc different dried specimens.

This particular plant Evander kept behind glass, because he'd never use it.

But Wren doesn't know about Ayc's past. Doesn't know he understands exactly what this plant can do.

"Fuck!" he snarls at last, as the last flicker of hope snuffs out within him.

There's music pounding from Ayc's cabin when he approaches it. Every note of the rapid beat slams squarely between his eyes. A headache has been building since he left the closet, still clutching Wren's pouch in his fist. The song is one he recognizes, one of his and Xylie's favorites from the recorders he left in his room back at Wyntra. His hand is on the doorknob when he hears the singing. A feminine voice, loud and off-tune, joins the band's gravelly ballad.

And it almost sounds like...

No, it can't be.

He creaks the door open, slowly, carefully, as to not make a sound and peeks through the slit in the door. Xylie stands closest to the door, rocking back and forth on her heels in time to the music. Bronwen twirls around the bedpost of the large poster bed, moving as though the music is part of her, her mouth fixed into a laugh.

And Lora is on the bed, barefoot, her armor traded for her soft, gray sweater. She jumps around, swirls her hips, and belts the lyrics of the song into the sheathed dagger she holds in one hand like it's an amplifier. For a long moment, Ayc's brain can't make sense of what he's seeing. And then it clicks.

Lora—his cool, vicious villainess—is *dancing*.

He clamps a hand over his mouth to hold in the delighted laugh that would give him away. If he does, she'll see him. She'll cease her dancing, and he'll be forced to stop looking at her. And he *cannot* stop. His eyes drink her in, wanting only more. She's an objectively *horrible* dancer, every movement at odds with the rhythm of the song, but there's a carefree, unguarded expression on her face that Ayc has never seen. The coils of her dark hair spring around her head, her brown skin shimmering in the candlelight.

Beautiful.

Divine, she is so fucking beautiful.

She always is, even when she looks terrifying and carved of impenetrable stone. But she's more beautiful now, when she looks soft and, for lack of a better word, *alive.*

Somewhere within him, he knows he's missing a wonderful opportunity to mock her, but he can't bring himself to embarrass her. He suspects moments like these are rare, that she trusts few people to see her unguarded, to see who she might be behind her stone. He has caught a glimpse, and he feels... grateful.

And so, he backs up and shuts the door as quietly as he came.

Ayc watches the earth move past thousands of feet below, turning the pouch Wren gave him around in his hands. Wren and Sterling and their party have since left, during a brief landing in Audori territory. Ayc was below deck then, in a common room made for ship passengers. He didn't even attempt to say goodbye.

Midnight. That's the common name of the plant in the

pouch Wren gave him. Evander told him it has exactly one purpose.

To kill.

With a single dose, the person would die a most violent and painful death. Yet, Wren looked Ayc in the eye and told him it would only *weaken* Lora. And Ayc doesn't know which bothers him more. That Wren is so willing to manipulate him to win her game or that she thinks him unintelligent enough to fall for it.

What if Loraphne wins? Wren's question rings in his head. Ayc sighs. It doesn't matter. It never crossed his mind that he'd actually poison Lora. He refuses. He won't be made to be a monster, no matter what the reason or cause.

"Do I want to know why you're pouting?" Peregrin asks as they position themselves beside Ayc, searching the sky— presumably in search of their gryphon. Ayc hasn't seen Tempest in a bit, but he trusts the gryphon will meet them where they land.

"I'm not pouting," Ayc says.

Peregrin grunts as though to say, *Who are you kidding, boy?*

Ayc studies Peregrin, gathering up his courage. "Why did you agree to be one of Lora's Five? You could have said no."

Peregrin arcs an eyebrow at him. "Why are you asking me now? You haven't bothered all week."

Had it really only been a week since Lora assembled her Five? It feels like so much longer and like no time at all since Ayc was dancing in his kitchen, drunk off fae wine.

Ayc shrugs. "I'm curious. You've never liked Yris or the way she rules. You hide it well, but I see it. Why support her daughter?"

"Lora is not Yris. Do you think I'd leave behind my family to help Lora if I didn't believe her worthy of being Sovereign?"

Peregrin is a deeply private person. Ayc is certain that, though they know him better than anyone, there's much Ayc doesn't know about them. But he's had the rare privilege of seeing who Peregrin is aside from a hardened warrior and wise instructor. He's seen how Peregrin picks flowers from the courtyard gardens every week to make a bouquet to present to Zinnia. Ayc has watched as Peregrin and Irving clean up after dinner, debating fiercely about whether the now-extinct wyverns only had two legs or if the excavations of their fossils were sloppy. They always end up in laughter. He's seen Peregrin teach Ember chess and not swordplay, because they hope he'll be a thinker instead of a fighter.

But mostly, Ayc knows, deep in his bones, that Peregrin is *good*, the kind of good Ayc hopes to be. Peregrin would never agree to help Lora if they didn't believe she was the best option for Everadyn.

"No. I don't," Ayc replies. "I just don't understand why."

Peregrin searches around them, but most of the passengers have remained under the deck and the crew are fast at work, cleaning and wielding ropes according to the captain's calls. Still, Peregrin lowers their voice. "It's the easiest thing in the world to become the people who raise us, if you aren't willing to fight against it. Yris certainly tried to forge Lora in her own image, and can Lora be vicious? Yes. Can she be unkind? Certainly. But I also see much of her father in her, and he was... good. Just. The very best."

"Was?" Ayc repeats.

Peregrin gives the smallest of flinches. Ayc might have

missed it, if he didn't know Peregrin so well. "I'm not going to tell you her story, boy. If you want to know, ask her yourself."

And have her snarl in his face to mind his own business? *No, thank you.*

Ayc looks away from Peregrin and down into the fields below. The same wind that billows out the sails, mixed with a static tint of magic, brushes the loose hair around his face.

"I don't blame you for mistrusting her or her motivations," Peregrin says. "I know Lora was never kind to you growing up. Yris pitted you two against each other for some kind of sport. It was a cruel game. But have you ever asked yourself what would have happened if Lora refused to play it?"

"To Lora?"

Peregrin nods. "And to you."

Ayc turns it over in his head. Yris would have let her daughter drown before risking Lora looking weak. What would she have done if Lora showed him kindness, something Yris thought of as the greatest of weaknesses?

Ayc doesn't know, but Yris has only ever been capable of cruelty. He knows Peregrin has taken to sheltering more than Ayc in their safe, cozy home. Perhaps not as often as Ayc, but many children have found their way there for a warm meal and the deeper warmth of being surrounded by genuinely good people who love one another. Maybe, Peregrin knows Lora so well, because she was one of those children who, just like Ayc, needed to escape Yris's long shadow, if only for a few hours.

Peregrin lets the silence linger, like they know Ayc needs the time to think, then they ask, "Do you remember when Yris left you in the pasture with the gryphon fledglings?"

"Yes."

"Who do you think told me you were there?"

Ayc squints at them. He has always assumed Tempest told Peregrin through their mental bond, but if that were the case, Peregrin wouldn't be dredging it up after all these years. "Surely, you're not trying to tell me *Lora* sent you to my rescue," Ayc says, unable to stop the laugh that follows. The idea sounds absurd, but Peregrin only inclines their head.

"If she hadn't told me, I wouldn't have known you were there."

The disbelief builds in Ayc's throat, and he swallows it down hard. "But why?"

Peregrin lifts the hand that holds their cane in a shrug and supplies no answer, only says, "We don't always have the luxury of choice. I know you reckon that better than most. I think we should judge people by the choices they made when they were able, and I like Lora's choices."

The knowledge that Lora saved him rattles Ayc, like stone catapulted against the wall he uses to protect himself. It's much safer to believe Lora a villain like her mother.

"Mostly," Peregrin adds. "I don't believe Lora truly *wants* to be Sovereign. I think she believes it is her destiny or, perhaps, her penance. And that's the type of person I want to have power: the one who never wanted it to begin with. They're the only ones who can wield it with any sort of grace." Peregrin reaches up and clasps Ayc's shoulder. "I know you don't trust her. After everything, you have every right not to. But trust *me*. Trust *Xylie*. We see her for who she is. Maybe, one day, she'll let you see her, too."

The words linger long after Peregrin descends back into the hull of the ship, leaving Ayc alone with the hum of the wind and the calls of the captain. His eyes close, and he finds Lora there.

For the first time, when he thinks of Lora, he doesn't force himself to think only of her ferocity and cruelty. Instead, he thinks about the tears in her eyes when her mother ordered her to kill a boy she didn't know; her standing on a river's edge and telling him to run; her hands around his neck as she clung to him in the same river eight years later, her breath soft on his neck; her bare feet on the bed as she danced far away from where her mother might judge her.

Maybe, he's already begun to see her. He's just not sure he wants to.

When Ayc opens his eyes again, he dumps the plant Wren gave him over the side of the ship. The leaves and flowers flutter down through the clouds like snow.

FIFTEEN

The first glimpse of Somnia Ignis is as terrible as Ayc imagined. A layer of fog covers the mountains so thickly that only the shadows of the craggy peaks are visible, even from where Ayc stands aboard the fisherman's ship that is anchored half a mile away. The white mist crawls from the island and reaches across the top of the brackish water, like clawing fingertips. Eerie silence hangs over the island, over the ship itself, and then it shatters. A distant roar rips through the air, so loud Ayc's bones tremble.

"Hey, Lora," Ayc says, his voice thin, almost a whisper. "What do you call six people who dare to venture onto an island full of dragons?"

Beside him, she crosses her arms and says nothing.

"Lunch," Ayc answers, leaning closer to her so Tavish, who stands on his other side, can't hear. "Served extra crispy."

Lora heaves out a breath. "Your leather armor is fire resistant."

"My face is *not*."

She finally looks at him and fixes him with a glare so fierce that a less foolish person might have stumbled away to safety. Ayc bites his bottom lip to keep from smiling.

"Maybe it'll be an improvement," she says.

"That's ridiculous, Lora. You cannot improve upon perfection."

She rolls her amber brown eyes. "You're welcome to stay on this ship if you're so scared. Otherwise, get your ass in the rowboat."

She doesn't wait for his response. Ignoring the rope ladder hanging from the ship's railing, she vaults over the side and lands lightly on the boat below, where Bronwen, Peregrin, and Xylie already await. In exchange for a very substantial bribe, the captain of the fishing vessel agreed to take Lora to the island, but refused to pilot his ship any closer than necessary. The Noxumbra are hearty people, used to the dragons who fly into their fields to snatch up the occasional cow or flock of sheep. But sailing into the dragon's nesting ground is an entirely different matter.

Fear clings like spiderweb to every nerve in Ayc's body, but he won't stay on this ship. The fear of watching them all sail off without him would be even greater.

Ayc assists Tavish to lower Saga to the boat below, using a cradle of ropes wrapped around the dog's belly. Saga whines at first but settles with a few soft words from Tavish, who then descends the rope ladder with an ease Ayc certainly won't manage.

From behind him, Ayc hears one fisherman cackle to another, "How much you want to bet they don't come back alive?"

"I give the two Adamant warriors a fifty percent chance. None of the others will come back, for sure."

"I certainly won't bet against you."

Ayc flips them off over his shoulder and swings over the railing, clumsily climbing down the ladder.

Another roar shakes his bone.

I just want to bake pretty cakes. Is that too much to ask? He laments internally but says nothing as he sits down in the boat and grabs an oar.

Ayc helps Lora heave the rowboat onto the shore, the loose shale that litters the water's edge cracking beneath his boots. He narrowly avoids stepping on a pile of bones half-buried in the rock, some remnants of an unfortunate animal. In the thick fog, he can barely see the others; they have become mere silhouettes as they make their way up from the water's edge. Tempest is not among them. She looked furious, her silver eyes narrowed at Peregrin, when they explained she could not come to the island before they climbed aboard the fisherman ship. Gryphon and dragons are natural enemies, and her presence would be a beacon that would make the journey even more treacherous. Tempest flew off in an angry huff, but not before leaving Peregrin with two feathers. One that Peregrin slipped into their own tea, and one Peregrin put into Ayc's.

"Everyone, come close to me," Bronwen beckons.

Ayc follows the sound of her voice until he finds her in the haze. When everyone has approached, she mumbles a few words beneath her breath, her hands entwined together. She spreads her palms, and light spreads from them. Ayc's skin vibrates as it passes through him. A perimeter forms around all six of them—transparent except for a few thin, blue lines that ebb and flow around it.

"Stay within the shield," Bronwen says. "It will protect us from outside forces and should hide our scents."

"You won't be able to hold it forever," Lora states. "We should move as quickly as we can. Tavish, which way?"

Tavish turns a full circle slowly, stops, and then reverses the opposite direction so not to be tangled in Saga's leash. Saga doesn't move, so whatever Tavish is sensing, it's not with his eyes. He pauses, facing the north, deeper into the island.

He points. "That way."

Lora doesn't hesitate, only squares her shoulders and heads in that direction.

The way Tavish instructs them to go is steep and covered in rocks that slip beneath Ayc's feet. Lora and Bronwen, who are in the lead, make it look like a leisurely hike. Lora offers her elbow to assist Xylie in scrambling up the slickest of the shale. Tavish holds onto the guide handle of Saga's harness to heave him up the slope, his cane sweeping on the ground before him, scattering rock. And Ayc pretends not to notice when Peregrin catches his forearm to steady themself. Sweat streaks down Ayc's back, his muscles twisting with every step. He grits his teeth and focuses on putting one foot in front of the other.

The rocky edge they traverse grows thinner as it leads up the side of one mountain. A steep slide veers down to the left, barely visible in the fog. One misstep would be all it would take for a nasty tumble. Rock juts out from their other side, rising into a sharp wall of stone.

Bronwen halts suddenly, causing everyone behind her to

pause as well. She searches around her. "Did someone say my name?"

"No," Ayc says, frowning, and it's echoed by a few others. In fact, Ayc heard nothing until she spoke. Nothing but the distant roars and the whistle of wind between the mountains and otherwise the eerie quiet which clings over the gray world.

Xylie's hands move. Lora translates for her. "She heard something. But to her, it sounds like someone screaming."

A shiver traces ever-so-lightly down Ayc's spine.

"We can't trust anything on this island," Peregrin says sharply from behind Ayc, the last in their line.

"They're right," Bronwen agrees. "This place is full of old, dark magic. Don't trust what you hear or—"

She stops, and this Ayc hears. The sound of the sky being disrupted, a sound he's heard when Tempest takes into flight, but louder, harsher. Distant at first but growing louder with each rhythmic pulse.

"Dragon!" Lora hisses. "Get down!"

Ayc flings himself beneath the overhanging rock that juts above their heads, yanking Tavish with him. Lora pushes Xylie behind her into a nearby crevice, and Bronwen and Peregrin flatten themselves against the side of the mountain. Saga growls low and pins his ears back. Tavish stoops and hugs his arms around the dog, hushing him softly.

The wings thunder louder, drawing closer. Ayc makes out an outline of mighty wings, a horned head, and a spiked tail as it passes overhead, so massive it momentarily blocks out the sun and plummets them into darkness.

The dragon tucks its wings and begins its descent—far,

far too close. Ayc's heart pounds against his ribs. The heat from the dragon's body dissipates the surrounding fog, creating rings as it darts toward the earth. The dragon's scales are a green so dark it's almost black, and its wings are darker still. Two horns curve back from its head, and spikes ripple down its spine until it forms a five-pointed club at the end of its tail. It looks utterly lethal, and yet, every movement the dragon makes is graceful, and when the little light that cuts through the fog brushes the wings, they shimmer iridescently.

Dangerous things shouldn't be so beautiful.

With one last flutter of those wings, it lands on the next mountain, only two hundred yards away. The cliff shudders, rocks sliding down the mountainside. The dragon shakes itself off, like a cat, and then prowls forward through the dark mouth of a massive cave. The fog slowly drifts to seal the hole the dragon created, concealing the cave and the mountain from sight once more.

Only then does Ayc let out a breath.

"Holy shit buckets," Tavish whispers hoarsely, pressing his hands into his knees as he crouches beside Saga. "I about pissed myself."

A small laugh escapes Ayc's lips. "That makes two of us, friend."

Bronwen and Peregrin straighten. Lora steps out from the crevice, Xylie following close behind.

Xylie catches Ayc's eye, grins at him, and signs rapidly. *"Did you see it? It was magnificent!"* She flaps her hands not in words, but how she does when she is very, very happy.

Ayc can't help but smile. Tavish, too, smiles as Saga fixes his attention on Xylie's little happy motions, Tavish's hand wrapped around the leash. "It was pretty amazing," he says, though he's only guessing at what she says.

The corner of Lora's mouth rises but falls just as quickly. Ayc stares at her lips, at that ghost of a smile, for a heartbeat too long. He forces himself to look away.

"That cave, uh—" Tavish begins, his smile tumbling as he pushes himself to a standing position. He clutches Saga's leash and stares across the space between the two mountains. He pulls at the leather armor around his neck, like it's suddenly too tight.

"What about the cave?" Lora demands.

"That cave is where we need to go. That's where the treasure is. I can feel it."

Ayc winces. *Fuck.*

Bronwen sighs. "I was afraid you were going to say that."

They find a path that connects between the two mountains, and far sooner than Ayc would like, they stand before the cave entrance. The massive, yawning mouth allows Ayc to fully grasp how large the dragon is. It had filled the entire entrance, and the five of them standing in a line can't even match its width.

The darkness within feels... Ayc can't quite find the word. But as he stares into it, it feels as though it stares back. It's unnaturally dark, turning to complete blackness far sooner than the light outside should allow. Every nerve in Ayc's body rattles. Every instinct tells him, *Do not go in there.*

But he will.

Perhaps they all feel the same as him, because they have not approached the entrance, keeping instead to the cliff's edge.

"What's the plan?" Bronwen asks, looking at Lora. She's a little breathless. They all are from the strenuous hike and change in altitude, but sweat beads along her hairline. She's exerting herself to maintain the shield. "We need to have a plan before we go in there."

Lora's hands clench and unclench at her sides as she stares into the darkness. She turns to Ayc. Her eyes are black as midnight, as inky dark as the cave itself. "Ayc, can you go invisible?"

Xylie's head snaps around to him. *"Yes, Ayc,"* her hands say, capturing her sassy tone with their sharp movements, *"can you go invisible?"*

If they'd been anywhere else, he would have flipped her off, but Lora is watching him intently.

"Yes," he says. "But it won't do much good. Just because the dragon can't see me doesn't mean the dragon can't *smell* me."

"They do have a remarkable sense of smell," Xylie agrees.

Lora looks back to Bronwen. "Will your shield repel fire?"

Bronwen hesitates. "Yes, but it'll take more effort, and I might only be able to do it for a few minutes."

"A few minutes is all we need for Peregrin or I to get a knife into the dragon's heart. Or Xylie to shoot an arrow."

Xylie's face contorts in horror, but she swallows and nods.

Peregrin says, "Aim low on its chest, between the scales. It's where it is weakest."

Lora turns back to the darkness of the cave, squaring up

247

on it like facing an army. "That's the plan then. We stick together, and if the dragon finds us, we kill it."

Bronwen shoves sweat-damp hair out of her face and gulps a breath. "Why do I get the sense that a dragon is the least frightening thing we might find in there?"

"Whatever we face, we face together," Lora promises, pressing a hand over her heart the way Ayc has seen Bronwen do in the past.

"Lora," Peregrin hisses, their voice low but urgent. They have turned their back to the group, staring off the cliff's edge.

Lora marches to Peregrin's side, and Ayc follows, curious to see what Peregrin has noticed. In between thin tendrils of fog, the ground far below is visible. On the path they all have just traversed, people are climbing. It's too far down to make out much, but Ayc can tell there are six people. And they're all dressed in the sky blue of Lux Aester.

"Marcellus." Lora says the name like it's a curse. "Do you think he's seeking the treasure, too?"

Peregrin shrugs. "Or he's coming after you."

"How would he know where we're headed?" Ayc asks.

"I don't know." Lora stares hard at the ground below. A line forms between her brows. She almost looks worried. Ayc's fingers itch to sooth that line from her skin, but he's certain she'd run a knife through his palm.

"Perhaps, he's tracking us somehow," Bronwen offers. She catches her bottom lip between her teeth for a moment, then adds, "Or someone gave him information. Someone in the fisherman's village who saw us leave, perhaps. Marcellus has connections everywhere."

"We can figure that out later." Lora turns on her heel

and marches toward the cave, drawing one of her swords from its scabbard. "Let's go. We need to get the treasure and get off this island before he finds us. Or I'm going to kill him."

They enter the cave in a cluster, Lora and Bronwen leading the way. Tavish and Saga on the left, Peregrin at the right, Xylie in the center, and Ayc at the back. Tension clings to all of them in a thrum that matches the frantic pulse in Ayc's neck.

Stalactites hang from the ceiling, and stalagmites as wide as tree trunks twist upward from the cave floor. The spikes all gleam in the light Bronwen has summoned, giving the illusion that they're walking through the mouth of some beast. The cave is utterly quiet, except for the soft *drip, drip, drip* echoing from some distant part of the cave.

Ayc tries to imagine they're on a leisurely stroll. Maybe if he pretends they aren't about to be eaten by a dragon, he'll forget it's true.

Lora and Bronwen suddenly veer to the right.

"Be careful," Lora warns, pointing to a spot on the floor.

The spot almost looks exactly like the rest of the cave floor. But when Ayc stares hard enough, he notices the difference in texture. It's looks softer, lighter, than the surrounding stone, and it ripples when their feet hit the stone near it, like mud mixed with water.

"A bog pit," Peregrin says.

"Aren't bogs normally outside?" Ayc asks.

"I don't think this place is normal," Bronwen says again. "Watch your feet."

Ayc carefully steps around it. Bronwen is right. Nothing about this place feels natural. His skin has not stopped prickling since he entered, and the air grows colder and colder. Bog pits, and dragons, and—

"Ayciah."

Ayc freezes in place; every muscle in his body growing tense. Surely, he didn't hear that. Surely—

"Ayciah."

He spins around toward the sound. A bubble pops in the bog pit, but everything else is still in the darkness. That name. He hasn't heard that name for twelve years. Even his own mother rarely called him by the full name she gave him. After she died, there was no one left who knew his name. Peregrin knows most things about him, but even they don't know that.

A light shock passes through his body as Ayc's group keeps walking, and Bronwen gets farther away, taking the shield with her. Ayc takes a few steps backward into the shield but keeps his eyes fixed into the darkness they have left behind.

"Ayciah."

Something moves from the shadow, and he stills again. Even the air in his lungs stops moving.

Mother?

It isn't possible, and yet that's who steps from the shadow. The same soft, wide form, same slightly upturned nose, same brunette hair she always wore piled in a messy ball on top of her head. Same smile that grows wider when she sees Ayc.

He cannot move, and the shield passes through him again. Goosebumps rise on the skin of his arms. He finally releases a breath, and it turns to smoke in the icy air.

The face of his mother transforms—the skin peeling back until rotten flesh and bone is left behind. The smile becomes sharpened teeth; the body fades to a skeleton dressed in tattered dark fabric.

Ayc's head chimes a single word of warning. *Wraith.* He doesn't even have time to scream the word, before the creature bellows a shriek and lunges at his throat.

CHAPTER
SIXTEEN

Xylie's scream echoes through the tunnel; it hasn't fallen silent before someone else's cry joins hers. *"Ayc!"*

Lora.

He can't respond. The force of the wraith took Ayc to the ground, and now its jagged teeth chomp inches from Ayc's throat. Ayc braces one hand on its forehead and the other on its lower jaw. His thumb slides into the thin, rotten flesh of the wraith's cheek. The foul smell twists his stomach along with the panic.

The wraith's hands claw at Ayc's leather, scraping at the fabric but not penetrating. Ayc can only see the darkness of the wraith's eyes—nothing but seemingly endless, black holes.

Of all the ways I thought I'd die, Ayc thinks absurdly, *being mauled by a skeleton is not one of them!*

Peregrin lunges and sinks a knife into the wraith's skull. It only turns to snap at Peregrin, who reels back, and then returns to gnashing at Ayc's throat. Saga growls and lunges for the creature, but Tavish yanks back on the leash.

A flash of metal tears through the air, coming far too close to Ayc's hand. The sword parts the wraith's cervical vertebrae, severing the connection between body and skull. But the creature doesn't halt. Its claws still scrape, and its jaw still snaps from the skull Ayc holds in his hands. Ayc chucks the head one direction and then kicks into the spoiled flesh where its abdomen should be, thrusting the body away from him. It lands in the bog pit and disappears beneath the mud. A skeletal hand shoots up, clawing at the air, before sinking.

Xylie shrieks again and stomps on the wraith's skull, over and over again. Each kick shatters bone until the corpse is nothing but fragments. Lora looms over Ayc, still clutching one of her swords. She offers her other hand.

"Thanks," Ayc says, panting, as he accepts her offer.

She yanks him upward and then shoves him back toward Bronwen. "Stay in the fucking shield!"

"If the dragon didn't know we were here before," Tavish says, his fists clenching on Saga's leash. "It does now."

Saga growls, ears pinned back.

Peregrin snaps, "We've got more company."

Past Lora, Ayc can see the shadows moving, materializing into more wraiths. The dozens of undead are worse than he ever imagined from the stories. No one knows quite what they are, though theories and myths abound. Some say they are ancient undead cursed by dark magic as punishment for evil crimes; others say that they are souls unable to find eternal peace who clawed their way back to corporeal lands. Ayc only knows that they are the most terrifying thing he's ever seen.

Their teeth snap together; their voices chant his name until it blurs into chaotic noises. Xylie clamps her hands over her ears and whimpers. The air chills to the icy bite of a winter storm. All six of their breaths turn to clouds before their lips.

"Might I suggest we run?" Ayc yells.

Clustered together within Bronwen's shield, they race down the tunnel. Peregrin takes the back, moving as fast as their legs will allow, but pain surges through their face at each step. Ayc offers his arm. Peregrin takes it. They move faster together, but not fast enough.

The wraiths chase them. Their hands claw at the shield. Bronwen throws a hand behind her as she runs and a pulse of light breaks from the field. The wraiths scream and stumble back, but more take their place. A few move alongside them and keep pace, claws scraping against the field. The tunnel before them splits into three, but they don't reach the split before Bronwen reels to a halt and forces everyone behind her to stop. Two wraiths now loom before them on the path. Their teeth gnash together with the sound of cracking bone.

Xylie scrambles through the pack on her side and draws out a bottle of green liquid. She steps around Peregrin and Ayc but remains within her shield. She heaves the jar over the heads of the first wraiths and into the center of the mass. It explodes in a blast of light. The wraiths shriek as they are set ablaze. They run in mindless circles, looking like matchsticks of green flame. But this only renews the franticness of the dozens who remain. Their skeletal hands scratch down the sides of the shield.

Lora swings her swords through the barrier and departs heads from the bodies of the two in front of them. But more replace them. Ayc releases Peregrin and draws his own blade, but his friends are too close to allow him to swing effectively with the large blade. Tavish barely restrains a snarling Saga. Peregrin holds a knife in their hand, but the short blade will do little to stop the undead.

Sweat shines off Bronwen's face, and a drop of blood trails from her nostril. A hole appears in the shield. A skeletal hand snakes through and grasps at Peregrin's face. With a flick of their knife, they slice the hand from the wrist. Panting, Bronwen utters a breathless spell and the hole seals. The severed hand creeps along the ground toward Ayc's foot, its fingers moving like spider legs, before Saga pounces upon it. With a strangled cry, Tavish yanks it from Saga's mouth and heaves it into the face of another wraith, where its fingers sink into empty sockets.

The shield flashes once, as though in warning. Lora stops her swinging to look at Bronwen, and Ayc can read it on both their faces. Time is nearly up. They are surrounded, hopelessly outnumbered, and their only shield is fading. Ayc positions himself before Xylie and Tavish and tightens his hold on his sword. The fear trembles through his arms, but if he's about to die, he'll die fighting.

A roar ricochets through one of the tunnels ahead. The stalactites shudder above them. The wraiths fall silent, their skulls and black holes for eyes whipping toward the sound. A four-beat rhythm picks up, each beat rattling the walls: the footsteps of a dragon. The wraiths whine in alarm and flee back down the tunnel, toward the entrance.

"Behind the stalagmites," Lora commands, pointing her sword at a cluster along the wall. "Go!"

They race behind the wall of stone and drop to the cave floor, moments before the rumbling footsteps arrive. The shield flutters and then strengthens again. Ayc stills his breath as he peeks through the crack between two stalagmites. The dragon fills the entire cavern, the horns scraping against the stone above them. The dragon inhales, seeming to suck all the air from the cave. The wraiths' cries intensify as they flee faster. When the dragon exhales, the roar comes with fire. Ayc flings an arm around Xylie and pulls her head into his chest. The fire doesn't break past the stone they hide behind, but the heat still singes at his hair, his skin.

"Get out!"

The voice comes from within the roar—deep and rumbling, but also touched with a lilt that rings of something feminine.

The dragon charges. Ayc can't see it happen, but the whole world trembles with the movement. Xylie shifts out of his protection to stare through the cracks. Ayc looks, too, just in time to see the wraiths departing the cave, racing back to wherever they were before they followed Lora and her Five into the cave. When the dragon reaches the cave entrance, it vaults into flight.

Ayc almost pities the poor wraiths who are facing that dragon. Almost.

For a moment, everything is still. The only sound is their panting breaths and that distant *drip, drip, drip.*

Then Xylie flaps her hands, stimming excitedly, before her fingers form words, *"It was even better up close!"*

Ayc almost laughs, but his heart still pounds too hard. There's something profoundly different about his friend, if that's her thought at a time of mortal peril. And he hopes she never changes.

"Well done, Bronwen," Lora whispers farther down, the

quiet of her voice loud in the stillness. She crouches over where Bronwen has collapsed to her knees. "But you have to drop the shield, now. You've used too much power."

The trail of blood on Bronwen's face now reaches all the way to her chin, but she shakes her head and holds the shield.

This time, Lora adds a growl of thunder to her voice. "Drop it, Bronwen!"

With a gasp, Bronwen releases her power. The wall around them disintegrates, and she presses the heels of her hands into her temples. She shudders, her breath still coming in gulps. "I'm sorry."

"You have nothing to apologize for, friend," Lora says, putting force behind her words. "You just saved all our lives."

"But if the wraiths or the dragon come back—"

"Hush. We'll worry about that when we come to it."

The gentleness Lora wields toward her First contrasts her mother so greatly that Ayc stares at her until she pushes to her feet. Ayc peeks through the gap in the stone, but he sees nothing. The air is warmer than before. The dragon has scared away the wraiths—for now.

"Let's go." Lora vaults over the wall, and everyone begins to follow, except Bronwen. She continues to sit with her head in her hands.

As the others round the wall, Ayc crouches down at Bronwen's side. He swings his pack off his shoulders and retrieves one of his pain relieving tonics. He uncorks it and extends it toward her. "Here, take this."

"Are *you* dealing in opium?" she asks, glibly.

"Yes, it's quite lucrative. Maybe, we should go into business together."

A breath of laughter vibrates her lips, as she takes the vial. She swallows it down. "By the divine," she sighs softly, blinking at the bottle. "That's the best tonic I've ever had. It's damn near magical. Did you make it?"

"No, Xylie did."

"Xylie," she repeats. She brings the vial back to her nose and sniffs. A bit of awe shines through her eyes. "She's brilliant."

"The best," Ayc agrees. He stands and offers his hand. She tucks the vial into a pouch at her side and takes his hand. He hauls her to her feet, and together, they round the stalagmites to where the others wait.

"Sorry," Ayc says. "I needed a minute. Turns out almost getting your face chewed off doesn't sit well with me."

Unconvinced, Lora looks to Bronwen. "Are you well?"

"Yes," Bronwen says. "I think I can put up the shield, again."

"Save it until we need it. We'll have to use it to get back to the boat, at least." She faces the three tunnels. "Now, Tavish, which way do we go?"

He points to one, and they start moving again. They weave past bog pits and avoid stumbling over great grooves left from the dragon's talons. Soon, the tunnel splits into two once more, and Tavish directs them to the left. Ayc thinks he hears the wraiths whispering his name or snapping their teeth. But the air is not frozen. It is only his anxiety playing games with him.

"*What did you hear?*" he signs to Xylie, trying to distract himself.

Her shoulders sag at the question. Her hands tremble as she signs. "*I heard my parents screaming.*"

Ayc's hands hover uselessly in the air, unsure what to

258

say. With all he's suffered, he knows words are useless in the face of such tragedy.

She spares him by asking in return, *"What did you hear?"*

"My name," Ayc signs back. A partial truth.

"Look," Bronwen says, pointing ahead of them. "Light."

A faint red glow breaks from the darkness a dozen yards ahead.

"It's there," Tavish says, excitement creeping into his tone. "That's where the treasure is."

Ayc releases a breath, but quickly sucks it in, unsure whether to be relieved or afraid. Lora picks up her speed, narrowly darting to one side to avoid tripping into yet another bog pit. The light grows larger, revealing an arch bathed in red as the tunnel opens into a wide chamber. Lora raises a hand in a signal to stop.

Ayc has heard a lot of stories about dragons and their caves. Some say they are collectors of treasures and that they sleep on piles of gold. Perhaps that's what he is expecting as they enter, but instead, there's almost nothing at all. The wide chamber has walls that are curved and smooth, except for a few deep gouges left by claws. Small boulders form a circle in the middle of the chamber. Each one glows a soft red as though fired to give off heat. In the very center sits another stone as large as both of Ayc's fists, but this one is as dark as a moonless night, except for the green veins that weave through it.

"Is that—" Ayc begins.

Xylie claps a hand over her mouth, her eyes wide with delight.

"A dragon egg," Lora murmurs, awe tinting her tone. Then she whips around to face Tavish, whose mouth gaps open. "Is the treasure a dragon egg?"

"I—I'm—" Tavish audibly swallows. "I'm just as surprised as you."

"But I don't understand," Bronwen says. "It's supposed to be a priceless treasure."

Xylie signs, and Lora translates, "Dragon eggs are extremely valuable in the right market."

"Who buys dragon eggs?" Ayc asks.

"Drakr," Peregrin replies. "Gryphons bond with their riders, and sometimes, though more rarely, dragons do the same for Drakr. But the Drakr government and armies don't find it necessary for the dragons to be willing. They will find, steal, or purchase the eggs and then break the dragons from the time they are born. They don't have many in their armies, but a few dozen is far more than I wish they had."

Fuck. Of course Ayc remembers the tales of Drakr having dragons, but he tries *not* to think about it. The only thing more frightening than the idea of Drakr is the thought of a Drakr riding a dragon.

"*We can't take the egg,*" Xylie signs to Lora.

Lora's lips form a thin line. She says nothing.

"*We can't sell it and risk the innocent creature getting into Drakr's hand.*"

"The mother dragon will hunt us into oblivion if we take it," Peregrin says as they shuffle back a step. "Facing a dragon is one thing. Facing a furious mother attempting to save her offspring? I'd rather not."

Ayc is with Peregrin on this. Not just because, Peregrin, as usual, makes a tremendous amount of sense, but because something feels wrong about taking an unborn baby from their mother who is clearly devoted to protecting it.

"We came all this way," Bronwen murmurs. "We have to take it. Don't we?" But she sounds uncertain.

Lora drags her bottom lip between her teeth, the only sign of her uncertainty. Ayc silently pleads that she has enough empathy that they'll turn and walk out of this place without touching that egg.

"Well, Loraphne," says a voice from behind Ayc, one silky and all too familiar, "if you're not going to take it, then I'll help myself."

Ayc whirls around. He sees only shadow in the tunnel behind him. And then Marcellus appears, pulling the hood of a bright blue cloak off his head. Who needs a divina gift when, with enough money—no doubt stolen from the tithing of his pious people—one can buy a cloak enchanted with invisibility?

Behind him, his Five appear, dropping their own hoods. And then more behind them, until almost a dozen fae stand before Ayc. All males, of course, wearing bright blue robes, and a variety of weapons. They fill the entire passageway, sealing off the path out of the chamber. The rules of the Trials are clear: no one can help but the Five, but clearly he's shattered that number by far. Perhaps, the six Ayc saw earlier are completely different people meant to be a distraction. Maybe, this group has followed them from the moment they stepped onto the isle.

Lora pushes through her Five, elbowing in front of Ayc to position herself before them. Ayc shifts to the side, and the chamber catches his attention. From the corner of his eye, he studies the abundant shadows that remain despite the red light. Perhaps, it's time that he uses his trick for something useful.

"Why does it not surprise me that you are breaking the rules of the Trials?" Lora demands.

"I follow only the will of the divine," Marcellus says. "I do not answer to rules of men."

"Convenient, isn't it?" Bronwen scoffs. She draws her staff from her back and grips it tightly. "When you claim to be the only one to know the divine's will. Perhaps, rather, you knew you couldn't win without treachery."

Ayc backs up into the chamber slowly. Both sides are too focused on each other to notice him. He undoes his bracelets and slips them into his pocket.

"Does it look as though I am not winning?" Marcellus holds up his arm and pulls back his long sleeve to reveal the chronicler. Three of the seven gems glow—purple, royal blue, and teal. "I don't see a single one on yours." He chuckles. "This can go two ways. You can step aside. Or we can kill you and your Five. I promise, it makes no difference to me."

From his position in the shadows, Ayc sees Xylie reach into her bag. Peregrin unleashes a dagger. Tavish fists his own cutlass and coils Saga's leash around his other hand. Saga bares his teeth. Now invisible, Ayc draws his blade.

"Two of my Five are divina," Lora says, her hands falling onto the hilt of her swords, telling Ayc she has every intention of fighting. She's simply stalling. "Would you truly risk your divine's wrath?"

"Perhaps, I will show them mercy. But you, Loraphne?" Marcellus drags his gaze up and down her body, in a predatory way, like he's trying to strip her bare. Lora doesn't flinch, but rage boils in Ayc's blood, tinting his vision in red. "I'll quite delight in killing you."

"Speaking of divina," says Marcellus's First, Erech, the burly one with more weapons than seems practical. "Where did the human go?"

Bronwen and Xylie whip their heads around and search the chamber, their gazes passing over Ayc twice before they swiftly look back.

"Showing himself for the coward he is," Marcellus says, sounding bored. "Spare the human and the blind one. Kill the rest."

A hiss of metal-on-metal echoes through the tunnel as weapons are drawn. Xylie steps forward and thrusts a handful of silver powder into the air above the Lux Aesters' heads. They fling up their arms to shield their faces as the powder rains down upon them. But nothing happens. The silver powder merely glistens over their cloaks.

"What was that, you little witch?" Erech snarls. He lunges for Xylie, his ax held high. Xylie scrambles back, but Lora effortlessly catches his ax between her two blades.

"It doesn't matter," Marcellus says, stepping aside to make way for his men behind him. "Pull up your hoods, and kill them. I'll get the dragon egg."

As Erech disentangles and aims another swing at Lora's head, Marcellus yanks up his own hood, a movement echoed by the rest of his party. The fabric of the cloaks disappear, but the powder remains visible, sparkling in the red light, outlining their bodies. Their weapons, too, are visible, seeming to float in the air. Imperfect invisibility. Not as good of a trick as Ayc's own.

Marcellus growls in rage as he realizes what Xylie has done. Peregrin aims a dagger, but the Marcellus-shape darts out of the way. The knife finds a mark behind him. Blood joins the floating powder, suspending in air before it crumples in a puddle.

Bronwen, Lora, and Peregrin surge forward to meet the Lux Aester blades. Xylie drags Tavish and Saga with her a few feet away, where she seizes three vials from her bag and shoves them into his arms. She draws her bow and aims an arrow, while Tavish issues Saga a command. When Saga fixes their eyes upon the battle, Tavish heaves the vial into the crowd, toward the back of the Lux Aester. A puff of smoke arises around them. There's coughing and sputtering and screams.

Ayc has been standing still for far too long. He starts toward the smoke, when a sparkle of movement breaks from the frenzy. Marcellus whips down his hood as he charges into the chamber. Two others follow him, fully visible as well.

Marcellus searches the chamber but doesn't stop walking. "Where are you, human? Don't you want to face me like a man?"

Ayc waits until Marcellus and his men march past him, and then he strikes. Peregrin has taught him well. He knows exactly where to land a blade to end a life and where to land one to ensure they are merely incapacitated. It's as though Peregrin knew one day Ayc might be in this situation, choosing whether or not to take a life. And Peregrin knew he would choose mercy.

The sword cleaves through the side of the fae's thigh, and Ayc's arms shudder as the blade grinds against bone. The man screams as he tumbles to the ground. Ayc steps back into the shadows, disappearing once more, before Marcellus and his follower reel around. His follower stops to render assistance to the injured fae. He throws back the torn cloak, and a wave of nausea surges through Ayc's gut at the gaping flesh and the pool of blood. Marcellus spares the fallen fae only the briefest glance, before he keeps walking, though now he watches over his shoulder as he goes, studying the darkness where Ayc hides.

Ayc inhales through his nose, forcing away the nausea, considering his next move. Marcellus vaults over the fire-hot stones and reaches for the egg. He jerks his hand back, narrowly avoiding the arrow that sails past him. His eyes blaze a molten silver, and he locks them on Xylie, who faces him from across the chamber.

Marcellus draws the sword at his hip and storms back toward her. "I will kill you, bitch."

He makes it only a few steps, when Ayc leaps the stones and blocks Marcellus's path, reappearing as he enters the light. "I don't think so, High Prick Marcellus." Ayc drives his sword down, aiming for Marcellus's shoulder.

Marcellus blocks the attack easily, their blades clashing. "It's High *Priest* Marcellus," he says through his teeth.

Ayc shrugs. "Close enough."

Ayc slams his boot into Marcellus's gut. Marcellus stumbles backward, eyes widening in surprise. Then he drives forward and unleashes a flurry of attacks that Ayc meets, blocks and parries. The muscle of Ayc's back snarl at him, but he shoves the pain back behind the mental wall and focuses on the rage. He hates this man, hates the way he treats the people who serve him, the way he threatened Xylie, the way he looked at Lora. It narrows Ayc's focuses and builds heat in his blood and behind his eyes.

Marcellus falters and blinks in surprise. "What?"

The brief hesitation allows Ayc to slip his blade beyond his defenses. Marcellus darts to the side, but the metal slices through the fabric of his cloak near his shoulder. Marcellus bares his teeth. His canines have sharpened, looking bloody in the crimson light.

"Forget what I said before. I'm going to—"

"Kill me," Ayc finishes for him and fakes a yawn. "Yeah, yeah."

Screams erupt at the entrance of the chamber, where the frenzy is being fought. Lora, Peregrin, and Bronwen scramble backward into the chamber, their mouths forming a single word, but they are drowned out by a roar that shakes the walls. For the first time, fear flashes across Marcellus's face.

"Oh, good." Ayc grins. "Mama's back."

CHAPTER
SEVENTEEN

One of the screams turns from panic to pain. The dragon stands in the tunnel, her great jaw open so every tooth is visible. Powder sparks near her tongue, right before she bites down. Bones crack, and blood rains from her jaw. The scream abruptly silences. She swings her head side to side and tosses the half-visible, bloody body to the side. Then she fixes her head squarely at Marcellus and Ayc, her red eyes vibrant in the darkness.

Ayc's ability to breathe succumbs to a mixture of fear and wonder.

Marcellus lunges for the dragon's egg. Ayc slides into his path once more, holding his sword at Marcellus's chest. The ground quakes as the dragon charges toward them.

Marcellus halts, but a smile twists on his lips. A force slams into Ayc and takes him to the ground. Ayc barely gets his sword up to block the fae—the same one who stopped to help his injured comrade—from severing his neck. The fae presses their weight down upon their sword, and Ayc's arms tremble to hold him back. Inch by inch, the fae's weapon creeps toward Ayc's throat. Cool sweat beads at Ayc's neck; his heart pounds at his sternum.

Then the fae slumps on Ayc, blood dripping from their neck where an arrow struck. Ayc kicks him off and jumps to his feet. Xylie races toward him, her bow still in her hand. In the center of the chamber, the dragon's progress has been interrupted by three Lux Aester, who swing their weapons, ready to do battle.

Fools, Ayc thinks. All of them.

"Fae scum!" the dragon growls, whipping her tail so fast it cracks with the force of the earth splitting. "I will end you."

She snaps her jaws at one. Another Lux Aester throws out their hand, and a shield, quite like Bronwen's, appears before the dragon. As the dragon's teeth collide with the shield, it explodes with a concussive *boom*. The dragon rears her head back with an enraged growl. The third fae thrusts a spear toward her vulnerable chest. With one swipe of her claws, she swats the spear holder across the chamber where he collides with the wall.

Using the moment of distraction, Marcellus sprints around Ayc, grabs the egg, and slips it into the pouch at his side.

"No!" thunders the beast.

Ayc lunges for Marcellus, but he leaps over the wall of stone and continues running. The dragon snaps at Marcellus as he races by. She inhales like she might breathe flame, but she doesn't have time to exhale. From across the room, Marcellus's First heaves his ax. It spirals through the air and slams into the dragon's chest.

The dragon *screams*. It isn't a growl or a cry. It's an

almost human scream. She buckles to the ground, her long neck splaying, her wings crumpling. Xylie's lips form a wordless cry as a river of blue blood pours from beneath the dragon.

The sorcerer near the dragon grabs a sickled blade from his side and holds it above his head. Ayc flings himself over the rocks, but he knows he won't get there in time. The dragon scratches out weakly, but she's dying, and soon her snarls turn to something else: a keening, whining sound.

She's *crying*.

She looks past her attackers and locks onto Ayc. Her red gaze bores into him, and she paws forward, her clawed hand reaching. Pleading.

"Save my baby."

Across the chamber, Lora dispatches the Lux Aester soldier she's been battling with and races toward the dragon. But neither she nor Ayc make it. The sorcerer's sword drops, slicing the dragon's head from her body. Lora slams her sword through the sorcerer's spine a moment later.

Fuck!

Ayc grinds his teeth against a scream and searches for Marcellus. The priest strides to the entrance alone, ignoring that his men are still locked in battle with Peregrin and Bronwen. Tavish, not holding Saga's leash, stumbles into Marcellus path, and they collide. Ayc and Xylie bolt his direction. Marcellus lifts his sword, and Ayc runs faster, even knowing he won't make it to his friend in time.

"I'm divina!" Tavish cries, flinging up his arm, the one with the mark. "Look! See! I'm divina."

Marcellus shoves him, and Tavish lands with his hands

behind him, pinned to the ground. Marcellus storms past him and into the dark tunnel.

Ayc pauses beside Tavish. "Are you all right?"

"Fine!" Tavish replies.

Xylie flies past Ayc and Tavish, charging after Marcellus.

"Wait!" Ayc calls, but she doesn't even glance back.

"Ayc, stop her!" Lora demands, from where she has rejoined Peregrin and Bronwen, somehow aware of everything even as she fights two opponents at once.

Ayc doesn't need the command. He's already racing after his friend. In the tunnel ahead, Xylie slams into Marcellus, hands clawing at the pouch where he put the egg. Marcellus catches her wrists and wrestles her backward a few steps. She kicks out, fights to be free, but her feet slide over the stone until he releases her with a thrust. Her small frame spirals backward and lands right where Marcellus intended.

In a bog pit.

For one strangled heartbeat, she lingers on the surface. Then the mud swallows her whole.

"No!" The word blazes like glass in Ayc's throat. He bolts the last few steps and drops to his knees beside the pit, as Marcellus escapes down the dark tunnel. Xylie's hand shoots out, and Ayc scrambles to grab her. Her fingers, slick with grime, slide through his grasp, and she completely vanishes beneath the dark surface once more.

"Lora!" Ayc screams, pawing at the mud, searching for any sign of Xylie. "Lora, help! Xylie!"

This can't be happening. He can't fucking lose her. Not his best friend. Not the one person who made him hold on when everything was more than he could bear.

"Ayc!" Lora calls, pounding down the tunnel toward him. "What's going on?"

"Xylie! Marcellus pushed her into the pit."

Every bit of warmth drains from Lora's cheeks, turning her gray and ashen. She flings her pack off her back and yanks off rope that is coiled on the side. She winds it around her chest, her arms, her waist and ties it with a quick knot. It takes only seconds, but every moment stretches out like eternity as Ayc reaches into the pit, up to his elbows, but still finds nothing within the mud.

"Ayc, catch!"

He pulls his hands out of the mud as Lora tosses him the end of the rope.

"Don't let go!" she orders. "When I tug on it, pull us out."

Ayc has just enough time to circle the rope once around his right wrist and grasp tightly before Lora leaps into the bog pit. She disappears instantly, just like Xylie. The weight of her wrenches against the rope, and it slides through his grip. He tightens his hold and cries out as the rope burns against his skin. He sits backward and anchors his heels against the stone. The mud drags at the rope, trying to rip it away, but he only grasps tighter.

Even as it bites into his flesh, even as his skin opens and bleeds, he doesn't let go. Lora has given an order, but that isn't why. He doesn't even sense the command. He only knows that Xylie and Lora are at the end of this rope, and he'll drown in this pit with them before he lets them go.

Footsteps pound down the tunnel. Half a dozen Lux Aester flee behind Ayc as though finally realizing their master has left them behind. Bronwen chases after them with power pulsing between her fingertips like lightning. Peregrin follows a dozen feet behind her, moving in a limping run. When one of the Lux Aester dares to look back,

Peregrin fires a knife straight past their nose. No one looks back again.

A sharp tug comes at the rope, different from the steady pull of the mud.

Ayc yanks, but the mud has cemented the rope in place. He digs his heels in, but it doesn't give.

"Help me!" Ayc pleads, and Bronwen and Peregrin turn their attention to him.

Peregrin and Bronwen rush to seize the rope. All three fight against the mud. Ayc grits his teeth against the burn, his own blood slicking the rope. Slowly, so slowly, the rope pulls upward. At last, a hand surges above the mud, and then two heads.

Mud masks Xylie and Lora's faces, but they both cough, and that means they're breathing.

"Grab her," Lora calls, thrusting Xylie closer to the edge.

Without releasing the rope, Bronwen maneuvers closer and grabs Xylie's outstretched hand. She heaves her from the pit. Xylie lands on her hands and knees, letting out a relieved sob. Lora drags herself along the rope, and Ayc surges forward, grasping her beneath her arms and ripping her from the mud. They collide together on the stone, Lora's weight falling onto him.

Her breath warms his neck. Something releases behind his ribcage, and Ayc sucks in his own gasp. He thinks he's held his breath the entire time she was in the pit, knowing she and Xylie couldn't breathe.

She lifts her head, and her midnight blue eyes find Ayc. They are the only thing visible in the mud. Without realizing what he's doing, Ayc reaches his fingertips—the only place on his hand not blistered—to brush away the mud that has coated her cheeks. "Are you all right?" he asks, a thread of panic still in his words.

She nods and stares at him. Her head tilts toward his fingers, but then she jerks away from his touch and rolls off him. Her absence crashes over him like a cold shock, like diving into the Bellum Sea. He sucks another breath through his teeth.

Lora pushes to her knees before Xylie, who now sits, gasping. Bronwen rests a hand gently on her back. Tears trail through the mud on Xylie's cheeks.

"*I'm sorry,*" her trembling hands say. "*It's my fault we lost the egg. You should have gone after Marcellus. You should have left me—*"

"Stop," Lora says, urgently, catching her cousin's hands in hers. "I would rather lose this entire Trial than lose *you*. There is nothing worth more to me than your life. Do you understand?"

Xylie nods.

"Good." Lora presses a kiss to Xylie's head then pulls her into a tight embrace. Xylie's shaking hands clutch Lora's back.

Ayc sits up, unable to look away from the two, forcing his chaotic head to believe his eyes. They are here; they are both fine. And—

Ayc squints and shifts closer to get a better look. When Lora leans back, he sees her chronicler more clearly.

"Lora, your chronicler!" Ayc calls.

She shoves back the dark material of her sleeve. A single pink stone is lit, casting its hue against her damp, brown skin. She pulls back her sleeve further, to the list of quests written there. One of the seven lines has disappeared.

"Unearth a priceless treasure," Bronwen murmurs,

273

glancing from Lora's arm to Xylie. She chimes off a quick laugh but presses three fingers to her lips. "Guess we didn't need a dragon egg, after all."

"Yeah." Ayc's own laughter is nervous, almost unhinged, releasing his remaining tension. "All we had to do was throw Xylie into a large mud puddle. Should have done it sooner."

Both cousins shoot him a vulgar sign.

"Didn't need the dragon egg?" Tavish calls, as Saga leads him down the tunnel from the chamber. He looks unscathed. Somehow, they've all made it through this fight. "Do you mean I stole this thing back for nothing?"

He pulls his other hand out from behind his back, and there, balanced in his palm, is the dragon egg.

"Holy shit, Tavish!" Ayc's voice booms through the tunnel, a grin splitting across his face. "How did you manage that?"

Tavish shrugs. "Most people don't expect a blind kid to be pick-pocketing, so Zephen taught me how to use it to my advantage." His eyes widen, and he swiftly adds, "Not that I do it often anymore. Or ever. I never do it. But I saw Marcellus take the egg and I just—"

"It was brilliant, Tavish," Bronwen assures. "Absolutely brilliant."

Xylie springs to her feet and races to take a closer look at the egg. Tavish lets her take it into her hands, and she cradles it gingerly.

"But what do we do with it?" Bronwen asks.

"We leave it here," Peregrin says with finality, but they glance at Lora.

She nods. She brushes mud from her armor and her swords as she stands.

Xylie hands the dragon egg back to Tavish, looks at Ayc and signals for him to translate.

"The egg won't survive, now that the mother is dead."

Ayc swallows. The brief elation he felt at Lora's chronicler and Tavish's rescue of the dragon egg implodes, leaving only heaviness. Like someone has rested an anvil on his chest.

Xylie continues to sign, and Ayc presses on, "Without the mother, the heated stones will go out and the egg will grow too cold. Or another dragon will come and destroy it. Dragons are very territorial."

"What do you want us to do, Xylie?" Lora asks. Her tone is not cold, but neither is it warm. It is merely blunt and factual. "We can't take it with us."

Xylie stares at her, but her hands remain frozen in the air, saying nothing.

"We have to put it back where we found it," Lora says. "I'm—"

A groan reverberates down the tunnel from the direction of the chamber. Lora stiffens. The groan comes again and forms words, "Help me."

"I injured one of them," Ayc says. "They must have left him behind."

"I'll handle it." Lora marches toward the chamber. She lifts her foot extra high on one step and yanks a knife from her boot. "And then we need to leave."

Ayc rushes after her. Surely, she can't mean to murder an injured man like he's a wounded deer that needs to be put out of its misery. Footsteps echo behind him as the others follow them.

In the chamber, they find two Lux Aester. The one who the dragon swatted across the room has crawled to lie beside the one who Ayc wounded. The former's legs bend at odd angles. The latter is so pale he nearly blends into the rock beneath him. Lora storms toward them, and the broken one utters a cry.

"Wait, wait," his words slur as they exit his mouth. He rolls onto his back and slides backward on his hands, dragging his legs. Blood and a clear liquid drip from one nostril, a sign Ayc remembers from Evander's teachings that a skull is fractured. Lora continues to advance on him. He finally sees the futility of the situation and stops. Lora kneels before him, resting her blade on his throat.

"I'm sorry," he says. "I won't help Marcellus again. I won't cheat in the Trials. I'll—"

"No, you won't," says Lora calmly, and she slits his throat.

Ayc clamps a hand over his mouth to silence an involuntary cry. Lora turns her blade toward the other Lux Aester. She places the bloody point against his sallow cheek.

"Can you hear me?" she growls.

A whimper is the only response.

"If you live or die is up to you. I don't care either way. But if you live and somehow make it off this island, I want you to give Marcellus a message for me. He harmed my family, and he threatened my friends. When I see him again, I'll kill him for that. Do you hear me?"

The injured man nods. She slides her blade back into the sheath in her boot and stands. She marches back toward Ayc, the cape flowing behind her, her face a mask of mud, blood, and relentlessness.

Perhaps, Ayc should hate the coldness of what she's done, but the feeling that erupts within him isn't hate. She is like staring at the sun on the horizon when you've lost all sense of time—unsure whether it's a sunset or a sunrise. She's all contradictions and contrasts; day and night, rolled into one. She is devoted to those she loves and utterly merciless to those who might harm them. He doesn't dare name this powerful feeling within him, but whatever it is, it's as hot as a dragon's flame.

"It's only a matter of time before the wraiths or another dragon return." Lora looks toward the others, resting her gaze on Xylie who is cradling the dragon egg once more. "Xylie, put it back where it was so we can go."

Ayc stands rooted in place as Xylie, head hanging down, carefully climbs over the hot stones. She kneels to place the dragon egg down. Ayc glances to the right, where the mother dragon lays motionless. Several Lux Aester bodies also lay on the ground. This place is a tomb, and the unborn dragon will just be another death among them.

Xylie sniffs, drags the back of her hand across her face, and gets to her feet. Ayc offers his hand to help her over the stones.

Lora squeezes Xylie's shoulder, a brief comforting touch, and then turns. "Let's get the fuck out of this place."

Xylie hesitates, her attention lingering on the egg, before following. Bronwen, Tavish, and Peregrin fall into line, but Ayc can't bring himself to move.

Save my baby.

The dragon's voice replays in Ayc's head. A mother who would do anything to save her child. A mother's love like that he remembers, oh so well. And how can Ayc ignore a final wish?

When Ayc is sure no one will look back, he steps back over the stones. As quickly as he can, he wraps the dragon egg into his blanket with his aching hands and slips it into his pack.

When they make it back to the rowboat, they find it smoldering—the wood black and crumbling from the blaze Marcellus and his men must have started. The sea is empty as far as the eye can see. The fisherman's boat that brought them is long gone. Had Marcellus used force or bribery to get them to leave their post? Not that it matters, because the effect is the same.

They are stranded on the Isle of Nightmares.

Bronwen's shield shimmers around them. As they retraced their steps through the mountains, the calls of wraiths followed them. No one admitted what they heard, but it was clear by the looks of pain that crossed everyone's faces that they heard something. Now that they are on the shore, Ayc has finally stopped hearing his mother whimper *"water, more water"* the way she did when she died in the thick of an intense fever.

Ayc wonders if it's only a matter of time before the wraiths creep out of the mountains and devour all of them on the beach. The sun above is sloping toward the western horizon, the shadows of the mountains deepening. It'll be nightfall in only a handful of hours. If wraiths wander around in the hazy daylight, what worse things come out to play at night?

Lora crouches toward the ground and places a hand on her chin, as though perhaps the position makes her think better. Like she's going to solve this, but the little line between her eyebrows reappears and tells Ayc she knows what he does.

They are completely and totally fucked, and even he doesn't have the heart to joke about it.

As though reading everyone's mind, Peregrin shakes their head. "We'll get off this island."

Lora glances over her shoulder at them. "Any ideas?"

"Just one," says Peregrin. They tilt their head upward, searching the gray skies above. A small smile tilts up their lips. "And look, here she comes."

Ayc narrows his eyes and sees merely a dark dot in the sky. It flies lower, out of the clouds, and Ayc recognizes it for what it is. Tempest's mighty wings beat through the sky as she descends. Ayc feels air, and hope, soar back into his lungs at the sight of the glorious gryphon.

Thank fuck.

"She noticed when the fishing boat came back without us," Peregrin explains.

The gryphon lands with a graceful flutter of wings. And then she swings her mighty head to narrow her silver eyes at Peregrin. Ayc doesn't need to hear the mental connection between rider and gryphon to hear the *'I told you so'.*

Peregrin ignores her ire and lays a hand on the gryphon's neck. "Thank you for coming, friend."

Ayc and Xylie are the first to be deposited on the Everadyn shores close by the Noxumbra fishing village of Pax.

Peregrin tells Tempest to "Fly hard and fast", and she does. The speed at which she flies makes Ayc realize how careful she was when she carried them before. He clings to her feathers, and despite the gloves he pulled on, his blistered hands ache. Xylie grasps his waist tightly and buries her face into his shoulder beside his pack until they dismount onto the sand, their legs trembling.

After Tempest rockets into the sky again, Xylie drenches herself in the ocean, scrubbing the silt and mud from her clothes, hair and skin. After, Ayc and Xylie set off for a place a little farther from the shore to wait, collecting driftwood as they go. They assemble the wood into a pile, Xylie sprinkles two different powders across the logs, and soon a fire ignites. They sit in silence, side by side.

The fire crackles, and the tide shushes as it slides against sand. Occasionally, sounds of life carry from the fishing village a little to their north: mother's calling, children playing, a cart rambling on the dirt road toward the village. To the south, a different set of mountains makes shadows against the horizon. Ayc has seen enough maps to know those mountains are still dozens of miles away, and deep within them, lies the school of Adamant, where Lora called home for years.

The sun descends impossibly fast toward the western horizon, and Ayc watches it cast streaks of pink and red across the waves.

"She'll be fine." Xylie's soft voice shatters the silence so suddenly, Ayc jumps. "Lora's strong. She will be back before nightfall. You don't have to worry."

"I'm not worried," says Ayc, forcing his lips to curl into what he hopes is a believable smile. But he is. His anxiety twists in a constant cycle of thoughts. What if Tempest's presence brings dragons to Lora's position? What if the wraiths return? What if, what if, what if?

"Uh huh, sure." Xylie twists her body to fully face him and crosses her legs beneath her. "Let me see your hands."

Ayc turns toward her and offers his hands. She strips off one of his gloves to survey the damage with keen eyes. Ayc looks into the fire instead, watching a blackened piece of driftwood glow red at its center. He already saw his raw palms, the area where the first layer of skin has been ripped off entirely, and the blisters that brand the bases of his fingers. He doesn't want a closer look.

Xylie clucks her tongue, takes a jar from her pack, and begins to slather a salve onto his hands. It eases away the pain, and Ayc is sure it holds something to help protect it from infection and promote healing. She carefully wraps his palms in a white bandage.

When she pulls his glove back on, Ayc finally works up the courage to admit, "I did something I probably shouldn't have."

She doesn't look up from her work. "You kept the dragon egg."

Of course she already knows.

"What are we going to do to keep it warm?" she asks.

The term *we* doesn't go unnoticed. She's now his coconspirator. "I wrapped it in a blanket before I put it in my pack."

"Good. Keep the pack by the fire at night. During the day, take my blanket too and wrap both around it," she says as she tends to his other hand. "If only I thought to bring *An Exploration of Dragons*, I could have done a lot more research, but that tome is much too large to carry."

Ayc pulls his gloves on over the bandages and teases, "How dare you not foresee me becoming a dragon egg thief, on top of court magician and baker extraordinaire?"

She snorts and glances toward the ocean. "Peregrin and Tavish are here."

As soon as Peregrin, Tavish, and Saga set foot on the sand, Tempest launches back in the air. Deep violet edges the eastern horizon behind Ayc. In the west, the distant mountains of Somnia Ignis are fading from sight. With only Lora and herself, is Bronwen able to maintain the shield for this long? If not, how long until the wraiths surround them, or a dragon picks up on their scents?

Ayc has to drag a breath through his nose multiple times before the constriction eases on his ribs. Every second that passes lands like a sharp sting against his skin. The four of them nibble on dried meat and bits of unleavened bread slathered in preserves. Xylie works a hand towel from her pack through the roots of her many braids and soothes oil that smells faintly of peppermint into her scalp. Tavish fills the silence by telling a fable he learned in Tenebra, about a leviathan who lost a race to a seahorse. It sounds like a similar tale to one Ayc's mother told him growing up, but that tale involved a rabbit and a turtle.

The moon rises, casting silver like fractured bones across the rippling waves. The stars appear one by one, blinking down upon them. And then finally, *finally,* a shape cuts before the moon. This time, Tempest lands next to the camp. The gryphon huffs, her barreled chest rising and falling, her lion fur slicked in sweat. Bronwen tumbles off first. Her own breaths come in pants.

"I'm going to sleep for ten days," Bronwen says, collapsing by the fire. Tavish offers her some unleavened bread, and she devours it in three bites.

Lora pauses by Tempest's side and runs a hand down her feathers. "Thank you, friend," she murmurs, before she turns and heads toward the fire. Lora must have washed while she waited, because her hair is damp and clings to her round, freshly scrubbed cheeks.

The strangest of desires ripples through Ayc, but he resists the urge to jump up and run to her.

Lora sits and accepts dried meat offered by Peregrin. She searches around the fire, taking in every person. She pauses on Ayc for a heartbeat longer than the rest. His nerves rattle at her attention, but when he dares to meet her gaze, she looks away quickly.

Saga, who was previously sleeping, bolts upright and turns to stare into the darkness. A growl forms deep in his throat. Everyone jerks to full attention. Ayc's spine snaps straighter as he follows the dog's focus. Past the perimeter of the fire, all Ayc can only see empty sand that transforms into emptier grasslands, broken only by the occasional farmers field and home. But all is quiet.

"What is it, boy?" Tavish asks, resting a hand on Saga's head.

"What does he see?" Lora asks.

Tavish touches the Kindred collar's leash. "Nothing. He doesn't—"

One moment there *is* nothing. Then a foot covered in sharp pointed steel crosses the plain from darkness and into the firelight. The body follows, towering as tall as Ayc but built wider and stronger. Every inch of that body is covered in plates of dark armor that appear black at first but gleam an effervescent crimson where the firelight touches. Spikes curl from the plates at his shoulder blades. He draws himself to a halt only five feet from Ayc and Xylie.

Lora, Bronwen, and Peregrin are instantly on their feet, drawing their weapons.

The newcomer holds up his empty hands, in a gestures that shows he is unarmed, that he means peace.

"Loraphne, daughter of Yris." His voice is somehow like both silk and like sandpaper—deep and rough, but elegant. "I mean you no harm. I've been looking for you."

He grins, presenting a full set of teeth. Every single one comes to a devastatingly sharp point.

Ayc feels like he's a little boy again, breaking out of the clutches of a nightmare. Except now, he is waking to find that the monsters who haunted him aren't a dream.

A Drakr is here.

CHAPTER
EIGHTEEN

Ayc leaps to his feet and pulls Xylie behind him. This can't be happening. There must be some sort of daily quota of how many monsters one is allowed to encounter per day. The universe simply cannot allow them to face wraiths, dragons, and a Drakr all within the same twenty-four hour period.

Ayc shuffles backward, keeping Xylie behind him. She clutches at his back with trembling hands. The Drakr whips his head in Ayc's direction. Shoulder-length dark hair contrasts against the cold, fair skin of the Drakr. Sharpness marks every line of his face, and his eyes look blue enough to be cut from a cloudless sky. He's devastatingly handsome. Yet, his every movement is predatory, like Ayc has found himself in a lion's line of sight. Not even the dragon made Ayc's nerves shudder like the Drakr's attention does.

"You travel with a human?" The Drakr's curious tone would feel harmless from anyone else, but from him, it's a threat. "How interesting. Or—" The Drakr cocks his head at

Ayc. He steps closer, and his nose wrinkles as he sniffs. "He smells different. What is he?"

A knife slices the air between Drakr and Ayc, still a foot from either of their faces, and sails into the darkness beyond. The Drakr's smile disappears. He jerks his head back toward Peregrin. His eyes flash red.

Everadyn fae's eyes glow silver; Tenebra fae blaze a cat-like green, but Drakr's eyes burn blood red. Ayc shivers at the sight.

His smile returns as quickly as it disappeared, the red fading back to blue. "Is that how you treat your guests, gryphon rider?"

Tempest growls and flutters her wings, pacing uneasily behind where Peregrin stands. Peregrin only folds their hands calmly on their cane. "Guests rarely sniff my friends."

The Drakr inclines his head. "That is fair. My apologies."

The knife sails back into the light, arches over the fire, and buries itself in the sand at Peregrin's feet.

"My fighters saw fit to return your weapon to you," the Drakr says. "To show we come in peace."

Ayc searches the darkness beyond the light but sees nothing.

Lora slides her swords back into their sheaths and rounds the fire toward the Drakr. As she passes Ayc, he nearly grabs her and hauls her behind him, too. But the instinct is ridiculous. Lora does nothing without careful calculation, and she doesn't need anyone's protection, least of all his. Instead, Ayc continues to walk backward until he stands next to Bronwen. Xylie clings to him tighter. Her entire body trembles like a leaf in the wind, and her terror cracks something in Ayc's chest.

"You said you've been looking for me?" Lora asks. She

squares her shoulders and lifts her chin. The firelight plays off her damp hair, and it shines like she might already wear a crown. "Who are you?"

"My name is Lahlis, lord of the Drakr's eastern territories and ambassador to the Everadyn fae."

That name. Ayc knows that name.

"*The Drakr lord is not one to trifle with,*" Fennix said ten years ago, as he and Yris coolly debated whether to spare Ayc's life.

"I'm hurt that you don't remember me," Lahlis goes on. "We've met before. Your mother and I are friends."

Friends?

Fear and disgust war in Ayc's chest. A mutually beneficial allyship exists between the Drakr and Everadyn, true, but to call each other friends speaks of an intimacy Ayc doesn't like.

Bronwen hisses a sharp breath at the word, but Lora doesn't flinch. Her stone-masked face gives nothing away. Perhaps, she knows about Lahlis and his connection with her mother. Perhaps, she doesn't. It's impossible to tell.

"What do you want?" Lora demands.

"You don't waste time with pleasantries, do you? I like that."

His smile twists into something a little more devilish, and Ayc seizes the hilt of his blade. The raw and blistered skin of his hand protests, but he doesn't let go.

"I've come to make you an offer," Lahlis states. "On behalf of my queen."

Lora stares at him. In the long silence that follows, Ayc's heart pounds a warning in his ears. Magic shimmers off Bronwen's skin, ripples of blue shining in the night. Saga interchanges soft growls with little whines, as though not sure whether to be fierce or afraid.

Finally, Lora breaks the silence, sounding almost bored. "Are you going to explain the terms, or are we going to continue to stand here?"

Lahlis chuckles deep in his throat. "I want to offer you the same deal I offered your mother fifty years ago in her own Trials. I want to help you win."

Xylie gasps as Ayc's hand spasms on the hilt of the sword. A pulse of power releases from Bronwen's grasp, and the campfire twists into a small cyclone before returning to its normal burning pattern.

"You..." Lora hesitates, and that hesitation speaks volumes, even if her mask does not crack. She didn't know. "You helped my mother win her Trials."

She doesn't ask if Yris accepted the offer. Three days. Yris won her Trials in three days, and then proceeded to turn the Drakr from enemies to allies. Yris made a deal with the Drakr, and she won the Sovereign throne.

Lahlis nods.

"What did you ask Yris for?" Lora asks. "In exchange for your help?"

"The same thing I would ask of you. A favor that I will call into play at a later time."

Lora scoffs. Her mask seems to be slipping, but Ayc isn't sure what is beneath the stone. Apathy? Anger? "Let me guess. You won't tell me what it is. You'll let it dangle over my head for the next forty years. Then you'll call it into play. And whatever it is will cost me nothing less than my own soul."

The realization creeps in like a snake slithering into Ayc's chest and yanking taut. Of course, he knows what happened in year forty of Yris's sovereignty. What happened ten years ago.

"Lahlis said everyone in this castle. That was the deal."

And Ayc cannot breathe.

Finally, he understands.

"Souls are such trivial things," Lahlis says with a shrug. "You don't have to worry about that until you're dead, and we are immortal beings." He pauses for a beat. "What do you say, Loraphne? Fifty years of reigning, for one small favor."

"Fifty years?" Lora repeats. "Everadyn law dictates a hundred."

The Drakr rolls his eyes. "Yet, that's what I'm offering. You can take it and get fifty years, or you can refuse my help and lose these Trials. It seems like a good deal, doesn't it?"

"And you'll simply take my word that, when you come ask your favor, I'll still abide by the terms when I have the power of all of Everadyn behind me?"

Why? Ayc wants to demand. Why is she asking questions like she's actually considering saying yes?

"That would be foolish of me," Lahlis says. He pulls at the string of a pouch hanging from his belt. He empties the contents into his palm. The green stone fits into his hand. It's engraved with a single rune and glows like a firefly in the dark.

Ayc takes an involuntary step back, every instinct warning him of the danger. And it's only a fucking stone. Except it isn't *just* anything. A Binding stone is a rare and expensive magical item. Few possess the power of both sorcery and alchemy required to create them, but once made, they are a valuable weapon in the right hands—and a *dangerous* weapon in the wrong ones.

"This is a Binding stone," Lahlis explains, "in case you don't recognize it. Few have seen one in person. We'll both swear on it. And we'll both be Bound to uphold our ends of the bargain."

Lora's arms shift backward, as though her hands are fleeing as far from possible from the eerie glow of the stone.

"Oh, of course," Peregrin mutters, and Ayc knows what they mean.

That was the reason Yris willingly surrendered her throne. She made a deal on a Binding stone for fifty years. If she refused to step down—as Ayc is certain she wanted to—the consequences would be painful, or even deadly, depending on the power of the stone.

"What do you say?" Lahlis asks, his blue eyes gleaming wickedly in the stone's light.

Lora's gaze shifts from the stone to Lahlis. No flicker of emotion corrupts her face.

Say no, Ayc wants to beg her.

There have been moments these past three days that have given him hope that she isn't a villain like her mother, after all. If there is ever a time to prove it, it's now.

But instead, she says, "I'll think about it."

Lahlis's smile disappears. He strides forward until only a foot separates them. "I'm not a patient male, Loraphne."

She doesn't flinch. "I wouldn't be a good leader if I didn't weigh such important decisions carefully, now would I?"

He looks her over once more, before he nods. "Very well, Loraphne. I'll give you two sunsets. And I do hope you haven't lost the Trials by then. It doesn't appear they are going well for you so far." He gestures at her wrist with the chronicler. "You're lagging behind all the other victors."

He sweeps around, and as soon as he steps into the shadow, he's gone. But of course, he isn't. He and his companions are still out there in the night.

Lora swings around and faces her Five. None of them move. Saga has sat down at Tavish's feet, panting uneasily. Tempest ruffles her feathers.

The pressure of what Ayc has learned builds until he fears he may explode. He needs movement, release, something. He storms toward Lora and gets closer than he normally dares.

Despite the heat in his voice, he talks so low into her ear he's convinced the others can't hear. "It was Creed Castle, wasn't it? That was the favor your mother completed."

Lora draws away from him, her narrowed gaze as dark as the surrounding night. "We aren't talking about this. Not until daylight."

He signs instead, "*Because you don't want to face what your mother has done.*"

Her hands snap in the air, capturing her rage. "*No, because if Creed Castle is the deal my mother made, then according to those Drakr, you're supposed to be dead.*"

Ayc's breath catches. One wrong word is all it would take for Lahlis to realize Yris didn't complete her bargain. He would certainly kill Ayc on the spot. What would happen after? Would the Drakr punish all of Everadyn because Yris spared one peasant boy?

"We should go to sleep, all of you," Lora snaps, turning toward the other four. "I'll take first watch. We'll talk in the morning."

She starts back toward the fire, but she freezes and does a double take of her cousin. Terror remains frozen on Xylie's face, her eyes so wide the whites of them shine in the dark.

After what she survived, it would be foolish for her not to be terrified of the Drakr. Ayc starts toward her, at the same time Lora changes course, but Xylie throws up her hands and shakes her head.

"I'm fine," she signs.

Bullshit, Ayc almost says, but she flings herself around and grabs her bedroll. In moments, she's rolled it out and pulled a blanket above her head. Ayc knows she's self-soothing. She's cocooning into herself because everything feels like too much, and even the most soothing things will feel unkind right now. Lora must know it, too, because she doesn't take another step. Lora remains frozen, unreadable, untouchable. Then she turns and flops down beside the fire. She draws one of her swords and balances it on her knees, staring out at the night.

Ayc releases the anger with a shuddering breath. Now is not the time to continue arguing with Lora. It'll upset Xylie further, and besides, Lora isn't wrong. There are likely still people out in the dark, watching them. Better to wait until daylight.

Tension hangs thick around the camp. The distant hiss of the waves against the sand seems louder in the silence. Peregrin runs a hand over their face. Tavish strokes the length of Saga's back, murmuring words of comfort, but it does little to soothe the dog who stares into the night. Bronwen studies Lora. Lines embed deeply beneath her eyes, so dark they look bruised. Finally, she tosses up her hands as though surrendering.

"I'm going to set up a ward," she says, pushing to her feet. She moves with a stiffness Ayc recognizes as someone who's hurting but trying not to show it.

Lora looks at her sharply. "You almost burned yourself out today."

"I'll use a blood ward. The use of blood will take minimal energy to cast and none to maintain." Bronwen draws a small knife from her side and continues talking, "Magic is a force, quite like nature. And like how certain things can influence nature—change it or make it stronger—certain things can make magic stronger. Blood is the easiest, because it is the essence of life."

Ayc isn't sure why Bronwen is rambling, but she glances over her shoulder at Xylie, so perhaps Bronwen thinks that Xylie will find this comforting. She's not wrong. Xylie loves learning.

"Love, death, sacrifice," Bronwen says. "Those can all leave their mark on the world and be drawn from to make magic stronger, but only by the most powerful. Such a thing can taint a soul and turn their magic dark. You have to be careful with such things."

"You're tired," Lora says, scowling at her First. "You always ramble when you're tired."

"I'm fine," she insists.

She runs the blade over the length of her palm. She doesn't flinch. Bright red pours onto her pale skin. As she paces the perimeter of the camp, she mutters under her breath and allows blood to drip from her fist. She makes the loop once, twice, three times. With each circle, her steps become slower, and the line beneath her eyes deepen. Lora watches her every movement, as Ayc rolls out a bedroll. When Bronwen completes the final round, a pulse of power sweeps through the camp. The fire flares once more before settling.

"There." Bronwen produces a smile, but it's thin. She

sways a little on her feet. "It's a smaller version of the wards that once protected Aluina."

Ayc flinches at the name of his homeland and tucks his head so his loose hair tumbles forward to cover his face, hoping no one notices.

"So long as I'm alive and do not leave the perimeter, this ward will prevent anyone from entering." She raises her voice, and Ayc is sure that, once again, it's to make sure Xylie hears. "And I don't plan on dying before morning." She laughs under her breath, but no one joins her.

"Sleep," Lora commands. She glares, as though daring Bronwen to fight her on it.

Bronwen doesn't. She looks to where she left her pack to find Ayc has already laid out her bedroll. She nods gratefully. She stumbles the few steps there, and Ayc reaches out a hand in case she collapses. She flops down on her roll and buries her head into her arms. Her soft breaths tell Ayc she's already asleep. He tucks the blanket over her shoulders, then moves to his own pack.

He positions his bedroll, and more importantly, his pack, as close to the fire as he dares without making Lora suspicious. He doesn't pull the blanket from his pack and from around the dragon egg, but the warmth of the fire should be enough. To his right, Xylie remains hidden beneath her blanket. His tongue aches to say anything that might fix this, but his jokes are powerless against the war within her.

"Is she all right?" Tavish whispers, after he settles his bedroll down at Ayc's other side. Next to him, Saga still stands at guard.

Ayc hesitates as he rolls onto his back. The stars have

come out, blinking in their blanket of velvet. After a long moment, Ayc says simply, "No."

Tavish leans close to Saga and whispers into the dog's ear. It's a different language, one Ayc doesn't know, but thinks it may be the tongue of Tenebra, shared by both the humans and the fae who live there. Tavish releases the leash. The dog pads around Ayc's hand and lays himself between Ayc and Xylie, nearly pressed to both their sides. Saga nuzzles his nose into Xylie's form, then retreats, resting his head on his paw. For a moment, nothing happens. And then a hand sneaks out from beneath the blanket and settles into the dog's fur.

Ayc draws in a deep breath, relieved the dog can grant a comfort that Ayc can't. Animals are special that way. He almost tells Tavish thank you, but Tavish speaks before he can.

"Why do I feel like I'm the only one around here without secrets?" He says it lightly. His head is turned past the flames, past Lora, toward the sea. Despite his tone, his black skin is tinged in gray as though today has exhausted him, too.

"Everyone has secrets, Tavish," Ayc replies. He, himself, could not bury all of his if he used all the sand on this shore.

"Not me. If we hide the truth about ourselves away, are we truly ourselves? Or are we just the lies we hope people can accept?"

The urge to laugh surprises Ayc. He bites down on the inside of his cheek to suppress it. "Are you secretly some three-thousand-year-old wise man, like the ones in all the fairytales who give sage advice to lesser mortals?"

He smiles, but the far-away look on his face and the fatigue that hangs over him makes him appear far older than his twenty years. He pushes his tight ringlets out of his eyes with a sigh. "No. I've just... I've had a lot of time to listen to the ocean and think."

Ayc's stomach twists as he thinks about it. Tavish, on a ship—a thing that was once a home and then a prison—alone and listening to the song of the waves. How many times has Ayc stared out at the Bellum Sea, wishing for the answers to questions he doesn't have the courage to ask? He hears a different part of that same sea now, exhaling as the tide rolls in, and inhaling as it draws back out.

"Does the sea ever give you answers?" Ayc asks.

"Generally, yes. If you listen long enough. Or maybe it's not the water. Maybe we find the answers in ourselves."

Ayc groans. "Go to sleep, old man."

Tavish lays down with a laugh. He tosses and turns for a while, searching for a comfortable position. Still, he falls asleep long before Ayc. It's not only that no position will bring him relief from his aching muscles. It's the way he sees blood-red eyes when he dares shut his own and the unknown of what tomorrow will bring. It's the way he can feel Lora looking at him, but every time he lifts his head to look back, she's already focused on the night or the fire or on the moonlight that dances on the dark waves.

He's thought a lot of what fate holds for him, how the result of the Trials will change his life, but he's never imagined this. He's never imagined that he'll be the Fifth of someone who willingly makes a deal with the conquerors of his people. His whole life seems to rest in the balance of the answer Lora has not yet given.

Yes...or no.

Such simple words.

Such powerful ones.

CHAPTER
NINETEEN

Sunrise has never looked so beautiful, even though the clouds in the sky dilute the dawn colors until they appear rather bland. A couple dabs of pink are all that mark the moments before the sun turns the sky from indigo to cyan once more. Ayc is grateful for every millimeter of light that stretches over the horizon as he stirs the cast-iron pot over the fire. With the new light, he searches the stretches of sandy beaches and then the lands beyond until they are obscured by a town in the east. The Drakr are nowhere to be seen.

"Time to wake up," Peregrin announces to the camp.

Peregrin has been keeping watch, even though Ayc has also been awake. Deep green streaks their face, the underlying skin grayer than normal. They have not spoken this entire time, but Ayc has caught Peregrin glancing at him. Perhaps, there's much they would *like* to say but will not.

Bronwen groans, lifting her face from where it has been

buried in her arms. "Please tell me I smell food, and I'm not hallucinating."

"I made cinnamon roll porridge," Ayc assures. "I'm also boiling water for your tea." He gestures to the kettle resting beside the pot. He still wears his gloves over the dressings Xylie placed last night. This morning, the skin doesn't pull and ache with every motion, but he's yet to inspect the remaining damage.

"I have no idea what cinnamon roll porridge is," says Bronwen, sitting up and crossing her legs beneath her. Hair sputters out of her braid in all directions. She slept in her armor last night. They all did. But the purple beneath her eyes looks less like bruises and more like shadows this morning. The smile that tilts on her lips—only after she too searches the area around the camp—is less strained. "But I'm afraid when I find out, I might fall in love with you just a little."

Ayc laughs quietly as he spoons the mixture into the bowls that he dug from Tavish's bag. Syrupy swirls of deep brown contrasts against the paleness of the creamy porridge. "My cooking tends to have that effect on people."

He hands bowls to Bronwen and Peregrin. He sets a bowl down beside Tavish, who murmurs a thank you without moving an inch. Ayc kneels longest at Xylie's side. Her eyes are open, peeking from beneath the blanket that lays over her nose.

He rests the bowl on the ground to free his hands and signs, *"How are you, friend?"*

She tugs the blanket down a little further, and her hands appear. *"How are you?"*

"Asked you first."

She sticks out her tongue. And that's at least

promising enough to make him almost believe her next signs. *"I'm all right."* He arches an eyebrow, and she adds, *"Promise. You?"*

"Why wouldn't I be all right?"

He turns away so he can pretend he doesn't see the protest in her hands, then ignores the soft chunk of dirt she heaves near his head to gain his attention back. Ayc dishes one last bowl of porridge and brings it to Lora.

For the last couple of hours, when Peregrin took over as guard, she hasn't even pretended to sleep. She has stared upward at the stars above. When Ayc nears, she sits up. Her hair frizzes around her face, the curls not forming the usual taut, smooth spring. She fiddles with the clips on either side of her head to re-secure it from her face. Questions sit on the tip of his tongue, but he swallows them down, sour and bitter. He learned long ago Lora is best not trifled with before she has some sort of food and hot beverage in her system.

He offers the bowl, and she blinks down at it suspiciously. "Did you put explosive powder in this one?"

"That was one time," Ayc says. "And we were kids."

"We were *sixteen*," Lora corrects. "It nearly blew up in my mouth."

Ayc shrugs. He could tell her that it was merely payback for when her Wyntra friends tied him upside down from the rafters of the stables. She stormed in to cut him down before the position made him pass out, looking utterly furious at him for wasting her time. Pouring the powder into her bowl was an impulsive, spur of the moment action the next morning.

He expected Yris to skin him alive, but she only looked at her daughter, whose nose was singed in the microexplosion on her spoon. "Are you going to let him get away with that?" Yris asked.

He spent weeks waiting for Lora to retaliate. It never came. Maybe, she believed watching him jump in fear whenever she came near was enough retribution.

"Everyone else is eating it," Ayc says. "It's clearly not explosive."

To prove his point, Bronwen swallows and hums in appreciation. "How do you make something as simple as porridge taste like it was crafted by the divine?"

Ayc arches an eyebrow at Lora. "See?"

Lora shoves a spoonful into her mouth and raises both of her eyebrows defiantly. She looks ridiculous, with a spoon between her lips and her nose wrinkling in indignation. It's a brief flicker of someone different than the fierce warrior he knows, and a smile tugs at his lips.

Then reality hits like a lightning bolt, striking him with the reminder that she did not tell the Drakr *'no'*. That she could be considering telling him *'yes'*. For a brief moment he'd forgotten, but now it's returned.

Ayc opens his mouth.

Bronwen stops him with a question of her own, "Who taught you how to bake?" There's a weight to the question. She's not just curious; she's attempting to distract him.

Ayc moves back to the fire to pour the tea from the kettle. "My mother taught me," he replies as he passes out mugs to everyone. Xylie and Tavish are sitting up now, Tavish feeding Saga jerky from his bag. Lora tracks his every movement. "She had a small bakery and I helped her from a young age."

Bronwen sprinkles her packet of herbs into the tea. She waves her finger in a gesture over the cup, and a whirlpool appears like an invisible spoon is stirring the water. She must be recovered from yesterday's strain. "Your father was a lucky man, then."

Ayc shrugs, settling back by the fire with his own bowl of porridge. "He wasn't around much."

He tries to picture the wealthy merchant who showed up in the village every few months, but Ayc barely even remembers his face, just a name. *Hayes Thornwell.* The fact Ayc doesn't share the man's surname, but instead, bears his mother's—Kendra Waylonder—should have been all Ayc needed to know about him. The merchant wanted only certain things from Ayc's mother, things Ayc was too little to understand, and Hayes wanted *nothing* to do with Ayc. He always left without notice, leaving behind enough coin to help Ayc's mother keep the bakery open for a few more months. When Ayc's mother died, he thought Hayes might show up to take him. Instead, it was Evander, a distant relative of his mother, who found Ayc and took him to Creed Castle.

"Why not?" Tavish asks.

"Didn't want to be," Ayc says simply. It's a less depressing statement than the truth, the truth Ayc didn't realize until a few months before Ayc was taken to Everadyn. At a festival in Creed Castle, Ayc saw Hayes selling his wares. Ayc was about to say something to the man, when two children and a beautiful woman approached Hayes. The reality hit Ayc like a strike across the face. Hayes was too busy raising his two legitimate children with his wife to have much use with Ayc.

"Is he who sold you into slavery to the Drakr then?" Bronwen asks, cocking her head at him. "You speak of your mother fondly, so I can assume you don't blame her for that.

But that's the story I heard at Wyntra. That Yris found you with the Drakr and rescued you from slavery."

The suspicion that creeps in Bronwen's otherwise lighthearted tone causes Ayc to freeze with a spoonful of porridge close to his lips.

Bronwen sips her tea, never taking her eyes off him. "Unless it isn't true, which based on last night, I suspect it isn't."

Fuck, Ayc thinks. His gaze shifts to Lora, whose eyes are narrowed at her friend.

Peregrin, too, watches Bronwen carefully over their drink.

"Bronwen," Tavish says, and it's both a question and a protest.

Bronwen ignores him. She balances her tea between her crossed legs to free her hands and then makes gestures that Ayc immediately recognizes as words. She's *signing.* *"Why exactly does Lora think the Drakr want you dead?"*

Ayc's eyes widen. As do Lora's.

"There was a sorcerer at Velphin who was deaf," Bronwen explains. "We were quite close."

A line furrows between Xylie's eyebrows. *"Why didn't you say anything?"*

Bronwen shrugs, like she doesn't know. But Ayc suspects it was for this reason. Bronwen didn't survive both Velphin and Adamant, schools known for their brutality, without having some craftiness and tricks and even a little viciousness up her sleeve. People say careless things when they think no one is listening, and she has an advantage people don't know about. She understood exactly what Lora and Ayc yelled at each other with their hands last night—

302

about Lora's mother and about how Ayc is supposed to be dead.

She's looking at Ayc like she can see straight through all of his lies. Sweat beads at the back of his neck. Ayc has too many secrets. They spin like a ball of yarn in his head. If one comes loose, the whole thing might unravel.

Lora stands. "We should pack up and go." Her bowl remains mostly full; her cup of tea untouched. The message is clear. She wants to be done with questions. Right now.

Bronwen rolls her eyes and opens her mouth, but Peregrin speaks first.

"Go where?" They drain the rest of the tea to down the gryphon feather they put within. "We have not yet decided what quest we will try for next."

Lora crosses her arms over her armored chest.

Peregrin sighs. "If you don't know, there is no sense running aimlessly around. We can sit and figure it out."

"Laud," Lora says with a finality of someone who has just come to a decision. "We should go to Laud."

Tavish sputters on his tea. "Laud? The land of the giants?"

Lora nods.

"Lora, *pirates* won't even go to Laud."

"Exactly." She brushes the fingers of her opposite hand against her chronicler. "Forge a new path."

Bronwen huffs, throws back the rest of her tea in two gulps, and stands. "Are you telling me you're so desperate to avoid a conversation with us that you're willing to sail all the way to fucking Laud? We're your Five. Don't insult us by pretending that last night didn't happen. What are you hiding? And what are you going to tell the Drakr?"

Lora stares past Bronwen at the shoreline. Gulls cry out

as they circle above the water. The fishing village to the north is already awake. Ships are setting sail from the docks and cutting across the sea. Ayc tries to deduct what the lines of Lora's face might mean, attempting to read motivations and plans in the curve of her jaw, the outward bow of her cheekbones. He desperately wants to see something there to prove that she is something other than clay that Yris has molded and formed into her own image. But Lora remains unreadable, like a book filled only with blank pages.

"Lora?" Peregrin presses when she's been silent far too long, using their cane to push to their feet. "What are you going to tell Lahlis?"

She inhales sharply through her nose and exhales the answer through her mouth. "I don't know."

Ayc's throat grows tight. The unspoken words are suffocating him, so he has to speak. "I can't be one of your Five if you make a deal with the Drakr."

Five pairs of eyes snap toward him, and they all bear different weight. Lora's are sharp as steel, Bronwen's wide with surprise, Xylie's soft with understanding. Ayc doesn't glance at Peregrin or Tavish. The others are enough to deal with on their own.

"I won't force you to serve me, Ayc," Lora says, ice edging her tone. "You're welcome to leave whenever you like."

Ayc bursts to his feet and paces a few steps away, before coming to an abrupt halt. "It's not that simple," he says. *And you know it,* he almost adds, but he grinds his teeth together, knowing the other four are marking his every word.

Lora scoffs. "It certainly is simple. I'll even pay for your passage on a ship back to Wyntra."

Oh, of course, she'd be ecstatic to have a reason to get rid of him. Heat boils on Ayc's tongue, begging for release.

Whatever he is about to say, he's certain it will begin a fire he won't be able to extinguish.

Peregrin interrupts him. "You might as well send me with him if you accept the deal."

The white broadens in Lora's eyes. "Peregrin..." Her voice cracks over the name, and she stops. She looks almost... hurt.

Bronwen flings her palms to her temples, shaking her head. "My divine, Lora, what is going through your head? I know you, and I know you want to tell that Drakr to go fuck himself. Don't you?"

"Of course, I do." Silver blazes in Lora's eyes. Her voice shakes, unsteady with anger... but there's something else there, too. Something a bit uncontrolled. "You of all people know what my mother's alliance with the Drakr has cost me. Has cost the people I love."

Xylie's breath shudders audibly as she pulls her coat around her tighter. Lora's stone mask fractures, giving a glimpse of empathy. Her hands raise, like she might sign something, then she drops them back to her sides. She looks from her cousin and back to Bronwen.

"And to hear that my mother made a deal to become Sovereign and that Everadyn should never have rightfully been hers, makes me so..." Lora growls as though she can't come up with the words. "I have exhausted myself these last few months trying to figure out why my mother would choose *now* to step down, when I'm half the age she was when she became Sovereign, younger than any Sovereign in history. All along it's because she bound herself to the Drakr all those years ago, and the price she was willing to pay in exchange–" Her voice doesn't break, but something groans beneath her flat tone, like steel placed under too much pressure. Her voice would shatter if she was made of something less strong.

Ayc, though, is made of weaker things. He is made of dough and cinnamon and other fragile creations. Hearing that creak in her voice nearly undoes him. It's evidence that he isn't the only one who remembers that day. Perhaps, he's not the only one who grieves what happened there.

"What did she do?" Bronwen asks, her voice gentler now.

Lora squares her jaw and says nothing.

Bronwen sighs. "Lora, we can't help you if you don't tell us what—"

"Creed Castle," Peregrin says.

Though their voice is quiet, its impact reverberates around the camp. Ayc closes his eyes to brace himself against it. He tries not to let himself go back to that day, but the memories live just a thought away. The blood. The screams. The fear.

"Peregrin, how dare you!" Lora snarls, fierce enough Ayc's eyes fly open. "You know what my mother has done to keep that secret."

Peregrin shrugs. "I know what your mother is capable of, Lora, but you chose me as your Third because I challenge you when you need it. And secrets have no place between you and your Five. We can't make decisions to protect you and Everadyn if we do not understand everything in play."

Lora's sharp canines grind into her lower teeth, then slowly recede back to points that match Ayc's own human mouth. Her fingers twitch at her side, like they would tremble if she let them.

"Creed Castle," Tavish repeats, dropping his fist that was

pressed to his lips. "Do you mean that your mother was responsible for the massacre at Creed Castle?"

Lora's shoulders fall. "Yes."

Tavish releases Saga's guide handle as his face blanches from its rich black to a muted gray. Even the blue brushing his cheekbones seems to dim its vibrancy. "Oh... fuck..."

Saga takes advantage of the new found freedom and bolts into the nearby grass. He yips happily. Tempest lifts her mighty head from where she's been slumbering, her beak still bloody from whatever her midnight meal was. Both creatures seem oblivious to the tension.

"In Adamant," Bronwen says in little more than a whisper, "in Battle Tactics class our first year, we learned about the massacre of Creed Castle. No one understands how the Drakr did it, because the wards should have kept out anyone not human or not escorted by a human. You suggested to the professor that Aluina was betrayed. It's because you knew."

Lora nods. She doesn't tell Bronwen that she was there, and Ayc doesn't speak. That is Lora's truth. She can confess it if she wants.

Bronwen goes on, "Your mother killed the royal family and everyone else within the castle. The wards were tied to the royal family bloodline. So long as someone of the royal family lived and remained within Aluina, the wards couldn't fall. So Lahlis had your mother kill them all. Nothing could stop the Drakr from overrunning Aluina, then."

Ayc tries to draw in a breath, but it gets stuck before it reaches his lungs. The memories rush in. *Blood. Screams. Silver at his throat.*

"But why everyone?" Tavish's voice sounds distant. "The

stories I heard... it wasn't just the royal family who were killed. It was everyone in that castle."

"I don't know," Lora says. Her fingers twitch again, and she wraps them around the hilts of her blades. The same black hilt she held in her hands ten years ago. "It was the order the Drakr gave. No one was to be left alive."

Her eyes flick toward Ayc. Ayc dares to look back, though he knows it'll make the little air he possesses in his lungs disappear entirely. Their gazes lock, and the tension sparks between them. They've never discussed what happened that day, but it lives like a wildfire between them, pushing them together and forcing them apart because it burns to be near. The connection blazes brighter in this moment, like a blade glowing red in the heat of a forge's fire.

Bronwen follows Lora's gaze and turns to Ayc. He watches the pieces snap together for her and hates the way her fierceness crumbles to sorrow.

"According to the Drakr, you're supposed to be dead," she repeats. Her hands press to her lips. "By the divine, Ayc. You were there."

Fabric brushes against Ayc's arm. Xylie stands beside him now, even though he never noticed her approach. She doesn't reach out again or look at him. She's simply there, at his side, and he's grateful.

"You're divina," Tavish says, tracing the circumference of the mark on his arm. "Did Yris spare you because of it?"

Ayc grinds his heels into the sand, anchoring himself against the rush of emotion, so he can keep his voice steady. "Our stories are quite alike, my friend."

Tavish tucks his head and runs the pearl at his throat between his fingers. "Really stings, doesn't it?" he murmurs at last.

Ayc barks out a one-syllable laugh—utterly humorless. "Yes, it fucking does."

Silence blankets over them, heavy with the truth. Ayc uses the quiet to calm the chaos with him. He inhales slowly, the air sharp with the salt, and watches as Saga continues to romp through the grass. He scampers around Tempest, occasionally dropping low and wagging his butt as though inviting Tempest to play. Tempest inspects her paw and the lethal claws at the end, as though coolly contemplating the consequences of ending the beast. Somehow, Ayc knows she wouldn't ever harm Saga. At least, not much.

Perhaps the innocence of the creatures gives him courage, because Ayc dares to speak. "Don't take the Drakr's deal, Lora," he pleads. "Please."

"I want *nothing* to do with the Drakr's deal," she snaps. "But I need time to consider the consequences. I suspect Lahlis won't take my refusal well. He could offer the deal to someone else. Can you imagine Marcellus with the help of the Drakr? Or maybe they won't form another alliance. Maybe they will just punish me instead."

"I doubt they would jeopardize their alliance with Yris by killing you," Peregrin states.

"You overestimate my mother's affection for me. Even so, that protection hardly extends to any of you. They could kill *all* of you. And even if somehow we survive it, what happens if I win without the Drakr's help? What happens if I start my role as Sovereign making it clear that I'm not interested in playing nice with them the way my mother is? I'll make an instant enemy. I understand that all of you hate this situation. Believe me, I do, too. But none of you are foolish enough to think it's a simple choice."

But that's just it. To Ayc, the answer *is* simple.

No. No. A thousand times *no*.

"I get it, Lora," Tavish says softly. "I get that sometimes we have to make allies of the people we despise, if only to survive." He stiffens, seeming to sense all the focus that locks onto him, and he hurries to add. "I'm not saying that you should work with the Drakr, but it would be foolish not to think it through."

"I need more time to think. So I plan to walk back to Duell." Lora points over her shoulder to the city in the distance, the one their airship landed in. The walls can be made out if Ayc squints, still a few miles walk. "And figure out when there is a ship headed east. Until then, give me time."

Another heavy silence falls. Ayc feels every little sound in his head. The fire's crackle, a gull's call, Bronwen's sigh, Peregrin's fingers drumming on their cane, Saga's yipping and Tempest's growl. Then one by one, everyone nods. Ayc nods last, reluctantly, but what choice does he have? Going back to Wyntra would only mean Yris sending him right back here, after inflicting whatever punishment she justifies.

Lora bends to roll up her pallet, and the rest turn to do the same. The porridge he made sits, almost untouched, in six separate bowls. Ayc dumps the remnants of the hot water on the fire. The flames sputter out and die, leaving only smoke curling up from the ashes.

CHAPTER
TWENTY

They make it a mile before Lora threatens Ayc with bodily harm, which he supposes is good progress.

"I swear to the divine, Ayc, if you don't stop dancing to whatever music only you can hear, I'm going to tie you to a fence post and leave you for the crows."

Ayc leaps and claps his heels together defiantly, careful not to trip in the ruts left in the dirt road by wagon wheels. He grins as Lora grumbles a string of curses beneath her breath. He doesn't really think she'll tie him to the wooden fence that stretches beside them, separating the road from a field with a flock of grazing sheep. In a small wooden tower built in the pasture, a guard clutches a bow and watches the sky, the only person besides Lora and her Five in view.

For the last half mile, Ayc has given into his incessant inability to sit still—even apparently when going on a long, but under-stimulating walk. He's hummed to himself, shimmied his shoulders and occasionally done a few jigs. Nothing that will make his pain worse, but enough to expend his nervous energy. Meanwhile, the irritation that billows off Lora like a storm cloud has merely been a perk.

Peregrin, riding on Tempest, leads the way of the group, followed by Ayc and Lora. Xylie and Tavish walk side by side just behind them, Tavish pulled along by Saga. Bronwen brings up the rear, her staff in her hand.

Ayc turns and walks backward so he can face Lora, giving her a cheeky grin. "You're just cranky because you didn't drink the tea I made you this morning. Everyone loves my dancing."

"I'm sure," she retorts. "Like people love a pinecone shoved up their ass."

"Can you two *not*?" Peregrin yells from where they ride on Tempest. More to themselves, they grumble, "It's too early for their shit."

Ayc swallows down his retort, and Lora presses her mouth into a hard line. Lora may be the leader, but Peregrin has been their teacher for so long that defiance feels unnatural. Still, Ayc can't resist one last comeback. So he crosses his eyes and sticks out his tongue.

She lunges for him, and he leaps away from her. Her fingers merely brush the protesting muscles of his back. If she really wanted, she would have thrown him to the ground with no effort, but she only wanted him silent. They've been doing this dance for a long time now, and after the tension and vulnerability of this morning, it's strangely comforting to be back to normal again.

From behind them, Bronwen laughs.

Ayc doesn't dance again, but he still needs a distraction. "Well, if no one else is going to ask, why Laud?"

"As I said," Lora says, "to forge a new path."

"There must be easier ways. Everadyn is in better terms

with the dwarves, right? Surely their tunnels in the Stella Rune Mountains have a few unexplored pathways they might let us wander down. Might meet a few more wraiths; they were just *lovely* creatures." The Stella Rune Mountains, which take up much of central Everadyn, south of the Elodie forest, is divided in ownership between the dwarves and the fae. Everything on top of the mountains, like the Lycendi villages built upon them, belong to the fae. But everything beneath belongs to the dwarves.

Xylie makes a sound deep in her throat, and Ayc glances behind to see her sign, *"I'm not going into those caves."*

"Not enough dragons for you?" Ayc asks. He adjusts the pack on his shoulders, the one now holding both his own and Xylie's blankets, keeping the dragon egg warm. His hands are still bandaged and covered with gloves. They left camp too quickly for Xylie to re-wrap them. But his hands don't hurt as he grasps the straps.

"Yes, we're on good terms with the dwarves," Lora says. Ayc slows a little, so he walks alongside her, but stays far enough away that he's out of her reach. "And Everadyn fae and giants have not had contact since the war at the beginning of my grandfather's reign. We're not enemies, but we're not friends. We simply... pretend the other doesn't exist."

"I'd like to keep pretending," Tavish mutters under his breath. Lora and Ayc glance behind them, and he shrugs. "It's mainly just the stepping on me thing. Giants are terrifying."

"How would *you* know?" Lora says, her tone flat. "How would *any* of us know? We just go off stories we are told as children. Giants are terrifying. Drakr are evil. Dwarves are greedy. Humans are weak."

Ayc hides his wince behind a crooked smile. "And from what *I* heard as a child, the Everadyn fae are vicious creatures who could kill me with a single look of their silver eyes."

"Exactly. It's all gryphon shit."

Not missing a step, Tempest twists her head to the side to glare at Lora.

"She didn't mean it, Tempest," Ayc assures.

Tempest snaps her beak.

Peregrin mutters, "Now, friend, you know you hate the way fae taste. Too much sinew."

Unfazed, Lora sweeps her hand through the tall grass that grows alongside the fence, running the tail between her fingers. This far south, the weather is more temperate, and the grass has already grown thick. Ayc studies the fine movements of her long fingertips.

"So, we can't trust the biases we're taught as children?" Ayc repeats, wondering if she truly means it. Does she really not think him weak because he's human?

Lora nods.

Huh, Ayc thinks. *That's... unexpected.*

"That's fair," Tavish says. "But still... why the giants?"

A wagon approaches from the direction of the city, drawn by a team of mules. They step to the side of the road to allow them to pass. The mules bray anxiously at the sight of Tempest, and only the skilled hands of the driver keep them from bolting in terror.

When they are walking up the road once more, Lora answers Tavish's question, "Like Bronwen said, the magic in the chroniclers is old." She rolls her wrist with the chronicler. It circles around her arm, the glow casting a faint light against her skin. "I don't trust that my mother didn't find a way to manipulate it somehow, but it would have been limited. Old magical items tend to take on a life of their own for whatever purpose they were created. And that is to prove whether the wearer is worthy of being Sovereign. All the quests seem designed to test the character of a person. Even the one that seemed simple—unearth a great treasure—was completed not from something of financial worth, but an intangible one. For friendship and family.”

It may be more words than Lora has ever strung together in Ayc’s presence. From the corner of his eye, Ayc studies the movement of her lips, noticing every tick and curve. He hopes if he says nothing, he won't break whatever spell has made her talk to him so much, without any sign of anger.

“So," she continues, "I think that the best way to solve the quests is to show what type of leader I intend to be and the world I want to create as Sovereign.”

Ayc turns so he can face her more fully. “And what is that world?”

She cocks her head. “Shouldn’t you have asked me that before you said yes to being my Fifth?”

Ayc rolls his eyes at the clear avoidance. “Probably.”

“Then why did you say yes so easily?”

Ayc senses the ones behind them watching, listening. “Probably for the same justifications as you asking me.” He draws a finger through the air like he’s spelling the word out. “Reasons. I had my reasons.”

She presses her lips together in a hard line. Fine, clearly she still means to be as transparent with him as a thick log. Three days ago, he thought he understood everything about Lora. He made himself believe she was Yris’s little copy, but now—he’s seen her defend Xylie and Bronwen and strangely, even Ayc himself. He's learned that she warned Peregrin when they were children. He's watched her fight to save the mother dragon and learned how she slaughtered pirates and freed human children. He's studied the regret in her eyes when she speaks of Creed. And fuck, if all her contradictions are not driving him to distraction. He doesn't know which is worse: that he realizes he doesn't know her, or how desperately he *wants* to know her, to finally glimpse beyond the stone she presents to the world.

"Do you delight in avoiding questions?" Ayc asks, unable to stop himself from the verbal jab. "Because nowhere in there was an actual explanation of why we're going to see the giants."

Lora has only uttered a syllable when a bird's shriek rips through the sky. The group freezes as a small, dark shape contrasts against the bright sunlight. Ayc sweeps his unbound hair out of his face as he squints upward. Dark gray wings beat hard as the bird of prey banks toward the ground, not slowing as it dives straight toward them. Ayc stumbles back, but Lora raises her arm. The bird lands upon it in, wrapping its talons around her armor. Talons that Ayc immediately notices are painted a bright pink. A small scroll is bound to one leg with an equally pink ribbon.

Vidar's falcon.

Lora reaches for the scroll, but the falcon snips at her fingers and she recoils. The falcon flutters its wings and screeches.

"Easy," Bronwen says as she appears at Lora's shoulder. She rubs a gentle hand over the bird's head, and it drops its wings long enough for Lora to untie the scrolls.

The bird hops from Lora's arm to Bronwen's shoulder, and Lora unrolls the scroll. Xylie slips between Ayc and Lora and stands on her tiptoes to see the letter, blocking Ayc from getting close enough to read as well. Tempest turns and carries Peregrin back toward them, as though she too can sense the tension rising from Bronwen and Lora.

Lora unleashes a tirade of curses. "The package was intercepted."

Bronwen pales. "Lux Aester?"

Lora nods, the very edges of her royal blue eyes flashing silver.

"Oh no," Tavish mutters, as Xylie flutters her hands near her face. Ayc begins to suspect he's the only one who doesn't know what's happening.

"Where?" Bronwen demands, with enough force it startles the falcon into flight. It settles on the ground a few feet away and pecks at the ground.

"The last known location was at the northwest border of the Forest of Elodie," Lora says. She presses the message into Bronwen's hand. The sorcerer quickly scans the rest.

"We have to go," Lora says, before shifting her attention from her First to her Third. "Peregrin?"

Tempest crouches low so Peregrin can slide off easily. "Tempest is willing to carry you."

"And Bronwen?" Lora asks.

"Yes."

Lora and Bronwen march toward the gryphon.

"Wait, what exactly is happening?" Ayc asks. "You're running off to go rescue some opium?"

Whatever it is, it *isn't* opium. He definitely knows that, but the words have the desired effect. Lora swings back around to face him.

"The *opium*," Lora snarls, the silver momentarily taking up her eyes, "is a sixteen-year-old boy attempting to flee from Lux Aester to avoid marrying a fae three times his age and being forced to live as a gender other than his true self."

Ayc blinks. "What?"

"Lora and I started an organization," Bronwen explains, so rapidly her words tumble over each other. "A group of volunteers throughout Everadyn who help people escape Lux Aester to freedom. Not everyone is lucky enough to have a magical gift and get sent away like I did."

For years, Ayc has watched other regents and other citizens come to plead with Yris to take actions against the Lux Aester—to stop them from ripping away the rights of the fae within their clan. She has been immovable, maintaining that each clan has the right to make their own laws. She has chosen time and time again to protect the rights of the oppressors, instead of the oppressed. Perhaps, because of the money the Lux Aester temples contribute to the royal treasury.

And meanwhile, Lora has been running an organization that saves the people whom her mother refused to help.

He stares at Lora. "Your mother doesn't know?"

"No, she would stop us if she did."

Just like she stopped other rebellions, like the one that helped Aluina.

"And you all knew about this?" Ayc asks, glancing at the others.

Peregrin, Xylie, and Tavish all nod.

Peregrin explains, "I've helped ensure that those allowed in Final Testing are placed in a position that will get them far out of Lux Aester reach."

Tavish says, "I've sheltered those who needed it."

And Xylie signs, "*I help with logistics and planning.*"

Of course she does. She's probably brilliant at it.

Ayc turns back to Lora, who lifts her jaw, wearing her invisible crown. He sees it clearly then, what he's only caught glimpses of before, like spying a glint of light off the edge of razor-sharp metal. Beyond the stone of her expression, beyond her ferocity and power, there is kindness.

And fuck, he likes it. It makes his long-buried hope burst like sunlight breaking out from behind storm clouds, until his skin blazes with familiar warmth.

For the first time, he understands why the rest of the Five follow her so willingly. If this is what she meant by the world she means to create as Sovereign—one where all people are free to exist as themselves—then perhaps Ayc is wrong. Perhaps, she's not her mother at all.

Perhaps, she is someone worth serving.

"We need to go," Lora says, taking another step toward Tempest and resting her hand on the beast's shoulders to prepare to mount.

Bronwen follows, then hesitates. The look she casts Ayc's over her shoulder causes his stomach to twist. "Lora, wait. I think you should take Ayc instead."

"*What?*" Lora barks, as the same time as Ayc mutters, "You're fucking kidding, right?"

Bronwen positions herself so she can face both Lora and Ayc. "Hear me out. Vidar's letter says there's at least a dozen Lux Aester. We can't slaughter them all."

Lora bares her teeth. "Watch me."

Ayc almost laughs. There's the viciousness he knows. Turned toward injustice, her ferocity looks wicked and beautiful all at once.

"I mean, you *can*," Bronwen amends, "but not without

outing the entire organization. We won't be able to keep it from Yris if we leave a dozen dead bodies behind us."

Lora's mouth twists—like she knows Bronwen is right and doesn't like it.

Bronwen gestures to Ayc with her staff. "But Ayc has a talent that would allow him to go unseen."

Xylie whips her head toward Ayc so quickly that her braids fly, doubt spelled out on her face. But Lora looks him up and down, her eyes lightening from royal to a sky blue. The warmth beneath his skin creeps up. She's considering it.

"Bronwen's right," Peregrin says. "We can't afford to expose ourselves and start a war. Not yet. Even if it's one worth fighting."

Three more heartbeats pound against his sternum as Lora studies him. Boom, boom, boom.

Then she draws in a long breath and asks, "Ayc, will you help me?"

Ayc's bracelets feel suddenly too tight upon his wrists. A promise long ago tugs at his throat, as potent as any vow. Nothing good could ever come from his tricks, his mother warned. He has used them only to survive. But Ayc only has to imagine that boy, who has lived his life in a prison. Prison —because what other word is there for an existence where you are hated for who you truly are, and therefore, must hide it at all costs?

And, for once, Ayc has power to make a difference.

Ayc is already walking forward, pulling his hair back from his face and securing it with the ribbon on his wrist. "Let's fucking do this."

CHAPTER
TWENTY-ONE

Ayc pauses only long enough to turn to Xylie, shrug out of his pack and drop it carefully at her feet. "There's rations in there. Better leave it with you." Ayc winks, just in case she doesn't understand.

She nods. Tavish tilts his head curiously as Saga sniffs the pack. Hopefully, Saga can't pick up the smell of a dragon's egg.

Ayc starts to turn. Xylie grabs his wrist. *"Your hands,"* she signs. *"I never redressed them."*

"It'll be fine," Ayc says.

Xylie makes a sound of protest, but he's already heading toward Lora who waits by Tempest's side. Xylie darts past him, yanks a bottle and some rolled bandage from her bag, and presses them toward Lora. *"Change his dressings, or he won't be able to wield a sword."*

"Thanks, Mother," Ayc says.

"Slip them into my pack," Lora says, twisting and crouching so Xylie can reach.

When Xylie steps back, Tempest bows her head and forelegs. Lora grabs a fistful of feathers and swings gracefully onto Tempest's back. Ayc doesn't hesitate to mount behind her, and so he doesn't realize his mistake until her spine nearly presses to his chest. The impact is instant—a lightning bolt that flares all the way to his fingertips and down to his toes, leaving his skin blazing in its wake. He did not properly consider the full consequences of his decisions—the repercussions of Lora's body being so close to his own.

Fuck me.

Tempest paces a few steps to the right and spreads her wings wide. Ayc wobbles, and he reaches instinctively toward Lora's sides to steady himself. He freezes before his hands can land on Lora's hips and tightens his legs around the barrel of Tempest's body. His muscles protest, aching, and he knows he'll regret leaving his pain tonics behind.

"Go to Duell and find a tavern," Lora says to the others. "We'll find you there."

"Get back before Lahlis comes," Peregrin warns. "You don't want to be out there alone when he finds you again. And for fuck's sake, Ayc, don't do anything foolish."

Ayc shoots him a childish grin. "Love you too, Peregrin."

Tempest flings herself into the sky without warning. Ayc bites back a cry of surprise and tightens his thighs, but the muscles that always ache only hold for a moment before the pain intensifies past his tolerance. He slips backward, pushing against Tempest's wings.

Lora catches both his wrists and steers them around her waist. "Hold onto me. We need to fly hard."

No. Just fucking no.

But she lays his hands on the outward bow of her stomach, and even through the gloves and dressing, it's too much. His awareness screams at the contact. Unaware of the chaos she has created, Lora seizes feathers once more. Tempest continues her ascent into the clouds, her wings sounding like thunderclaps. Lora bends herself lower to Tempest's neck to shelter from the wind that roars past them. Her back arches away from Ayc, but her hips slide backward until only an inch separates her bountiful ass from his—

Fuck! Ayc thinks again. *I'm so fucking fucked.*

The heat fills every inch of him, turning his blood from a simmer to a full boil. He hardens at her nearness. If her ass slides back any further, there will be no hiding exactly how much his entire body is betraying him.

And not just his cock. His hands are traitors, too They long to press tighter into the soft flesh of her stomach, to measure the exact curvature of her wide hips, to slide down the hills of her thick thighs. Instead, he forms them into fists, hard enough they tremble.

He's generally better at controlling his emotions than this. He's learned how to mitigate pain: to treat it with tonics, or to drown it out with music or sex, or to seal it behind mental walls so it's only a hollowed echo—ever present but survivable. He has always dealt with the way his traitorous body longs for Lora the same way. He hides his desire behind locks and walls and ridiculous jokes. When he keeps her at a distance, it's so easy to pretend he does not want her.

He even managed it when they were in the Ever River, when they both had far fewer clothes. But that feels like months ago. Before Peregrin told Ayc about the way she rescued him, before she risked her life to save Xylie, before he found that she secretly defies her mother to free the innocent.

Before she began chipping away all the reasons he's supposed to hate her.

Tempest flies slower now. Vidar's falcon is in the sky before them. Its wings beat hard, straining to stay ahead of Tempest, leading the way.

Ayc inhales the crisp air through his nose. The wind blows Lora's loose hair back into his face, and he catches the scent of it. They have been traveling for days, but the scent is strong. After everyone fell asleep last night, did she work oils into her hair like Xylie had, in an attempt to rescue her curls from the saltwater? The scent is rich and smooth, like heavy cream, but within lies another scent. Sharp, sweet, and earthy, all at once. Familiar, but it takes a moment to place it.

Is that... anise?

Fuck, why does she have to smell like anise? He loves anise, loves the star-shapes they come in and the potent taste it gives his baking creations.

Lora tightens her hands in the feathers. He can't see her face, but he is sure her expression is fixed in determination and focus. She is utterly composed, and she has no idea that he's hanging on by a thread.

This is... this is how he dies. This is surely going to kill him, if he doesn't figure out a way to regain control.

"Hey, Lora," he calls over the wind, "have you heard the one where—*oomph!*"

Her elbow sails back and collides with his ribcage. It's

what he needed; a sharp stab of reality. She hates him... and he hates her.

I hate her. I hate her. I hate her.

It's the mantra he fills his head with until he can forget the truth, until the fire at his skin slowly begins to recede.

"How long ago did you start this organization?" Ayc asks, wanting to focus on anything else.

She straightens, putting some distance between them. With each fraction of an inch, Ayc can breathe a little easier. "My second year at Adamant."

The ground sails by far beneath them in patches of farmer's fields surrounding a village. He can tell they're still in Noxumbra by the large training arena found at the village's edge. Fighting is a sport that almost all Noxumbra participate in. Tempest lets out a vibrating cry, and the hawk responds with a shriek of its own. The heat in Ayc's skin continues to relinquish to the coolness of the wind, but it never fully surrenders. He's still keenly aware of Lora's every move.

"How do you fund it?" Ayc remembers the coins Lora pressed into Vidar's palm. "Surely an organization like this costs money, and I'm certain your mother makes you account for every bit of spending with the money she gives you."

"I don't need her money," she states. "I earn it."

"With the opium?" Ayc teases.

"No, I pay for it with my art." She says it quietly, almost like she hopes he won't hear. Vulnerability creeps into her voice. Instinctively, his arms tighten around her, a strange longing to comfort her. She heaves a quick breath, in and out, and he releases the hold.

"I weave tapestries," Lora continues. "And knit clothes. And I sell them at fairs and festivals throughout Everadyn."

"I know," Ayc admits.

"You do?"

"I've seen the booths at the festivals." But he knew about her talent before then. Since the time he arrived at Wyntra, he would see her hiding in dark corners with her books and her knitting needles. He knew she created Xylie's treasured multi-colored coat. And at every festival he's attended, he's walked through Lora's booth, letting the buttery material of her creations flow over his fingertips. He would always tell himself he wouldn't go, but he responded to the booth's presence like a siren's call, like he couldn't resist being near something Lora created with her own hands.

Lora never runs the booth herself; she has always been at Adamant. Instead, it's tended by a Totus Omni fae by the name Hellevi, an elder female with deep brown skin and eyes that shift in color, just like Lora's. She sits in the corner, knitting so quickly her needles look as fearsome as knives. She's always kind to the people who wander in, but her ability to negotiate the best price for the artwork is ruthless. It took a lot of charming—and bribing with baked goods— for Hellevi to admit what Ayc suspected: that she's Lora's grandmother, the mother of Lora's father.

Ayc hesitates before adding, "Your art is really beautiful, Lora."

Lora glares at him over her shoulder, as though thinking he's teasing her. But she must see his sincerity, because her face relaxes. "Thank you. My mother always believed it to be a waste of time."

"Your mother believes a lot of foolish things. If the only thing your art does is bring you joy, it isn't a waste of time."

The corner of her lips creep up and then fall. Fuck, what he'd give to see her fully smile. Or laugh. He's done so many foolish things to get her to laugh. He'd do even more.

He'd do such foolish things for her.

Ayc, you're being an ass. Stop it.

"I heard you have a booth at many of the festivals now as well," she says. "Does it bring you joy?"

It's such an odd question, but Ayc replies honestly, "Yes. There's something about creating something beautiful from nothing that makes me feel—" He trails off, certain that whichever words he chooses will seem ridiculous.

"Important?" Lora suggests. "Powerful? Like you've done something worthy of existing?"

Those words are not quite what Ayc imagined, and yet, they are perfect. "Yes."

He didn't think that this would be something he'd share with Lora. The headiness of mutual understanding settles over them. Perhaps, Lora feels it too, because her body relaxes. It brings her closer to him, her pack pressing into his chest. He inhales, the anise filling his nose again, and the fire awakens. But this time, it isn't blistering hot. It's warm and comfortable. Like sitting before the hearth after a long winter day.

And somehow, that feels even more dangerous.

"Why do you stay at Wyntra?" He tenses at her question, but she presses on. "Why don't you go out on your own and create a business? Own a bakery like your mother did? People love your baking. I am certain it would be successful."

Ayc frowns. Why is she asking? Surely, she already

knows the answer. "Well, your mother would hate to lose her favorite baker."

Lora's back tenses once more, and a sharpness gnaws at her tone. "My mother says you are free to go and do whatever you please. Is that not true?"

Ayc's mind whirls at the question. Lora knows that Ayc isn't free, doesn't she? She must understand the power that Yris has over him. But if Yris lied to her, then maybe—

Tempest follows the falcon in a sudden, steep dive. Ayc tightens his grip around Lora, his palms blazing at the place where it contacts the outward curve of her stomach. Tempest pulls up just as quickly. She soars below the clouds now, and the air becomes a little less thin.

Lora's fingers uncurl from around the feathers; the heat of them flutters near his hands. His breath stills, and the moment stretches on with the uncertainty of whether she'll touch him. Then her hand curls around Tempest's side once more.

Ayc exhales. There are hours left of this flight, and he's not sure he'll survive.

"Ayc?" Lora presses. "Why have you stayed in Wyntra for so long?"

"It's..." Ayc looks around him, as though the right words might be written in the sky. "It's complicated."

When she turns her head once more, her eyes are a startling lilac, a lighter purple than he's seen before. "What hold does my mother still have on you? I suspect it's something strong, just like I suspect it's the only reason you agreed to be my Fifth."

He searches her face, the line that forms between her eyebrows. For the first time, he's certain. She doesn't know. Fuck, *she doesn't know*. The astonishment knots his tongue.

Even if he could manage to untangle it, he can't tell her, not if he doesn't want his head to feel as though it's splitting open. Besides, she has enough power over him already.

When he doesn't answer, Lora heaves out a breath. "Fine. You can keep your secrets." She shifts forward again as Tempest picks up speed, her ass sliding back once more.

And fuck, this gryphon ride cannot be over soon enough.

By the time they reach the northern edge of the forest of Elodie, Ayc's pain has passed his normal threshold. Every jolt rocks his sore muscles as Tempest slips between the entwined branches of the towering evergreen trees and lands heavily on the forest floor. When he slides off, his knees threaten to buckle, and he clasps ahold of Tempest's side. A cold sweat breaks out on his neck. Blackness tints his vision. No, he will not let this pain get the best of him. Not today. Not when a boy's life depends on him.

"Are you all right?" Lora asks, as she slides down beside him.

"Fine," he says through his teeth.

She arches an eyebrow, unconvinced.

He unlocks his jaw and says it again, "I'm fine. Just a muscle cramp. I only need a minute."

Her brow remains furrowed, but she walks away to give him space. Ayc focuses on his breathing, the way Peregrin taught him. In through his nose; out through his mouth.

Tempest clacks her beak and brushes her wing against Ayc's shoulder. Ayc turns to see one silver eye fixed upon him, as though attempting to tell him something. She rustles her wing again.

"Are you sure?" Ayc asks.

Another clack of her beak.

He glances over his shoulder, but Lora's back is turned as she drinks from her canteen of water. He quickly finds a small, noncritical feather in Tempest's wing and plucks it. He hides it in the palm of his hand as he approaches Lora. She turns at the sound of his footsteps and offers her canteen without a word, before surveying the clearing where they stand once more. The falcon waits on a broad branch of one of the towering trees, shuffling its wings impatiently.

Ayc swallows the feather with a bit of water. Without a warm beverage to ease the passage, it gets stuck in his throat. Sputtering, he gulps down another drink, his eyes watering.

"Are you dying?" Lora asks.

Ayc coughs. "Not today."

"Pity." But her lips tip upward, the dry sarcasm clear for once.

The gryphon feather works its magic, like a breath of fresh air. The pain diminishes but does not completely fade. It turns instead to the stiffness that he would expect of any other body that underwent hours on the gryphon.

The falcon calls out to them and then glides to another tree branch, farther away.

"I think he wants us to follow," Ayc says.

Lora already moves over the forest floor, a hand resting on one of her swords. The bird leads them through the trees. The forest is denser here, on the border, than further south where the Totus Omni build their homes. Here, the trees nearly touch, and their branches entwine to form a roof above them. Ayc and Lora squeeze between the trunks and slip through the shadows as the falcon darts from one tree to the next, leading them closer to the edge of the forest. Tempest prowls after them, occasionally taking a different route when her massive body doesn't fit in the tight path between trees.

Lora holds up a hand to halt Ayc. She cocks her head, listening, and soon Ayc hears it, too. Voices. Footsteps. The snort of a horse. Lora crouches low and creeps forward in the brush. Ayc copies her movements, thighs shaking from exhaustion as he holds the position. Thorns scrap across their armor as they go. They stop at the very outskirt of the forest. An open plain stretches before them.

Fifty yards away, a party of at least a dozen men on horseback pick their way across the trodden path in the field. Each Lux Aester fae wears the traditional sky-blue tunics, embroidered with suns. In the center of the group, one horse bears two riders, one rider's arms bracketing the boy before him. The boy looks utterly hopeless, his hair sheared crooked and messy, his tunic two sizes too large, ropes biting into his wrists. Ayc grinds his teeth together.

Lora curses beneath her breath and draws her sword.

Ayc grabs her arm. "We have to wait," he says, keeping his voice low.

She shakes him off. "For what?"

"Until nightfall."

"You can't go invisible *now?*"

"I can sneak *in* now, but I have to be able to get him out, and *he* can't turn invisible. If we go now, we risk him getting hurt."

Lora stares out at the party. She fists her hand so hard around her sword that it trembles.

"You're right," she spits out, like she hates the taste of

the words. Her eyes turn silver, bright in the dimness. "I want to rip every single one of them apart for doing that to him."

Ayc's shivers, but he knows now her viciousness doesn't frighten him. It thrills him.

"What's his name?" Ayc whispers.

Lora sighs. "Ohen."

"Have you met him?"

"No. Does that matter?"

Ayc shakes his head. "No, it really doesn't."

Ayc and Lora follow the Lux Aester party from the shadow of the trees for two hours. Vidar's falcon has disappeared, but Tempest remains close by. Despite her size, her paws make no sound as she makes her way through the brush, though occasionally Ayc hears the snap of bones as another unfortunate squirrel runs into her path and becomes a lovely snack.

As the sun dips toward the west, the Lux Aester stop to make camp. Crouched low in the shadows, Ayc and Lora watch them pitch tents and start a fire to cook food. One bastard drags Ohen into a tent, still tied up. When they are certain the Lux Aester will remain for the night, Lora and Ayc retreat farther into the woods to wait until the sun has fully set.

Nervous energy builds beneath Ayc's skin as they gnaw on provisions from Lora's bag. It settles the ache in his stomach, but does nothing to ease the tension, the heavy responsibility of knowing that boy's fate rests with him. He pushes himself to his feet, debating whether pacing will release the energy or merely worsen his pain, but Lora stops him.

"Let me dress your hands."

A little constriction at his throat tells Ayc that he won't be able to resist. He flops down in front of where Lora sits next to a tree with gnarled roots sprawling in all directions. She opens her pack which sits beside her and pulls out the vial and dressings Xylie put there. Ayc peels off a glove and unwinds the old dressing. He stares at the skin of his palm. What was once a raw and blistered mess is now nothing but smooth skin.

Lora's hands tighten on the vial. She blinks at his hand. "It looks... fine." She draws a finger over the skin, from the heel of his hand to the tip of his middle finger. Her touch is featherlight, but fuck, it awakens Ayc's nerves to sing an entirely different song from the anxiety.

I hate her, he tells himself. *I hate her.*

She grasps his other wrist and gently—almost too gently—removes that glove. A few more careful movements and the dressing fall away to reveal that hand healed as well.

Lora's brow knits. "I saw your hands yesterday. They were... much worse than this."

"That salve Xylie put on them must have worked wonders," Ayc says, pulling his hands away and fisting them against his thighs.

"She *is* powerful," Lora agrees, but her brow doesn't relax.

"She's going to be the best alchemist of this age. Evander would be jealous."

Lora cocks her head, like he's a puzzle she's trying to solve. But then she looks away and shoves the bandage and salve back into her pack. She opens the pack wider and shuffles a few things inside in her search for something else.

"Who's Evander?" she asks.

The knot that's already in his stomach tugs tighter. He shouldn't have said anything. He was just trying to distract her from his hands. "The master of the apothecary at Creed Castle. He was a bit of a physician, too. Brilliant, though not formally trained."

She stiffens, every muscle drawing taut. She withdraws slowly from the pack, a book in her hand—the one she carries for reading, not for writing. "Is that the man I..." She trails off.

"Yes," Ayc says, softly.

She stares hard at the book's cover, the one that bears dark swirls, but no title. The silence hovers between them, thick and slow as molasses. Somewhere in the deeper shadows of the woods, a squirrel shrieks and bones crunch as Tempest finds yet another snack.

"What book is that?" Ayc says, to save them both from this moment. Growing up, he saw Lora with a book as often as he saw Lora with a sword, but he's never dared to ask. Now seems as good a time as any.

"What?" she says, her voice rising an octave. She clutches the book to her chest, splaying her hands over it to hide it from his view. "It's nothing."

Ayc frowns at her odd reaction. She's acting almost like she did when he stripped his clothing at the river. "Your book is called *Nothing*? What a peculiar title."

She narrows her eyes.

"If you're embarrassed to be reading such a stuffy classic," Ayc teases, "you could just say so."

She ticks up her chin and returns to her cool tone. "If you

think it's stuffy, there's no reason to discuss it with you, is there? And maybe you should keep your nose out of my business before I remove it from your face."

Ayc throws up his hands in surrender. "Very well, then. I'll leave you to it."

He paces a few feet, but the release of energy does little to expel the tension in his skin, so he keeps moving. Lora settles back against the tree, nestled in between two arching roots. She cracks open her book, somehow finding her space without anything to mark it, and begins to read. Tempest returns and stretches out on a patch of moss, soaking in the few rays of swiftly fading sunlight that make it through the evergreen branches above, preening at her feathers.

Pages turn, the wind whispers, and pine needles crunch beneath his feet. It's too quiet to drown out the sound in Ayc's head. He torments himself with all the scenarios of the plan before them. He imagines all the way tonight might end disastrously, of how he might ruin everything.

Lora sets the book face down over a root, stands and stretches her arms above her head. Ayc forces himself to look at his feet so he doesn't stare at the arch of her spine.

"I'll be right back," she says, before slipping between the trees and heading deeper into the forest. No doubt to relieve herself out of his earshot.

Ayc paces a few more steps, and then his focus draws back to the book she left. He thinks of the way she reacted earlier, like she had something to hide. And here is the perfect opportunity to settle his curiosity. As soon as the idea enters his mind, he knows it's a tremendously bad idea. But he knows he's going to do it anyway.

Glancing the way Lora went to make sure she's still gone, he hurries to the tree and snatches the book up.

Keeping his finger in the book to mark her place, he flips back to the title page.

A Measure of Perfection by Allari Rose.

Very well, certainly not a classic he's ever heard of, not that he's the most knowledgeable in literature. He's never been able to force his mind to focus all the way through a book. He turns back to the page Lora is on and reads the top line.

...the baker's tongue trails up my inner thigh, tracing the path of chocolate pudding that leads straight to my...

Oh...

Ayc nearly drops the book in surprise.

Oh!

A delighted smile yanks at his lips as he continues to read. This is definitely *not* a classic book. This is filthy and dirty, and he didn't know that books like this existed, but he thinks he might have finally found a novel he'll enjoy—

"What are you doing?"

Ayc snaps his head upward. Lora stands a few feet away. His heart skitters.

Well, if she's going to murder him, he might as well have some fun with it.

"I was curious about what you were reading, and since you wouldn't tell me, I thought I'd take a peek," Ayc says, keeping his tone warm. Teasing. "I have to say, the baker in this is really creative with his use of chocolate pudding. And, of course, his other non-baking tools."

Her eyes fling wide with horror. It's perhaps the most expression he's ever gotten from her face, and a crow of delight escapes his mouth before he can stop it. He slaps a hand over his lips, but her face has already locked into a look of pure mercilessness.

She charges toward him, and he jumps back and holds the book up out of her reach. He has few advantages over her, but his height is one of them.

"Is this the sort of book you normally read?" he asks.

She doesn't answer, only twirls to reach the book from a different angle. He spins out of her way, and for the second time, surprise fractures her face.

Her eyes darken with fury. "Lots of people read those books."

"I'm not judging you. I'm rather impressed, actually. Is that the sort of thing you like?"

He wants to yank the question back down his throat, because no sooner has he uttered it than he imagines it. Lora spread out and bare, every curve of her abundant body on full display as his mouth forges a pathway to the core of her. Hot. Fuck, he is instantly so hot that red tinges his vision. Closing his eyes, he rapidly retreats from Lora, trying to buy enough time to take a cooling breath.

A branch snaps beneath Lora's foot, clumsy in her haste, and he opens his eyes in just enough time to see her lunge. He jumps back, but too slowly. She slams into him, her hand wrapping around his neck as she propels him back into the tree. She pins him there, chest-to-chest, her fingers curled around his throat. She doesn't squeeze, doesn't constrict his airway, and yet he cannot breathe. The air around them surges and vibrates the way it does during an electrical storm, the hair on his arms standing at attention. He holds the book up still, but she doesn't reach for it. She's just as frozen as he is. Her full lips part as though she has surprised *herself*. And those lips are so close to his—so painfully close—that he can feel her unsteady exhale.

Ayc has survived many things.

He will not survive this moment.

It aches and longs and bleeds in his chest, and he cannot stand here, sharing air with her. A moment more, and his hold on his control will fracture and he will haul her mouth to his and erase the distance between them.

So, he gives her his best wicked grin and covers her hand with his. He presses her fingers in, just enough to feel the pressure against his pounding pulse. "Harder," he whispers. "I like it harder."

Just as he predicted, she reels back, her eyes flashing silver. She paces away from him, then spins back, planting her hands on her hips. Her breath comes in quick bursts, like she's run a dozen miles. He forces himself to lean casually on the tree and inhale through his nose so she doesn't notice how unsteadily he's breathing, too.

"I swear you were put here by the divine just to torment me," Lora says, through her teeth. "You will be my ruin."

"You're already mine."

Lora goes utterly still, and Ayc wishes he could bite back the words. He swiftly holds the book out to her. "Here."

She eyes it wearily, like it's a trap. Then she snatches it from his grasp. It snaps closed, losing her place.

"Maybe you'll let me borrow it sometime," Ayc says.

She clutches the book closer to her armored chest. "No, because then you'll dogear it or spill coffee on it, and I'll have to kill you. I don't let people borrow my books."

In the last few days, Ayc has learned so many new things about Lora. She dances when no one is watching. She risks everything to rescue kids her mother has abandoned. *And* she reads filthy, sexy books and loves them enough to kill for them. It might be his favorite detail yet.

"All right, I'll get my own copy," Ayc says. He snaps his

fingers. "I have a brilliant idea. We should start a book club. I can bring treats."

Her narrowed eyes are cold enough they would freeze his blood, if he hadn't nearly been set on fire a few moments go. "I fucking hate you," she snaps and then whirls around with enough force her cape waves and her hair sails around her. "It's almost dark. We should go watch the camp."

She marches away, and Ayc fixes his eyes on the back of her head and nowhere else on her body—definitely not her swaying hips—least his mind return to images he has no business entertaining.

From her spot in the dim light, Tempest clacks her beak repeatedly, like she's laughing at him. Like she knows.

He gives the beast the finger and follows Lora.

Long after darkness has fallen, the Lux Aester finally go to sleep, taking their places in the tents or spread out on bedrolls on the ground. One stretches before the tent where Ohen is imprisoned, and another remains awake, pacing around the perimeter of the camp. Their fire has burned low, casting only the dimmest of lights over the camp.

"I'll take out the guard." Lora's voice is scarcely louder than a breath. "Are you ready?"

Ayc nods. He can do this. He *will* do this.

"Good." Lora hesitates, then adds, "And... be careful."

Moonlight drapes over her face. She gnaws at her lower lip, like she's afraid for him. He chuckles at the thought.

"Careful," he warns. "Keep saying things like that and I'm going to start thinking you like me."

Lora looks away swiftly. "That'd be remarkably foolish of you."

"Truly." Ayc removes his bracelets and tucks them into his pocket. "And there's nothing to be worried about. Court magician and baker extraordinaire, remember? What could possibly go wrong?"

He takes one last deep breath, steps into the darkness, and disappears.

CHAPTER
TWENTY-TWO

Ayc creeps around the first slumbering fae and avoids the light of the embers still burning in their fire. The night itself seems to hold its breath —silent save for the soft sounds of breathing, the crush of tall grass beneath the marching guard's feet, and Ayc's own heartbeat in his ears. Then, a soft *oomph* sounds in the darkness. The guard circling the camp has disappeared from sight. Lora strikes as silently and as deadly as a spirit.

Ayc freezes, but none of the fae stir in response to the thud. He moves on toward the central tent, forcing each step to be light, soundless, a warrior's footsteps, the way Peregrin taught him. He doesn't approach the fae sleeping at the entrance of the tent, but instead, he angles toward the back.

Quiet, shuddering sounds come from within the tent. Sobs. A fist clenches around Ayc's heart. He knows a thing or two about being a boy feeling totally alone and trapped. At least, this one, he can save.

He kneels and works out a tent peg that fastens the

canvas to the ground. It loosens the cloth just enough for him to crawl beneath. Ayc is still invisible, but the movement of the cloth is not. Ohen shoots upright, his eyes wide. Ayc allows himself to reappear, and Ohen reels back. A scream begins low in his throat, and Ayc slams a hand over the boy's mouth.

This close, Ayc can see the tear tracks that streak down Ohen's face.

"It's all right, Ohen," Ayc whispers. "I'm here to get you out. I was sent by the organization. I'm going to remove my hand, but you can't scream, all right?"

Ohen nods.

Ayc drops his hand and unties Ohen's wrists. Ayc points to the loose canvas. "Crawl underneath. I have a friend waiting out in the darkness. We just have to get you back to the woods, and you'll be safe."

When they are both outside the tent, Ayc doesn't return to being invisible. There isn't a point if Ohen cannot also be invisible. Ayc clasps Ohen's upper arm, and they move slowly, soundlessly, back through the camp. Ayc holds his breath the entire way, but no one moves. When they are several yards past the edge of the camp, Ayc shoves Ohen forward.

"Run to the trees," he hisses. "Go."

Ohen sprints forward, and Ayc follows right on his heels. He watches over his shoulder, expecting to see someone pursuing them. But no one comes. They rush into the tree-line, and Ayc finally breathes again when he sees Lora step from behind a trunk.

Lora assesses Ohen quickly, as though marking any wounds. And then she turns to Ayc. "You did it," she breathes, something close to wonder in her voice.

"You sound surprised. I'm almost offended," Ayc says, but he's grinning too wide for it to be convincing.

Ohen blinks at her, with eyes still so wide they glow like a blanched moon. "You're... you're Loraphne, the Sovereign's daughter."

Lora almost seems to flinch, but the motion is small and Ayc might have imagined it. "We have to go," she says, spinning around to lead them deeper into the forest.

"Where?" Ohen asks.

"Somewhere you'll be safe."

The wind chimes that hang from the eaves of the Totus Omni homes whisper in the stillness of the night. Ayc hears them long before he, Lora, and Ohen reach the outskirts of Avia, the Totus Omni village. Some of the homes wrap around the bases of the mighty trees, while others climb into the branches. They are all still and peaceful. Only a few candles remain lit in the windows, glowing like stars high above Ayc's head. No matter how many times Ayc sees the Totus Omni villages, he never ceases to be amazed by them: their simplicity or their beauty.

As they enter the village, a voice calls to them from above, "Who goes there at this unholy hour?"

Ayc's feet plant on the trail and his hand jumps to the hilt of his sword, but Lora doesn't even tense. "Don't worry. I know him."

Still, Ohen shies a little closer to Lora.

Lora tilts her head up, looking toward a platform built into the branches of a towering tree. "Hello, Veni."

A lantern turns on, illuminating a handsome, fair-skinned fae, dressed in a knee-length tunic. Strands of turquoise hair fall into his eyes as he leans over the railing. "Lora? What are you doing down there?"

"I could tell you," Lora says, "but—"

"Then you'd have to depart me of my tongue. Aye, aye, I know." He squints down at them, and a slow smile curls up his face. "And who is that handsome thing with you?"

Ayc returns the grin and waves up at him. "I'm A—"

"He's nobody," Lora interrupts.

"Nobody?" Veni says, a dimple flashing in his cheeks. "What a peculiar name. Hi, Nobody!"

Ayc laughs. It's a terrible joke, one he might have made himself. He winks in return, a gesture that makes Veni's smile grow wider.

Lora's mouth twists into a scowl. "I don't have time for your flirting, Veni. We're in a hurry."

Veni twirls his hand dismissively. "Oh, very well. Go ahead then. Should I expect anyone to follow you?"

"I don't think so," Lora says. "But if you happen to see a few Lux Aester wandering around in the dark..."

"You know me." Veni kicks gently at a crossbow leaning against the trunk of the tree beside her. "I tend to shoot first and never ask any questions. I *loath* questions."

Lora bids Veni goodbye and leads them through the silent village. She glides between houses and beneath great arching roots with an ease that says she has traced this path hundreds of times before. She finally pauses at a home with a half-moon shaped porch. Wind chimes hum from the overhang. Vines trail around the posts and over the roof. A swing hangs beside the porch, attached to the lowest branch of the tree that is still a dozen feet overhead. Potted plants crowd every inch of the porch and the space before it. Some

Ayc recognizes as common plants, while other blooms turn as the three of them pass, as though tracking their movement. One nips at Ayc's fingers, and he tucks his hands into his pockets.

Lora knocks on the door. A lamp on the porch flicks to life. The glass fills with tiny lights that whirl and spin, like fireflies are caught within. The light glistens off Lora's dark hair.

The door jerks open. Hellevi's ample frame fills the doorway, and the resemblance to her granddaughter once again strikes Ayc as uncanny. Lora has never resembled Yris's pale, wraith-like shape, but Lora is a reflection of her grandmother's warm brown skin and wide, soft curves, and tight, black curls. Even Hellevi's scowl speaks of Lora, as the elder woman straightens her purple robe and looks them up and down.

"Aren't you supposed to be off winning the Trials?"

"Something important came up." Lora nods her head toward Ohen, who stands behind them with his head tucked.

Hellevi takes the boy in, her face softening. "What's their name?"

"His name is Ohen," Lora replies.

Hellevi steps to the side. "You best be getting in here." She pins Ayc with a glare. "But *you* better have brought some of your biscuits with you, or I'll make you sleep on the porch." She says it sternly, but one side of her mouth tips upward to reveal she's joking. Ayc realizes that subtle expression is another thing Lora inherited from her grandmother.

Ayc leans an arm on the doorway and grins down at her. "Oh, Hellevi, you know you love me."

"You mistake my undying love for your lemon drizzled biscuits as my limited affection for you."

"Limited affection is still affection."

"Only for the desperate." Hellevi snorts and moves into the house.

Lora casts a frown between them as she steps inside. Ohen sticks close to Lora's heels, and Ayc shuts the door behind all of them.

The home forms around the trunk of the tree, like the numbers on a clock. An arched hearth carved with vines is formed into the wood directly at the center. Before it, two armchairs sit on a colorful, woven rug. On the right lies a tight kitchen with a small, round table and a dozen oddly angled cabinets. On the left, a staircase winds up the trunk to another level. Ayc glazes over all of it, and then looks again to mark the more important details of the home: the basket of yarn by the fireplace; the soft, knitted blankets draped over the chairs; the floating shelves lined with books; the sketches hanging from the tree of two children throughout their lifespan. One, a boy with a beaming smile, and the other, Lora. Sometimes, in the sketches of Lora, the first boy is clearly grown and holding her in his arms. Her father, Ayc guesses.

"Are you hungry, Ohen?" Hellevi asks.

Still looking at the floor, Ohen shakes his head.

"Tired?"

Ohen nods.

"Come with me." She beckons him toward the stairs, but Ohen hesitates.

"What happens now?" he whispers. "What's to stop them for coming for me again?"

"Me, of course," Hellevi says, a silver gleam passing over her eyes.

Just like Lora, Ayc thinks.

"No one is going to come for you here," Lora assures him, her voice soft, gentle. "So long as you stay here, or with someone within the organization, you're safe."

He folds his arms over his chest and runs his hands up and down his biceps, like he's cold. Ayc wishes he possessed the right words, the right actions, to make Ohen feel less alone, less afraid. But anything Ayc can think of feels too small. So, he simply remains, lingering next to the closed door, like he's disappeared into shadow once more.

"Does this mean I'll never be able to see my parents again?" Ohen asks. He drops his head back down, his jagged hairline falling before his face. "I mean... that's a foolish question, isn't it?"

"You're not trapped here, Ohen," Lora says. "Your life was a prison before, and I don't mean for your future to be one. But no, there's no going back, not unless you mean to return to the cage they put you in."

Ohen slumps into the nearby chair and buries his face in his hands. Hellevi takes a step forward, but Lora is already there, slipping into the chair across from him. She leans in and speaks so softly, Ayc has to move closer to hear.

"Sometimes, the ones who are supposed to love us aren't capable of seeing us and loving us for who we truly are. And eventually, we have to make the painful choice either to be our true selves or to be the person they can accept. You cannot be both. And, Ohen, a love that doesn't see you— *really* see you—isn't love at all."

The light of the fire plays in Lora's dark eyes, like starlight on a seemingly never-ending night. Ayc feels as though he's twelve-years-old again, seeing Lora for the first time, being struck with awe, because he never knew such beauty existed. He tries to pry the emotion from his chest, but it will not budge.

I hate— he tries, but he can't. He can't even think it.

Ohen finally lifts his head and sweeps the back of his hands over his cheeks.

Ayc clears his throat to be rid of whatever emotion has accumulated there. The sound draws Lora's attention to him. The look on her face is not a guarded mask of stone. It's the opposite. It is an entire book written in a language he doesn't know. Infinite and timeless, the way certain stories are. He can't begin to interpret what it means. And he cannot breathe, with her looking at him like that. She's shaking the very foundations of him, laying siege on the walls he's used to separate them, and he can't bear it. If they fall, he'll be left in ruin.

"Yes," Hellevi agrees, and Ayc yanks his attention away from Lora so his lungs can expand with air. "And if they choose not to see you, well, that's their fucking loss."

Ayc laughs, pleasantly startled, and Ohen joins him nervously. Lora's lips tug upward.

"And you shouldn't steal my speeches, sweet pea," Hellevi says to Lora. "Not without signed and written permission."

"Sorry, Grandma." Lora leans back in the chair. "It's good advice."

Ayc forces himself not to think too hard about the implications of those words. If he does, he'll picture Lora sitting in these exact chairs as a child. Then he'll have to think about whose expectations she found herself imprisoned in and whether or not she chose to free herself.

"You ready now, boy?" Hellevi asks.

A soft smile tugs on Ohen's lips at the word 'boy'. He stands. "Thank you." He looks between Lora and Ayc. "Both of you. For everything."

He disappears up the steps with Hellevi, and Ayc and Lora are alone—in this home of hers. This must be where she disappeared to each summer, and where she returned from, looking so miserable. She relaxes into the chair, the tension in her shoulders fading. She looks far more comfortable here than she's ever looked at Wyntra, under the shadow her mother casts. Perhaps it didn't make her unhappy to be here. Perhaps it simply made her unhappy to leave.

Ayc's mind is a chaotic mess, spinning around the events of the last full day. The Drakr's visit, Lora's uncertainty, the organization, the gryphon ride, the rescue, her body so close to his, her fingers around his throat, her shuddering breath on his lips. It all spins faster and faster through his head, a blur of images and sensation, until it almost hurts. The pain is building around his spine, and he needs a distraction.

He looks to the kitchen and starts toward it. Baking is always a good idea. "Do you think your grandmother would mind if I used her kitchen?"

Lora frowns at him from around the chair's tall back. "Not if it means that you're making her lemon drizzle biscuits."

He finds the right ingredients in the cabinets, all carefully labeled in crystal blue jars, including lemon extract. It's not fresh zest like he prefers, but such things can be difficult to come by this far north. Not everyone has Yris's financial means and insistence for fresh ingredients. He eases into a familiar pattern: tending the fire in the oven, then measuring and mixing, stirring and dividing. Meanwhile, he knows Lora watches him. Her gaze teases down his back like a stinging caress of fingernails. He focuses on his baking, until everything else fades. He barely hears the stairs creak as Hellevi descends to join them.

She pauses beside Lora and rests a hand on her shoulder. Still stirring, Ayc watches them over his shoulder.

"How are you really, sweet pea?" Hellevi's gaze fixes on the chronicler on Lora's wrist and the single lit stone there.

Lora yanks down her sleeve to cover it. "I'm well."

"Are you, though?"

Lora's scowl makes it clear she isn't in the mood to answer. Ayc faces them and leans his back against the counter, still whisking the dough.

"Do you call her sweet pea because of the flower?" Ayc asks.

"No," Hellevi replies, "it's because of the time she laughed so hard peas came out her nose."

"Grandma," Lora protests through her teeth.

"It was at your own joke, too. The one about a witch having twins. What was the punchline, again?"

Ayc's hand misses a beat before he starts to stir again. The look on Lora's face is downright murderous, and he likes it too much to stop himself from creeping a few steps closer to see it better. "Yes, Lora," he urges, "*what* was the punchline?"

She stands and directs that murderous glare fully on him. She responds in a flat tone, "You can't tell which is witch."

A chuckle rumbles deep in this throat. It's unbelievable, the thought of Lora sitting in this house and telling jokes.

His jokes. The ones she never laughed at, at least, not where he could see her. But maybe she *did* eventually laugh, and the idea makes him smile wide enough his cheeks ache.

Lora gives him the look he knows too well, the one that tells him he's one misstep away from seeing his own heart pulsing in her hand. He turns around to hide the glee on his face and begins to evenly lay out the biscuit mixture onto the pan.

"Your father laughed so hard he sprayed peas from his nose, too," Hellevi adds.

"Does your father also live in this village?" Ayc asks.

Silence.

That's all that follows that question. A silence that stretches out so long and so heavy that Ayc's skin pricks with discomfort. When he peeks over his shoulder, he finds shadows shifting over both their faces.

"Forgive me," Ayc says. "I've clearly brought up something painful, and I'm not making near enough biscuits to repay you for it."

Hellevi flicks her hand. "Best get on that, then."

She gives him a twisted smile and a wink, to tell him no permanent harm is done. But Lora looks back to the wall, and the sketches of her father there, her face behind a veil of hair. He can sense it now. Loss clings to this house like a ghost. Ayc turns back to his baking, before he does something entirely reckless. Like close the distance between them, pull Lora into his arms and hold her.

While the biscuits bake, Ayc prepares the lemon glaze topping. Lora helps Hellevi carry blankets and pillows from upstairs and makes up two pallets on the floor before the fire. Hellevi hums as she works, the same tunes Ayc has heard coming from Lora's booth. Lora strips off her armor and pulls her gray sweater from her bag. She selects a book from her grandmother's shelves and stretches out on one pallet, her back to the kitchen. By the time the biscuits are cooked and drizzled with the lemon glaze, Ayc is uncertain if she's still awake. Her breaths rise and fall easily.

Fuck, he shouldn't be so aware of her breathing.

"Thank you for the biscuits," Hellevi says, coming to Ayc's side with a crystal-blue plate in her hands. "You didn't need to."

"It relaxes me," Ayc says, wiping down the countertop. "It's been a day."

"That it has." Hellevi layers a few of the fresh biscuits onto the plate. "Leave the mess until morning and get some rest. Days always seem less long after some good sleep. This village looks after itself, and the guards here are some of the best. No one will bother you. I'll handle it if they do."

Ayc chuckles. "I'm certain you will."

She carries the plate up the stairs, turning out lights as she goes. She leaves only the one in the kitchen and the low embers of the fire. Ayc doesn't leave the mess. Despite the ache in his muscles and the pull at his eyelids, he doesn't yet trust his mind to surrender to sleep. Only after he's washed, dried, and put away the dishes does he slip onto the pallet of buttery knits. The blankets smell like the home, like thyme and basil and maybe a hint of Lora's shampoo, the sweet and sharp smell of anise.

He's surprised to find that Lora is not asleep. Her book is still open, upside down on the ground before her to mark her place. He considers, briefly, asking her if this is another one of her dirty books, but the joke dies on his tongue as he takes her in. She stares instead at her forearm where the quests are written. She traces the fingertips of her other hand across one of the lines.

"Undo an unforgivable wrong," Ayc reads. "I thought for sure it would be completed from helping Ohen."

Lora's sigh sounds tired. No, *exhausted*. "But how many more people are still in need of help? The wrong is far from undone. I still have much to do to make it right."

Ayc shifts to his side. Only a foot of the woven carpet separates them. He could so easily reach out, so he tucks an arm beneath his head and folds the other within the blankets, so that he's sure his hands will obey. "Will you try to change it? If you become Sovereign?"

"Yes," she says without hesitation. "I'm not sure how, but I will. I won't be my mother, Ayc. Not after everything she's done, especially to my fath—" Lora stops, her fingers curling into fists.

"What did Yris do to your father?" Ayc presses gently, knowing he's touching a tender bruise. He doesn't expect her to answer, especially after her eyes shutter closed.

The silence lengthens between them. A log snaps in the fireplace.

"My mother had him exiled," she says at last. Coolly. Like she can pretend she doesn't feel the impact. "He was a part of the Aluina rebellion." She pauses and opens her eyes to search Ayc's face as though looking for recognition. She must find it because she goes on. "He was exiled seven years ago."

Ayc remembers it again: the day seven years ago, when Wren's mother was executed. But this time, he remembers it differently. Lora banished him from the courtyard that day.

Did she do so to spare him from the sight of what was about to happen? And when he returned from the shore, she wore tears on her cheeks. He tried to ask, to approach her, because the sight of her hurting was fundamentally wrong and he *needed* to fix it, but she snarled at him to go away. He didn't know what caused those tears then, but now he understands all too well.

"Yris did that to someone she bore a child with?" Ayc asks, even though he knows what an unintelligent question it is. Yris's cruelty knows no bounds or affections.

"She never intended to have children. I was an accident. She told me she thought of ending the pregnancy, but she thought, if I was strong enough willed to be conceived despite all her precautions, perhaps I would amount to something."

Disgust burns deep in Ayc's throat. "Fuck, Lora. That's awful. She never should have said that to you."

Lora lifts her hands in a shrug-like gesture, like those words didn't hurt. Like they aren't half as cruel as other things Yris has said to her. Which is probably true.

"Have you seen your father since he was exiled?" Ayc asks.

Something glistens in her eyes, but she blinks, and it's gone. "No. It was forbidden. As part of his punishment."

"I'm really sorr—"

"Don't!" Her voice explodes from a whisper to a snarl. "Don't fucking apologize."

Ayc's eyes widen.

"I don't need or want sympathy, especially not from *you*." She tempers her volume, but the heat in her words doesn't ease. "Fuck, why are you always so nice?"

Ayc bites back on his frustration, so he doesn't yell, too. "I don't know what you mean."

"I was there at Creed Castle. I murdered that man, Evander, right in front of you. You're supposed to hate me, but no matter how cruel I've been to you, it's never mattered. All you've ever done is tell jokes or make me desserts or give me a pretty smile or just be so fucking kind."

Ayc closes his eyes to block out the fury on her face. But she's there, behind his eyelids, too. He sees her how she looked ten years ago, in Creed Castle, the silver of tears gleaming in her eyes.

"We were twelve, Lora," he says softly.

"So?"

"So, you were a *child*. You never should have been there that day."

He opens his eyes again to find her mouth parted. Her breath shudders as it passes her lips. He's too far away to feel it, and yet he does, vibrating like a shiver on his skin.

"I'm just saying," she says, a sharp force in her voice that doesn't quite match the width in her eyes, "that this would be a lot easier if you weren't so nice all the damn time."

"*What* would be easier?"

She scoffs and makes a vague gesture between them. "This."

"And what exactly is *this*?"

Lora snaps her mouth shut. Words that she doesn't say and that he cannot fathom play over her expression. Her gaze traces over every line of his face: the slope of his nose, the stubble on his jaw, the curve of his lips. There, they linger.

And linger.

And no. *Fuck.* She absolutely cannot keep looking at him like this. He's going to lose his fucking mind.

Hope is such a dangerous, painful thing. But for a moment, the space between them doesn't feel like a chasm. The distance feels manageable, like they could reach across it. Like she is close enough to touch. To kiss.

Her body tilts forward, coming closer.

CHAPTER
TWENTY-THREE

Just as quickly, Lora stills. She angles her focus away, somewhere past Ayc's head into the darkness of the room. "I don't know," she exhales, and with that breath, the chasm between them reappears. "It's... nothing."

Nothing.

There's no reason that one word should feel like a sword driven through his sternum, but it does.

"Very well, then." He flips back onto his back and presses his eyes closed, feeling utterly foolish for even thinking for a moment that she might kiss him.

I'm such a fucking ass.

Silence blankets them, broken only by wind chimes jingling close to the window and the snap of the firewood. When her voice comes again, it's so soft he almost loses it beneath the delicate noises.

"Fuck, I'm trying to apologize, and I'm getting it all wrong."

A bark of laughter escapes Ayc's lips, more surprise than humor. "You're trying to apologize?"

"Yes."

He twists his head to look at her once more. "You're right. You're doing an absolutely wretched job of it."

"I know." She shakes her head, a coil of hair springing forward to cover her nose. "I've never said sorry for the role I played at Creed Castle. And I am. Truly."

Ayc has never once imagined he would hear those words from her lips, but they tremor with sincerity. A pool of emotion stings to his eyes. He blinks hard at the ceiling and clears his throat, lest the emotions building make him do something that others might consider unmanly. Like cry.

"Like I said, you were a child," he says, when he's sure his voice won't betray him and his vision is clear once more. "Your mother is responsible for that injustice. It's not your fault."

"Is injustice still not your fault if you have the power to change it and choose not to?"

Ayc doesn't have an answer to that, but it's clear she doesn't need one. Instead Ayc asks, "What would have happened to you, then? If you chose not to participate?"

She hesitates, tracing the pattern of the rug between them with a finger. "I didn't know what was going to happen until I got on the ship to go to Creed. My mother told me nothing beforehand. She only gave me a choice. I could get on the ship and follow her every command, or I could spend that week in the dungeons of Wyntra."

"The *dungeons*?" He's known that Lora hasn't been completely spared from Yris's cruelty. But Yris has always been careful with Lora, never leaving the scars and marks she leaves upon others. It made it too easy to believe that

Yris was kinder to Lora than most. But the fucking dungeons? "She would lock you in the dungeons?"

Her fingers pause briefly, before continuing along a different color. "Not often, just sometimes."

Rage, hot as the crackling fire nearby, broils in his blood. He presses his eyes closed as the heat gathers there as well, threatening to blur his vision. He barely manages to keep his voice steady. "Fuck, Lora, I—"

"Do *not* say you're sorry."

It's an order; it pricks like a knife at his sternum. But he wasn't going to say sorry to begin with. He rolls back on his side, and the space between them narrows once more. He rests his hand on the floor, where her own hand is only a breath away.

"I was going to say that I know what it's like to be your mother's prisoner," Ayc says. "But at least she locked me in a pastry kitchen, and not a dungeon."

"I didn't kill that man because I feared being put in the dungeon." Her tone contains a sharpness, reminiscent of how she snapped at him about being too nice. Perhaps, it's a defense, meaning to restore distance between them. But this time, Ayc remains steady and doesn't recoil when she hisses the final words, "I killed that man because I hoped it would make my mother proud."

Ayc should add that to the long list he's carefully assembled in his head of why he should hate her, a weapon he holds to cleave unwanted affections. But he can't do it. He was a son once, too, who loved his mother enough he would have done anything to make her proud. The oaths he made to his mother are still as binding as the bracelets on his wrists. The fact that his mother was worthy of such affection and Yris is not would scarcely matter to a child.

Maybe love can be a prison, too.

Ayc pulls his lower lip into his mouth to keep back the words. Lora tracks the movement. And she *has* to stop looking at him. Her gaze means nothing; he *knows* this. But still, it's filling his head with all kinds of ridiculousness. It's making the space between their hands on the floor feel like millimeters and not like miles.

Wanting a distraction, he asks, "Is that why you want to be Sovereign? To make your mother proud?"

"I gave up on making her proud the day she sent my father away without even letting me say goodbye." A little flash of silver punctures the dark, before her irises return to the deepest of purples. "The only way to make her proud is to be exactly like her. There was a time I tried, but I gave up on that."

"Then why become Sovereign? To undo your father's exile?"

"That'll be one of the first wrongs I undo. But the list is long."

Ayc dares to hope that maybe, just maybe, Aluina is on that list. She is looking at him with an intensity that certainly implies it, but he can't hear her say it. If she says it, he's going to do something—say something—entirely too reckless. So he says, "And let me guess, that list involves giants somehow."

Her eyes lighten slightly, from a near-black-purple to a royal purple. "Precisely. Before the beginning of my grandfather's reign, we were friends with the giants. I suspect my grandfather did something to ruin whatever friendship existed before. I've tried to search for what it could be in the library, but neither I nor Xylie have found much. The ones in power always write the history that comes after. So I want to hear Laud's side of the story, and then I want to fix it."

"So you want to fix what your mother and grandfather have done?"

She nods. She's being vulnerable and honest, and the trust she's placing in him to do so is not lost on him. The fire casts patterns over her cheeks, her neck, and just like when she danced on the ship, she looks alive. A shield has come undone between them, and he likes seeing her like this, probably too much.

Perhaps that's why he pushes, seeking an answer he's wondered since the night Yris announced the Trials would begin.

"Is that the only reason you are competing to be Sovereign? Because you feel as though you must? That it's your responsibility?"

Her brow knits together, but she nods again.

"That isn't the same thing as *wanting* to be Sovereign," Ayc says. "That's obligation, not desire. Lora, do you *want* to be Sovereign?"

One shoulder tilts toward her ear. She responds with just as much apathy as the shrug suggests. "It's my destiny."

Ayc growls in frustration. "Fuck destiny. Is it what you *want*?"

"My people need me. What I want doesn't matter."

"It does," Ayc insists. "Because *you* matter."

Her eyes widen, and he wishes he could yank the words back down his throat. He's always been a reckless fool, who doesn't always think before he blurts out words. And words have power. With them, he's shown far too much of the hand he tries to hide. The air around them grows heavy. Neither of them speak. Neither of them move.

Then her littlest finger flexes on the floor between them. It shifts, sliding just a little closer to him. It's millimeters, and it's miles. The space between them is filled with only a tiny sliver of carpeting and ten years of barbed words and shared wounds. More than ever before, he longs to reach across it. He wants to trace the lattice-work of light the fire casts upon her skin, first with his fingers, then with his lips, then with his teeth. He wants to scrape away his lists of reasons and excuses and his measly walls of protection until there is nothing left between them. He wants to know if she would let him. And in this moment, when he's beginning to see who Lora is behind her stone, he's beginning to forget all the reasons he shouldn't cross the line in between them.

He spreads his fingers, until his own little finger brushes against hers. The sparks in his blood ignite. Her breath shudders past her lips once more.

Then she whips back like she's been burned and tucks her hand beneath the blanket. "There you go again, cinnamon roll," she says, with a roll of her eyes. "Being far too kind to me."

He forces a smile; it feels like lifting a thousand pounds with the corners of his lips. "It's what I do."

"Well, stop it," she snaps, and then she flips herself around, giving him her back. "Good night, Ayc."

"Good night, Lora."

He rolls himself onto his opposite side, so he doesn't look at her. But the embers play off the walls of her childhood home, and the faint smell of anise taunts his nose with every inhale. His head is a merciless sea, thoughts of her crashing over him again and again. Normally, he's better at suppressing them. But not tonight. Tonight, they are his torment until he's finally dragged into sleep.

362

He doesn't know how long he's slept when he wakes to hushed voices, but the fire has gone out and dark has overtaken the room. The blankets warm his core, but a chill bites at his cheeks. He holds still and keeps his breathing even, lest someone notice he no longer slumbers.

"The baker, huh?" Hellevi asks. A lilting laugh hides beneath her voice that carries from the kitchen.

"He's my Fifth," Lora explains.

"Which guidance is he?"

"What do you mean?"

"The guidance the rest of the Council gave you." Hellevi clears her throat and deepens her voice as she recites, "Someone who is more powerful than even you. Someone who thinks differently than any other, and someone who sees things others cannot. Someone who challenges you when you need it the most. And someone you hate, to teach you how to make enemies your friends. Which one is he?"

The realization hits Ayc like a punch in the gut before Lora lets out the truth with a sigh. "The last one."

There it is: the reason he's here—to ensure that Lora earns the luck that comes with following the guidance of the Totus Omni's Council of the People. She needed someone she hated, and that's a complicated prompt to fill. How do you put an enemy on a team you're supposed to trust? But Yris knew something about Ayc that Lora did not.

Ayc can be controlled. Yris made damn sure of that.

Fuck.

"Someone you hate?" Hellevi repeats.

"Yes."

Hellevi exhales a long, long breath. "Oh, sweet pea, you chose poorly then."

The words land like a much needed slap on his cheek.

Of course, he's only here because Lora hates him. Of course, even Hellevi sees Ayc as the foolish, weak choice he is. The little hope from earlier explodes like the fragile, porcelain thing it is. Tiny shards of glass embed deep. It hurts, but it's all a fool like him deserves. Really, when the fuck is he going to learn?

"Where is that damn bird?" Lora demands, staring at the branches overhead as she stomps through the forest. The sky past the trees is an angry gray, heavy clouds rolling past, leaving the forest below dark as dusk.

"She's probably sulking because she heard you call her bird," Ayc says, as he follows after Lora with far less urgency.

Lora woke him before dawn, eager to get back to the others and back to her quests. Ohen and Hellevi weren't awake yet, and so Lora and Ayc left without so much as a goodbye. They've been roaming through the woods, headed south, for an hour now, but Tempest is nowhere to be found. They haven't seen her since last night when they neared the village, and she suddenly took to the skies without warning. Ayc assumed that she went off to hunt something more satisfying than a squirrel, but he also assumed she'd be back by morning.

"We're running out of time." Lora aims a frustrated kick at an unfortunate fallen and rotten branch. It cracks beneath her boot, but she keeps walking.

It grows darker still. the temperature shifts down a few degrees. He can feel the coming rain like spikes into his spine. He grinds his teeth to push past the discomfort, but after a long night tossing and turning on the floor, he could really use one of Tempest's feathers right now.

Ignoring the pain, Ayc rushes to catch up with Lora. He catches her by the arm, which is covered in armor once more. "Lora, a storm is coming. Maybe we should go back to Hellevi's and wait it out. Or at least wait until Tempest finds us. There must be a reason she hasn't come yet. She wouldn't abandon us."

Lora retreats a step. "I can't go back. I only have until night fall before Lahlis returns, and I don't want to draw the Drakr to Ohen or Hellevi or the dozens of other people in that village."

"That's fair," Ayc agrees. "But we have hours until nightfall. Tempest will find us before then. And—"

He stops, his words freezing on his tongue as he catches movement behind Lora. They were not there before; he's certain of it. But they are now, standing in one of the few remaining patches of sunlight, only half a dozen feet away. Lahlis stands in the center, a smile curled on his face, with two other Drakr—tall and muscular and pale as death— standing by his side. All wear the same dark, spiked armor that gleams red wherever the light touches.

Lora must see it in his face, because she tenses. "What's wrong?"

Ayc nods his head behind her, and she spins around, her hands flying to the swords at her side. Ayc's hand is already wrapped around his own, the blade an inch out of its sheath.

"I grew impatient," Lahlis says, stalking toward them slowly, like the predator he is.

"How did you find me?" Lora demands.

How can her voice be so steady, when Ayc's own heart is

beating much too fast for survival? He ignores the fear and steps to Lora's side. Are there only the three Drakr he can see or are there more out in the shadows or hiding behind the trees?

"You shouldn't underestimate what I do and don't know about what goes on in Everadyn," Lahlis says with a callous shrug and a cool smile. "I wonder what your mother would have to say about abandoning the Trials for your little side quest. Kidnapping is illegal here, isn't it?"

The rain doesn't start in a drizzle, but in a downpour. The leaves rattle overhead in warning moments before water pours down, raindrops pelting Ayc's face.

Lora raises her voice to be heard over the rain. "What I did is none of your concern."

"Perhaps you're right, but do you know what *is* my business?" Lahlis pauses, as though giving her a chance to guess. Lora doesn't. "The proposition I gave you. I want an answer, Loraphne. I won't wait until tonight."

He reaches into the pouch at his side and brings out the Binding stone. The stone's green light highlights his pale cheekbones as he holds it toward her. Instinct demands Ayc run from the stone, but he presses his feet into the earth, determined to remain at Lora's side.

Lora lifts her chin, stoic and strong, despite the water that streams down her face. Ayc can picture her, wearing a crown made just for her—a mighty, fearsome Sovereign. He holds his breath and waits for her to prove to him, once and for all, the queen she might become.

"No."

Lightning flashes so brightly everything goes white. Thunder cracks, shaking the world. When the light fades, Lahlis's smile is gone.

A low growl creeps into his words, "Try again."

"No," Lora repeats, her voice firm and powerful. "I do not want your help. *No,* I will not be your butcher in exchange for it."

Relief releases some of the tension in Ayc's shoulder. He knows it will be short-lived; that the consequences of her choice will be swiftly delivered. But he is grateful, so very grateful, that she said no.

Lahlis tucks the stone back into the pouch at his side. "How very disappointing. You surprise me, Loraphne."

"Only because you know my mother," Lora says. "But you don't know my father."

The men behind Lahlis grasps the curved blades hanging on their belts. Lora marks their every movement. Ayc tightens his hold on his sword and shifts closer to Lora's side.

Lahlis stares at her for a heartbeat more, then flicks his wrist in the air like brushing off dirt. The rain streaks down his face as his smile returns. "Fortunately for us, Marcellus said yes to the offer. It's a pity. At this point, he's best positioned to win the Trials, but I would much rather have worked with *you*. He's a tiresome fool, and you're such a pretty plaything."

A hiss of metal rings out like another crack of thunder. All eyes snap toward Ayc, and it's only then he realizes it's his own sword that has been partly drawn.

"She is no one's plaything," Ayc growls, in the voice that reverberates deep in his chest.

Lahlis rolls his eyes toward Lora. "Your human's devotion to you is quite—" He hums and then spits the word, "Nauseating. And it won't spare you from consequences. Your mother would be quite furious with me if I killed you, but your human has no such protection." Red spreads through Lahlis's eyes, overtaking the blue like blood spilling across water. "I'll take his life as payment for your refusal."

Another flare of lightning blinds Ayc. When his vision clears, Lora's blades spin in her hands, and the Drakr hold their curved red blades. Two more Drakr have joined the others, making the ratio an impossible five to two. Lora is powerful, and Ayc is well-trained, better than he's ever dared let on, but they're no match for five Drakr warriors.

And still, Lora steps in front of Ayc. "If you want him, you'll have to go through me."

Ayc wants to scream at her to move. She's being foolish. The Drakr are sparing her, but she's giving them the perfect excuse to tell Yris that killing her was unavoidable because she got in their way. And she is *not* allowed to die for him.

But Lahlis laughs. "You can't protect him. You're hopelessly outnumbered. You'll lose."

"Maybe," Lora says coolly, lifting her blades. "But not before I make it hurt."

"Lora, don't do this," Ayc hisses lowly. He tries to step around her, but she moves with him, so her body remains his shield.

Lahlis chuckles again, turns on his heels, and sweeps away from them, back into the darkness he came from. As he passes his four fae, he says, "Kill him. And if she gets in the way, kill her, too."

The four Drakr smile, every one of their teeth elongating and sharpening, until they form an entire mouthful of grinning daggers.

"Ayc," Lora says. "Run."

The command wrenches through him like his spine

might be ripped through his stomach, but no. *No!* He won't leave her. He *can't* leave her.

"No," Ayc says as he plants his feet. His disobedience feels like a hand sealing around his throat, cutting off his air.

"Ayc!" Lora snarls, as all four of the Drakr march forward. "Run! Leave me, and do not come back!"

The invisible hand clamps down harder. He gasps for breath, his eyes watering from the pain, blurring his vision. He has no choice. His feet are already moving, willing him to survive. With a scream of frustration, Ayc turns and runs as the clash of swords thunders behind him.

CHAPTER
TWENTY-FOUR

yc hates himself more with every step propelling him farther from Lora, but still he runs deeper into the woods, his sword still in his hand. The rain pours down his face, and the sound of swords grows fainter. He's leaving her behind, and it hurts in a different way. Not visceral, but deeper, like each step is pulling him apart. Yet, the command and the magic that binds him doesn't let him stop, even as his very soul screams back.

I cannot leave her!

She will die, alone. For him. And then the Drakr will find him, and it'll be for nothing.

A sharp, high-pitched cry of pain rings out. He freezes. The hand tightens back on his throat, but he forces himself to pull air in through his nose. That was Lora. He's certain of it. He feels it.

The Drakr hurt her. She is being hurt. While he's running away, like a fucking coward.

Fuck this.

He sprints two more steps forward, sucking in every

ounce of air he can into his lungs, steeling himself for what is to come. Then he turns and races back the other direction. With each step, the invisible force constrict his throat more. He tells himself it cannot actually kill him. No matter how he feels, air is still entering his lungs, but his wheeze as he inhales proves otherwise. Perhaps it *can* kill him.

It doesn't matter. Not when every heartbeat pulses the same roar.

Lora. Lora. Lora.

He pulls at the buckle of his bracelet with his teeth and shoves it into the pocket of his trouser. He transfers his sword to his other hand and does the same with the other. Then, in his next step, he wills himself invisible.

In a small patch of light that breaks through the clouds and trees above, Lora holds a solitary line before three Drakr. The fourth lays dead at her feet. One attempts to dart around Lora. She disengages from the Drakr her blades are locked with and spins to meet him. She kicks out and her boot slams into the Drakr's gut. He stumbles back, but she can't take advantage of his unsteadiness, because she must fling herself back the other direction to stop the first Drakr from getting past her.

She is far too focused on ensuring none of them make it past her, trying to buy Ayc as much time as possible. It has made her careless. A gash parts the flawless curve of her cheek. Blood pours down her jaw, her neck, and onto her armor. They have hurt her, and anger erupts in Ayc's veins.

Dead.

Ayc wants them all *dead.*

He doesn't know which he should be more scared of: the dangerous, deadly wrath that rises up inside him, or that, really, it doesn't frighten him at all. In fact, it temporarily eases the pain of the hand around his throat and gives him something greater to focus on.

One Drakr breaks from the others and works his way toward Lora's side, just as two of the other Drakr lunge. She flings up her sword to engage two, but the third grins, showing every single one of his pointed teeth. Ayc charges across the remaining distance, reappearing in the light as he brings his sword high. He swings the blade downward into the Drakr's neck. Blood spurts, showering Ayc's face. A thud sounds as the Drakr's head lands on the ground and tumbles through the leaves.

"Ayc!" Lora yells. She holds her blades high above her head, catching both Drakr's swords. "I told you to run!"

It's not another command, but it's a reminder, breaking through the haze of rage. The strangle-hold of Ayc's disobedience pulls taut, and he gasps for air. It refuses to fill his lungs. But he ignores it, ignores the way his vision tinges with black. He leaps forward. He brings his sword down in an arch at one of the Drakr's heads, and they disengage from Lora to meet him.

Ayc's teeth rattle as their swords clash, and a second later the Drakr's boot slams into his stomach. He stumbles back, and his vision blurs further. He fumbles with his sword and barely catches the next blow. He tries to yank a breath through his teeth, but it won't come.

He won't be able to do this long, but he doesn't need long. Lora is a blur of motion, a dancer with two blades. The Drakr barely keeps up. It's only a matter of time before Lora finds a weakness and ends him. Then only one Drakr will remain. Ayc just needs to be a distraction for a little longer.

Ayc gasps as the Drakr's blade slams into his own. The Drakr shoves him back, pinning him against a tree. Ayc strains against their locked weapons to keep distance, but long daggers of teeth snap close to Ayc's throat.

A call echoes above their heads, starting as a shriek and ending with a roar. Ayc dares to look upward. Through his blurred vision, he makes out mighty wings and claws.

Tempest.

She dives between the branches, paws outstretched, talons bared. And she is not alone. On her back is Peregrin and Bronwen.

A knife flies from Peregrin's hand toward Ayc and embeds into the side of the Drakr's throat. The Drakr slumps toward Ayc, who shoves him away. He crumples at Ayc's feet, dead within moments. From above, Bronwen releases a force of power from her outstretched hand. It collides with the other Drakr, knocking his sword from his hand and propelling him away from Lora. A moment later, Tempest crashes down upon him. The Drakr screams, but Tempest silences them quickly, roaring and clawing and stabbing with her curved beak. Bronwen clutches Peregrin's waist to stay on the rearing beast. Soon, the Drakr is nothing more than mangled flesh beneath her.

The four Drakr are dead. Lahlis might still be out there, watching, but surely he will not face the four of them and a gryphon on his own. Lora is alive. And Ayc—

Ayc cannot *fucking* breathe.

The pain drives past the wall forged from Ayc's need to save Lora. It encircles his throat and rages through his body. He feels it everywhere, into the very marrow of his bones. The world tilts on its side. He drives his sword into the ground, and he clings to the hilt to keep himself upright.

In a distant echo, he hears Lora's voice. "Tempest, you incredible beast! Thank you!"

And then, Peregrin shouts, "Ayc!"

Ayc needs to run, but the pain is too much, and his knees buckle. Blurred images whirl before his eyes: Peregrin tumbling off Tempest and, without their cane, scrambling and stumbling toward him. Horror painting itself across Bronwen's face. Lora falling to her knees before him. He can barely make out her bloody, beautiful face.

"Ayc, what is it?" she demands. Her fingers brush against his cheeks, but he's so numb he can't feel them. There's only pain. He can no longer feel anything good. "What's happening?"

He opens his mouth, but all that comes out is a choke. His vision disappears completely. The ground rises up to meet him. Maybe he was wrong. Maybe this can kill him. Perhaps, it's the compounding of all his years of disobedience. The stone let him get away with it once. It won't allow it again.

Their voices are so far away now.

"Bronwen!" Lora cries. "Help him."

"I don't know how."

"Please, Bronwen. I'm *begging* you."

"This isn't a spell. I'd feel it!"

"Come on, boy," Peregrin pleads. "Tell us. Dammit, Lora, did you give him a command?"

"What?"

"Did you give him a command?"

"I told him to run. To leave me. I—"

"Tell him to *stay*."

"*What?!*"

"Do it, Lora! Now."

A hand sweeps across his forehead. Gentle and loving. Maybe, it's his mother. Maybe, he's already dead.

Then, "Ayc, stay with me."

The invisible hand uncoils from his throat, and oxygen races into his lungs. He gasps, gulping a breath and then another. His lungs burn, but the pain ebbs until it's tolerable, until he can feel other things. The ground beneath him. Hands in his hair.

He opens his eyes to find four pairs of eyes peering down upon him. Peregrin, Bronwen, Lora, and even Tempest stare down at him with mixed looks of worry and confusion. He must be lying on the ground, because a rock juts into his back and his head rests... in Lora's lap. Her fingers brush against the damp hair at his forehead. The rain has stopped, the thunder now distant.

Ayc wants to remain here, wants to beg Lora not to stop touching him. Her blood-stained fingers feel better than anything he's felt before. But he can't bear the way they're all looking at him.

He cracks a smile and pushes himself upright, trying not to wince as his back protests. "What do you call dangerous precipitation?"

Bronwen utters a small laugh of relief. Peregrin's head falls into their hands. Tempest shoves her beak against Ayc's arm like a cat does when it demands to be pet.

And Lora growls between her teeth. "What the fuck was that?"

"You call it a rain of terror," Ayc finishes.

"Stop it!" Lora shoves to her feet, so she towers over him.

When Ayc looks up, he finds the blood has dried on her face, the wound already knitting itself back together with the supernatural speed Everadyn fae possess. She's doesn't seem to notice it as her voice crackles like lightning. "I want to know what just happened, and I want to know *now*."

Ayc runs a hand over his own blood-soaked face. He can't explain it. If he tried, he would be right back to gasping for air, the consequence of his disobedience. Yris told him to never tell a soul what happened eight years ago, the way she trapped him in Everadyn forever.

Peregrin looks around them. "We shouldn't talk about this here."

The clouds are thick enough that the shadows are dense. Anything could be here. And they are still standing among the corpses of the Drakr, their blood seeping into the mud and leaves.

"I want—" Lora begins, then she presses her lips together. "Fine. Ayc and Peregrin will go first. Tempest can take them out of here as quickly and as far as she can go in a few minutes. And then come back for Bronwen and me."

Tempest bobs her head as though listening, and then bows. Peregrin swings themself up and then gestures for Ayc to follow. Ayc stumbles to his feet. Every muscle screams at him, angry at every tiny movement. He nearly buckles, and Lora's hands reach to steady him.

He steps back and forces another dazzling smile. "It's fine. I'm fine."

Her narrowed gaze tells him she's unconvinced.

Ayc bends to pick his sword out of the earth. Blood drenches the blade. The same blood he wears splattered on his face and clothes. He wipes it off on a patch of grass that isn't also stained in blood. His stomach twists as he avoids the slain bodies. They are Drakr soldiers, who willingly take innocent lives to ensure their own power. They act like monsters, but they are men, nonetheless. He killed one, took them away from those who loved them. And yet, as he mounts Tempest, the guilt is not nearly as strong as it should be. Because given the choice, he would do it again, if it meant that Lora is here. What does that say about him?

Perhaps, that his worst fear is coming true.

Maybe he can be a monster, after all. Perhaps he's not so different from the man whose life he took.

Tempest races through the sky to a spot farther south and dumps Peregrin and Ayc at the banks of the Ever River. It is only a few miles from where the Drakr's attacked.

"Shouldn't we go farther?" Ayc asks, as he watches Tempest vault back into the sky. They must be near a village here. Over the melody of the Ever River, Ayc can hear the symphony of children's laughter, though he cannot see them through the dense foliage. The storm clouds have disappeared, but heavy white clouds cling close to the tops of the towering trees, turning the air around them a hazy blue-gray.

"We'll be safe here," Peregrin assures, lowering themself onto a fallen log with a grunt. "Totus Omni are mainly composed of artisans and lovers, but their guards are some of the fiercest I've ever seen. Lahlis is bold, but he's not so foolish to harm a village just for the mere sake of getting petty revenge."

It does little to ease Ayc's fear, because the Drakr have attacked villages in the name of revenge before. And because Lora is still out there. He paces a few steps. Each one of them hurts, so he slumps against a nearby tree. "You talk as though you know Lahlis."

"I suppose you can say that. We fought against one another before. Back when he was leader of the armies attempting to take Aluina, instead of ruling over it. He is... not a good man."

Ayc shrugs a single shoulder. "Well, he's a Drakr."

"Don't do that," Peregrin snaps. "Most Drakr are my enemies, not because of who they were born, but who they choose to be. Their rulers care nothing about the harm they cause others so long as they get what they want. And the people who follow them do nothing to stop it, because it's profitable to them. That doesn't mean they are incapable of goodness, only that they do not choose it. You could say the same of many Everadyn fae."

Ayc doesn't have the energy to argue. He slides down the bark of the tree until he's sitting on the ground, his knees bent before him. "Where are Xylie and Tavish?"

"At a tavern in Silvae."

Silvae is a large town with an air dock on the outskirts of Elodie. Ayc has landed in it many times when he attended festivals.

Peregrin explains, "We got on a ship shortly after you flew yesterday morning. We wanted to be close in case you needed us. Tempest found us in the early hours of the morning. She suspected that you were being hunted by the Drakr and confirmed it during hunting last night."

"Good girl," Ayc murmurs.

"The best," Peregrin agrees. They run a thumb over the smooth top of their cane. "You're going to have to tell Lora the truth, Ayc."

"You know I can't."

"But I can. With your permission."

Ayc presses the heels of his hands into his temples, a dull

throb starting there. He knows Peregrin is right. Lora will not let go of what happened, and there's nothing that will satisfy her other than the truth.

"All right." He drops his hands and notices the blood streaking across his knuckles. Heaving himself to his feet feels as difficult as trying to uproot an entire stone wall from its foundation. He leans heavily against the tree, steeling himself before he takes the few steps to the river and kneels beside it. The turquoise water washes away the blood stains, and he splashes the ice-cold water against his face. He's tempted to slip in and let the chill ease away the ache in his muscles, but instead, he fastens his bracelets into place.

"How bad is it?" Peregrin asks.

"I'm managing," Ayc replies.

"Aye." Peregrin massages a hand over their leg, the one that took a blade decades before. "That's what we do. We manage."

Ayc has returned to sitting against the tree, focusing on his breaths, when the familiar crack of wings beats against the sky. A second later, Tempest's paws slam into the mud near the river. She quickly side steps out of the mud until she's on dry ground, glaring down at her dirty paws like it's a personal offense. She must have flown fast, because Bronwen's braid has come completely undone, the wispy, pale strands clinging to her face. Lora's own curls are taut, whipping over her shoulder as she vaults off Tempest before the gryphon even stops. Blood still streaks across her face. As she charges toward Ayc, she reminds him of the storm from earlier, roaring in swiftly and filling the air with electricity.

"It's a Binding stone, isn't it?" Lora demands when she stands before him. He once again climbs to his feet, using the tree for support. "Bronwen said it's the only enchantment that could have caused the reaction. You're Bound to someone, aren't you?"

Ayc can barely swallow, let alone speak.

"Dammit, Ayc!" Lora snaps, her voice trembling. He expects her eyes to flash, but they don't. "Ans—"

Ayc flings up a hand. He dares to put a finger in her face, driven by a flare of anger and a spark of terror. "Don't. Do *not* give me an order I cannot follow. Not again."

"He can't answer you," Peregrin says, coming to stand beside Lora. "Do you really think your mother would have Bound him to obey her and then given him the ability to tell anyone of it?"

Ayc shutters his eyes closed. For a moment, he's fourteen again, with Onanna's magic draping around his throat as a cool threat, and Yris holding the Binding stone between her pointed fingernails. He remembers thinking the stone was such a tiny thing. Surely, it couldn't harm him. But it had the power to ruin his life. Yris Bound Ayc to be obedient, and with her first order, she commanded him to tell him the truth of his power, of who he really is.

And he lied.

"I'm divina," he told her.

He's been in pain ever since.

The first day he could barely stand it. Irving must have been in that room, lurking in a corner while Ayc was too terrified to notice, because Peregrin found Ayc hiding in the stables, crying like he was a little boy once more. Peregrin only said, "Come along, boy." Then they helped Ayc to stand and led him to their home. There, Ayc drank his first gryphon feather, mixed into tea that Zinnia made him, served in a cup he cracked and she called his own.

Peregrin taught him something that words cannot. People live in pain every day. They adopt strategies to survive. And it doesn't make it easy. It makes every day, every simple task, really fucking hard. Some days are easier. Some days are *almost* good, but there are other days that breathing feels like the only thing he can manage.

Peregrin helped Ayc train his body and taught him mental techniques to block out some of the pain. The other things—how to get lost in baking and music and sex—are things he taught himself. He survives. He is still surviving. And he hates to think of Lora knowing, of thinking him weak.

But he's losing his secrets. One by one.

When Ayc opens his eyes again, he watches as the stone of Lora's face fractures. He's always imagined her being gleeful of the power Yris has over him... of the power she might one day have. Of the way she might exploit it. But she doesn't look happy, now.

She looks... devastated.

She stares at him, her eyes a watery, crystal blue. "Please, tell me it's not true," she begs. That's the only word for it. It isn't a command or even a request. She is *begging* him to tell her.

"I can't," Ayc replies.

"Oh, Ayc," Bronwen murmurs from where she's dismounted from Tempest's back. He doesn't look at her. He doesn't want pity.

Lora shifts her head away, blocking his view of her face in the cascade of her hair. Little raindrops still sit on top of her curls, sparking in the blue-gray light. "When?" she asks, her voice tight, like she's clinging to control.

Ayc shakes his head. He can't, so Peregrin answers for him, "Eight years ago."

"Eight years? After you ran away?" Heat rises in Lora's voice with every word, her horror shifting to anger. Good. Ayc knows better how to deal with that emotion. "That's why you never tried to run away again. That's the power she still holds over you. My mother has kept you prisoner at Wyntra all this time?"

Lora doesn't need an answer this time. Ayc's silence is confirmation enough.

"Fuck!" She flings herself around and paces away, her hands rising to her hair, forming into fists around the roots, before spinning back around. "Then why was it *my* command that hurt you?"

Ayc rubs a hand over his face, uncertain whether to answer. But Yris didn't command him not to tell that part. "Before we left, she ordered me to obey you like I obey the Sovereign."

Lora looks as though he just told her he's going to throw her into this river, the one she's terrified of. "So if I give you a command, you have to follow it?"

Ayc nods.

"No!" Lora barks, her canines bared. "No, I don't want this. I always suspected you didn't agree to be my Fifth of your own free will. I came to your kitchen expecting I'd have to beg you to help me, and you agreed as soon as you heard my mother knew I'd picked you. You knew you couldn't say no. You never had a choice. You've never had any choices."

He lifts his hands in a helpless gesture. "What do you want me say, Lora? Choices aren't a luxury I will ever have."

"No," she says again. He understands the feeling. It's what his soul cried out for years, until he accepted his fate.

He simply doesn't understand why *she* is feeling this so strongly.

"Ayc?" Bronwen says softly.

They all turn to look at her.

Bronwen approaches slowly, like she's afraid she might startle one of them away. "You said Sovereign."

"What?" Ayc says.

"You said that Yris commanded you to obey Lora like you are bound to obey the Sovereign. Not Yris. Did she Bind you to herself or did she Bind you to the *Sovereign*?"

Damn, she's smart, and the other two must realize it, too. Peregrin hisses through their teeth sharply. Lora closes the distance between her and Ayc in two strides. Her hand rises, and he nearly leaps into the river, concerned she might grab his throat again. Instead, her fingers curl around the front of his shirt. She doesn't pull taut, because the action isn't done in anger, but in desperation.

"Look at me," she says, her voice scarcely a whisper.

Ayc doesn't believe she meant it as a command, but it is one, nonetheless. Before the pain can warn him, he meets her eyes. They are a swirl of color, flickering between the deepest of purples and the deepest of blues, a subtlety of shades reflective of the chaos within.

"Please, tell me that your Bond will not pass to the next Sovereign."

"I... I can't tell you."

"Because of the oath?" Peregrin demands. They clutch their cane so tightly their knuckles lose all color.

"No, because it would be a lie."

Lora releases him and stumbles back a step.

Peregrin presses their fist to their forehead. A brutal string of curses flies from their mouth. Lora looks at them, and they shake their head. "I didn't know the exact wording. Irving couldn't tell me. He has his own oaths he's bond with."

"So if Marcellus wins," Bronwen says, leaning heavily on her staff, "you will have to obey his every command?"

Anxiety flares under Ayc's skin. He fidgets with the buckle of one of his bracelets. "Yes."

"No!" Lora snaps back. "No, I won't allow it." She spins her body to fully face her First. "How do we fix it, Bronwen?"

"There's only two ways that I'm aware of," Bronwen replies. "One is if the original person who Bound them chooses to release them—"

Ayc barks out a laugh at the absurdity of that statement.

Peregrin glares. "Nothing has been less funny to me, boy."

Bronwen ignores them both. "And the other is a Severing stone."

"Then we'll get a Severing stone," Lora says.

Ayc snorts. "Do you think it's so simple? Do you think I haven't thought about it? Severing stones are rare and cost a fortune. I could save until I grow old, and I wouldn't have enough money to purchase one."

"Then *I* will buy one!"

Lora advances on him until she stands only inches from his chest, lifting her chin so that her eyes blaze into his. They've settled on the deep purple, but silver lines the edges. He feels no fear, only the exhilaration, the fire of having her so near. He still doesn't understand why she is reacting in such a heated way. Is this because he is yet another injustice that she now feels she must set right? Or is it because of something... more?

It doesn't really matter, because either way...

"I'm not letting you use the money that's meant for helping people escape Lux Aester on a Severing stone," Ayc says.

She growls in frustration. "Why do you have to be such a damn noble hero, cinnamon roll?"

"I'm not your damsel in distress that needs rescuing, villainess!"

"Keep your voices down before you scare the whole village," Peregrin warns.

Ayc locks his jaw, and Lora presses her lips into a fine line, both still glaring at one another. The laughter of children and the call of a mother floats through the woods. The river rushes by like it too is shushing them.

Bronwen breaks the calm with a scoff. "You two are ridiculous." Ayc and Lora break their locked gazes to look at her. Bronwen still leans against her staff, but it seems more relaxed and casual now, her head resting against the place where the blade begins. "If you would stop fighting each other for two seconds, you might realize that you both are trying to fight *for* each other. You're both just too proud and stubborn to admit it."

Ayc casts his eyes above him to avoid looking at any of them. He watches the branches that stretch over the river sway and cast shadows. Somewhere near here, Lora tried to buy him time as he ran away; he stayed behind to rescue her, knowing that it would cost him.

Maybe both of them have been prisoners of Yris in their own way, both obeying when they must and rebelling when they could. They've fought each other as she meant them to—Lora with knives, and Ayc with jokes—but perhaps, along the way, they've found ways to save each other, too.

"Shut up, Bronwen," Lora mutters, almost beneath her breath.

Bronwen smirks. "The only time you tell me to shut up is when you know I'm right."

She is, Ayc thinks. *Dammit.*

Lora exhales slowly, before looking up to meet Ayc's eyes. "Ayc, what can I do? I can't let you be her prisoner."

"You want to help me, villainess?" Impulsively, Ayc reaches for her hand. She lets him wrap his fingers around her palm, soft skin gliding beneath his fingertips. He lifts it so her chronicler is at eye-level. "Then *win.* Win so I don't have to be stuck for the rest of my life serving Marcellus or Wylder."

Lora doesn't look away from his eyes. "I don't want that power over you, either."

Isn't that what Peregrin said about Lora? That she didn't want the type of power that came with being Sovereign. Ayc hadn't believed it when they said it four days ago. But Ayc has lived lifetimes since then. The walls and the half-truths he's used to protect himself have crumbled to dust at his feet. For so long, he has forced himself to believe that she can't be both a villain of stone and a beautiful, caring soul.

But two things can be true all at once.

She is vicious. *And* she is beautiful.

And perhaps, one day he'll be courageous enough to admit he likes *both* sides of her.

"I don't want *anyone* to have power of me," Ayc says. "But if someone must, you're the only person I trust to have it." He adjusts his hand against hers, and their fingers lace together. She doesn't pull away, and Ayc finds himself lost in the feel of her skin on his. Then her eyes shift from him to her wrist, and his own gaze follows.

"Two stones," Ayc murmurs, when he sees it. "There are two stones lit."

"Really?" Bronwen rushes forward to see.

Ayc drops Lora's hand like he's been caught doing something he shouldn't.

"Which quest did you complete?" Bronwen asks.

Lora pushes back her sleeve to look at her forearm. "Forge a new path." She blinks. "How?"

"You said no to the Drakr," Ayc says. "You forged a path different from your mother, from what your mother wanted from you."

Lora rolls her eyes. "Divine, that's really obtuse, isn't it?"

Ayc laughs. "It is a little, yes."

Lora smiles. Not a quirk of one corner of her mouth or something forced and strained. A quiet, sincere smile. And, fuck, he could stare at the curved line forever. He could build dreams upon its peaks and make himself home in the valley.

Ayc reels back, shaking his head. What the fuck is the matter with him? He's never been one for poetry and yet one smile from Lora and he's composing sonnets in his head. He needs help. Or a cold dunk in the river. That might set him straight.

"I told you the quests could be completed in obscure ways," Peregrin says.

"And you were right. As always." Lora stares at her forearm a moment more, and then she pulls down her sleeve. A gleam of determination passes over her face.

"Oh no," Bronwen says. "I know that look."

"What look?"

"That determined look. It used to mean you were about to do something that might get us expelled from Adamant. You have an idea."

"Maybe I do." Lora sweeps her gaze across the three of them. "Two things. First, Ayc, I want you to understand that you are free to choose. With me, you're free to choose. I'll do my best not to issue a command, but if I slip up and do, tell me to—I don't know—fuck off or something."

He smiles at that. "Fuck off, Lora."

A soft line appears between her brows. "That was a command?"

"Little bit, yes"

"Fuck. Sorry."

"And look at that," he cheers. "You just apologized without insulting me first. That's progress."

Her eyes narrow. "Oh, shut—" She snaps her mouth shut so audibly her teeth clack.

Damn, she's serious about this. Relief floods through him, a soothing balm to wounds that are far deeper than physical.

Bronwen rolls her eyes at them, the corners of her lips twitching. "What was the second thing, Lora?"

"Second," she says, "we need to get back to the others as soon as possible. If the Drakr mean to help Marcellus, we don't have much time. Forget Laud for now. I know how to complete the next quest."

CHAPTER
TWENTY-FIVE

I t doesn't come as much of a surprise to Ayc that he and Peregrin don't find Xylie at the tavern; they find her at the library.

The buildings of the Silvae public library live within the branches of six towering trees. Within the buildings, bookshelves spiral around the tree trunks, each level containing a different genre. Walkways pass between the trees, some mere rope bridges, but two are enclosed with walls and a roof. These passageways contain rows of tables and chairs. Ayc finds Xylie and Tavish in the passageway between nonfiction and accessible books.

Xylie bends over a heavy tome, while Tavish sits across the table, his fingers tracing over the embedded letters of the book. Saga sleeps beneath the table but perks his head up when he hears Ayc and Peregrin's approach. A pack sits next to Saga, between Xylie's feet—Ayc's pack, and within it, the dragon egg.

"Learning any dark secrets?" Ayc asks, slipping into one of the unoccupied chairs.

Xylie doesn't look up as she signs, *"Oh, you're not dead. That's good."*

"What are you reading?"

Xylie halfway closes the book—not so far that she can't keep reading, but enough he can see the title: *An Exploration of Dragons.* Ayc should have known.

"Who's with you, Ayc?" Tavish asks. He's not holding Saga's leash.

"Just me," Peregrin states. "Tempest went back for Bronwen and Lora, but we should still have a couple of hours before they arrive. It's a long flight." They settle into a chair with a groan. Tempest left them both with gryphon feathers, and Ayc and Peregrin guzzled them down at the tavern. But the grey sheen of Peregrin's sweat reveals that today it is not enough. The feather gave Ayc a much-needed relief, though the remnants of pain feel like distant screams lodged in his muscles.

Xylie snaps her fingers to get Ayc's attention and then says, *"Your lover is here."*

"Which lover?" Ayc teases with a grin. "I have so many."

Xylie snorts. *"The one with the blond hair and ugly scowl."*

"I have no idea who you're talking about." Ayc looks to the other side of the table. "Tavish, who's here that I know?"

"Sterling and their Five," he replies.

Oh. Wren. The blond hair and ugly scowl. *Got it.*

Xylie's assessment is rude, but fair, and certainly not the worst thing that Xylie has said about one of the people that Ayc has taken to his bed. She's never liked any of them. Someone who didn't know Xylie might think her jealous, but Ayc knows better. Xylie has admitted that she doesn't feel sexual attraction toward anyone, lest of all him. It's simply the way she naturally is, the way Ayc is naturally attracted to any and every expression of gender or lack thereof. She desires romance and companionship, but believes she'll never find someone else willing to have one without also wanting sex, no matter how Ayc has tried to encourage her otherwise.

But no one ever passes Xylie's scrutiny when it comes to Ayc. He's never actually had a sister, but he imagines Xylie and he are quite like that.

"They're here in the library," Tavish continues to explain. "I think they're looking for something, but I'm not sure what. They're staying at the tavern, too, and I worked up the nerve to talk to a couple of them, but they're a lot harder to get information out of than drunk pirates. I think they're in a foul mood because Sterling hasn't completed any quests since we last saw them. Xylie tried to give me truth weed to slip into their drinks."

Ayc arches an eyebrow. "You carry truth weed on you?"

Not taking her eyes from the book, Xylie riffles through the bag hanging from her hip. She pulls out a small, drawstring pouch and tosses it to Ayc. He opens it and looks to see the rare plant. It looks almost exactly like the common weed, green foxtail, but it's the smell that sets it apart. He inhales. It is both sweet and sour. Like dill and honey.

Oh.

The moment comes back to him. The strange taste on Wren's tongue when she first pulled him into the storage room back on the ship leaving Bromalis. The way, when he resisted answering her questions, she fucked him so sweetly, buying time for the truth weed to work its way into his bloodstream. And then, after, how he couldn't stop the truth from pouring from his mouth, even though he tried.

Fuck.

His hand fists around the pouch, and he hands it back to Xylie before he crushes the precious ingredient inside. She tucks it back into her bag.

"Where did you say Wren is?" Ayc asks.

Peregrin shakes their head. "You don't listen to a thing I say, do you, boy?"

"I'm a notoriously foolish boy," Ayc says. Because he is. He is so fucking foolish. But he needs to see Wren. They have a conversation that is now overdue.

Peregrin narrows their eyes at Ayc, but Tavish responds, "Last I knew she was in the mythology section."

Ayc starts to stand, but he settles back down. No, this conversation could end poorly, and he doesn't think having it in the middle of a public library will go well. He suspects that Wren is far more volatile than he's given her credit for.

"I'll wait until we're back at the tavern," he says.

Peregrin opens their mouth, like there's a lot they would like to say. But they snap it closed again and make a flicking gesture with their hands as though washing themselves of the situation. Xylie taps Ayc's shoulder and signs for him to translate.

"Did you know that dragon eggs incubate for an entire decade?" Ayc says. "Tavish, when did you first start sensing the egg on Somnia Ignis?"

Tavish leans back in his chair, rubbing a hand over his jaw. "I don't know. Right before the *Maiden's Tears*. So maybe nine or ten years ago."

So, the egg could be preparing to hatch at any moment.

Peregrin snaps up straight. "Why do you ask, Xylie?"

Shit. Xylie should definitely not have brought it up in Peregrin's presence, but it's far too late now.

"No reason," Ayc says, quickly. "She was just curious."

"Ayc," Peregrin says, in a familiar tone. One that Ayc recognizes as calm—but only because they are trying very, very hard to remain calm. "Did you take the dragon egg?"

Ayc springs to his feet, grabs his pack from beneath the table and swings it over his shoulders. "Who is up for a drink? Or food? I am starving. Tavish, I know Xylie has probably kept you here for hours. Want to get some lunch from the venders near town central? I think I can smell it from here."

"Actually, I *am* starving." Tavish grabs Saga's guide handle and stands. The dog sneaks out from beneath the table and leads Tavish toward where Ayc is slowly backing toward the door. Saga takes long strides, stretching out each leg as he goes.

Peregrin's cheeks flush with red. "Ayc, if I open that pack, am I going to find a dragon egg?"

Ayc turns around and hurries toward the door. "What are you in the mood for?" he asks Tavish.

"Anything," Tavish says. Then he grins, leans close, and whispers, "You know I can sense the dragon egg, right? I knew you never left it in that cave."

"Don't tell, Lora," Ayc warns, flinging the door open.

"Of course not, but if she finds out, I'm going to deny ever knowing. I'll help Xylie throw you a beautiful funeral, friend."

Ayc laughs. "Fair enough."

"Ayc!" Peregrin hisses, trying to keep their voice at library volume. They are halfway out of their chair, but Xylie hasn't budged from the table, and Ayc knows Peregrin won't leave her alone.

Once Tavish is through the door, Ayc turns around to

toss Peregrin and Xylie a wave. "See you at the tavern. I'll get you something from the vendors."

He lets the door slam shut, far louder than any library should allow. He's immediately shushed by at least three people, and then more as Tavish and Ayc barely contain their laughter like two teenage boys getting away with something foolish.

Ayc's stomach is filled with meat pie and fried cheese by the time he and Tavish make their way back to the tavern, both carrying food wrapped in cloth for their companions. The center of town buzzed with crowds of people shopping at the carts and stalls set between the trees. Ayc imagined, as he often does when he comes across such places, what it might be like to have a stall of his own, where he'd spend every morning baking new and extravagant creations. But he shook the thoughts away as quickly as the thoughts came. Such dreams aren't meant for him.

When Tavish and Ayc enter the tavern, people crowd every table. He spots Peregrin in the corner, their feet on one seat and a cane on the other, saving places. They wear a deep scowl. Xylie isn't anywhere to be seen, and Ayc suspects she is in one of the rooms on the floor above them. The laughter and talking of the Totus Omni who fill the place shakes the walls, and a feminine-presenting fae is on a makeshift stage in the corner, drunkenly crooning the lyrics to a love ballad. Sitting on a barstool nearby, their clearly-smitten lover, a sweet looking faun, giggles behind their hand and sways their petite hooves. A nearby table of friends cheer for them. It is absolutely adorable.

"I brought you food," Ayc says to Peregrin as a peace offering, setting one of the bundles before them. "Lamb and sweet potato pie. Your favorite. This other one is for Xylie. What room is she in?"

The scowl on Peregrin's face doesn't budge. They move their cane for Tavish to sit but keep their feet on the other remaining chair. "She's in room 3. If you think I've forgotten, you're greatly mistaken. What's in your pack?"

Just then, the love ballad ends, and the lovers entangle with each other so hard they tumble off the stage and back into their chairs.

"You know what?" Ayc says, pointing his thumb over his shoulder at the stage. "I think I'm going to sing."

Ayc ignores the choice words Peregrin heaves at his back as he approaches the stage. Applause breaks out as Ayc jumps over the two steps and lands on the platform. His blood thrums with excitement. A few recorders sit at a thin table at the back of the stage, marked with the titles of songs. He spots a title he recognizes on one shaped like a unicorn. He taps to play it.

The music fills the cramped space, and the crowd begins to cheer. It's a popular song, played at all the festivals hosted by the Totus Omni. He's danced to it at several parties. There's a strong beat, and a traditional dance and clapping that pairs with the rhythm. Several fae jump up to make the motions. Others still sit and beat their goblets and fists on the table, three beats and then two claps.

Ayc lifts the rose-shaped amplifier left on the stage and brings it to his lips to belt the lyrics. Ayc suspects most of the crowd can't hear him, because they are belting the familiar lyrics, too. Instead, he works the crowd. He dances in a way that he knows he'll feel in his muscles later, but he's too engrossed to feel it now. He tilts the amplifier in his hand to one audience member and then another to pick up their voices. The goblets on the tables tremble with the delight of the crowd.

> "I'll be brave enough to fight dragons for you.
> I'll be daring enough to sail seas for you.
> I'll be whatever you need to be,
> For you to see me."

He's through the first verse and chorus when the door opens, and he misses the next line as Lora enters the tavern. Bronwen is right behind her. Ayc lifts his hand to wave. Lora backs away like she might bolt from the tavern, but Bronwen beams, grabs Lora's arm, and hauls her into the crowd. Ayc brings the amplifier to his mouth and sings the next lines even louder.

Bronwen abandons Lora in the center of the crowd and flings herself across the room to Tavish, who she pulls from the table to dance with her. Tavish can't see the standard moves to the song, so Bronwen doesn't even try. Instead, she leads him to twirl and spin her beneath his arm. Lora slowly weaves through the crowd toward the stage, where she stops, her arms crossed over her chest. The wound on her face is now scabbed; the blood has been washed from her face. The furrow in her brow speaks of disapproval, but when he croons a line especially off-key, her lips spasm like they might betray her with a smile.

He works for that smile: acting even more ridiculous, dancing so badly it should be embarrassing. When her smile forms, it's worth it. She shakes her head at him, but that smile awakens her face, making it glow all the way to her violet eyes that glimmer like the stars on a clear night. Like the tapestry that hangs in his bedroom.

He's so distracted by her that he doesn't realize how close he's come to the edge of stage, until he does a playful leap and tumbles right off. He lands flat on his stomach as the crowd roars the last line of the song.

> *"And in the end, I learned that*
> *What you really wanted was me."*

As the song and the crowd fades, he hears it. A sound like wind chimes and bird song, the fairest melody he's ever heard. He tips his head back to look up, certain he's hallucinating. But Lora is there, laughing.

After all these years, he finally made her laugh.

Victory. It is sweet, sweet victory.

She bites her lip to silence the sound, then reaches down to offer her hand. He takes it and lets her help him to his feet. "By the divine, you are utterly ridiculous."

"I'll gladly be ridiculous, if it means I keep getting to hear you laugh."

Fuck, did he say that out loud?

He must have, because her smile wanes. Her face transforms, and she's looking at him again, like she did in her grandmother's house, tracing the lines of his face and then following them down to linger on his lips. The moment is intoxicating. It's the sweetest of cinnamon rolls and the lightning of her villainy and every melody that has ever made him feel free. His breath shudders from his lungs, because he's quite certain that this moment will end in him going up in flames.

Good. He wants to *burn.*

He's already burning. He's been burning for so fucking long.

She tugs at his hand, and he takes a step. Millimeters, not miles, separate them now.

"Hi, Ayc," says a different voice. Wren.

Ayc's heart plummets into his stomach. *Dammit. Not now.*

He longs to seize hold of the moment and refuse to let it go, but Lora whips away from him. The absence of her touch scalds.

He represses the urge to bare his teeth at Wren and works his expression into a smile instead. Wren wears her cloak clasped down the front, covering her all the way to her ankles. She carries two goblets and a bottle of wine. Her hair is free of her braid, spilling around her shoulders in ringlets. She's certainly not dressed like she's looking for a fight. Ayc searches the room, but Sterling and the rest of the Five aren't here.

"Hello to you too, Lora," Wren says.

Lora fixes her with a glare that could have peeled the skin off a lesser person. She says nothing in return.

"Ayc, can we talk in private?" Wren asks.

"Sure," Ayc says, perhaps too quickly.

Wren nods toward the staircase and steps in that direction. Ayc follows, but Lora snags his sleeve. "Ayc."

Ayc turns around. He hopes she's about to say something like *Stay with me* or *I don't want you to go.*

Instead, she lowers her voice and hisses, "Do you not have even a single ounce of sense left in your brainless head? If you would stop thinking with your dick for two seconds, you'd realize that she could kill you the moment you're alone."

Those words are as effective of a slap across his face, a reminder of how Lora truly thinks of him. A foolish ass whose only brain exists between his legs. He pulls away from her, the heat in his skin morphing from desire to anger.

Thanks for the reminder, he almost says. *I needed it.*

He forces an easy, playful smile. "She's not a preying mantis. She's not going to fuck me and then bite off my head. If she was going to, she would have done it on the ship from Bromalis."

"What?" Lora's eyes darken with some emotion that Ayc can't place. Anger? Jealousy? That dark, monstrous thing that lives deep inside of him hopes it's jealousy. It is a vengeful, petty thing.

"Fine," she growls, "do whatever the fuck you want. But we're taking a ship out of here first thing in the morning. If you're not here, I'll leave you behind."

She storms toward where Bronwen and Tavish stand. Bronwen fixes her eyes on Ayc and shakes her head. But Ayc ignores whatever message she's trying to send and marches to where Wren waits at the bottom of the stairs

"She really doesn't like that you're with me, does she?" Wren asks. She grins, like the fact amuses her.

Ayc shrugs. "Let's just go."

"I'm glad I ran into you, Ayc," Wren murmurs as she leads him up the stairs. "I missed you."

"Did you?" he muses back, playing the part. When they reach the landing, he says, "Give me a minute. I just want to drop off my pack."

Room 3 is locked. He knocks. "Xylie, it's Ayc."

When Xylie appears at the door, she frowns at the sight of Wren down the hall, but opens the door wide enough for

Ayc to slide in. Ayc kicks the door shut behind him, slips off his pack, and hands it to her.

"What are you doing, Ayc?" Xylie says with a sigh, taking the pack and cradling it against his chest. "Neither Lora or Peregrin trust Wren, so I don't either."

"Good, neither do I." Ayc signs the words, in case Wren has wandered too close to the door. *"I'm going to try to get information from her. I'll explain everything later. Don't say anything to Lora, please."* He wants to be able to explain everything to Lora himself.

Xylie's hands hover in the air, as though unsure what to say. Finally, she only signs, *"Be careful, all right?"*

Ayc nods and steps back into the hallway. Wren unlocks the last door in the hallway, and Ayc follows her inside.

There's only one bed, made up like no one has slept here. Only one pack sits in the corner, but perhaps, Sterling has rented multiple rooms for their Five and this belongs to Wren alone. Wren sets the wine and goblets down on the stool sitting beside the bed and then unbuckles her cloak. She tosses it on the bed. Beneath, she's wearing a loose tunic that glides off one shoulder and stops just below her hips.

She really is beautiful. His body remembers the tightness and warmth of being inside her, and he almost desires to give in as she saunters toward him, letting her hips sway with her intentions. He longs to fuck just so he can banish the ache beneath his sternum and extinguish the fire in his blood. Or, at least, damper it back to a simmer. He's an expert at burying pain behind pleasure and sex. Only this time, it's not the pain of his physical body he desires to hide from.

He won't, though. Right now, he's not able to lie to himself. It's not Wren he wants. Maybe, it never has been.

It's never been anyone else. Every person—every fling, he's fooled himself into thinking he might be falling for—is just a poor substitute for the person he knows he has no business wanting.

When Wren steps into his space and stands on her toes to kiss him, he presses a finger to her lips. She grins, and he brings himself close, so she'll feel his words.

"You—" he growls "—are a manipulative, vindictive *bitch*."

She reels back. "Excuse me!"

He retreats a few steps and crosses his arms over his chest. "You're going to have to swallow the truth weed in your mouth. I'm not falling for it this time."

Fury crackles over her face. He thinks she might deny it, but then she rolls her eyes. "I don't understand why you're so angry."

She returns to the goblets and wine. He watches her carefully as she pours the wine into each goblet—a gold and silver. She shifts to obscure his view of the silver goblet. All the while, she talks. "You don't seem to understand that this is a game. You could have chosen to give me information willingly, but you proved to me the night before the Trials that you weren't going to do that."

The night before the Trials? That was the night she showed up in his kitchen and told him she wanted him. It was a game, even then. Maybe it was before that, on the very first night. She certainly came with questions about Yris and the Trials. Ayc has been nothing more than a pawn in Wren's game this entire time. It shouldn't hurt, but it does. All the things she whispered in his ear, the way she laid against his chest, the way she made him hope that he could be something important to someone—it was all just pretty lies.

Wren turns with a goblet in each of her hands. "You know I gave you plenty of chances to make a choice. Me or Loraphne? You profess to hating her, and yet, you always chose her."

She sips from the gold goblet, licks the wine off her lips, and then offers him the silver one. Does she truly think him unintelligent enough to fall for that? He ignores the silver goblet and pries the gold from her fingertips. She frowns but lets it go.

"If I hadn't chosen Lora, she'd be dead right now," Ayc says. "You gave me midnight, thinking I wouldn't recognize it, let alone know what it could do. You *lied* to me."

"I didn't lie," Wren corrects, setting the goblet back on the nightstand untouched, confirming his suspicion that she was trying to poison him. "I couldn't. I'd ingested truth weed, too, after all. Technically, it *would* have weakened her, before it killed her."

Her words are cold and unfeeling, as vicious as Yris. Ayc thought he knew a lot about who the villains were in his life's story. He so adamantly kept Lora in her role of villain while he easily cast Wren to be something good. As it turns out, he's just a terrible judge of character.

"And *I* would have had to live with the guilt of her death forever," Ayc says. "And you didn't give a fuck."

"Don't act so perfect. It's not like you've *never* lied to me. Do you think I didn't recognize that it was Loraphne's tapestry on your bedroom wall?"

Ayc nearly drops the goblet.

"It must have cost you a fortune," she sneers. "Yris can't

pay you that well. How many months of wages did you pay just to have a *piece* of Loraphne?"

An entire year's worth.

That was what it cost him.

How many festivals did he wander over to Lora's booth to stare at that tapestry, transfixed by it? It was like he could see a piece of Lora—something beautiful and good, sunlight gleaming off the iron blade that she is. Ayc suspects now that Hellevi refused to sell it to anyone else after noticing his admiration, even though he told her the first time he saw it that he'd never be able to afford it. Fair after fair, the tapestry remained. In the end, he scrounged up enough to offer half of what the tapestry was worth. Its destiny was to be hung in some wealthy merchant's home, but it hangs in his broom closet of a room.

At least now, Ayc knows that the money went to a valiant cause. Whose freedom did he buy?

"Tell me," Wren taunts. "Were you thinking about Loraphne while you were fucking *me*?" He doesn't answer, and Wren laughs cruelly. "You're so desperately in love with her. It's *pathetic*."

I'm not, Ayc wants to say, but the words hover in his throat, choking him. It's like he's swallowed down truth weed, after all.

I hate her has only ever been a poor coping skill to protect him from the truth he's too cowardly to face. The truth that will destroy him. Love is the type of pain that magic and tonics can't touch. He will shatter for her, one of these days. It is only a matter of time.

He gulps down a few mouthfuls of wine, craving the numbness he knows it'll provide.

"Do you know what I really don't understand, Wren?"

he says, pointedly changing the subject to why he actually came here. "Is why you would work with Marcellus?"

Again, he expects her to deny it. She only glares at him, a silent admittance.

"You told him we were going to Somnia Ignis. And you told him about Tavish and Xylie, because I was foolish enough to trust you."

Wren shrugs. "The enemy of my enemy, Ayc."

It's the confirmation that he needed. Wren gave every bit of information she gathered from Ayc to Marcellus. And it was all Ayc's fault. *He* betrayed Lora. He has to walk out of this room and admit that to her and hope she doesn't wring his neck the way he deserves. Or worse, expel him from her Five.

"And you really think Marcellus is better than Lora?" Ayc demands. "He would make it so that your sibling cannot exist as themselves."

"I have a plan."

"I hope for the sake of all of Everadyn that you do, because if you help him win, I swear I'll make you pay for it." Red flashes before his vision, fueled by the rage erupting through his veins. He closes his eyes just as quickly, and the room tilts and sways. He stumbles to the side and flings his eyes open.

What the fuck was that?

His head steadies as he focuses on Wren. She's grinning at him. Not the reaction he wanted from his threat.

Fear trails up his spine like a ghostly touch. He needs to leave this room. Now. "I hope you drink that other goblet and get a taste of your own poison," he snarls, taking a step past her. The room tilts again, and he careens sideways, crashing into the wall. The goblet tumbles from his hand, wine splashing across the floor.

She faces him, still smiling. "I didn't poison the *goblet* of wine, Ayc. I poisoned the *bottle*. I've built up tolerance to my own methods. A taste can't hurt me."

Fuck! Fuck!

Ayc sprints toward the door, but he only makes it a step before Wren seizes his leathers and heaves him backward. He timbers like a tree, landing hard on the floor. The ceiling above him spins.

Wren sighs and mutters, "I wish it hadn't come to this."

And then everything goes black.

CHAPTER
TWENTY-SIX

- LORA -

This time Lora is *really* going to kill him.

She paces in her armor in the common room of the tavern. Despite the singing, partying crowd of last night, the place is silent now. Whether the patrons have gone home or are simply sleeping off the hangover upstairs, Lora doesn't care. Only Tavish, Peregrin and Bronwen sit in the corner table. And, Saga, of course, nestled beneath Tavish's feet. Xylie signed that she intended to wait upstairs until they were ready, perhaps afraid that the place would still be overstimulating.

But Ayc is not here. Lora hasn't seen him since last night.

She and her Five only have another fifteen minutes before they all must leave if they hope to arrive at the air dock on time. They are supposed to board the ship that will carry them to the Lux Aester city, and from there, find an ocean ship that will sail them to Velphin. She threatened Ayc that she'd leave without him, and she really doesn't want to find out whether she actually meant it.

And all because he's up there fucking Wren.

Lora's fists coil so hard she nearly breaks the skin of her palms. "I'm really going to kill him this time."

"You know," Bronwen muses, sipping her tea with a calm that sets Lora's nerves even more at edge, "if you had just told him you were jealous, none of this would have happened."

"I am *not* jealous!" Lora growls.

Tavish snorts into his own mug. "And *I'm* the one who's blind."

"I'm not," Lora insists. "He's late because he's sleeping with an enemy. I have perfectly valid reasons to be angry at him."

Bronwen twirls the end of her braid around one finger. "Are you upset that he's sleeping with an *enemy*, or you upset that he's sleeping with someone who isn't *you*? I've seen you with other males, Lora. And a female or two. You've never let *any* of them get under your skin the way Ayc does. Not even Wylder."

"I really don't want to be part of this conversation," Peregrin groans, rubbing their temples.

"That makes two of us," Lora says through her teeth. She paces away from her First, before she surrenders to the urge to pretend she and Bronwen are back in their first year at Adamant. First years are pitted against each other, battling until one of them is unconscious or bleeding. It's not how most friendships are made, but somehow, it worked for Bronwen and Lora.

Bronwen snorts, and Lora almost tells her to shut up, but that will only grant her more satisfaction. What had

Bronwen said? *You only tell me to shut up when you know I'm right.*

Xylie can see facts and solve puzzles and divine logic in ways that defy explanation, but Bronwen understands people. She watches everyone from behind a teacup and then can tell them things about themselves that they never dare to face. Lora hates that about her. And also loves it.

Bronwen must have noticed how Lora laid awake for most of last night, knowing Ayc was in another room. She listened quietly, wondering if she might hear the moans of pleasure, but the night was still. She heard nothing at all, except for the whispers of a late-night traveler leaving their room and departing the inn. Or perhaps, Bronwen saw the way Lora so foolishly pulled Ayc toward her last night. She hadn't thought about the people around her. For a reckless moment of time, Ayc was all she could see, and she'd almost given into the impulse to haul him to her.

But Bronwen is wrong. Lora understands how it looks, but it means *nothing*. When it comes to Ayc, Lora's mind and body simply betrays her sometimes. The way it betrayed her when she and Ayc rode Tempest and she found herself unable to control the way his hands on her stomach built an ache between her thighs. It betrayed her when her hand wrapped around his throat and he taunted her to squeeze harder, making her eyes flare silver, but not in anger. And most devastating, it betrayed her when she watched Ayc in her grandmother's kitchen and foolishly wished they could both stay there forever.

This was why asking him to be her Fifth was a mistake. She thought that, after four years apart, she would somehow be immune to the way he always crawled beneath her skin. She was strong enough now; she could handle him being so close. She was wrong.

But I'm not *jealous,* Lora insists to herself. Whatever complicated things she feels for him, she refuses to call it jealousy. Ayc can go and fuck whoever he wants. But why does it have to be Wren? Wren, the woman who, seven years ago, pinned Lora in a dark corner of Wyntra and told her that one day she'd kill Lora to get revenge for her mother's death. Even though she knew Lora, too, lost a parent that day.

I'm not jealous, Lora repeats it like a mantra in her head. *I'm not jealous. I'm not* fucking *jealous.*

A creak of stairs draws Lora back to reality.

Xylie frowns around the room. She approaches, her hands already speaking. "*What's going on? What are we waiting for?*"

Lora grunts. "Ayc."

Xylie's eyes fling wide. "*Is he still sleeping?*"

"I don't know," Lora says. *And I don't want to think about it anymore.*

"*Has no one checked the room?*"

"I don't know what room Wren was in," Lora says. Or she might have dragged him out of there by his ear already.

Color drains from Xylie's face, turning her warm black skin grayish, like she might be ill. "*What do you mean he never came back from Wren's room?*"

Lora frowns, unsure what's caused the horror on her cousins face. "I mean exactly what that sounds like. He's apparently found her company far more appealing than ours."

Xylie shakes her head so quickly her braids lash side to side. Her lips move, mouthing with no sound, *No, no.*

Alarmed, Lora rushes a step toward her, but Xylie retreats backward.

"No." This time it makes a hoarse sound.

"Xylie, what's wrong?" Bronwen says, pushing to her feet and rounding the table.

Xylie's hands tremble as she signs. Lora translates, and as she does, Xylie's panic spreads toward her like a dark, creeping smog. With each word, Lora grows colder.

"Xylie saw Ayc before he went with Wren. He said he didn't trust her, but he wanted information. He said he'd explain later, but Xylie didn't see him again. She just assumed it got late, so he went to Tavish and Peregrin's room after."

"No," Tavish says. "He wasn't with us."

Peregrin shoves to their feet, bracing themself on the table. "He said he didn't trust her? Then where the fuck is he now?"

Xylie mouths the word one more time. *No.*

Lora's heart stops utterly and then takes up the same cry as it restarts again. *No, no, no.*

She catapults herself toward the front desk and rings the bell to summon the innkeeper. A fae with gold-hued skin stumbles from the kitchen, clutching a mixing bowl and blowing a strand of green hair from her face. "Yes?"

"What room was Wren of the Bromalis staying in?"

"I can't tell you where my guests were staying without significant reason."

Lora hesitates, trying to decide whether significant reason means a blade or a coin, but Bronwen slaps a stack of silver down on the counter.

Bronwen gives a smile that hides a threat behind its sweetness. Lora has seen her friend offer someone that

410

smile right before she's cast a spell to turn them inside out. "Is this significant enough?" she asks.

The innkeeper sets down her mixing bowl. "That ought to do." She wipes her hand on her ale-stained apron and reaches toward the ledger sitting on the counter. "Ah, yes, Wren. She checked out about one after midnight."

"Was there a man with her?" Lora demands, her heart slamming in her eardrums.

"Wasn't any mention of a man. Isn't any of my business. But—" She taps the book. "Says here she left a letter." She shuffles back a few pages in the book and removes a folded piece of paper. A name is scrawled across it. "You wouldn't happen to be Loraphne, would you?"

Lora snatches the paper from her hand, ignoring her protest. She marches a few steps away and fights to control the shudder in her fingers as she unfolds the letter. Somehow, she knows what she will find. Still, when she reads the words, she drops the paper. It flutters from her hands and drifts down to the floor.

Her vision turns silver. With fear and a flash of tears, yes, but that's gone quickly and replaced with something else. Something that burns so bright, her eyes blaze and her soul trembles. It should make the world tremble, too.

Rage.

Lora is going to kill them all.

"What does it say?" Peregrin demands, as Bronwen grabs the letter from the floor.

Lora replies through her teeth, her canines growing to deadly points, "If you want him, come and get him."

411

CHAPTER
TWENTY-SEVEN

- AYC -

Everything hurts.

The realization comes to Ayc slowly—the burn between his shoulders, the pound at his temples —and then all at once as his eyes fly open. His skin blazes like it's been lit on fire; his nerves rattle like they are screaming for relief. His arms suspend above his head by metal handcuffs, high enough his toes barely brush the stone beneath him.

He groans, fighting past the wall of pain to make sense of his surroundings. His vision swims and blurs, and in the darkness, all he can make out are the stone walls of a circular room, barren save for a few wooden benches. And then Ayc focuses enough to see *him*, standing near the wood door with his arms crossed and a smirk on his face.

Marcellus.

Ayc's lips curl back in a snarl. "So this is eternal torment, huh? Always knew I'd see you here someday."

"You're not dead, human," Marcellus says. "Though I suspect you probably wish you were. I hear dazewood burns like eternal torment when you come out of it. Wren said it should be out of your system in an hour or two. Maybe longer. She had to give you multiple doses for you to stay under until you got here. You have incredible tolerance..." He pauses and then adds heavily, as though trying to make a point. "For a human."

"Where am I?" Ayc wishes he growled the words, but his head still spins, and it sounds more akin to a gasp.

"In the lower levels of a Lux Aester temple. Consider yourself blessed. This is a small sanctuary in the priest's quarters, and you certainly aren't worthy to be in it, but I needed to make due."

"Do all priests get chained to the ceiling here?" Ayc asks, finding strength behind his voice. "If so, sign me up. Sounds depraved in the best sort of way."

The smile tumbles from Marcellus's lips. "You're a degenerate."

"I take that as a compliment."

Ayc assesses his situation carefully. Looking down at his body, he appears to be physically unharmed, despite the pain. They have stripped him of his leather armor, leaving only his breeches and linen shirt behind. They've left his leviathan's tooth, dangling from the cord around his neck. His chains are secured to a rafter, above which the ceiling is painted with a golden sun in the bluest of skies. His bracelets press tight to his skin where the iron chain digs into his wrists. If only he could snap the chains in half, he would willingly be at Marcellus's throat, but these chains were made to hold fae, likely a blend of iron and tungsten. A Drakr warrior couldn't break free.

413

Ayc forces himself to breathe. In and out. He imagines the pain as a wave, slowly receding, until he isn't drowning; he's swimming. He focuses on Marcellus. With his arms crossed, his chronicler is visible. All but two of the gems gleam in the dim light of the two torches that hang on either side of the door.

"I guess working with Drakr has been profitable to you in a very small amount of time, huh, Marcellus?" Ayc asks.

The bastard doesn't flinch.

"Doesn't the divine have anything to say about cheating?"

He drops his arms to his side. "Is it cheating to use all the resources available to you?"

"Did the Drakr tell you to kidnap me?" Ayc asks, even though that doesn't seem right. Wren was already in Silvae before Lora told Lahlis no. This plan was in place long before that.

"The Drakr have nothing to do with me completing the last two quests," Marcellus says. "Right now, they're busy making sure the Noxumbra and Lycendi victors don't see tomorrow."

Fuck. Ayc almost feels bad for Wylder, and if there are gods or the divine, he would send a prayer for Wylder's Five, particularly his brother. They are all strong warriors. Surely, they'll survive.

"So what's your plan for me, then, Marcellus?" Ayc changes the subject. "Can't get enough of my baking? Want me to perform for you?"

"Isn't it obvious? You're bait."

Ayc was afraid he was going to say that, but he makes his voice sound bored. "Lora is too smart to fall for your stunt. She'll know this is a trap."

Marcellus leans back against the door, and his smile returns. "I'm sure she will. And she'll still walk right into it to keep me from killing you."

"Me?" Ayc snorts. "I annoy her far too much. You'd be doing her a favor by getting rid of me."

"Is that why she threatened to rip our hearts out? Is she truly so blood thirsty to threaten people over someone she hates so much?"

"You truly don't know her at all, do you?"

Marcellus's smile creeps higher, curling up his pale cheeks like slithering snakes making tracks in snow. "Oh, but I think I do."

Ayc responds with an exaggerated roll of his eyes that does nothing to quell Marcellus's smile. But Ayc isn't certain which of them is right. Nor does he know who he *hopes* is right. Lora has demonstrated she cares for Ayc in some way and has chosen to protect him before. But she must know he's not worth the risk of losing the Trials. Ayc's suffering will be a small price to pay for defeating Marcellus. And yet, some part of Ayc hopes he's wrong, and that she cares enough to come for him. A truly foolish part of him.

"But if she doesn't—" Marcellus lifts his palm in a gesture that says *'Oh, well'* "—I'll just send your heart back to her tied in a lovely pink bow."

Ayc refuses to let fear flicker on his face. Instead, he grins right back. "I hope you have fun with those three generations of bad luck."

Marcellus's cold laughter echoes through the room. "Lying is a sin, human. And I'll be happy to deal the divine's judgment upon you when the time comes."

A shiver trails down Ayc's spine. He doesn't think Marcellus is bluffing. Whatever Marcellus saw when he dueled Ayc in the dragon's lair, Ayc revealed far too much. And now, he's fucked.

Marcellus opens the door. Two priests, identifiable by their blue robes, enter. "Watch him closely. Don't let your guard down even for a moment. He's not what he seems."

Marcellus slams the door behind him, and the two priests stand still as statues before the door, their Lux Aester blue eyes never leaving Ayc. They look almost like ghosts— so pale they're nearly translucent. They barely seem to blink.

Ayc swallows down the fear and the pain and anchors a smile onto his face. "Hey, have you ever heard that one about the merfolk who swam into a bar?"

TEN YEARS AGO

- LORA -

The human boy wore a smile that didn't make sense. Lora studied it like a puzzle as Ayc spooned a perfect dollop of chocolate pudding into the bowls in front of Lora's mother and her Five. The smile illuminated his entire face, making the sky-blue eyes glimmer like a bright summer day. Surely, he couldn't be that happy. She wondered if that smile was real, or a disguise, or perhaps a weapon.

The young fae who rotated through the Wyntra school never smiled at her. They were all too terrified of Lora, too busy whispering behind her back. They called her "the little villainess"—evil, just like her mother. They were only repeating things they had heard their parents say; they didn't really know what it all meant. Lora knew she should do as her mother always said and make her skin thick as stone, so nothing could touch her, certainly not silly words. But it hurt, anyway.

Ayc served Lora last. She always sat at the very end of the table, separated by a couple of seats from the others— always there but never really present. She quickly looked down at her plate so he wouldn't notice that she'd been staring at him.

"Hey, Lora," he whispered in a familiar, teasing tone, as he spooned the delicious looking chocolate into her bowl, "do you want to hear a joke?"

Lora peeked at her mother, but Yris currently had her head bent toward Fennix. Still, Lora's heart hammered against her breastbone unsteadily. Ayc did this a lot, whispering jokes when he noticed her mother's attention lapsing. Lora had no idea why, but she wished he wouldn't. She wasn't sure what her mother would do if she caught him.

Yris had warned Lora the very first day. As the fae ship crossed the sea from Creed to Wyntra, Lora had tried to sneak food to Ayc where they had him bound in the hull of the ship. But Yris had caught Lora and forced her to throw out the food.

"Do not get attached to that boy, Loraphne. Kindness is weakness."

Though Lora said nothing, Ayc went on with his joke anyway. "Have you heard the one about the merfolk who swam into a bar? They said, 'Sure is sandy in here'."

Lora frowned. Then, *oh*. Bar. Ocean bar. The desire to laugh bubbled in her throat, and she bit down on her bottom lip to staunch it, lest anyone hear.

His smile wavered, like he was disappointed. And Lora didn't understand why her laughter meant anything to him.

"Human," Yris snapped from the other end of the table, "what are you lingering for? Go back to your kitchen."

His smile vanished completely. "Yes, my l-lady."

He hurried to the door, and Lora's heart sank lower at each of his retreating steps. She often wondered about him, though she tried not to. Did he ever feel as lonely as she did? She understood how this castle could be a prison, because it was hers as well. She carried a journal in her pocket, something her father had given her, to write down all her thoughts and feelings, her plans and her dreams, her ideas for tapestries and clothing she would get to make when she returned to Avia in the summer. At the very front, she kept a tally, tracking all the days left until she could return.

At the door, Ayc cast a look over his shoulder. He arched one eyebrow. Dammit. He'd caught her staring. Before she could look away, he pulled a ridiculous face, eyes crossed and his tongue sticking out right before the door slammed behind him. And she couldn't stop it. One burst of laughter broke from her mouth. She bit down hard on her lip, hard enough she tasted the sharp metallic sting of blood. But it wasn't enough to keep Yris from hearing.

Her mother's gaze could cut deeper than any blade. It slices into Lora's spine, slipping between her vertebrae.

"Leave me alone with my daughter." Yris's command rang through the dining hall.

Only Fennix hesitated, sending Lora a concerned glance. He always looked concerned, but Lora learned long ago he'd never actually help her. He was the last to leave, but still he left, shutting the door behind him.

Yris's chair screeched against stone as she stood. Lora

continued to stare at her plate, fisting her hands in her lap to keep them from shaking. Her mother hated when Lora shook, when she sometimes flapped her hands or fanned her face when the tension in her body became too much. She had learned long ago to hide it. She forced herself to breathe in through her nose and out through her mouth, the way Peregrin had taught her.

"I thought I had made myself clear about that boy," Yris said as she stopped beside Lora, looming above her. "And yet, you continue to be merciful. Do you think I don't notice how you look at him with such sympathy?"

The back of Lora's eyes burned. *Don't cry. Do not cry.*

Her mother would slap her if she cried.

Her vision blurs as everything inside her trembles. One day, she will learn to take this feeling and turn it into rage. She will understand that it's easier to be angry than to be afraid. But she hadn't yet learned that. So she stared at the pudding and imagined a merfolk swimming into a sand bar until her vision cleared.

"Loraphne, look at me!" Yris didn't give her the chance. She seized Lora's face and yanked it toward her. Her long nails threatened to pierce Lora's cheek, but her mother was too careful for that. The poison in Yris's fingernail paint would lead to scars, and Yris couldn't accept her daughter's face being scarred. "Kindness is weakness. And I will not tolerate my daughter being weak. Your destiny is to be Sovereign one day. You must be as immovable and as unfeeling as stone. If I believe for a moment that you've let yourself get attached to the human boy, then the divine be damned. I'll see him dead, and I'll make you do it."

Something imploded within Lora's chest. She didn't have words for it then; she still doesn't. She only knows that it hurt. She only remembers it as the day she learned how painful it is to want things that she cannot have.

So she stopped wanting.

Or at least, she thought she did.

NOW

Xylie digs out the map from Tavish's pack, before he can even take it from his back. She flings it open on one of the tables.

"Find him, Tavish," Lora orders, but Tavish already bends over the map.

He flattens his hands on the paper, sensing. It takes him only moments, and he taps a finger on a spot in the northeastern regions of Everadyn. The Lux Aester lands take up nearly all the eastern border of Everadyn, through the plains and over the eastern edge of the Stella Rune Mountains before finally giving way to the warmer lands held by the Sal Maris. The expanse of their lands grants Lux Aester power. Each clan has its shares of farmers and hunters, but Lux Aester has the most, their production of food vital to every other clan except perhaps to Noxumbra.

Not much is marked on the map in the Lux Aester territory, but they have made sure to include their temples, their proportion disproportionate to the surrounding structures. Tavish's finger poses above one of those symbols, a steepled building. Throughout most of Lux Aester, people cram an entire family into a single room house, while everything they earn goes into tithing. Tithing that the religious leaders than use to build temples lined with marble and crowned in gold. The buildings are beautiful and magnificent and an utter waste.

Bronwen squints at the letter she now holds, the one that fell from Lora's fingers. "It matches the coordinates you were given. At least, Wren wasn't lying. Ayc is there."

Peregrin reaches for the letter, and Bronwen hands it over. "It says to come alone and unarmed." Peregrin grits their teeth. "It's a trap."

"I know," Lora replies. Just as she already knows what she must do.

Protect him.

Just as she's always tried to do. Admittedly, she's never done it very well. She could never make it obvious to her mother what she was doing, lest Yris follow through with her threat to make Lora kill him. But Lora did what she could.

When Yris nearly drowned Ayc by tying him to the cliffs above the Bellum, Lora waited until the water was at his chest, hoping he would do something to save himself, before she ran to get Fennix. When she heard Ayc was sent into the gryphon pasture, she warned Peregrin who hurried to intervene. Later, when Yris enlisted some of the students in her games to continually torment Ayc—long past when Ayc showed his powers, long past when he would have been Bound to Yris—Lora always threatened them not to take it too far. Yes, sometimes Lora even tormented him herself, but only did it when she feared Yris suspected her of becoming too soft. Or sometimes, just for Lora to convince herself she hated him again.

The protection wasn't enough; she knows that now. She should have found a way to help him escape. Maybe, she should have run away with him and never looked back. But she never was brave enough.

Until now.

Bronwen brushes a hand on Lora's shoulder. "Lora, I know what you're thinking—"

"No, you don't."

"You think you can storm in there and save him with nothing more than hands and your teeth."

All right, so maybe Bronwen knows exactly what Lora is thinking.

"That is exactly what Marcellus wants you to do," Bronwen continues. "He will exploit any weakness he can find, and he thinks he's found yours."

Lora means to deny it, but Bronwen lifts a single eyebrow and Lora finds herself lacking the energy to lie to her. *Kindness is weakness.* Her mother's words ring in her ears, even now. But her mother was wrong to fear kindness. Lora has never been particularly kind. *Villainess,* the children at Wyntra called her, first as an ode to her mother and then because she earned it. *Relentless,* Peregrin always told her instead, while her instructors at Adamant preferred, *Merciless.* Even Lora's own father worried about the influence her mother had on Lora before he was exiled, even as he and Hellevi taught her—showed her—what she should truly be fighting for, what is worth being ruthless for.

Kindness has never been her issue.

But Ayc...

"*Has* he found your weakness?" Tavish asks, breaking the thick silence hovering in the air.

"What am I supposed to do?" Lora snaps. "The letter says that Marcellus will kill him if I don't go."

Xylie sniffs, and Lora can't bear to look at the flicker of silver tears in her eyes. Xylie loves Ayc, with the same adoration that Xylie holds for Lora. Maybe deeper, as their bond has only grown while Lora has been away at Adamant.

"I'm not asking you not to go," Bronwen says. "I'm asking you to think it through. Marcellus *cannot* win."

"No, he cannot, but I can't—" Lora snaps her teeth together to silence the next words. *I cannot lose him.* Unspoken, they tremble throughout her body. In her throat, in her head, through her very soul.

She knows everything that is at stake. Everything that is good about Everadyn will die if Marcellus rules, and with the Drakr now helping him, they only have days to stop him. Lora has watched Marcellus wreak ruin on countless lives, lives she's tried to save. She's listened to Bronwen in the dark of the night, explaining all the damage Marcellus did to her and to others. Lora loves her people, and they will suffer if Marcellus wins. She would sacrifice anything to prevent him from becoming Sovereign. Anything.

But Ayc?

Please not Ayc. She cannot sacrifice him. The very idea of something befalling him feels like she is cutting open her sternum and ripping her heart from her chest.

She can't explain why. She doesn't want to look too closely at this feeling inside of her, the feeling that only lives and breathes when Ayc is near, the one she's spent years trying to pretend doesn't exist. But Lora thinks she finally understands why Ayc jumped into that river eight years ago to pull her from the water, knowing it would cost him his chance to be free. If it felt anything like how *this* feels, he had no choice. She won't be well again—will not feel like she can breathe again—until she sees him still breathing with her own eyes.

And then—*then*—she might kill him herself for not listening to her and choosing instead to face Wren alone. Even if his reasons were utterly different from what he led Lora to believe. If he told her what he was thinking, all of this could have been avoided. But no, he had to be a stubborn and obnoxious ass, like always.

Bronwen presses two fingers on the back of her elbow, a familiar, comforting gesture. They've done it dozens of times before duels and tests at Adamant as a subtle signal of support. Lora shifts away. Her skin already feels like it might be peeling from her muscles, and the sensation is simply too much, even if it's meant to be comforting.

"He's divina," Tavish says. "Marcellus can't kill him. He won't. He didn't kill me."

Peregrin groans, and beside them, moisture floods Xylie's eyes. Her hands move swiftly, despite the way they tremble.

Lora translates, "Marcellus will kill him, like the letter says. He was going to kill him in the dragon's cave. I heard him say so."

"But why?" Tavish asks. "Surely, he wouldn't risk the anger of the divine."

Xylie's hands move, and Lora's mouth goes dry. Surely, she read the signs wrong. She blinks rapidly at Xylie. as she repeats the sign, but Peregrin speaks.

"Ayc isn't divina." Peregrin's eyes are closed, their fingers pressed to their temples, like the words hurt them to say. "That man at Creed Castle told a lie to spare his life."

"What?" Bronwen chokes out.

"But I've seen him turn invisible," Lora protests. She

never bought the other fancy tricks—the slight of hand, the little fire that always seemed to backfire and set him ablaze instead. But the invisibility...

"It's a trick," Xylie confirms. *"The fire is just magic powder, and I'm not sure how he does the invisibility, but I know it's a trick."*

Bronwen gasps. "Lots of things could render him invisible. An enchanted object, maybe." Clearly, Bronwen believes them then, or she would not offer solutions so quickly.

But Lora can't accept it. "And he's admitted this? To both of you?

"He's never denied it," Peregrin says. "I told him years ago that he had to find a way to convince your mother, and I suppose he did."

Lora shakes her head. "I know my mother suspected he wasn't telling the truth. I think that's why she got the Binding stone. Surely, she would have commanded he tell her the truth about his powers, and he couldn't have lied to her. If he had, he'd have suffered consequences. He would have been in pain this entire time. And he can't—"

Lora's voice cuts off as Peregrin's face contorts. Her teacher is a warrior through and through, always careful not to give anything away with a careless expression or show of emotion. But the truth is written plainly on their face now.

He's been in pain this entire time.

Her heart plummets from her chest. It feels as though it falls forever.

Memories flicker through her head of subtleties to which she never paid attention, from as far back as before she moved to Adamant. A wince turned quickly into a smile, a hand braced against a wall to hold him upright, tonics swallowed down when he thought no one was looking. And more recently, she saw the look of pain as he slid off Tempest after the long ride. She saw Tempest give him a feather.

Lora glances to Xylie, her last hope that this isn't true. But a tear glides down her cousin's face. Xylie only learned about the Yris Binding Ayc with the stone last night, when Lora told her. Ayc would have had no choice but to keep it a secret from Xylie, and perhaps, Lora had no business telling Ayc's truth. But Xylie is her Second and she needs her help to do what Lora has planned. But now Xylie knows, and she's put the pieces together, just like Lora.

"I never asked why he needed my tonics," Xylie signs. More tears rain down her cheeks, and she lets them pour. *"I didn't think it was my business why he needed them, but I should have asked. I should—"* She releases a sob and drops her face into her hands.

Lora should go to her, but her feet are stitched to the ground. Tavish reaches toward her. No one has translated for Xylie, but her sobs seem to beckon him. His hand hovers near her back uncertainly, before his fingers curl and he presses the fist to his lips instead. Saga whines.

Ayc has been in pain for eight fucking years. Behind his smiles and his jokes and his silliness he has been *suffering.* And it is all Yris's fault.

A scream swells in Lora's chest. She bites down on her tongue to suppress it. She's afraid if she surrenders control than she will not stop screaming, that she will let out the rage and tear apart everything around her.

Lora has wanted to hurt her mother many times—when she kept Lora away from her father all but three months out of the year. When she banished her father without letting

Lora say goodbye. When she threatened to not let Lora go see her grandmother again until Hellevi showed up with multiple other council members, and the regent of Totus Omni themselves, stating calmly but firmly that Lora was Totus Omni too and their claim on her remained. If she wanted to come, Yris could not stop her.

But this—this is a new level of rage.

Lora lifts her hand to fist her hair, not caring if she rips it out, and her chronicler catches her eye. Three stones are lit now.

She claws back her sleeve to see what line has disappeared from her flesh.

Reveal a long-concealed lie.

Has this been her mother's plan all along? Is this the reason she suggested Ayc? Yris loves to play games. She must be so furious that she suspects that Ayc has somehow bested her for ten years now. A Binding stone couldn't break him, but maybe the Trials could?

I'm going to make her pay for this.

Lora is certain the four around her note the chronicler's change. Xylie has dropped her hands and drags the edge of her coat's sleeve across her cheeks. But no one comments.

"I would not have told you the truth," Peregrin says. "It wasn't my place, but I need you to understand that the threat to him is real. And maybe, you won't want to save him now that you know he's lied—"

"Fuck you!" Lora snaps, because it's easier to be angry than to feel the sting of Peregrin's lack of faith. They have known and trained her since she was a small child barely big enough to lift a wooden sword; they have sheltered her within their home when she needed an escape from her mother. Do they truly think she is the sort who might doom

Ayc because of a lie—a lie that spared him as a child and he has been forced to keep ever since?

Peregrin holds up a hand. "Easy, Lora. I don't know how Marcellus knows the truth, but if he does, then he *will* kill him."

"But you go, and Marcellus might win," Bronwen says. There's no judgment in her tone. "It's your decision, Lora."

None of the four before her offer any opinions or even a clue on what they themselves might choose. Instead, one by one, they press their hands over their sternums, the way Bronwen and Lora started when their bond truly forged when Adamant dumped them in the middle of the ocean. It is an oath and a reassurance.

My heart is with you. You are not alone.

Whatever she decides, they will follow.

Ayc or the fate of her land? Which is she willing to sacrifice? She knows what she should choose, what is right. A hero would choose to save their land. One life for millions is a fair trade. But Lora is not the hero.

She is the villainess.

CHAPTER
TWENTY-EIGHT

The twin steeples of the Lux Aester temple loom above Lora as she ascends the front steps, which are so white they blaze like untouched snow in the afternoon sunlight. Grand double doors tower at the top, formed of twirling golden wire and blue stained glass. It's far more grand than the chapels and sacred groves in Totus Omni, where anyone, from any race or continent or faith, is welcome to find peace any time day or night. But these temple doors only open once a week for worship and on holidays, and even then, only citizens who have met certain strict conditions may enter.

She studies the doors for a second, sizing them up, before glancing behind her. A dark shape soars in the distant sky, far enough away to look like a large bird, but not far enough away that Tempest can't see everything that is happening.

Half an hour. That is what Lora has before the rest of her Five will storm this place. They are within a copse of trees nearby, ready to act sooner if they sense anything going wrong.

Lora has done what the letter asked. She is unarmed, her faithful twin blades handed over to Bronwen. The enchantment around the temple ensures she would not have been able to climb the steps of the temple if she—an outsider—carried a blade on her person. Marcellus and Wren have made a foolish mistake thinking that has weakened her. Adamant warriors are not allowed weapons their entire first year, not until they grow to fully understand what their greatest weapon is.

Themselves.

Their minds and bodies and unbreakable spirits.

Lora brushes her fingers against the leather cord around her neck, ensuring it is in place and that the end is still tucked within her armor. She snaps her focus back to the doors—these fucking doors that keep out the people they should serve. She charges toward them and kicks them open with a force that slams them against the inside wall. They shatter, and she enters in a shower of blue glass.

Inside, a half dozen priests leap from the pews and draw their swords. Warriors of the divine, they like to call themselves, armed with faith and silver. She doubts few priest have trained past the limited time they were granted at Wyntra and the Noxumbra specialty school; Lux Aester can never release its grip on its people for long. But they continue to train with one another here in their temples and are at least formidable.

Six of them, against one of her. Good. At least it will be a challenge.

"Where is he?" she demands. Her voice echoes in the

sanctuary, all the way to the altar at the front and into the spiraling dome above.

"The high priest stated you are to wait for him here," answers one priest, taking a step from the line they have formed. "We will go get him." He nods to another priest, who turns and saunters toward a door on the side of the sanctuary.

"Wait!" Lora barks at him.

The priest turns back, and all six of them stare at her with sneers upon their faces.

Whatever happens to them, she will feel no remorse. They are helping Marcellus; they may have harmed Ayc. And even if they are innocent of anything other than being guard dogs, they have still participated in the oppression of the Lux Aester people. They've arranged the marriage of fae who aren't even out of childhood; they have done unmentionable things to Bronwen and fae like her to 'break' them of what they see as sins. Maybe, they will cooperate, and she won't have to hurt them.

She hopes they don't cooperate.

"Fuck Marcellus," she snarls.

The lead priest's pale face turns a molten red. "I will ask you to show some respect. This is a holy—"

Lora advances a step. "Don't try me with your pious shit. If someone doesn't agree to take me to Ayc by the time I count to ten, I'm going to see how black your hypocrite hearts are and then find him myself. One—"

"You are not in charge here," the lead priest snaps.

"That's where you're wrong. *Two.*"

"You're unarmed!"

"I know." Lora smiles. "But you're not. *Three.*"

The priests exchange an uncertain look. They adjust their grip on their blades.

"Four."

The head priest gives a nod. "As the high priest ordered. If she doesn't cooperate, kill her."

Four of the priests prowl forward, their blades held high. Something flares to life within Lora, like a simmering storm releasing its first bolt of lightning. It sharpens her focus and makes her eyes burn with silver.

Anger.

Lora is angry, but then, she's always been angry.

Angry at her mother and all the things she saw her do. Angry about how, no matter what Lora did, it was not and could never be enough to make her mother proud. Angry at her father—unfair as it was—for leaving her. Angry at every injustice she saw—Creed castle and Aluina and Lux Aester —and the powerlessness she often felt to make it better. And here, in this moment, angry that her enemies dared lay a hand upon Ayc—*her Ayc*—someone who is good and kind and silly, despite all that has been done to him.

Sometimes, the anger builds within her until she thinks she might erupt with it, until the most dangerous place to be is within her own body and mind.

Peregrin has always seen it. When she was young, they gave her exercises to work out the tension. Taught her breathing and how to hide the way she fluttered her hands and sometimes, simply gave her a safe place in which to scream and slap the ground and implode upon herself when it all became too much. Peregrin trained her, and then told her to go to Adamant, where she trained even more. And, somewhere along that journey, Lora learned something more important.

She is not helpless. And her anger does not make her weak.

It makes her *powerful*.

Lora grabs the strand around her throat and yanks it free of her neck. She grasps the bottle that hangs from the end, the one Xylie gave her, and heaves it at the feet of the priest. It explodes in a cloud of gray dust. The priests cough, stumbling back, rubbing at their now-burning eyes. The protective charm Bronwen placed on Lora holds as she lunges into the cloud after them.

The first priest's neck snaps like a twig. She pulls his sword from his lifeless fingers. She swings toward the others, all five of them.

Then Lora unleashes her rage.

- AYC -

"If he tells one more joke, I'm going to stab him," one of the priests says, seizing the hilt of his sword and taking a step toward Ayc.

His fellow priest grabs his shoulder. "We can't. The high priest said he wants him alive."

Ayc grins at them cheekily from where he still hangs from the ceiling by his wrists. He's needed distraction from the agony rippling from his suspended arms all the way down his back, acute pain morphing with the chronic. If he focuses too much on it, he'll lose himself to it. So he's been telling joke after joke, from the childish ones he torments Lora with, to the raunchy ones he generally reserves for special company. Seeing a grown man blush has been the most delightful experience. Ayc pities their wives.

"Did you hear the one about what the sign outside the out-of-business brothel said?" Ayc asks.

The priest bares his teeth and growls. This time, his fellow priest releases him, and he stalks forward.

Ayc keeps smiling. "The sign said, 'We're closed! Beat it!'"

He laughs as the fae stops before him, but the sound turns into a croak as the fae slams a fist into Ayc's right cheek. The force propels Ayc backward, swinging on the chains. His feet collide with the altar behind him, but he's unable to latch a foot on the top before he swings back around.

"Or how about the one—" Ayc begins.

The next punch lands straight into his nose. Black interrupts his vision, and blood pours down his face. But the force is enough that he spins on the chains. He uses whatever remains of his strength to curl at the waist and then plants his feet at the top of the altar. Relief, blessed relief, ripples through his arm muscles as he stands.

"What are you doing?" demands the priest.

Ayc really isn't sure. He's kind of just... improvising.

"Thought I'd take up praying," he says, facing them. "Is this not how it's done?"

The priest grabs for his leg, and Ayc kicks out, slamming his boot into the priest's face. The priest stumbles backward, but the other priest surges forward. His sword hisses as he pulls it from his scabbard.

Then a sound rips out from outside the doorway—loud and piercing and dripping with terror. It's echoed by more.

It's such a departure from the quiet of the temple that it takes a moment for Ayc to register it.

Screams.

"Oh," Ayc says, and this time the smile that crawls onto his swollen cheeks is genuine, "I think Lora's here."

The priests whirl toward the door. The one closest yanks it open. A long stone hallway stretches before the sanctuary, lined with doors. And there's Lora, her face already drenched in blood as she pins a trembling priest against the wall, her hand curled around his throat.

"Where is he?" Lora demands, and the priest thrusts a finger in his direction. Her eyes snap toward Ayc. They burn silver, bright in the dimness. She tosses the priest to the side and draws a sword from where it's been tucked in her belt. She holds two swords, longer than her own, matching the ones the priests carry, as she charges down the hall. Her cape ripples behind her.

Ayc's heart stands still. She is magnificent. Glorious. He has never believed in any higher being, but at that moment, there is a goddess of life and death. And it is her.

Another priest flings himself through a door in the hallway and swings a sword at her head. She ends his life in a merciless and effortless spray of blood. And Ayc should not like that. Her violence certainly shouldn't strike his body like lightning, lighting it on fire, and yet he is burning for her, as he always does.

She's come for him.

The priest who struck Ayc leaps forward to grab the door and slam it shut. It's closed only for a moment, before it's propelled open again. It collides with the priest, flinging him backward against the wall. He slumps to the floor with a gasp. The other priest defends one of Lora's blows, but her other sword drives into his gut. When he lays on the ground, Lora's narrowed silver eyes focus on the other priest, but he holds up his hands weakly. In them, he holds a set of keys.

"To the chains. Just take him and go."

Lora kicks the priest's blade from where it fell. It slides across the bloody stone, out of the priest's reach. She whirls toward the altar. Her eyes fade from silver to black. Ayc wills a grin upon his face, hoping to hide the way his very soul shivers in her presence.

"Fancy meeting you like this," Ayc says.

She searches him over. "Who did that to you?" she growls, her eyes flashing silver once more.

He blinks, and she gestures at his face with her sword. He forgot about his swollen cheeks and the warmth of blood still trickling down his chin. "Oh, this?" Ayc shrugs and flicks his fingers toward the slumped priest. "He didn't like my joke."

She weighs one of her swords in her hand. "Is that right?"

Without looking, she throws the sword like a spear. It pierces through the priest's right shoulder and pins him to the wall. He screams.

Ayc fights to keep his smile from curling wider. There's something deeply wrong with him. "Seems a steep price for a poor sense of humor."

"What do you mean?" Lora asks, marching toward the altar. "That was merciful."

The heat in his blood burns brighter as she vaults onto the altar. Her body presses against his as she stands on her toes to reach the chains. He takes a deep, calming breath, trying to focus on anything but her presence. Anything but her strength and beauty and the fucking smell of anise in her hair—least his body betray him to the point she'll notice.

The chains release. He rubs at the raw skin, right above where his bracelets sit, and recalls the reality of their situation. "You shouldn't have come, Lora. This is a trap."

She bares her teeth, revealing those sharp canines. "I'm not a rabbit to be ensnared."

"No, you're a dragon."

She meets his eyes, the irises lightening from black to the deepest of purples. His heart betrays him once more. If it keeps stopping like this, surely it'll kill him.

"Let's get you out of here." Lora leaps down from the altar, and Ayc takes the opportunity to breathe.

Ayc hurts too much to jump, and so he sits and slides off.

Lora reaches toward him but drops her hand before she actually touches him. "How bad is it?"

"How bad is what?"

"The pain."

Ayc studies her, noticing the way that now-familiar line of worry has appeared between her brows. She said it almost like she knows. But *what* does she know, and who told her?

"I'm fine," he says.

She narrows her eyes skeptically, but only says, "Never mind. We can discuss not lying to me later." She adjusts her grip on the one sword she still holds. "We have to go. We only have ten minutes before the other four storm this place."

She pauses before the door and peers out into the hallway, before beckoning to him. The hallway beyond lies empty and quiet. Still, goosebumps tease over Ayc's arms.

He listens, but all he hears is Lora's soft exhale as she steps into the hallway. Ayc follows.

He sees only a flash of silver before sharp, blinding pain rips through him. When his vision clears, he finds a blade protruding from his side. Blood pours across the linen of his shirt. A hand wraps around the hilt, floating in the air momentarily, until another hand rises and pulls down the hood of a cloak that has rendered him invisible. Marcellus appears, grinning that snake-like smile.

Ayc feels the doors of the trap slam shut. As he collapses to his knees, he closes his eyes, red flashing behind them, and grinds his teeth against a scream. *This* is the trap.

Ayc has always been the trap.

- LORA -

It's a familiar sound. The soft, squelching sound of flesh parting beneath a blade. Fear, thick and rancid, boils on Lora's tongue as she reels around to see Ayc collapse. Marcellus tears back his blade and lets Ayc go. The blood drains from Ayc's face, the light shuttering out of his brilliant eyes, before he closes them. The world tinges in silver. Rage, like she has never felt before, rattles through her soul.

"You're a dead man," she snarls, charging toward Marcellus.

"Ah, ah, ah." He takes a step back, wagging a finger. She lifts a blade to sever that hand, when he says the next words like a rush. "If you kill me, I'll never tell you what poison I put on my blade. Nor will I give you the antidote."

Lora freezes, realization dawning. Marcellus's whole trap felt too easy, insultingly so, because it was. This was the plan all along, and Marcellus has pulled the noose taut before she realized it ensnared her.

"What do you want?" she demands.

"Lora," Ayc begins, his voice strained. He clutches his side, his hand already soaked red. "Whatever it is—"

"Not now, cinnamon roll," Lora snaps, before he can be sickeningly noble and say something like *"Let me die."* She swears she'll punch him right in the face. "What do you want, Marcellus?"

The high priest is still grinning. "What would you be willing to pay for his life?"

Anything. Everything.

Lora grits her teeth against the words, her sharpened teeth digging into the inside of her lip. "Let me guess? You want me to take off my chronicler?"

"No," Ayc growls, but Lora only glares at Marcellus.

"And win by default?" He laughs. "I don't want you to bow out, Loraphne. I want to beat you. I want you to stand down and do nothing for three days. If you—and your Five —do nothing but wait for three days, I will return and give you the antidote."

"No." Ayc grabs the door to the sanctuary and tries to haul himself to his feet. More blood drains from his face, and Lora shoves him back down with a hand on his shoulder. "He only has two more quests left, Lora. You can't agree. He'll win."

Lora counts the lit stones on Marcellus's chronicler to confirm what Ayc said. Her hands want to flutter; her throat aches to scream so she can release the rising pressure. She forces herself to inhale slowly. In and out.

"You could have just stabbed him back in Totus Omni and given me your ultimatum then," she says, buying time to think. "Why go through the trouble of bringing me here?"

"For two reasons. First to confirm my suspicion that he's your greatest weakness. And second, once all of Everadyn finds out you slaughtered a mass of fae priests just to save one human, who will ever willingly follow you?"

He's right, of course. When Lora began these Trials, she swore she wouldn't be like her mother. She wants to be a leader whom people love, not fear. But Yris's frequently-offered advice drifts back to Lora, a haunting echo.

Who needs love if you can have fear? Both will give you devotion, but only fear can keep it.

Lora shakes the thoughts away. It's a worry for a different day. "Three days? And you swear you'll have what it takes to heal him."

"Just three days."

It is not just three days. It might as well be a lifetime, because Marcellus will win by then. Ayc is right. This is more than *risking* Marcellus win the Trials. It is *guaranteeing* it.

Ayc bares his teeth and growls in frustration. "I could be dead in three days, anyway."

Her hands flutter, her sword vibrating. She tightens her grasp. "Will he survive?" she demands of Marcellus.

"If he's strong, he'll survive until then. If not—" Marcellus shrugs. "It's a risk. You must decide if you're willing to take it. The choice is yours."

She says nothing, only imagines all the ways she'll kill Marcellus when she gets the chance. Slowly. Piece by minuscule piece.

Ayc seizes her wrist, so tightly his fingers dig in. All her nerves hone in on that bit of flesh where his skin touches hers. A drop of sweat weeps down his face. She studies his face, but she can't tell if he's in pain. He must be, but he's had so much practice hiding it.

"Lora, don't. I'm begging you. I'd rather be dead than face what happens if he wins."

She shuts her eyes to shield herself from the desperation that contorts his face. She knows he's talking about more than just the fate of Everadyn. Ayc will suffer personally, Bound to obey Marcellus's every wish. How long would it take for Marcellus to realize the power he holds over Ayc? It would take only seconds for him to decide to abuse it.

She shudders, but then she imagines the alternative: Ayc, cold and gray with death. No more smiles. No more ridiculous jokes. No more sparkling light in her gray world. And her, left to survive the aftermath.

Perhaps she should have listened to her mother, all those years ago. She should have been stone, should not have let herself get attached. But it's too late. Perhaps, it was too late from the moment she burst through that door ten years ago to find him holding a pan of cinnamon rolls.

"Decide, Loraphne," Marcellus says. "Do you agree?"

Lora opens her eyes. "I agree."

CHAPTER
TWENTY-NINE

- AYC -

Ayc curses Lora and pleads with her while she looks at him with unemotional eyes, until at last, Marcellus calls a couple of priests. At first, Ayc fights against them, but quickly realizes that the more he struggles, the more he bleeds. He lets them lay him on a stretcher. One of them drips something down his throat. It makes the world go fuzzy and soft, and soon, he's unconscious.

Fragments of reality break through the darkness: pain in his side, hands pressing into him, murmuring voices, someone crying, a voice that sounds like Lora: "He will not die. I promise you; he will not die."

Ayc tries to speak, but only manages a grunt before he's pulled into an unwilling slumber once more.

He wakes an unknown time later to the sight of two Peregrins, sitting beside the bed where he lies. Both Peregrins wear scowls so deep Ayc is convinced it'll leave a permanent imprint. Strangely, Ayc doesn't hurt, but he's freezing, despite the fur blanket that covers him.

His teeth chattering, he tugs the blanket higher. "F-fuck, you th-think with two of you n-now, one of you would have l-it a fire."

"What?" the two Peregrins say.

Ayc shuts his eyes and reopens them again. Only one Peregrin frowns down at him now. Fuck, it seemed so real.

"N-nevermind," Ayc says quickly. "Where are we?"

He looks around the room. It looks like any generic tavern he's ever been to, except far cleaner. Pristine almost. The walls are a crisp white and the floor gleams as though scrubbed. His bed lies in the center, and a fireplace stands on one end, devoid of any fire. The room is dim, lit only by lamps on either side of his bed. Outside the one window, open to let in a cool breeze, the sun hovers near the horizon, but he isn't sure if it's sunset or sunrise. How long has he slept?

"You're at a hospital in the village near to the temple," Peregrin says. "The priests brought you here."

"You only bring p-people to hospitals when you think they're going to d-die. Oh." Ayc presses a hand to his forehead, finding it damp and fiery to the touch. "You all think I'm d-dying."

Peregrin's throat works visibly as they swallow. "You are dying. But you will *not* die."

"B—" Ayc grinds his teeth to keep them from chattering. "Because you actually trust Marcellus to keep his word?"

"We have no choice but to trust him." Peregrin rubs their hand over their face. Their skin matches their gray armor; crevices form beneath their eyes, as purple as a bruise. "The Lux Aester healers have been very knowledgeable and attentive, and they are running tests, but so far they have not been able to identify whatever poison was on Marcellus's blade."

"Or they are under orders not to reveal it."

"True. We sent Tempest with a message to get a Totus Omni healer. Hopefully, they'll be here soon."

"Where's everyone else?"

Peregrin lifts their cane to gesture at a door at the side of the room. The one near the front is barred close. "They are in an adjoining room meant for waiting families. Marcellus left his First, Erech, to watch us and make sure that none of us leave."

"You need to talk to Lora," Ayc says, trying to put force behind his words. "Tell her this is foolishness. She shouldn't risk everything for my life. She—"

Peregrin cuts him off with a slicing gesture. "We've all talked to Lora. She understands the risk she is taking. She is certain of her choice."

"But why?" Ayc demands.

Peregrin pinches the bridge of their nose, their eyes pressing closed. "Boy, if you don't know, I can't tell you."

Ayc opens his mouth, but no words come out. He's much too tired to argue. And too cold. He pulls the fur blanket up to his chin. The room blurs at the edges, and he isn't sure if that's the poison or a side effect of whatever medication he's been given. A rattling sound ripples through the room, and it takes a moment to realize it's his teeth chattering again.

"C-can we s-shut the window?" Ayc asks.

Peregrin rises, leaning heavily on their cane. They close and latch the window. "I'm going to go get the healers. I think your fever has returned."

Ayc says nothing as Peregrin exits through the side door.

He lifts the fur to inspect what has become of his wound. He's shirtless and his abdomen is bound with dressings, covering the laceration. He vaguely remembers the sharp sting of a needle as someone sewed him back up, but the memory slips away like sand through his fingertips.

Xylie rushes through the door and closes it behind her. She pauses to assess him before she makes her way to his side. Like Peregrin, she appears worn, her eyes drooping and a frown creasing her cheeks. "You're awake."

"How long have I been asleep?"

"About fourteen hours. It's morning now. The healers have wanted to keep you unconscious and calm. They think it'll slow down the poison."

Ayc catches movement and turns to look at the end of the bed. He blinks, trying to make sense of what his eyes are seeing. "Xylie, when did the dragon's egg hatch?"

Xylie follows his line of vision, her frown deepening. "What are you talking about?"

"The dragon. It's at the end of my bed. It's really cute. I think we should name it Muffin."

She searches over his face, then turns away briefly, just long enough to run the edge of her sleeves over her cheeks. Then she says sternly, "We're not naming the dragon Muffin."

He casts her a glare. "You never let me do anything fun."

She brushes her fingers over his forehead, an uncharacteristic touch. "You should go back to sleep. You need your strength."

"Bossy," Ayc mutters, but no matter how he tries to fight them, his eyes fall closed, anyway.

"He's hallucinating," Xylie signs as she reenters the room, her hands weaving around her head.

Lora blinks her weary, aching eyes at Xylie. Bronwen, who has been snoring softly on Lora's shoulder, sits up at the sound of the door. On the floor, Tavish curls around Saga on a bedroll within the circle of chairs, the only furniture within this room. But his eyes are open, too. None of them have slept much, and Lora doesn't think Peregrin has slept at all. They are currently out of the room, speaking with the healers.

Marcellus's First has positioned himself upright against the door, slumbering with loud snores, but jerking awake at every word they speak. Erech adjusts his hand on the sword that lays over his knees, an ever-present threat. If one of them attempts to break Lora's deal, it's not any of their necks he'll aim for. It's Ayc's, laying helplessly in the next room.

It's been less than a day since Ayc was stabbed. The healers are doing all they can, and Peregrin has been dissolving gryphon feathers and dripping the tea down Ayc's throat. Still, per the reports Lora has gotten from her four who have been taking shifts, he is fading: the color leaching from his face, sweat pasting over his skin, a fever that comes and goes. Lora has remained outside for most of it, after she was certain the healers here would not harm him. She feared her presence would only make him angry if he woke to find her, and the healers have warned he needs to be calm.

But also, she simply cannot watch him slip away.

"We should tell the healers about the hallucinations,"

Lora says, pushing to her feet. "Maybe it will give them an idea of what the poison is."

Erech shoves to his feet the moment she steps toward the door, instantly awake. "You know the rules. Only one of you out of this room at a time."

"Then open the door and yell for a healer," snaps Lora.

"I don't take orders from a woman. You can wait until the gryphon rider returns."

Lora advances a step. Rage boils through her blood. She doesn't have her weapons. She and her Five voluntarily surrendered them when they stepped into the hospital, but she would go into Erech with her teeth if she could. She longs to hurt someone, hurt them the way Ayc is hurting, the way *she* is hurting. The idea of him dying is already a permanent hitch in her side; she feels it with every move, every breath.

As though sensing her thoughts, Erech wiggles the blade in his hand. "Or I can visit the human now."

Silver floods Lora's vision. "If you touch him—"

"Lora," Bronwen warns softly.

It's enough to rein Lora in. If Marcellus returns to find his First dead, he will never hand over the antidote. Lora marches back to Bronwen, Tavish, and Xylie. The door wheezes as it opens, and Peregrin stiffly limps into the room. Their movements seem particularly painful today. Peregrin once admitted that stress and emotion can make their physical pain worse, so Lora can only imagine they are suffering.

A young girl follows. She's dressed in the modest garb of the Lux Aester women, a gown buttoned high up her neck and hiding all but her fingertips and the tip of pointed shoes. She looks scarcely older than seventeen, and Lora hasn't seen her before. She carries a bottle as Peregrin leads her toward the door to Ayc's room.

"Who are you?" Lora demands.

The girl jumps. "I, um, sorry," she stammers. Her pale face flushes a brilliant red. "I— my husband is the head healer, and he's resting, so he asked me to bring the tonic for the patient's fever."

Husband? Lora met the head healer. Age is subtle in the fae, but he is marked with it, beneath his eyes and around the corner of his lips. He has to be a century older than her. Maybe even two. Lora's lip curls in disgust, and Bronwen gives a sympathetic sigh. Peregrin nods in confirmation of the fae's identity.

"I'll go with you," Lora says. Peregrin steps aside as Lora moves toward the door.

"A-all right," the girl says, as Lora passes her.

Lora opens the door carefully and peeks in. Sweat shines on Ayc's brow, but his eyelashes drape softly, peacefully. Good. He's asleep. She releases a breath as she enters the room. As she slips past, the girl turns sideways to keep her body as far from Lora as possible, like Lora is a frightening monster. Like she still wears the blood of all those priests on her face.

The girl stills her trembling when she reaches Ayc's bedside, instantly seeming a little more confident. She pulls a dropper from the bottle she holds. The others have simply dripped medicine onto his tongue, prying his mouth open at times. But she gently slips a hand behind his head to steady him. His eyes fly open, and he jerks back.

She squeaks and whips her hand away. "I'm sorry. They said you've been so sedated you would not notice my presence. I brought you medicine."

Ayc squints at her, a sliver of blue peering behind his lashes. Lora doesn't move from the door, hoping Ayc won't notice her.

"I th-think I know you," Ayc says, his teeth chattering. He yanks the blanket up to his chin. Lora has not heard his teeth chatter so hard since they were twelve, and she held a sword at his spine.

The girl gives a slight smile. "We met only once. At the celebration for the Sovereign."

"Avabeth."

"Yes." She flushes and ducks her head. Her hair comes forward like a veil. "Thank you for my wedding cake. It was beautiful."

Lora remembers now. The night she came to ask Ayc to be one of her Five, she found him dancing and laughing drunkenly in the kitchen. She paused to watch him at the door, transfixed by the light in his face, his eyes, before she forced herself to enter. She remembers the letter and the exquisite cake and how she hadn't been surprised at all. Baking a cake for a Lux Aester girl sounded exactly like something Ayc would do. He's always been far too kind for his own good.

Ayc studies the girl's face. "Are you h-happy?"

"I—" Avabeth begins, and then says swiftly, "My husband is a good man."

He manages to make his voice firm. "That's not what I asked, Avabeth."

Avabeth looks down at her feet, making a sound like honesty strangles her. Then she simply says, "Please. I brought you medicine. For the fever."

He sighs, but when she offers the dropper, he takes it and drops the medicine onto his tongue.

Avabeth stands. "That should help with the shivering, but I'll get you more blankets."

She bolts for the door. Lora twists to follow, relieved he did not notice her, when he barks, "Lora, don't you d-dare leave without talking to me."

Lora steels herself and closes the door. She supposes she's avoided him long enough. She faces him but keeps a safe distance like always. Like she's afraid of him. And with the way her heart hammers, of course she's afraid of him. Him and deep bodies of water. They are the only things that can make her heart do these strange things.

"What are you doing?" he growls. It's a voice she hasn't heard often, deep as a dragon's roar, something that doesn't sound like him at all. It makes her heart bound harder, and something deep in her stomach clench. She shakes off the feeling. Or at least, she attempts to. The feeling sticks to her skin like glue.

"You need to stay calm, Ayc," she says. "The healers say—"

"Fuck the healers!" He pushes himself upright, leaning heavily on one of his elbows. Agony ripples across his face as he does, and she rushes a step forward before halting. "You should never have agreed to Marcellus's trap."

Her jaw tightens, and she clings onto the flash of anger. That's a simpler emotion to deal with. "So, I'm supposed to let you die?"

"Yes!" The medicine must be helping swiftly, because he's not shaking anymore, though his hands still fist the blanket at his shoulders. "Don't you realize what happens if Marcellus's wins? The freedoms he will take? The people whose lives will be lost because they can't bear the world he'll create? My life is not worth all of theirs."

"For divine's sake, why do you have to be so fucking noble? It's obnoxious."

Ayc throws up his hands. The blanket tumbles to his waist. Lora's instinct is to snap her gaze to anything other than his bare chest. But it's too late. Her focus gets trapped there. She's used to shirtless males. Male students at Adamant, like Wylder, never seemed to be able to keep their shirts on when sparring and training. Lora is familiar with the hard lines of muscle, the way they do not give under a punch or even a caress.

Ayc is not built like them. There's strength to him, yes, from all that time swimming in the hazardous waves of the Bellum Sea. But there's softness there, too. She could touch him, and he won't break, but he *will* give. Smooth and soft and strong. She's never been able to see him and not have her fingers ache to touch him. She nearly did in the river a few days ago, but instead grabbed the leviathan's tooth—the one that still hangs around his neck. Now, she fists her hands at her side.

Perhaps, if she touched him, he wouldn't feel like stone like the men before. Perhaps, he would feel alive.

She rarely ever lets herself look at him, but now that she's begun, she can't seem to stop. She drinks him in, savoring every detail: the earrings across his curved ear, the chipped paint on his fingernails, the lines of his shoulders and chest, the fullness of his lips that, sadly, don't hold their usual smile.

"Are you listening to me?" Ayc snaps.

"Yes," she hisses. A lie.

She drags her attention back to his face. That is not necessarily safe either. His long hair clings to his face, and he should not look handsome when he is so sick. But he does.

"Then explain to me why you'd want to save me when you hate me so much. I heard what you said to your grandmother. I'm only here to fulfill the prompt, the one about having someone you hate. And you chose poorly. I'm utterly useless. Even your grandmother knows that."

Lora's heart stutters, and she presses her eyes closed, afraid he might see how wrong he is. Her grandmother needed only to be in the room with Lora and Ayc, and she knew what Lora tries so hard to hide.

Lora doesn't hate Ayc.

Not even a little.

"I'm not good enough to be one of your Five," Ayc continues, and she hates every single word coming out of his mouth, but she does *not* hate him.

"Stop," Lora snaps. "This won't make me change my mind."

He doesn't stop. "I'm the reason that Marcellus found us at Somnia Ignis. I told Wren where we were going. I didn't mean to. She laced her kiss with truth weed, and I didn't realize it. But still, I didn't listen to you. She was using me, and you tried to warn me, and I didn't listen."

Lora tenses. He's hurling the words at her like he thinks this is the thing that should change her mind. But it's nothing she hasn't sorted out already. She's had a lot of time to sit and think and put pieces together.

"Do you want to hear me say I'm angry with you, Ayc?" Lora asks, letting heat singe her words. "Fine. I'm *angry* with you. After you survive this, I'm going to kick your ass. You should have listened to me. If you had, you wouldn't be poisoned right now. So yes, Ayc, I'm fucking pissed at you. But I'm still not changing my mind."

"Fuck." He buries his face in his hands and growls in frustration. Good, for once, she's not the only one driven to distraction by their conversations. Or maybe she is, because in the silence that descends, she's left thinking about him and Wren. Yes, Wren was using Ayc, but Ayc was only with Wren because he wanted to be. And that's a knife that still twists in Lora's gut.

"Did you love her?" The question is out before Lora can stop it. She wants to claw it back, to plug her ears and never hear the answer.

I'm not jealous, she tells herself.

He snorts and drops his hands. "No. I didn't even really know her. I just hoped that I could be... *something* to someone. But I'm not. I'm no one, and nothing. I'm certainly not worth sacrificing everything for."

The way he's talking about himself hurts. Every word slices against her skin, and she wishes she could rip apart everyone who has ever made him feel that way. Except, she's probably on that list.

Lora draws in a breath, making sure her expression and voice are stone. That they give nothing away. "I can't let you die, Ayc."

He presses his fists to his forehead. "Dammit, Lora, what can I say to get you to change your mind?"

"Nothing."

"Why not? Because I'm divina and my death might anger the divine? Then let me make it easier for you. Evander lied. I am not divina, and I never have been. It's all a trick. All of it!"

He stares are her, his hands fisted in the blanket,

waiting. Like he knows he has thrown down a card that will finally, *finally* win him the game.

But she only shakes her head. "I know."

"You..." he starts and then trails off. Understanding slowly dawns on his face. "Fuck. Peregrin told you, didn't they?"

"They felt they had no choice. I needed to understand that Marcellus might truly kill you." Lora pulls back her sleeve and approaches so he can see the quest that is no longer written on her arm.

A muscle ticks in his jaw. He sags back on his pillow, glaring hard at the ceiling. "I suppose your mother got what she wanted. She'll kill me when she finds out."

Lora's canines sharpen at the thought. She drags her tongue over the points, giving herself time so that she can temper her tone. "If I have my way, the bitch will go to her grave not knowing. A premature one, hopefully."

A single beat of a laugh escapes from his lips, but it's followed by a groan. He clutches his side, and Lora's hand spasms as she restrains herself from reaching out. She grasps for her swords instead, but they aren't there.

"Either way," Lora adds, "I'll end her before she harms you again. She's hurt you enough."

He does not speak, nor look at her. Instead, he stares up at the ceiling, and she follows the rise and fall of his chest, counting his breaths to distract herself from all the emotions broiling within her. Emotions are such painful, complicated things, and he makes her feel more than anyone.

"There's really nothing I can say to change your mind, is there?" he asks.

"No."

454

He turns his head and captures her with his endless eyes. She's never been able to decide what shade of blue they are, whether they more closely resemble the sky or the ocean or polished gems. Maybe because they are all those shades put together.

"But, why?" he asks.

Fuck, she hates that question. What is she supposed to say? The truth? She can't even admit it to herself, let alone face the consequences of what might come after. He is mortal human, and she is immortal fae. She can't surrender to what she feels, knowing she will one day watch him die. It would doom her. It already does. Denial is her only chance for survival.

She shrugs and says the closest thing she can say to true. "I owe it to you after everything, don't you think?"

He cringes, fisting a hand in his blankets. Perhaps she should find a healer or Avabeth, for another pain tonic, but before she can move, he asks, "What will you do? When Marcellus wins?"

A shiver passes down Lora's spine. The rest of her Five have asked her the same thing. To them, she lied and told them he wouldn't. That he would fail at whatever his quest and come back in three days to release them, and then they'd fight to finish the Trials. But she's too tired to lie right now.

"Then I'll protect my people," Lora says. "Even if that means leading a rebellion to overthrow him."

Ayc turns his head to look at her. The smallest of smile breaks against his lips. "Sounds very villainous of you."

Her heart flutters at that ghost of a smile. And maybe she's wrong. Maybe, she does hate him a little, for making her feel like *this*.

Ayc surges upward. He barely angles himself over the side of his bed before he heaves. Hot green bile splatters on the floor. She rushes to him, reaching out to sweep the hair from his face, but before she touches him, he snarls, "Get out!"

He vomits again, coughing, his body trembling. Trembles that turn into convulsions. He writhes on the bed, his eyes rolling back into his skull, his teeth bared.

"Help!" Lora calls. She leaps on the bed and tries to hold onto him, but his movements are so violent she can't contain him.

The door slams against the wall, and Avabeth flies across the room, dropping an armful of blankets. "Turn him on his side!"

Lora rolls him over, and Avabeth cradles his head. Lora hears Erech barking from the next room as Xylie and Bronwen run in. Peregrin and Tavish ignore him and follow shortly after. Peregrin hurries to call more healers.

Lora clings to Ayc harder. "It'll be all right," she says, in case he can hear her. But she doesn't know that. She looks up into the faces of her friends. Xylie is crying again, like when they first brought Ayc here and Lora promised Xylie that she wasn't going to lose him. And now, Lora isn't sure.

They still have two and a half more days.

THIRTY

- AYC -

Reality slips away.

Sometimes, Ayc awakes to find a dozen wedding cakes and bowls of chocolate pudding leaping and dancing around the room and sometimes he falls asleep to find Tavish wearing Saga on his head like a hat. Or perhaps it is the other way around.

He wakes to find a baby dragon nipping at his toes, and when he jerks away, he wakes again to find Avabeth telling him he's all right—or no, it isn't Avabeth. It's Wylder laughing in his face and giving his most common taunt, *"You'll never have her, fool. Lora is immortal. You won't even be a line in the chapter of her life."* Wylder always did see things about Ayc no one else noticed.

Ayc dreams of Peregrin teaching him to fight and Lora working skilled fingers at a loom to weave the tapestry that already hangs above his bed at Wyntra. All of it seems both profoundly real and not real at all, wrapped in a dreamlike quality. The only moments that hold any clarity are when he wakes to vomit and retch until a healer comes with more medicine. Those are the moments he wishes he could forget.

He dreams of Bronwen kneeling beside his bed, her hands curled together on the side of it, the way he has seen people from Lux Aester pray. That's how he knows it's a dream.

"What are you doing?" he asks.

Saga, who is snuggled close to Ayc's side, raises his head. Saga's body is warm, and for once, Ayc isn't cold.

Bronwen lifts her head. "Praying."

Ayc rubs a hand over Saga's ears until the dog rests his head back on Ayc's chest. "I would have thought you would want nothing to do with the divine," he tells Bronwen.

She climbs off her knees and sits on the chair beside his bed. "I didn't for a while, and I certainly understand someone who would abandon everything they've been taught and not look back. Marcellus and the priests preached so often about how the divine hated me for who I am. But there was a sorcerer at Velphin who taught me that the divine created me, and so therefore, cannot possibly hate me." Her voice fades, becoming more distant, like an echoing lullaby. "I don't believe in the divine Lux Aester teaches about. That divine is merely a weapon they choose to use to oppress others. But I do believe in the divine as the Totus Omni believe in. The divine is in everything. In nature. In you and in me. It's a force that connects us and loves us. I feel it within me, and most certainly in my magic."

Ayc shrugs and murmurs, "If you say so."

"Growing up in Lux Aester, they tried to take a lot of things from me. They can't take my faith, and no one else can judge me for choosing to hang on to it."

She blurs and multiplies into two. Ayc blinks rapidly but can't make the two Bronwens forge together. "What were you praying for?"

"You."

"Waste of prayer, don't you think? I'm a lost cause. You should pray Lora sees sense and gets back to the Trials."

Bronwen scoffs. "She could no more leave you than the Ever River could flow backward."

Ayc narrows his eyes, but that only makes his vision worsen, so he relaxes his face again. "Why?"

"Go to sleep, Ayc."

"I *am* asleep."

Saga with wings.

Endless pans of cinnamon rolls piled on every inch of floor and towering toward the ceiling.

His mother tightening the bracelets on his wrist.

Avabeth giving him more medicine.

Gryphons the size of toy horses galloping around Ayc's head.

A healer with earrings shaped like leaves bending over Ayc with a frown upon their face. But this image appears sharper and more real than what has come before. When Ayc tries to open his eyes fully, the sunlight in the room slams into his temples like hammers. He shuts them again.

"Well?" demands a voice. Lora. He knows her voice, like a song stuck in his head, repeating over and over though he's tried desperately to make it stop.

"The Lux Aester healers are correct," the healer says. Their voice is soft, feminine, but confident. Ayc remembers vaguely that Peregrin said something about a Totus Omni healer. Perhaps, this is them. "I do not recognize the poison. The test that might show us comes back muddled. Perhaps, it is undetectable, or perhaps, it's many different poisons."

A body shifts beside Ayc, fur wrestling beneath his hand. Saga is still here, and Ayc brushes a hand down his back to confirm that no wings have grown on the dog. Yes, Ayc is awake. Maybe. His head is so full of clouds, and his bones are sos leaden from whatever medication he's getting, he's not quite sure.

"I spoke to the head healer," the Totus Omni healer continues, "and I think you can trust him. Marcellus has power here, yes. But the healer's oath is a sacred one, and not one any of them will break. They are doing all they can to help him."

"That's it?" Lora asks. "You can't do anything else?"

"I'm afraid not."

"Then what good are you?" Her words are a hiss, cold and cruel.

The healer's own voice remains gentle. "I am sorry for your pain, Lora. Keep giving him the gryphon feathers. Keep reminding him why he needs to stay. That's the only thing advice I can give."

Footsteps pound against the wood; a door slams. Saga whines. A moment later, Ayc hears Lora's laughter as he tumbles from a make-shift stage, over and over and over. He could live in this moment forever. It's a good moment.

Good things. If he is to die, he will make sure he only dreams of good things.

Ayc wakes with silver at his throat and before his eyes. Shadows swirl around him, stroke his skin with unseen fingertips, and block out the entire world except for the woman before him, her burning silver eyes, and the knife she holds at his throat. Lora, his Lora, holds a knife to his throat like she has countless times before. But this time, it feels different. She is looking at him differently, her eyes unguarded as she stares, transfixed at his mouth.

A voice says: "Do you want something, villainess?"

It's his voice, but it's a challenge he would not normally utter. She yanks her gaze up to his, and he raises his eyebrows in a dare. Her own eyes harden, deepening in a near-black purple. And then she buries her other hand in his hair, holding his head in place as she marries her lips to his.

His first thought is: *This is a dream. It must be a dream.*

And his next is: *Fuck it, I don't care.*

Then there are no more thoughts. Warmth and sweetness overpower every one of his senses, until his existence broils down to the places where their lips connect. Her tongue darts out and drags a line across his mouth, and he opens for her and sucks her in. This is... this better than he ever imagined. Here is the fire he's always felt, burning hot as she nips at his bottom lip, flaring even hotter as she moans when he bites back. They burn as bright and sharp as every tongue lashing they've exchanged, as hot as every profession of hate. And more. It is so much more than anything he has ever felt before, so much sweeter than anything he's ever tasted, so much better than... anything.

She breaks away and shoves him in the chest. He falls backward, spiraling downward through the swirling shadow. And he lands on a bed. His bed. In the midst of the shadow swirling above him, Lora is astride him in the dark.

And fuck, she's utterly bare. And so is he. Her naked, wide thighs press against either side of his hips. Her breasts hang, full and heavy, as she hovers over him. Her curved stomach grazes over him. There isn't an inch of her that is not perfection, that fails to live up to his every imagination. And fuck, he has imagined her a lot, laying in this same bed, taking himself in his hand. He always knows he'll hate himself after, for letting his feelings and fantasies loose, but he could never stop himself. He's certainly not about to stop now.

He reaches toward her, but sharp steel whispers near the skin on his sternum. "If you move," she taunts, "I'll cut you."

Ayc places his hands obediently back at his side. She trails the knife point over one side of his chest and across the other, never breaking skin. She grins viciously as his cock jumps behind her, grazing over her full ass.

"This is what you want?" she taunts as she reaches the hand not holding the knife between them and wraps her fingers around him. He pulls so hard on the sheets he hears a rip.

"All you have to do is say please, Ayc," Lora says.

Some part of him wants to fight, because fighting with her is *so fucking good*. But who is he kidding? He's a desperate man dying of thirst, and she is the only thing that will quench his need. And if this is just a hallucination of a dying man in a hospital bed, then he wants this one last dream to burn vivid in his brain when he draws his last breath.

"For fuck's sake, Lora," he growls. "*Please*."

Her eyes burn silver as she lowers herself onto him. At the first inch, she lets out a groan, like she, too, is relieved this game between them is done. That he's let her win.

462

"For the record," she gasps, when she's fully seated upon him, "I still hate you."

The shadows shift, concealing everything once more. And when it clears again, she's moving in the dark above him. She fucks him like she hates him, with a mercilessness he has admired as she dances with her blades. The shadows give him only brief fragments of images, and each one is perfect. Her hair streaming behind her as she throws her head back. The moonlight brushing against her brown skin. Her free hand clamping around her breast, as his own fingers ache with jealousy.

The tip of the knife slides along his skin. The fierce stroke of silver, compared to her softness, makes him groan. He is already on the edge, and he barely clings onto it. But, no, not yet. He's not done yet. Not done watching. Not done listening to the little noises she makes as she uses his body for her pleasure. All these years, from the time he met her, he made it his unspoken mission to make her laugh. And when she finally did, he thought he never heard a sound so beautiful, but he likes these just as well. And he hasn't had enough; he's not sure how he will ever have enough of her, but he will cling to every moment he has.

So, he seizes her thighs in his hands. A sharp sting pricks at his skin, and a drop of blood, hot and sticky, slips down his side. Shadows overcome him, and when they clear, his hand is already between her thighs, his thumb working slowly around her clit. Her whimper vibrates his tongue as he kisses her. The knife has moved back to his throat, but it doesn't stop him as he thrust up inside her, burying himself deeper and deeper.

He buries his face in her neck and breathes her in. Fucking anise.

This is better, so much better than anything he has ever felt. Because no one has ever been *her*.

"Did you know I've spent my whole life wanting to make you laugh, villainess?"

She shakes her head.

"And now that I have..." He circles his thumb faster, drives into her harder. She throws back her head. "My new life's goal is to make you scream."

"Ayc!"

It's not Lora's voice that yells his name. It comes from Ayc's right, loud enough his eyes fly open.

Open?

Ayc's breath comes uneven. He searches around him, frantically trying to make sense of his surroundings. The hospital room. Tavish who leans over him, shaking his shoulder. Saga whining on his other side.

Fuck, he was dreaming. Of course, he knew all along he was dreaming. Only in dreams does Lora ever want him back.

"You were groaning," Tavish says, worry written in the lines between his brow. "Are you all right?"

A wretch of nausea rips Ayc's stomach open. He manages "Don't tell Lora," before he turns to heave into the chamberpot beside the bed.

Yes, this is reality.

- LORA -

A hand taps Lora's shoulder, and she jerks her head upright. She must have finally dozed off for the first time in over thirty hours, her head slumped against the wall. Xylie sits in the chair next to her, the white of her eyes wide in the light of the single lantern on the wall. In the window, the darkness of night has faded to a deep violet. Peregrin and Tavish are asleep on the floor. Bronwen and Saga must be in with Ayc.

Tavish's faithful dog has hardly left Ayc's side. After the convulsions stopped the first time and Ayc slipped into sleep, sedated by whatever drugs the healers gave him to stop the seizure, Ayc's teeth still chattered and his whole body shook. No amount of blankets Lora piled around him did any good. As though knowing, Saga jumped onto the bed beside Ayc and rested his head gently on his chest. Only then did Ayc stop shaking. Saga has been there ever since, only leaving when Tavish takes him outside to stretch and take care of his basic needs.

Lora is grateful that *something* has given Ayc relief. Nothing else has seemed to help. Whatever poison Marcellus gave him is merciless and fierce. If not for the gryphon feathers Tempest has donated, Ayc would certainly have been dead by now. The medicines the healers give him stop the convulsions—but only for a time. They stop the vomiting—but only for a time. None of them have seemed to stop the hallucinations.

Ayc is breaking, right in front of her eyes. The poison will steal his life, but first, it is robbing him of his sanity, of his silliness, of everything Ayc is. And it is *killing* her.

Every moment she's wanted to scream, to make a deal with the divine to swap their places, to burn everything down to the ground if it means she can save him. But she can do none of it. She can see the hope slipping slowly from the other four: the tears that crust Xylie's lashes, and the grayness that deepens in Peregrin's face. She must be strong for them, so she's tried to force herself to be numb, like her skin is made of ice. If she lets herself feel, she feels the ice cracking, whining as though it threatens to shatter. She fears that, soon, even a snowflake might send her plunging beneath, drowning in the pain.

But for now, she simply takes a deep breath.

Xylie's hands move in the dark. *"I have a plan. I had to observe for a while to be sure, but I think it will work."*

Lora glances to Erech, who is asleep against the door once more. Still, she signs back. *"A plan to do what?"*

"For me to escape here and go to Velphin."

Lora blinks at her cousin, but she looks absolutely serious. *"No,"* Lora signs swiftly. Whatever plan Xylie has, Lora is sure it'll work, but that's beside the point. She isn't going to Velphin alone. It's too dangerous.

The door to Ayc's room opens, and Bronwen slips out. At the click of the lock, both Tavish and Peregrin stir. Lora's eyes shift again to Erech, and this time she finds him watching.

Peregrin sits halfway up, but Tavish says, "I'll go. I need to check on Saga."

Tavish grabs his slender cane from the floor beside him and rises to his feet. The cane sweeps across the wood as he finds his way past Bronwen and into the room with Ayc. The door shuts, and Erech works his neck before settling back down on his pallet before the door and shutting his eyes.

From across the room, Bronwen locks onto Xylie and Lora, and she must sense something because she draws near.

"What's going on?" Bronwen signs.

"I want to go to Velphin," Xylie signs back. *"I have a plan."*

Lora watches Bronwen carefully for her reaction. Bronwen is the only one who has been to Velphin. She'll uniquely understand the dangers that Xylie would face. Bronwen's eyes widen, only a fraction, but enough that Lora sees it.

Xylie must see it too, because her gestures grow more urgent. *"I can't do anything for Ayc here, but I can help him—and you, Lora—if I go to Velphin."*

"Marcellus is going to win," Lora signs, hating every gesture she makes to spell out the bastard's name. To Xylie and Bronwen, it's time she admitted it.

Xylie's shoulders slump as she gazes at the chronicler on Lora's wrist, and Bronwen goes pale as the moonlight, all color draining from her cheeks. She's paler than when they were in that pit of snakes. After all, Bronwen has told Lora of the cruelty Marcellus wrought upon her as a young child. He made Bronwen feel that she was wrong and broken, lies that inflicted wounds Bronwen still struggles to heal. This must be Bronwen's most dreaded nightmare.

And Lora hates herself for failing them both.

"I know," Xylie signs. *"And that's why I need to go. Let me do this, or at least, let it be my choice. I know I can do it."*

Lora swallows, her mouth dry. She understands Xylie's desire to help her friend, but Xylie is her cousin. More than that Xylie's father and Lora's own were friends. From the time Xylie was a toddler, they ran through the trees of Elodie and in the heights of the Stella Rune Mountains. And when they both suffered unimaginable loss seven years ago, they survived it together. If there is one thing Lora cannot sacrifice to save Ayc, it's Xylie.

But Lora has lived her life on a path she was forced to take; she will not take a decision from someone else.

She looks to Bronwen who studies Xylie carefully. Then Bronwen's hands move. *"If you're going to do this, there are some things you need to know. Do not accept any deals with the Supreme sorcerer. Offer to pay them money. Nothing more. The Supreme is ancient and their magic is old. They know and wield magic that has otherwise long been forgotten. No deals. Understand?"*

Xylie's motion is confident. *"I understand."*

Bronwen's hands hover in the air and then fall. She nods at Lora.

Lora hesitates for one more breath before she signs, *"Tell me your plan."*

Lora watches as Avabeth fusses over the blankets on Ayc, who still lays sleeping. Lora avoids looking at him directly, least she notice the signs that he is not comfortable, not at all: the sweat on his brow, the sallowness of his skin, the hitch in his breath. She focuses solely on Avabeth.

The girl would make a great healer, if she was born in a different clan or a different sex. Maybe, her husband sees it too, and that's why the male has allowed her to come back and tend to Ayc, which she has done frequently over the last day. It has been Avabeth's movements that Xylie has been watching, the one who Xylie's plan formed around. They need her help if this is to succeed, and Xylie cannot ask her, so here Lora is.

Before Lora entered the room, Bronwen insisted, *"Ask her. Do not threaten her."*

Pity. That would be far easier.

"Can I ask you something, Avabeth?" Lora asks, trying to stick to the script she rehearsed in her head.

Avabeth keeps her eyes low and folds her hands demurely before her. "Yes, my lady."

"Did you like the cake Ayc made for you?"

She blinks. "Yes. It was incredibly kind."

"Would you repay him if you could?"

She shifts uncomfortably. "I don't know what you mean."

Lora moves around the bed that separates them. Avabeth freezes in place, her eyes wide. Lora knows that she shouldn't intimidate her, but she can't help it. She has no time to be more gentle. She is taking a risk, telling Avabeth their plan. But it's the only chance they have.

"I need your help. *Ayc* needs your help."

Avabeth studies Ayc, breathing softly in the bed, his skin nearly blending into the white blankets beneath him.

"What do you need me to do?" she says at last, looking back at Lora. A spark flashes briefly in her blue eyes.

A little bit of courage. That's all she has. It's all Lora needs.

Twenty minutes later, Lora watches Xylie walk from the waiting room into Ayc's room. The other three pretend they are still sleeping, exhausted from the lack of rest they got the day before. Erech glances up from sharpening his sword. He notes Xylie at the door, carefully counts who else is here, and then resumes dragging the stone over the edge of his blade. Xylie peeks back at Lora. Her face is framed in the hood of the colorful, blocked coat that Lora made her.

Lora makes a gesture, a single simple one: "*I love you.*"

Xylie signs it back and then closes the door behind her.

It's a couple of hours later when the door opens again. The hooded head hangs low as she hurries out and sits hard on the chair, her back to Erech. Erech watches her come out and Peregrin go in.

Even from her spot across the room, Lora can see that her hands shake. Her pale hands.

"Hide your hands," Bronwen whispers from the chair beside Avabeth, and she tucks her hands into her sleeves.

Xylie's coat and spare clothes fit Avabeth perfectly, just like Xylie knew they would. Xylie put them in a cupboard in Ayc's room, just before she slipped out the window onto Tempest's back. Avabeth snuck the spare key from her husband's office so she can use the front door of Ayc's hospital room. Erech is a brutal and efficient man, but he's hardly an observant one. All he needs to see is the right number of bodies, and occasionally, a girl in a colorful coat.

The plan is working, and by now, Xylie and Tempest are flying toward the sea and the island of sorcerers who are Ayc's last hope.

CHAPTER
THIRTY-ONE

- AYC -

Ayc dreams of Xylie crawling through a window and a Xylie who now has Avabeth's face, or perhaps, it's an Avabeth wearing Xylie's clothes. But mostly, Ayc dreams about Lora. He clings to those dreams. They are more comfortable than the reality.

He isn't sure if he wakes up or falls asleep, but Peregrin sits beside him in armor now made of feathers. Ayc's teeth chatter, and yet the blankets cling to his skin, damp with sweat. And everything, everything, *everything* hurts. He's not a stranger to pain, but this feels like there is a beast inside of him, clawing to get out. He tries to form words past the pain, but all he can manage is a choke.

Peregrin bolts from the chair. They lift Ayc's head and press a mug to his lips. "Drink."

It's difficult to get his muscles to follow commands. He sputters and gasps but manages to get down several gulps of the tea. As he drinks, relief floods through him, not complete, but enough that when Peregrin lets his head fall back on the pillow, Ayc can breathe. There must have been a feather within it, because the beast grows quiet. That was what he saw when he first awoke. Peregrin doesn't wear feathers, but there's a pouch at their neck and a few feathers poke out.

Ayc's teeth still chatter, and he pats at the empty bed beside him. Something is missing, but he can't remember what.

"Tavish took Saga outside," Peregrin explains. "He'll be back soon to keep you warm."

They reach for a blanket crumpled at the end of the bed and pull it over Ayc, tucking it around his shoulders. The gesture makes Ayc feel young... and loved, but it shifts something on Ayc's chest. The sharp object scraps along his skin. Ayc seizes it beneath the blanket and tries to thrust it away, but he only tugs at the cord around his neck.

It's just the tooth, the one Ember laid in Ayc's palm, like it could ensure Ayc would come home.

But with the scream of pain echoing through his muscles, with his head full of hallucinations and dreams, Ayc is more certain than ever it isn't going to happen. It takes Ayc a few tries of opening and closing his mouth, but eventually, he speaks.

"How long has it been? Since I was stabbed?" Surely, it's been an eternity.

"Nearly forty-eight hours now."

How many more hours does he have left until the three days are over? He can't do the math in his muddled head. Too long. It'll be too long. And it doesn't matter anyway. Marcellus won't keep his word.

Ayc pulls the tooth out from beneath the blanket and

holds it up to Peregrin. He doesn't have the strength to lift his head and free the cord. "Peregrin, if I die, will you take the leviathan's tooth back to Ember? I want him to—"

"Shut up!" Peregrin snaps, silver sparking in their eyes. "Shut the fuck up, boy. I am not going back and telling my child and my loves that we've lost you—that *I* lost you. So you're going to hang on. You're going to survive."

Ayc's chest hurts, but this is a pain deeper than physical. Tears burn in his eyes. He wants to sob, the deep, relentless type of crying he hasn't done in a long, long time. But he blinks the tears away. He clings to the remnants of his strength like it's the very edge of a cliff about to crumble.

"Marcellus isn't coming back," Ayc reasons.

"Yes, he is. Tempest and I will hunt him to the ends of the earth if we must, but he is coming back. You will not die. You won't—" Peregrin's voice breaks, and the silver fades from their eyes to make way for a flash of something else.

Ayc looks away, unable to bear it. He tells himself this isn't real. He must be dreaming again, because Ayc has never seen Peregrin cry.

It cannot be real.

- LORA -

Lora paces at the end of Ayc's bed. It's noon on the third day, and Marcellus said he would be back at sunset. Only a few hours to go, but overnight, Ayc has been fading faster.

This is the first time Lora has seen him in nearly twenty-four hours. Avabeth has limited time when her absence won't be noticed, and if she's not sitting in Xylie's place, no one else can leave the waiting room. It means that most of the time Ayc has been alone, or at least alone except for Saga. But Avabeth is currently in the waiting room, ensuring that Erech lays eyes on who he thinks is Xylie so he doesn't get suspicious. Lora took the brief opportunity to see Ayc, and she noticed the change as soon as she laid eyes upon him.

Ayc's breaths have become shallow, and his skin has turned a sickly yellow. He hasn't been seizing or vomiting, but he hasn't woken up since last evening when Peregrin sat at Ayc's bedside. The healers and nurses must now give total care to him: repositioning his body to prevent sores, cleaning his mouth every two hours to keep away infection, and frequently monitoring his breaths and heartbeat. Per the healer's reports, he doesn't even stir.

Lora understands the signs all too well.

Just a few more hours, she reasons. They just need a few more hours. By now, Xylie has surely made it to Velphin, though the flight would have been long and hard. She will try to bargain for what Ayc needs, but it'll surely be another day until she's back. Ayc doesn't have that long. Marcellus is his only hope.

Still, two words echo in her head, a haunting refrain.

He's dying.

...dying...

Lora's eyes sting, and she presses them shut.

"Water." The request isn't stronger than a croak. She whirls toward Ayc. His eyes are still shut, but his lips move again.

"W-water."

Lora rushes to the pitcher on the stand beside his bed and pours water into a cup. When she looks again, one of

Ayc's eyes has peeked open. She offers the cup, and he raises a hand, but it trembles like the last leaf of autumn clinging to a barren limb.

"Here." She lowers herself gingerly to sit on the bed beside him. She cradles one hand behind his head and helps him lift it as she brings the cup to his lips. He drinks it down, his body shaking.

Lora grits her teeth. She hates this, hates how fragile he seems. No matter what the kids around her thought, she never once thought of him as weak. Disadvantaged, perhaps. Different, certainly. But not weak. The way he could smile with a knife at his throat always made her admire him a little too much. She wants that now. She wants him to tell her a joke, one that is so ridiculous she'll want to punch him, but he slumps backward onto his pillow.

"Thank y-you," he says, his teeth chattering.

She sets the cup down on the stand and pulls the blankets up to his chin, hardly registering her own movements.

"C-cold," he says, though sweat shines on his brow and he's covered with three blankets. A fire still roars in the fireplace. It's sweltering in this room.

Lora looks to the side door, wondering if perhaps she should get Tavish and Saga, but Lora has only a short amount of time before Avabeth must leave. She forces herself not to hesitate, knowing if she does, she'll let fear get the best of her. She stands and swiftly strips out of her armor with practiced ease until only her tight black shirt and breeches remain. She kicks off her boots and then lifts Ayc's blankets.

"W-what are you—" Ayc begins, but Lora ignores him

and slides beneath the blankets. The bed is narrow, meant only for a single person. She has to press her body against his side to fit. She tucks the blankets back around them but keeps her body stiff and rigged. She hovers her head above his shoulder, trying to touch as little as possible.

"O-oh," he whispers softly into her hair.

She isn't quite sure what to do with her hands, so she keeps the one that is not beneath her awkwardly pressed to her shoulder. Then, slowly, she lets it relax, resting it on his chest, careful not to let her pointed nails touch his skin. His breath stills beneath her touch, pausing for a small eternity before he releases a shaky exhale. And she finds she was right about touching him: he gives beneath her touch. He is not stiff and unmoving. He is soft and alive.

Her fingers flutter with the desire to explore his chest, trace the lines of it, explore the hills and the valleys, but she forces her hand to be still.

"Better?" she asks.

His teeth are not chattering now. "Yes."

"Good."

Her neck aches in the position she has been holding it, so she allows her head to fall onto his shoulder. He adjusts his arm from beneath her and curls it around her. Goosebumps prickle along her arms, even though heat blazes from Ayc's skin. She has never been the type to lay for hours in someone's arms. She's never seen the point. But she might like this a little too much: his heartbeat beneath her palm, the steady rhythm of his breath, the way his fingers absently trail over the taut muscles of her back, convincing them to ease. She takes a breath, and despite herself, her body fully relaxes against him.

They fit together, the two of them, like a sword resting in

its sheath. The strange sense of well-being and warmth settles over her, the same tenderness she felt as she watched Ayc bake in her grandmother's kitchen. She could stay here forever, live in this moment and make it her home. Here, with him.

Ayc's voice vibrates in her ear, "Hey, Lora, why didn't the wall trust the stairs?"

Lora tilts her head up. She catches the smallest of grins playing on his lips, though his eyes are still closed. Her own lips tug up on one side. It feels so good to hear him speak. Perhaps she was wrong in her assessment. If he has the strength to joke, perhaps he's doing far better than he first seemed.

"Because they're always up to something," she replies.

"Damn, I've already told you that one, huh?"

"Twice."

"Pathetic of me, really. I ought to do better."

Almost without realizing what she's doing, she fiddles with the cord around his neck, the one connected to the leviathan tooth. His eyes open at last, revealing that stunning blue.

"Will you read to me?" he asks. A grin curves fully up on his lips, now, and her heart swells with hope. "From that dirty book of yours."

Warmth stings her cheeks at the reminder that he not only read her book, but he read the portion she paused on. "No. Absolutely not." As much as she's relieved to see him so alert, she's not giving into that request.

"It's not kind to deny a dying man his last wish."

The words wound more than any weapon. Her hand clamps over the tooth. It's larger than her fist. She grasps it so hard her hand shudders. "No, because you will *not* die," she snarls. She pushes herself up on her elbow so she can look down at him. "Do you hear me, Ayc? Do not die."

His smile disappears. A muscle in his jaw jumps as it tightens. "Fuck off, my lady."

She forgot for a moment—the power she has over him. She drops the fossil tooth with a growl of frustration. "That isn't an order. I'm *not* giving you an order. But you can't die, Ayc. Do you understand? You can't."

He searches over her face like she's a book whose words are written in a foreign language. Then he shrugs, shuts his eyes, and sinks deeper into his pillow.

No, he isn't taking her seriously enough.

"Will you look at me, Ayc?"

When he doesn't, her hands fling to his cheeks of their own accord, framing his face. "Ayc!"

His eyes flutter open.

"I need you to promise me you won't die." The words open a vein, and she can't make her mouth stop. She bleeds out the words, one by one. "I need you to keep being a pain in my ass, all right? I need you not to die. I just need—"

You.

She stops before that last traitorous word can leave her lips.

"Promise me, Ayc," she insists. "That's not an order. Just... please."

"Why?" he demands.

He searches her eyes, and he's much too close. Their noses nearly touch. His breath teases her lips, smelling of the wash the nurses have kept his mouth clean with and the sharp, bitter smell of whatever tonic the healers last gave him. This close, and he can see right through her. Yet, she can't bring herself to draw away. His face fits into her hands far too perfectly. Her thumb glides against the stubble on his chin, across those white crescent scars where the stubble doesn't grow.

And fuck, she *does* hate him for this. Hates how being this close to him is such fucking torture, and yet she doesn't ever want to be anywhere else.

"Why, Lora?" he snaps again. His hand lifts and cups the back of her head. The pad of his thumb presses against her jaw, and all of her senses narrow down to that spot.

"Why w-what?" she asks, hating the way her voice trembles like she's the one with a fever.

"Why do you care so much about what happens to me?" Something burns in his eyes, too hot for the blue. And that heat blazes into her. She closes her eyes to block him out, but it only serves to heighten her senses. She's aware of every millimeter of his skin when he guides her closer and presses his forehead to hers. "Don't tell me it's only out of guilt for what your mother has done. I don't believe you. Why did you *really* come for me? Why can't you leave me now?"

"I just... can't."

The tip of his nose brushes down the bridge of hers. "You can do better than that. I deserve more than that."

His voice is his own, but deeper. Stronger. It makes the hope grow wings and soar around her chest. Perhaps, the healers are wrong. He's stronger than anyone gives him credit for. He's fine. He's going to be fine.

"I don't know how to explain," Lora manages. The emotions clattering around inside her can't be illustrated in a few sentences. It would take twelve tapestries to capture, and at least six dozen books. It would take *decades* to explain all the things she feels for him.

479

"Try."

She shakes her head, her eyes still closed, and something soft as rosebuds trail across her cheekbone. Lips. His lips.

Her heart slams against her sternum. One small tilt of her head, and she could meet his mouth with her own. And she *wants* to kiss him. She wants to know what his mouth would feel like against her lips, against her body, between her thighs.

A shudder passes through her, and perhaps he feels it, because he chuckles. When she peeks her eyes open, he wears a wicked smile, like he now knows that he's winning this game that exists between them.

"You're supposed to hate me," he says.

"I do," she lies. Or perhaps it isn't a lie. She hates him for how much she wants him.

"Then leave me."

It's a dare. A challenge. And she doesn't care when she fails it.

"Never," she snarls.

His hand glides back to tangle into her curls ever so carefully, not tugging on the strands. "Why are you always so stubborn?"

"Why are you such an obtuse asshole?"

Their foreheads still touch, and her fingers drift of their own accord, down his neck and onto his chest. His breath releases in another unsteady exhale, and she barely controls her own breath. They are so close, and yet, still so far away. Between them are millimeters and miles and this game— this ridiculous, foolish game that has existed between them since they met, that has been present every time she's held a knife to his throat. A game of tension and half-truths and words unspoken and risks they do not dare to take. A game

480

that will end as soon as they close the distance between them. But neither one of them moves, neither of them able to be the first to surrender.

And so he does what he always does when the tension rises between them. He tells a joke.

"Do you know what you get when you cross an obtuse asshole with—"

"Shut up!" she growls. "For once in your life, cinnamon roll, just shut up!"

And she kisses him.

It isn't a conscious choice. It is inevitable.

They have always been charging toward this moment. But when she closes those millimeters of distance, she understands why she resisted so long. There's power here, a magic that can't be cast with words. Walls crumble, and the world utterly changes in the moment that her lips collide with his.

He stiffens in surprise, but his hesitation lasts only a heartbeat before he responds. His hand tightens at the back of her neck, and he pulls her until their bodies are flesh together. They come together like swords clashing. Sparks ignite, and the heat roars through her. If he keeps kissing her, she will go up in flames. She will die with him.

Die. Dying.

Reality crashes back to her. She yanks herself back, managing to pry herself only a finger's breath away. She gasps for a breath. "I shouldn't have done that."

"Yes, you should have," he argues. "You absolutely fucking should have."

His hands slide down her back, pressing her toward him. It takes every shred of her will to turn her head. His lips find her jaw instead and forge a path across it. Every warm caress of his lips sends a shiver through her, melting the tension in her muscles, chipping away at her resistance.

"You're sick." Her protest is weak. Breathless.

"And it's a miracle," he says against the curve of her neck. "I suddenly feel fine."

He lays a kiss where her pulse thrums. Slowly, first with his mouth, then with his tongue. When he kisses her again, he's only moved millimeters, like he means to devote time to every inch of her skin. She trembles and bites hard on her lower lip to keep back the whimper that rises in her throat.

"You've been given medicine," she says, and she isn't sure if she's convincing him, or herself. "You may not be thinking straight."

He rests his head back on the pillow, creating space she desperately needs. His eyes are bright, and the look he gives her is unguarded, but she still can't define it. She only knows she wants to weave tapestries using only the shades of blue in his eyes.

"Medicine can't make me want something I've wanted for years."

"Years?" she repeats. "You've wanted—"

"Lora." Her name growls off his lips. The vibration of it rattles her all the way to her core. "Shut up, and let me kiss you."

The last of her reasons fracture, and she can only nod. He guides their mouths back together, and she realizes she's fucked. Completely and totally fucked.

Because no one has ever kissed her like *this*.

Males have kissed her like it's a task to be completed before moving on to more exciting things. But Ayc kisses her slowly like he cherishes every brush of their lips, like he could kiss her for the entire rest of his life and never bore of it. Then, when her mouth parts for him, his kiss becomes more urgent, desperate. Like he is dying of hunger and she is the only thing that will satisfy.

And his hands—oh, his hands. They glide lightly across her back like she is something to be worshiped, something so priceless he must handle with care. Then, just as quickly, he grasps her to him tightly, his fingers sinking into her soft flesh, like she is something he longs to devour. And then back again.

Worshiped and devoured, devoured and worshiped.

It's too much. Every long withheld emotion ignites within her, and she blazes so hot she thinks she might explode at the seams. This is too much. It's *everything*.

"Lora," he groans against the skin of her neck. The next time, her name's a growl again. "Lora."

And nothing—not anything in this divine forsaken world—could keep her away from him now. She arches against him, sinks her fingers into his hair to hold his face to hers, drags her hands down his body. And he meets her every violence with tenderness, her yearning with ferocity. Of course, kissing him would be like this. Like an endless battle and final salvation, all at once.

There's still too much between them, too many clothes, too many words unspoken, so many wounds unforgiven. She longs to rip it all away until there is nothing left but *this*. These kisses and his skin and something to satisfy the damp ache building between her legs.

He is everything.

When he presses against her, she allows him to change their positions, until they are both on their sides and every last inch of their bodies weld together. His fingers pluck at the hem of her shirt, but he hesitates there, as though seeking permission, Yes, she's about to demand. Fuck, she'll *plead* if he must, if he'll just *touch her*, skin to skin. Every part of her aches for him. She can't make the words form in her throat, so instead she yanks on his bottom lip with her teeth. She expects a groan or a curse, but she's rewarded instead with a grin. His lips curve against her own, and the brightness of him glows in her chest, like she's swallowed sunlight.

His chuckle shudders through his body as he maneuvers away from her mouth and back to her neck. He grazes his next words playfully against her throat with his teeth. "My vicious, beautiful villainess."

"Ayc," she whispers back. *My Ayc.*

"Do you remember what I said about my new goal?"

"No. When were we talking about goals?"

He whips his head back so quickly cold hits her like an avalanche. She's about to yank him back, but the cloud of confusion in his eyes halts her. He searches her face, looking bewildered, lost, as though he can't quite remember where he is.

Then a look of crushing disappointment crosses his face. He sighs, and the sound is as bitter as the darkest of chocolates. "Oh, fuck, I'm dreaming again."

"What?" she mumbles. "What are you—"

He flops onto his back and flings an arm across his eyes. "Ayc?"

But his breath already moves in the slow pattern of sleep. At least, he looks comfortable. A red flush colors his pale cheeks. A sign of life.

She takes a moment to catch her own breath. Every nerve still feels alive from his touch. But honestly, what the fuck is wrong with her? He seemed fine, completely within his senses moments ago, but of course, he isn't. He can't even tell that their kiss isn't a hallucination. Maybe, when he wakes up again, he won't even remember that this happened.

And she will never forget. His kiss lingers even now, on her lips, on her jaw, on her neck.

A knock sounds at the door. It's probably Avabeth. Lora has been in this room far too long.

She climbs from the bed and gathers her armor, strapping it back in place, like it can shield her from all the things that she feels for him. She makes the mistake of looking back at Ayc, at his beautiful face and mouth still puffy from her lips. She cannot stop herself from bending and brushing a kiss upon his forehead. He smiles in his sleep, and she hopes his dreams are good ones.

He's fine. He's going to be fine.

"How is Ayc?" Avabeth whispers, when Lora opens the door.

Lora glances past her, into the room, but Erech is absent. Probably only stepped outside to relieve himself.

"I spoke to him," Lora replies, "and he seemed fine a minute ago. Normal almost."

Avabeth frowns. "I've seen that happen fairly commonly when people are this ill. They regain strength and seem fine, right before—"

She stops. As the blood drains from Avabeth's face, the hope in Lora's chest plummets like its wings have broken.

"Right before what?" Lora snaps.

Avabeth doesn't meet Lora's eyes when she answers. "Right before they die."

485

In the waiting room, Lora watches the pattern of sunlight change on the floor. Avabeth comes back every two hours and allows Lora to peek in. Whatever fresh energy Ayc felt when he kissed her disappears. He does not wake up again. At times, the spaces between his breaths seem too long, and at others, he breathes far too quickly.

The healers are honest. Ayc will likely not make it another day. Perhaps, not even through the night.

The shadows on the floor grow longer. Through the window, Lora, Peregrin, and Bronwen watch the sun slip beneath the horizon. Tavish sits with them, and he doesn't ask for the time, but perhaps he can feel the end coming.

The sun sets.

Darkness falls.

And Marcellus does not come.

Lora's entire world tints with silver, her very soul shaking with rage, as she storms toward Erech. "Where the fuck is he?"

Erech shrugs, sheathing his sword for the first time in three days. "He must have gotten held up. Either way, your end of the bargain is done, and I don't have to babysit you anymore."

He turns around and saunters from the room. Lora almost follows him, intent to tear him apart with her bare hands, but she sucks in a breath. *Focus. Time is running out.*

She snatches Tavish's pack from where it lies on a chair. She yanks out a map of Everadyn and spreads it on the floor before Tavish. "Find him."

He leans over the map, concentrating. Bronwen kneels beside him, and Peregrin moves to the door of the hospital room. They open it, so they can watch Ayc and the map all at once. Lora forces herself not to look into that room.

"Find him," Lora commands again.

"I'm trying," Tavish says, rubbing the heels of his hands against his temples. "But I can't. It's like he's shielded himself or something."

No, no, no, this can't be happening. Lora can't lose Ayc. She refuses.

One more chance enters her head, and she changes the request, "Find Wren."

Tavish hesitates, staring past Lora's right shoulder. "What are you going to do?"

"I'm going to find out if she knows where Marcellus went." *And then I'm going to kill her.*

Wren is a traitorous bitch who played with Ayc's affections like it meant nothing and then handed him over to his death. Lora will enjoy every moment of disassembling her body.

"Lora," Bronwen says, because surely she knows. But Lora shoots her a look, and she only says, "Throw an extra punch for me."

Tavish's hand shudders a moment, before he stabs a finger onto the map. A village that is close, perhaps only an hour's hard ride away.

Perfect.

Lora jumps to her feet. "Bronwen, Peregrin, stay with Ayc. Tavish, ride with me in case she moves. Those priests better have a fast horse."

There will be one less bitch breathing come morning.

THIRTY-TWO

Lora rides as hard as the horse can bear. Tavish clings on behind her, but he never once asks Lora to slow down, and Lora is so grateful to her friend for it. Saga has been left at Ayc's side, curled up to keep him warm. When they reach the inn, Lora swings off the horse before it's fully stopped. She offers Tavish a hand as he slides off and then hands him the reins.

"You all right?" she asks.

He nods and inclines his head toward the inn. "Try not to destroy *everything*, Lora."

"I make no promises."

She swings around and charges toward the door.

The inn has no boisterous music. It's dimly lit, sitting in the midst of shops that have been locked up for the night. This is Lux Aester; there won't even be alcohol within the place. Instead, it'll be full of wealthy patrons eating a hearty meal and poor workers tending to them hand and foot. It'll be quiet and peaceful and demur.

So, when Lora enters, she enters like a storm.

The door slams against the side of the wall. Strings shriek as the violinist in the corner stops their melody. The tables of patrons look up with startled cries. Lora searches through her silver-tinted vision for Wren and finds her at a corner table. Wren stands, dressed in her rainbow armor, and draws her sword. Only Sterling sits at the table with her, the other members of the Five nowhere in sight.

"Where's Marcellus?" Lora demands as she eats up the distance separating them, both swords already in her hands.

"Lora," Sterling says calmly as they climb to their feet, "maybe we should—"

"Where the fuck is Marcellus?" Lora roars again.

Some diners creep toward the door, while others remain seated and gawk. Lora focuses only on Wren, barely able to restrain herself from clawing that too-calm look from Wren's face.

"Why would I know where Marcellus is?" Wren asks.

"If you lie to me again, I'm going to rip out your tongue. *Where is Marcellus?*"

"Wren would never work with Marcellus," Sterling protests.

Wren's gaze flicks to Sterling, while Lora laughs coldly. She doesn't like the sound of her own laugh; it's too much like her mother's, but she can't stop it. "Are you going to tell your sibling the truth, Wren? Or shall I?"

Wren visibly swallows. She stares at her sibling, and Sterling must see it in her face, because they murmur, "Oh, Wren, no."

Wren flinches, but then hides it behind a glare, "All I've done is what is necessary to help you win."

Sterling swears, lifting a hand to their lips.

"What you've done," Lora spits, "is ensure Marcellus's

victory and get Ayc k-" Her voice breaks over the word, and she grits her teeth. "Killed."

Wren snaps her head back to Lora. "Ayc is dead?"

Those three words rob Lora of all her air, and she has to suck in multiple breaths before she can respond. "He will be soon. Marcellus stabbed him with a poisoned blade, but you knew that would happen all along, didn't you?"

"He was supposed to return after three days—"

"He lied!" Silver explodes in Lora's vision, and she swings her blade at Wren's neck. Wren throws up her sword in defense. The clash rattles Lora's teeth. The remaining diners race for the door.

Lora leans into their locked blades. Wren grits her teeth and attempts to resist. She doesn't match Lora in strength, and slowly, Lora's sword makes progress toward Wren's face.

"I gave Marcellus golden root!" Wren explains. "He swore Ayc wouldn't get hurt."

Lora disentangles their blades and steps back. "You found golden root?" Hopes blooms once more. That would work. It would really work. "Where's the rest of it?"

Wren hesitates, but Sterling quickly answers, "We turned what we harvested over to the Splendor in Lycendi already, for the lottery. Except the one bottle that Wren gave Marcellus, I guess," Sterling adds, shooting their sister a disgusted look. "But we didn't harvest all of it."

"Where is it?" Lora asks. "We can make more."

"No, you can't," Wren says, her voice wavering. "I—I destroyed it."

Lora's hope crumbles like sandcastles beneath a wave.

Sterling's eyes fling wide. "You *what*?"

"So no other victors could use it to fulfill their quests,"

Wren adds quickly. Her explanation does nothing to ease the look of horror in Sterling's eyes. Or the hate rising in Lora's throat.

"You destroyed dozens of people's chance to be healed, so that I would win," Sterling chokes out.

Wren swallows again, saying nothing.

"You really don't know where Marcellus is?" Lora asks.

"I would tell you if I did."

"Then there's no reason for you to still be breathing."

Lora aims her blade for Wren's neck. Wren jumps back and lifts her sword to parry. Lora unleashes a barrage of moves, honed into her from all those years of training. Never mind that she thought it was her destiny to be Sovereign. She is and always will be a warrior first.

Wren barely keeps up, blocking blows only inches from her stomach, her heart, her face. But she doesn't manage to block the boot Lora lands in her gut. She flies back into a table and tumbles over it, landing on the other side with a gasp of pain. The table tips over, and dishes shatter around her.

Sterling yells, "Stop! Please!"

Lora rounds the table. Wren grasps desperately through the broken glass for the sword she dropped, but Lora's foot finds it first and kicks it away. She sheaths one sword, so she can wrap that hand around Wren's throat. She clamps down hard. Wren's eyes water.

"I'll surrender!" Sterling cries. "I'll take off my chronicler."

Wren's vision snaps to Sterling first, and only then does Lora let herself look. Sterling is the only one still standing in the inn. Even the workers must be hiding in the kitchen. Sterling grasps their chronicler.

"It'll take it off right now. It'll just be you and Marcellus. Just spare my sister."

Wren croaks out a noise of protest. Sterling doesn't even look at her.

Lora loosens her grip on Wren so she can inhale a breath but places her sword against Wren's sternum, so she doesn't dare move. "What do you mean just me and Marcellus? What about Wylder? Ruatha?"

"Ruatha is dead," Sterling explains. "And Wylder removed his chronicler yesterday. He lost his brother trying to complete a quest. It completed the quest to make a great sacrifice, but I think he felt the price was too high."

The silver in Lora's vision fades. Sweet Ryker. Poor Wylder. No matter what transpired between them, Lora would never wish that upon them. Wylder was good sometimes, as cruel as Lora at others. But Ryker was good *always*.

This will crush Bronwen. Their friendship ran deep, and sometimes, though Bronwen denied it, Lora thought it was more.

"You have four stones lit, Loraphne," Sterling says. "There's still time to beat Marcellus."

Four? Lora glances down at her chronicler, near the hand that is currently clamped around Wren's throat. Four lit stones wink back at her. Not releasing her sword, she hooks a finger on her sleeve and pulls it down to find a quest now missing.

Make a great sacrifice.

Three days. That is what she sacrificed in her attempt to save Ayc. Three days, and the likelihood she would be Sovereign. The fate of her people for one man. It didn't feel like a sacrifice; it didn't feel like a *choice*. But whatever magic rules the chronicler must see it differently.

"I don't want you to forfeit," Lora says. "I want her dead." She tightens her grip on Wren's throat once more. Wren opens her mouth, but no sound can come out now. Blue tints the skin around her lips, and Lora finds that shade beautiful. At the very least, a fair trade for what she did to Ayc.

Metal rattles, loud in the silence, as something lands near Lora's boot. Sterling's chronicler, now cold and dim, sits in the rubble of broken dishes.

"If her treachery is how I would win, then I don't want it," Sterling says.

Lora's hand loosens around Wren's throat, and she lets out a sob. "No," she wails, a dam of tears breaking in her eyes and flooding her face.

"Let this be her punishment," Sterling says. "I know she doesn't deserve it, but please spare her. She's the only family I have left."

Lora glares down at Wren. She hasn't changed in the years since she threatened Lora's life for a crime she didn't commit; she's still beautiful and treacherous. But Lora never blamed Wren for her hatred. Not when Lora watched her mother behead hers. Lora lost her own father that day, but still, the guilt of what Iris took from Wren and Sterling weighs upon Lora.

Lora thrusts Wren away from her, dropping her onto the ground, and stands before she changes her mind. She pivots to meet Sterling's eyes. "Her life, for what my mother took from you. It doesn't repay the debt, but—"

"It wasn't yours to repay," Sterling says softly. They incline their head in gratitude. "Now go and win this thing."

Behind her, Wren climbs to her feet. Lora watches her out of the corner of her eye, not trusting her not to draw the knife at her side and aim for Lora's spinal cord.

Instead, her tentative words land just as sharply, "I'm sorry about Ayc. I truly did care about him."

Lora strikes before she's consciously makes the decision. Her hands swipes across Wren's face, nails digging in. Three long scratches are left in her wake across Wren's pale cheek. Wren gasps and presses her hand to her face. Blood seeps between her fingers, but neither she nor Sterling move to retaliate. The three ugly lines are beautiful to Lora, and they will last, ever a reminder of what Wren has done. Yris has given Lora the same gift every year on her birthday, a small pot of nail paint. Yris understood Lora well enough that she would never wear the garish red that Yris favors, so the color is different, but the formula of the paint is the same. The poison within is rare and expensive but serves to slow the fae's ability to heal until any wound inflicted by her nails is certain to scar.

"You didn't deserve a single moment he granted you, you traitorous bitch," Lora seethes between her teeth.

"And you do?" Wren fires back.

No, Lora thinks, but does not say. *And that's the point, isn't it?*

Instead, she says, "You speak his name to me again, and I'll do more than scar your pretty little face."

The inn door bangs open. Lora expects to see town guards running in to stop what is happening, but it's Bronwen who flies in, clutching her staff like she's preparing for battle.

Lora rushes toward her. "What's happening?"

Bronwen swiftly assesses the scene in the inn, before

answering. "It's Marcellus. He came back only a quarter of an hour after you left. He has the antidote."

Profound relief pours like a balm over Lora's skin that has, up to this point, felt like a raw and open wound. But then Bronwen adds, "But Ayc won't take it."

"Why the fuck not?" Lora asks.

"It's golden root, and he says it should go to someone else."

Lora is going to kill him. She's going to stab his stubborn, noble ass repeatedly, but first she has to save him. Without a backward glance, she races out of the inn and back toward Tavish and the horse. A dapple gray mammoth of a horse stands behind Lora's own, sleek with sweat. Up the street, Lora hears the pounding of boots. Ah, there are the guards.

"I'll take Tavish," Bronwen says. "You ride as hard as you can. We'll catch up."

Lora mounts her horse and digs her heels into its sides. The horse snorts, but bolts out into the night, back toward the hospital. She can see the steeples of the temple near the hospital in the distance, rising high above the plains, the lanterns casting a gold gleam in the dark. Each yard the horse eats up feels like a mile, so Lora bends low, riding harder than she's ever ridden in her entire life. She so rarely prays, but she prays then. All she wants is time. Time enough to make it back to the foolish baker, who has always been too kind for his own good.

"Ayc, listen to me—"

"No, Peregrin." Ayc's voice croaks, but he at least has the

strength to speak. Lora finds that encouraging as she runs through the waiting room and into Ayc's hospital room.

Peregrin leans over where Ayc still lies in the bed, face riddled with fury. Ayc glares back just as hard. The sickly yellow shade of his skin has deepened since she left; he nearly glows against the white sheets.

Marcellus and Erech stand in the corner. Marcellus's brow pinches in annoyance as he fiddles with a blue, ceramic vial. His sleeve is rolled up, revealing his chronicler, only one gem unlit. She registers the words on his wrist, familiar from this distance because of how long she has stared at her own arm.

Upturn the hands of fate.

Lora releases a breath that has been hitched in her ribs. She feared Marcellus would have given up and taken the antidote with him, but there's still time.

She can save Ayc.

"Good," Marcellus says with a heavy high. "We were about to leave. I'm wasting my time if he won't take the antidote. I did not think him to be suicidal."

Lora moves to Ayc's side. "Ayc—"

"Don't," Ayc interrupts, shaking his head. He meets Lora's eyes defiantly. "The golden root could save someone who needs it more, who deserves it more."

Saga whimpers softly, the dog's head still resting on Ayc's stomach.

"You will die without it," Lora tries to reason.

"Give it to Peregrin," he snaps.

"I don't want it," Peregrin growls back.

"You're in pain every day. With the golden root, you could be in the aerial army again. You could have your life back—"

496

Peregrin hits their cane hard on the side of the bed. The whistle of it through the air cuts Ayc off. "Boy, you don't get to tell me what I want from my life. You don't get to assume that I want to be rid of my pain. It's *mine*, and only I get to decide what I do with it. Without this injury, I wouldn't have Irving and Zinnia. I wouldn't have Ember. And I would not have *you*. And I would rather walk with this cane for the rest of my days than bear the pain of losing you. So, shut up and drink it."

Moisture pools in Ayc's eyes. Lora thinks for a moment it will convince him, and then he tightens his jaw into a hard, immovable line. "Give it to the Lycendi for the lottery. It's only fair."

Lora takes a breath. She hoped it wouldn't come to this. He'll hate her for this, but it's a price she's willing to pay.

"Drink the antidote, Ayc," Lora orders.

His body jerks as he realizes what she's done. Sweat beads across his nose as he shakes his head. "Fuck off, Lora."

"Drink the antidote," she repeats.

"No." It's a groan, like it hurts to say. Because it does. She is hurting him, but she can hate herself for that later.

"I command it."

She watches whatever shred of affection he feels for her die in his eyes. It's like the setting sun. It leaves the world cold and dark. She reaches her hand out to Marcellus. His brow furrows, curious, but he gives her the vial. She uncaps it and offers it to Ayc.

"Drink," she orders again, sealing both their fates.

Ayc rips the bottle from her fingers and brings it to his lip. He can't even lift his head, so he throws the liquid down his throat, sputtering before swallowing. He glares at Lora, the rage billowing off him. Hate. That's the only word for how he looks at her now.

But it doesn't matter, because he's here. He'll be all right. He's going to—

His hand falls to the side of the bed. The bottle tumbles from his grasp and collides with the floor. It shatters. The remnants of green liquid scatter amongst the shards of glass. *Green.* Not gold. Ayc still stares up at her with those wide, blue eyes, but he doesn't blink, doesn't move. Doesn't breathe.

Ayc has always been motion and energy and ridiculousness, but now he is still. Deathly still.

"Ayc!" Peregrin calls, shaking Ayc. "Wake up, boy! Come on!"

Saga barks and nuzzles Ayc with his nose.

Ayc doesn't move.

Air. There is no air. Lora can't draw in a breath. She has seen the face of death, and Ayc wears it now. He was there and gone in an instant. A crack forms in her chest, growing larger and larger. She is stone, and now she is shattering.

This can't be happening. He can't be gone. He can't, because she cannot survive this. This agony ripping through her is not something that can be survived. It is river water pouring into her lungs and the slap of her mother's hand and the day her father was banished and every beating she ever took at Adamant to make her stronger. This pain is unfathomable.

I can't breathe.

I can't...

"Oh dear," Marcellus murmurs, "it seems I gave him the wrong vial."

The world bathes with silver. Lora unleashes a scream as

she flings herself at Marcellus. Erech thrusts his sword between them, and she freezes. She surrendered her own weapons before she was allowed back inside the hospital, but she might impale herself on Erech's blade just to get one swipe at Marcellus's throat with her elongated teeth. But he holds up another vial. This one is clear, and gold liquid shines from within.

"If I give it to him now, it will reverse this poison too and should revive him," Marcellus says.

Lora swipes for the vial, but Marcellus moves it out of her reach. Erech presses the tip of the sword to Lora's chin. She stills, tilting her head back.

"I'll be the one to give it to him," Marcellus says.

Lora doesn't know what game he's playing, but it doesn't matter. "Do it!"

"Are you sure that's what you want?" Marcellus asks. "You know he's not divina, but you have no idea what he is, do you?"

"I don't care!" Whatever Marcellus knows, or thinks he knows about Ayc, it doesn't matter. Because Ayc is still just *Ayc*, who is worth saving. Who her life will be in ruins without. "Just do it!"

Marcellus shrugs. He crosses the room toward the bed. Peregrin opens Ayc's limp mouth so that Marcellus can drip it down his throat. Lora watches with Erech's sword still at her throat. All the cracks and seams within her groan, threatening to explode at any moment. Each second crawls by as Ayc doesn't move... doesn't breathe...

How will she breathe again if he does not?

And then Ayc gasps.

Peregrin lets out a sob of relief. Lora's own sob can't make it past her lips. It gets trapped inside, ricocheting around, deeper and deeper. It's only the sword at her throat that keeps her knees beneath her, that stops her from falling to the ground to thank the divine for giving Ayc back to her.

Erech drops the sword and looks at Marcellus. "Did it work?"

A wide grin breaks over Marcellus's face. He lifts his wrist to show off his chronicler. All seven gems are lit.

Ayc was dead, and now he is not. Marcellus has upturned the hands of fate.

And he will be the next Sovereign.

The cracks within Lora turn to a chasm, and she crumbles, piece by piece. She failed. She failed her destiny and her Five and her people. The Totus Omni–who embraced her not as Sovereign's daughter, but as just Lora– chose her to be their victor. They gifted her with the cape she now wears. Dozens of hands took their turn stitching the leaves and branches as a form of blessing. And Lora failed them. She will not be able to protect her people or make right what has long been broken. She will not be able to end her father's exile or send Aluina aid.

She has *failed*.

She always feared, deep down, that she is not enough. And here reality is—proving it to her.

She forces her chin higher, so those around her cannot see the way she is ashes and dust on the floor. Marcellus saunters toward her.

"I will see you in Wyntra for the crowning," Marcellus says, grinning wickedly as he looks down upon her. "And I will so enjoy watching you bow."

He wants a response, and she refuses to give him the satisfaction. She only stares at him coldly, until he walks away. Until he and Erech leave. Only then does she give herself five seconds to come undone. Only five. Her hands flutter near her face, attempting to release the tension, but it's too much.

Her own chronicler catches her eyes. She counts again. Five stones. Not four. She glances at the writing on her arm to see which task was completed.

Face your worst fear.

She isn't sure which moment it turned—in the moment she thought Ayc was dead, or in this moment, as she realizes she is not enough. That everything her mother whispered— that she is too soft, too naïve, too weak—has all been true after all. She's not sure which of those is her worst fear, but whatever the case, she has completed five of the seven quests.

Not enough. Not nearly enough.

"Lora," Ayc says softly from the bed.

She looks at him. His skin is no longer yellow, and as he sits up in bed, he looks strong. Perfect. Like nothing even happened. Peregrin slumps down into the chair and places their face in their hands.

Ayc's hands fist in the blankets, even when Saga licks his fingers. "He won, because you let him save my life, didn't he?"

Lora can only nod.

"I hate you," Ayc growls.

"Good," Lora replies. "That means you're still alive to hate me."

CHAPTER

THIRTY-THREE

- AYC -

He's alive.

Ayc scarcely believes it, even after he unwraps the bandages at his side to find the flesh there healed so completely it has not scarred. He plucks out the thread of his stitches as he listens to the voices in the adjoining room. Lora explains to Bronwen and Tavish—who have just returned from somewhere—what has happened. How Marcellus has won. He will be Sovereign.

And Ayc will be forced to obey his every command.

Ayc's usual pain rattles through his nerves, an ever-present reminder of the curse he must follow. He would rather be dead than obey him.

"There's still light in your chronicler," Bronwen says in the other room, her protest shaking with the fragility of someone who already knows their protest will do no good.

"Perhaps if we complete the quests and make it back to Wyntra before he does, we'll beat him."

"A message already came onto my arm saying someone has completed the quests, and we should return to Wyntra," Lora explains. "It's over, Bronwen. I failed you, and I'm s—"

Ayc stiffens when Lora's voice cracks, a fracture in the coolness she showed him right after she lost. She clears her throat before she finishes.

"I'm sorry."

Ayc grits his teeth and yanks out the very last stitch. A knock sounds at the front door to his hospital room before it opens tentatively. Avabeth pokes in her head, keeping her eyes low.

"Peregrin said you needed clothes."

"Come on in." He rises from the bed. His legs wobble, weak from the days he was in bed, but he steadies quickly. He takes the clothes she offers him. "Thank you."

She starts to leave, but he can't quite let her go.

"Avabeth," he says, lowering his voice. "If there's ever anything you need, if you ever decide you want out—"

"Out?" she repeats, staring at her feet.

"If you want a different life, find a way to send me a message. I can help you."

She peeks up at him through her hair, and her lips part. But then footsteps sound in the hallway. She darts out and slams the door closed without a goodbye. Ayc sighs as he shrugs into the new clothes, relieved that the linen shirt is white and not the Lux Aester blue. The leviathan tooth scraps against his skin as he adjusts the shirt, somehow still sharp all these years later. He untucks it from his shirt and runs his thumb over the point. It could be a weapon. Just the right force propelled into a neck. A way out...

He shakes his head, forcing the thought away. He pulls back his sweat-damp hair and secures it with a tie that's still on his wrist. Then he approaches the other door.

In the small sitting room, he finds Tavish, Bronwen, and Peregrin all slumped in chairs, wearing expressions that can only read as defeat. At the sound of the door, Lora stops her pacing, clamping her previously fluttering hands into fists.

"Ayc," Bronwen says with a sigh of relief. She rises from her chair, closes the distance, and folds her arms around him. "I'm so glad you're alive."

Ayc returns the embrace, before she steps back. "Where's Xylie?" he asks.

Bronwen glances at Lora, who hesitates before saying, "She slipped out to help complete a quest."

"What quest?"

Lora says nothing, and none of the others do either. Do they not trust him now, because they realize that Wren used him?

Ayc fiddles with his bracelets. "Is she safe, at least?"

Lora shifts her weight, but Peregrin reassures him. "Yes. Tempest is with her. She will protect Xylie."

Ayc tries to imagine Xylie riding Tempest for any length of time, but he's unable to conjure it in his head. Her loyalty to Lora must make her do terribly great things. "Is this why I have memories of seeing Avabeth dressed in Xylie's coat?"

Bronwen nods with a little smile that wobbles and then falls. "You were a bit out of it. You kept hallucinating a baby dragon."

Tavish's cheeks pucker as he presses his mouth into a hard line. One look at his face is all it would take for Lora and Bronwen to know he's up to something. Luckily, they don't look at him.

"A baby dragon, huh?" Ayc says. "I was hallucinating some very strange things. You were praying, Bronwen."

"That wasn't a hallucination," Bronwen says, her lips parting with what Ayc thinks would have been a laugh if he hadn't interrupted such a hard conversation.

"Wasn't it?" Ayc thinks over the last few days. Only a few memories are sharp prior to when he awoke after the golden root.

The memory of Lora giving her command—taking away his choice after she swore not to—is vibrant, as is the rage that blazes over him. But then, the heat is dampened by what else he remembers. The tightness of being inside of her, the sharpness of the knife against his throat, the sweetness of her soft moans as she slowly unraveled for him. *That* was certainly a dream. He even knew it at the time, no matter how vivid his intoxicated, dying mind made it.

But there is something else, too, something that lingers on his lips like the echo of a dream. He remembers kisses and teeth and her name growled on his lips. Was that a dream, too? Or was it real?

No, of course not. In what world would she ever kiss him?

But then Lora came for him, saved him, sacrificed for *him*.

Why?

It's a question he doesn't want to ask again. He doesn't trust her to be honest. She told him it was only out of obligation, guilt after everything, and as much as it stung to hear at the time, he's not sure he believes it. But even if she were to tell him the truth, he's not sure he wants to hear it—

whatever *it* is. Not when he's furious with her for her betrayal.

The door opens, and a healer steps in. Age is written in the lines of his eyes and around his mouth, and Ayc wonders if this is Avabeth's ancient husband.

"Ah, good," the healer says. "I'm glad to see the patient is well, but this is a hospital. Not an inn."

"It's the middle of the night," Bronwen says, twirling her wrist toward the window. The darkness outside is heavy, barely touched by moonlight.

"And we never know when a patient and family will need these rooms."

The message is clear. Ayc is stable and Marcellus is done with them, so the Lux Aester healers are done with them, too.

Bronwen snaps her head side to side, her braid flaring. "That's rid—"

"It's fine," Lora says. "We need to be in the nearest air dock by morning, anyway." She looks to Ayc. "If you're feeling well enough."

He nods. "I'm fine, but what about Xylie?"

"Tempest will be able to find me," Peregrin says.

"Then let's get out of here."

They walk through the plains of Lux Aester toward the nearest air dock for a few miles, until the exhaustion becomes plain on their faces. Ayc's anxiety still demands movement, after being sedated for the last three days, but Ayc fakes fatigue so they will agree to rest. They make a fire and spread out the bedrolls. Lora insists on taking the first watch, and Ayc pretends to sleep for an hour before a gnawing in his stomach becomes too much to ignore. How long has it been since he's eaten? He can't remember.

He sits up, but Lora standing beside him, holding a bowl. She crouches down and offers it to him. It's filled with unleavened bread he baked before they left, squashed but smeared in preserves.

"Your stomach is so loud it's going to wake everyone," Lora explains.

Ayc takes the bowl. He should thank her, but all he can manage is a grunt. He stuffs a bite in his mouth, half to ease the stomachache and half to have an excuse not to talk.

She folds her knees beneath her. The firelight plays over her face, highlighting the curve of her cheeks. Her eyes look dark at first, but when the light hits them, they turn a royal blue. The very air feels different between them now. Charged. Like the air between two people after confessions are spoken and cannot be taken back. But Ayc can't remember what that confession was.

"You're angry with me?" she says.

He takes his time chewing and swallowing, long enough to decide to be honest. "Yes."

"Because I agreed to Marcellus' deal or because I forced you to drink?"

He shrugs. "All of it."

Her hands start to flutter, and she clamps them around her knees. "I never wanted to break my promise to you, but what was I supposed to do? You would have died to save some hypothetical person you thought deserved it more."

"It was my choice to make."

"Fuck." She throws her head back and glares at the stars. "I'm not going to apologize, Ayc. I'm not sorry I did whatever it took to save you, because I believe *you* are worth saving."

A comeback is halfway up his throat when he fully hears her words, and he's left with his mouth parted, unable to say anything at all. The words fit like a key into an empty space in his chest, a hole created when he watched his people be slaughtered and knew he should have died with them.

You are worth saving.

It echoes in his head, a new melody, a sweet refrain. Maybe one day he'll believe it. For now, he shuts his mouth and stares at her, wondering how they got here, how his beautiful villainess was the one to say such kind things to him.

She always did have a way of leaving him breathless.

When she meets his gaze, her eyes look like the stars themselves, the firelight blazing within. She is close and yet too far. The inches between them feel like miles and decades, and he both aches to reach across it and run from it. Her breath catches, and she pulls her bottom lip between her teeth, and he *remembers*: her tongue dancing with his, the softness of her body melding to his bare chest, the stab of her teeth against his bottom lip.

Was it real? Or was it only a dream?

And if he leaned forward now, would she let him kiss her or stab him in the neck like he deserves?

Saga lets out a loud, long snore from his sleep. Ayc jumps and then laughs. Lora's lips tilt up on one side, and whatever comes, however angry he is at her, he's grateful that he's still here to see that smile.

"I meant what I said about fighting Marcellus," Lora says after a long moment. "I won't let him take away everything I love about Everadyn, and in the meantime, my organization will help as many people as we can."

Ayc licks preserves off his fingers and sets the bowl aside. His hand absently wraps around the leviathan tooth at his throat, his thumb plucking at the sharp end. Another idea is forming in his head, like a phantom hovering at the edge of his vision.

He asks, "And can I help in this plan? I know, with being Bound to the Sovereign, I might not be able to do much, or be more risk than I'm worth, but—"

"I would very much like your help." She says it firmly, as though she's not teasing or doubting. Like she means it. "First, we will free Everadyn, and then, we will find a way to help Aluina. I promise you."

The words rattle the earth beneath him, shaking his very foundation. He stares at her, searching for any sign that she is being dishonest. Her eyes of starlight do not lie. He sucks in an unsteady breath. He has hoped, with all she's told him, that she longs to help Aluina, like her father did before her. Here she is, confirming it. And damn, if it doesn't doom him to sink deeper into an affection that already feels bottomless.

She stretches out her hand to him. "Deal?"

He takes her hand, and the static pulses between them. For a fraction a moment, it feels as though no distance exists between them. That they are entirely united. It is an exhilarating feeling... and a terrifying one. He drops his hand and shifts away. "Deal."

To fracture the intensity of the moment, he grants her a teasing tone and a small, genuine smile. "But it'd be irresponsible to make dastardly plans of rebellion and mayhem on no sleep. Best leave the treason until morning."

When she doesn't budge, he flicks his hand in a shooing motion. "Go on now."

"You—" she begins to protest, but he cuts her off.

"I'm not tired. I've slept for three days. You look like you haven't slept at all."

It's true, now that he lets himself really look. It's clear in the darkness in her eyes, the heaviness of her shoulders. She doesn't fight him but lays down on her bedroll. He moves closer to the fire, taking his pack with him. Tavish told him that Xylie left it in his care, and now Ayc has it back, still heavy with the weight of the dragon's egg. He keeps it close to the fire.

He pretends not to notice how Lora watches him, like she's afraid to take her eyes off him. But how can he not notice? His skin, his nerves, and very heartbeat come alive when she looks at him, singing out a familiar, haunting tune he can no longer ignore...until her eyes finally drift shut.

Long into the night, Ayc studies the twisting, forked tongues of flame and thinks about sacrifice, about evil men and blood and monsters, about wars and rebellions and ways to stop them. He clutches the tooth hanging from his neck and ponders it for hours until something forms fully in his head, something that terrifies him. It is downright... villainous.

But perhaps there's a time for villainy.

The cry of a gryphon startles Ayc awake. He has only just fallen asleep, after Bronwen took his place at guard. The sun has begun breaking over the horizon. A dark shape, framed by the hazy pink and orange sky, approaches rapidly.

Peregrin bolts upright. "Tempest!"

Xylie! Ayc ignores the protests of his muscles as he shoves to his feet, the way his nerves rattle in fury. Lora stands and shields her eyes as she gazes into the sun.

"I can see her. She's here." She exhales softly.

Ayc echoes the sigh as relief settles his soul. His best friend has returned.

Saga barks excitedly but remains still as Tavish uses the guide handle to stand. Tempest lands in a flare of wings. Xylie clings to the beast's neck, her body trembling, her face buried in the feathers. Ayc races toward her, but Lora passes him, reaching her cousin first as she half dismounts, half tumbles off Tempest. Lora steadies Xylie then yanks her into a hug.

Where did she go? Ayc wonders. *How long has she flown?*

"*I am never flying again,*" Xylie signs.

"Did you get it?" Lora asks.

Xylie lifts the deep purple, velvet pouch she clutches in her hand. Lora takes it from her, and then Xylie turns. When she sees Ayc, she cries out and flings herself at him. She clings to his leather armor, and he returns her embrace with the tightness of a snug blanket, the way he knows she needs to be hugged.

"Hey, friend," he whispers. "You all right, there?"

She nods against him and takes a step back, wiping at the tracks of tears that descend her cheeks. Her trembling has stilled. "*I thought you'd be dead,*" she signs.

"Can't get rid of my obnoxious ass that easily," he says.

She sends him a crude gesture then hugs him again.

Tempest trots over to Peregrin who runs a loving hand down the beast's wing. "Thank you, friend," they say, before looking back to Lora, Xylie, and Ayc. Bronwen already watches the trio. Tavish holds the Kindred leash and gives Saga a command. The dog obediently turns his focus from Tempest to Xylie. It's as though they all know something is about to happen.

Ayc frowns. "Xylie, do you want to tell me what you were doing?"

Lora looks up from inspecting the contents of the drawstring bag. She pulls the strings taut again and tosses it to Ayc. "It's for you."

He catches it and weighs it in his hand. Whatever object lies within fits within his palm, smooth and hard and heavier than he imagined. "What is it?"

"Reach in and find out," Lora says it like a dare, her lips tilting upward in a brief smirk.

He arches an eyebrow at Xylie, who signs, *"Do it."*

Everyone watches him intently. He shifts uneasily. He would think that this is a set up for a prank, but he trusts Xylie. And Lora, too. He unties the pouch and reaches within. His hand wraps around something cool and hard. An impulse shocks through him, rushing through his arm, down his spine, all the way to his toes. It knocks all the air from his lungs, and he gasps. But it isn't painful. It's the opposite. It feels as though he's jumped into the Bellum Sea and the icy waves are covering him like a balm. It soothes over the pain in his body, calms his nerves, quiets the protests of his muscles. In its wake, the pain remains, but different, not as strong or sharp. Instead, it feels like a ghost, a haunting, the last remnants of an eternal torment that no longer exists.

His hand trembles as he pulls the object from the bag. In his palm sits a stone, which is the same deep purple as the bag. A rune marks its smooth surface. He has seen similar runes before, only those stones were green.

"It's a Severing stone," Bronwen explains, at the same time as Xylie signs it. "It'll undo any Binding on the first person who touches it."

But it can't be...

Because that would mean that Ayc is free.

Free. It's a strange word, an impossible word, a word that makes his knees shudder and threaten to buckle. It *cannot* be true. Ayc shakes his head. "I don't... I don't understand."

"Xylie went to Velphin to get the stone from the sorcerers there," Lora says.

Moisture pools in his eyes, and his vision swims. They were all headed to Velphin, before Wren ruined those plans. Getting a Severing stone was Lora's plan all along. As soon as she found out about Ayc's Bond, she intended to go. He blinks rapidly and clears his throat, before he trusts himself to speak.

"Xylie, you flew all the way to Velphin?"

Xylie nods.

"It must have cost a fortune," Ayc protests. "Too much."

Lora flicks a hand dismissively, and Xylie signs. *"The sorcerer didn't want much, at least of money. I made a deal instead."*

"You made a deal," Bronwen snaps, all joy dropping from her face. "I told you not to make a deal. What was it?"

Xylie shrugs. *"Nothing I didn't part with willingly."*

Despite Xylie's nonchalance, uneasiness settles in Ayc's gut. What would some of the most powerful people alive want from Xylie? Bronwen and Lora exchange a look, like perhaps they're thinking the same thing.

"Why would you do that?" Ayc demands, looking between Xylie and Lora. "You shouldn't have risked so much. Neither of you."

Xylie flicks him on the shoulder and signs, *"Because you're my best friend, silly."*

"I told you, Ayc," Lora says, steadily. "I believe you are worth saving."

Ayc swallows hard. He clutches the stone in his hand, still not quite believing it's real.

"You're free, Ayc," Peregrin says, a smile dawning on their face. "You do not look as though you yet believe it. But you're free."

It's that smile, the joy in his beloved friend's face—the only one who has known how Ayc suffered all this time—that makes the truth settle.

He's free. No longer will he be forced to follow an order. No longer will Wyntra and the kitchen within be his unlocked prison. No one will have power over him. Not anymore.

Free. A word so big and so wide he doesn't know how to bear it, contain it, make sense of it. It bowls him over, and he has no choice but to sit down, right there in the grass. Emotions wave through him. Relief, then joy, then grief for the boy who believed he'd always be a prisoner, and finally, hope for a future that is his—only *his*—to choose.

Hope is a beautiful thing.

And Ayc is laughing and he's crying. He drops the stone and covers his face in his hands, knowing how he must look. He tries to slow his breathing, but he's unable to stop the tidal wave of emotions. A head rests on his shoulder, bringing with it the scent of peppermint, and he knows it's Xylie. When he finally gathers control of himself, he lowers his hands to confirm Xylie is indeed at one of his sides. And Lora crouches at the other.

The tears he sees in Lora's eyes disappear in a blink. But they were there. He's sure of it.

"Are you all right?" Lora asks.

He grins, wiping at his cheeks with the back of his hands. "I've never been better. I'm *free*."

Her smile lights up her entire face, and she's the most beautiful thing he's ever seen. "You're free."

"Thank you." Those words are not enough. They are a drop of water in the ocean of his gratitude, but he has no more words, so he lays his hand over his chest, over his heart.

Lora returns the gesture.

Bronwen inhales a sharp breath. "Lora, look at your chronicler."

Lora stands and lifts her hand. The sixth stone shines, and Ayc knows which one has disappeared from her arm.

Undo a great wrong.

Days ago, Ayc might have believed that fulfilling the quest was Lora's only reason for giving him the stone. But that was before she stormed a temple to save him, before he saw tears in her eyes. She wants him to be free. Whatever anger he held toward her for forcing him to drink the supposed antidote is gone now. After all, if their positions were reversed, he knows he would have done whatever it took to save her.

"If the chronicler turned on a stone even now," Bronwen says, "perhaps there's still a chance."

Lora shakes her head. "I'm sure by now my mother knows Marcellus won."

Xylie jerks her head off Ayc's shoulder, reminding Ayc

that she didn't know. She sways, and Ayc wraps an arm around her shoulders.

Lora looks down at her and signs, *"I'm sorry."*

Xylie only signs back, *"I'm proud of you."*

Lora turns away, walking back to her pack and withdrawing Xylie's coat from it. The cousins say nothing to one another as Lora gives the coat back. She merely returns to her bedroll to begin to pack, a silent signal that the others should do the same.

Ayc only watches Lora for a long moment, and he thinks again about sacrifice, about how she sacrificed her chance to be Sovereign to save him. He considers the plan he's been toying with, the one that will certainly bring his worst fear to life, but one that might give them a chance.

He has a choice now, a choice between who he has always wanted to be and what he could become. He fiddles with his bracelets, trying to decide.

Man or monster?

Hero or villain?

He stares at Lora, his beautiful villainess. The one who set him free. He feels once more like he's on the bank of the Ever River, waiting for her to rise. Asking himself: what would he do for her?

The answer is as clear as when he jumped into the dark unknown of that water.

He would do anything.

Everything.

CHAPTER
THIRTY-FOUR

- LORA -

Wyntra's main street bears the flag of the Lux Aester. The blue banners embroidered with a sun flutter in the salt-tinged breeze, bright against the heavy, indigo clouds that block out most of the late morning light. The air promises oncoming lightning. The electricity causes Lora's hair to stand up on her arms as she walks across the cobblestone. Before the Trials started, she tried to imagine her clan's symbol flying in victory, but she never could envision it. Perhaps, she always knew she would not be enough.

People wander in and out of the shops that line the main street, flowing around Lora and her Five like a steady river. This is the street Lora has traversed thousands of times. As a child, she picked flowers in the narrow garden beds at the center of the street. She weaved them into crowns she never wore, lest her mother see. She threw coins in the fountains that mark every cross street, making wishing she knew wouldn't come true. The shops that line the outskirts are the ones Lora explored as a child, generally with a guard or Fennix or Onanna following her, because her mother couldn't be bothered to spend time with her child. On the corner lies the small, but perfect public library where Lora found friends in the form of characters in books.

This city should be her home, but she's never felt like it was, even as a child. Now, with the strange faces clogging the streets, this place feels even less friendly. The crowd has been brought here for the ceremonies and celebrations to follow. Today will be the official declaration of the winner and tomorrow will be the coronation. But none of it can begin until Lora, and the rest of the victors who remain alive, arrive.

Still, Lora and her Five have taken their time getting here. They even stopped to spend the night at the Pink Elk. There, Yris's messenger hawk found Lora. She barely glanced at the first three words scrawled on the paper— *Where are you?*—before she crumbled it and tossed it aside. Lora leaned back in her chair and watched as Ayc and Bronwen guided a tipsy Tavish to a makeshift stage to do an uproarious rendition of a popular Sal Maris song. Xylie happily stimmed, moving her head and shifting in her seat in a way that was almost dancing. Peregrin rested their feet on another chair, nursing a mug of tea infused with whiskey, and basked in the joy with Lora, because they both knew tomorrow would be a dark day. But that was tomorrow's problem.

Tomorrow, though, is here now.

Bronwen stays at Lora's elbow as they walk down the road, toward the castle gates at the end of the road. The other Five form a line behind them, with Peregrin aboard

Tempest bringing up the rear. Some of crowd fall silent as they pass by. Some openly gawk. She pretends not to notice. This crowd seems more subdued than others who have come for celebrations in the city. Only the ones decked in a particular shade of blue are wearing smiles. One male in Noxumbra black is ranting at someone who runs a stall of ale. He's loud enough that most of the people can hear his condemnation of Marcellus. The shop owner's face is strained as he offers a mug. A Lux Aester male glares over his shoulder in their direction.

Lora wonders what will become of the man. He may be in stocks as soon as Marcellus is crowned. That's what powerful, cruel rulers do. That's what Lora's mother would do. Criticism can never be tolerated by those who fear to lose control.

As they crest the top of the hill, the castle gates part for Lora, directed by the castle guards above.

"Tell the Sovereign her daughter is here," one of the guards says.

Lora's feet falter, but Bronwen presses two fingers to her elbow. Today, it steadies Lora. She lifts her chin as she enters the entry hall, but her fingers nervously move to the cord she now wears around her neck. She tugs, feeling the weight of the leviathan's tooth she has tucked beneath her armor. It scrapes against the skin between her breasts.

The entry hall basks in the multi-colored light cast by the stained glass high above them—a map of Everadyn. Straight ahead is the door to the great hall, towering as high as the entry doors. A cluster of people have gathered before it. She thinks she catches a glimpse of Adamant armor and rainbow chain mail, but before she can approach, she hears her name called from the hallway to her right.

"Finally," says a voice that makes Lora go instantly cold. She suspects most people don't feel that way when they hear their mother's voice, but it's a survival instinct Lora can't shake. But there is something else that is stronger now. A rage that roars and crackles, that threatens to make her eyes burn silver. Lora has always been angry at her mother, but it was a fire before. Now, after all the truths uncovered during the Trials, it is an inferno.

Yris wears a regal, black, velvet gown much too dark for her complexion. Her hair is pulled high, through the golden circlet of her crown. It's the last day that she will wear it.

"You should have been here yesterday," Yris says, surveying Lora. She scowls, and Lora wonders what it is she's found displeasing this time. The dust on her armor, the way she wears her hair unbound, or just everything in general.

Lora doesn't give Yris the chance to tell her. "We're here now."

"I can see that." Yris sweeps her scowl over Lora's Five. Tempest has remained outside, but Saga stands at Tavish's side. The dog's hackles rise, and he growls lowly.

"Easy, Saga," Tavish says, with a comforting pat, but Ayc praises, "Good dog."

Lora bites the inside of her lip to keep from smiling as Yris shoots Ayc a glare. He grins cheekily back, and Lora is glad to see it. His defiance can still come with consequences, but at least now, he can choose his risks.

"The ceremony is starting now," Yris says.

Lora's heart beats a warning. "Now?"

"Yes. It was meant to be last night, but you could not be bothered to get here on time so it had to be postponed. You can join the other victors and wait for your cue to come in.

When you face Marcellus, you will bow and forfeit your claim to Sovereignty, do you understand?"

Lora grinds her teeth. The idea of bowing makes her want to rip off her own skin, but she forces out the words. "I understand."

Yris steps closer until only a knife's width separates them. Even though they are equal in height now, Yris seems to look down her nose at Lora as if she were still a small child. There's a shift of fabric behind Lora. One or more of her Five are ready to defend her. She makes a flicking motion with her hand, and they still.

"It should have been you up there," Yris snarls, showing her teeth. She keeps her voice low. "If only you'd—"

"If only I'd *what*, Mother?" Lora says without flinching, without attempting to lower her voice. "Accepted a deal with the Drakr? I'm not a cheater like you."

Yris's gaze shifts toward the group standing before the entrance to the great hall. Lora identifies them this time. It's Wylder and Sterling... and Marcellus, standing near the guards stationed at the door. They all stare back down the hall at Lora and her mother.

Yris draws herself up taller. She appears unphased by the accusation Lora has just hurled, but she soothes her hands over the waist of her dress, even though the fabric still lies perfectly. A subtle tell, but one, nonetheless. Yris curls her upper lip back, baring the points of her teeth. "I'll deal with—"

"Run along, Mother," Lora interrupts again. She allows herself to focus on the anger, enough that her vision flashes a silver warning. "Your people are waiting."

Yris sniffs and lifts her head. She cuts one last glare at Lora's Five. "Have your Five use the side entrance."

Yris marches toward the doors, her heels clattering on the stone. Her crown still gleams in the light of torches, reflecting shades of green and blue back from the stained glass. Disgust boils on Lora's tongue as Marcellus takes his place at Yris's side. The doors of the great hall swing open, revealing an aisle lined with flagpoles that interchange the Noxumbra and Lux Aester symbols and a crowd that gathers on either side of it. Marcellus raises his arm above his head to display his chronicler and enters as the crowd cheers. The guards close the door behind them, dimming the sound.

Wylder and Sterling remain outside, waiting for Lora to join them. She will be expected to walk in, declare her allegiance to Marcellus, and bow at his feet.

I can't. I won't.

Her hands shake, and she grasps the hilts of her twin swords to steady herself.

"It's just a bit of theater, Lora," Bronwen whispers, stepping back to Lora's side. "That's all."

"I know," Lora says calmly, like the idea doesn't make her skin feel like it's peeling from her sinew. She hates theater, even though most of her life feels like theater. She steels herself with a breath and turns toward her Five.

"I will see you all in there. And—" She hesitates as an ocean of emotion crashes through her chest. They look back at her as though nothing has changed over the last few days, without a trace of disappointment. Like she did not utterly fail them. And she is overwhelmed that she found Five talented, kind, and good people who were willing to follow her. If she'd become Sovereign, all of them would have made Everadyn better. They would have changed the world.

She clears her throat. "Thank you all. For everything." The words are not enough, so she forces a smile, but it's so uncharacteristic that Bronwen frowns at her, concern deepening the lines of her face.

"Hurry," Lora prompts them.

Bronwen hesitates, then leads the way down the hallway. As they pass, Xylie bumps her shoulder against Lora's arm and Peregrin studies her from the corner of a narrowed eye, like they know what she has planned. Tavish murmurs, "Still waters, Lora" a Sal Maris expression that wishes good fortune. Saga wags his tail as he leads Tavish away.

Ayc pauses before Lora. She doesn't face him at first, watching the others go, watching her cousin longest.

"Keep looking after Xylie," Lora says.

"I'll be looking after *you*," Ayc says softly, solemnly.

She finally meets his eyes. The blue looks too dark in here, like a troubled sea, even as a hint of a smile plays on his lips. He reaches forward and runs the cord around her neck between his fingers. She shivers as his soft skin brushes against her neck, right where her pulse hammers, right where he kissed her and growled her name. She's certain he doesn't remember, and she certainly can't judge his feelings from a kiss that was stolen out of desperation and illness and sedative tonics.

Even if it was a kiss that will haunt her forever.

Even if she wants to steal just one more right now.

He tugs on the cord, a reminder. "Good luck in there, villainess."

She nods, knowing what he means. He says the name—villainess—with a tone of affection, and she lets it grant her courage.

He pries himself away, his face contorting like it pains him to do so, and she forces herself not to watch him walk away. She listens to the fading of his footsteps, before joining Wylder and Sterling at the door. Inside the great hall, Lora can hear her mother's amplified voice introducing Marcellus as the winner. Her stomach roils, but she manages to nod to Sterling. It takes a little more effort to look at Wylder. He's already staring at her.

He truly is handsome, with his black hair and chiseled features. There was a time she told herself she was in love with him, because he was everything she has been conditioned to want. Strong, unbreakable, ruthless. She chased sparks of emotions and convinced herself they were enough to keep her warm, even as they bounced in and out of a relationship. But when his poison hit her, and she grew cold at his betrayal, she realized she never was that warm to begin with.

It wasn't nothing. If she felt nothing, his actions wouldn't have hurt. But whatever she felt toward him disappeared like a candle snuffed out in the wind, far too easily. If she's honest with herself, that candle was nothing compared to the wildfires that she's felt. Those feelings are impossible to put out, no matter how hard she tries.

Now, she's not sure what she feels for Wylder, except, perhaps, pity.

"I'm sorry about your brother," Lora says.

He winces, like it hurts. Of course it does. She still hasn't told Bronwen what happened to Ryker. She's trying to only deal out one tragedy at a time.

"What happened?" Lora asks.

"The same thing that happened to Ruatha and all of her Five," he seethes. "Drakr."

Guilt creeps over her skin like wandering fingertips. Perhaps, Lora should have sent a message to Wylder and warn him of the deal Marcellus made. She's not sure why she didn't, why she never even thought about it. But it's too late now.

"I'm sorry," she says again. "Your brother was a good soul."

His throat bobs as he swallows, and he turns away without another word.

A voice clears to gain Lora's attention. "My lady, your weapons cannot enter with you," one of the guards by the door says.

Lora removes her weapons swiftly—the two swords at her hips, as well as the daggers from her side and boot. The guard raises his hand, and a sensation like a shiver passes over her. A spell to ensure she's armed with nothing. The guard places her weapons carefully in a nearby cupboard, kept in the hall for this purpose, already filled with weapons from the guests. "You can have them when you leave."

Lora grunts, but silently says goodbye to the weapons that have served her well.

Within the great hall, Yris calls, "I present our remaining victors."

"Let's get this over," Wylder says.

Sterling murmurs their assent, and Lora shoves the doors open. The three of them enter side by side, their heads held high. The great hall is darker than normal. The storm has rolled in and stolen the light that would normally pour through the stained glass above. Candelabras scatter throughout the room, casting shadows over the crowd as they applaud, a bit solemnly. In a section of earth-colored clothing, Lora spots the familiar leaf-embroidered cloak that wraps around her grandmother's shoulders. Lora looks away before she can meet Hellevi's eyes. Lora didn't think her grandmother would come, and she wishes she hadn't. She doesn't want her grandmother to see this.

Marcellus waits for them at the head of the great hall, where the head table and Sovereign throne has been removed and replaced with a dais. Yris has stepped to the side, while Marcellus remains at the center. He grins at the victors as they approach. Lora's Five wait at the very front of the crowd, even Xylie with the noise-dulling cuffs on her ears. As Lora passes them, they all lay their hand on their chests. They are with her. She draws comfort in that.

The three come to a stop before the dais. Marcellus positions himself before Sterling first, and his lip curls in disdain as Sterling takes a knee. "I recognize your worthiness as Sovereign," Sterling says.

Marcellus moves to Wylder, who copies the action. Anyone who didn't know him might have thought it gracious, but Lora hears the tension in his voice, notes the way he closes his eyes to keep the silver from showing. And then Marcellus approaches Lora, his smile twisting even wider.

Lightning flashes, light momentarily filling the room from above. It blanches out Marcellus's pale face, until he looks like a smiling skull. Like the wraiths on Somnia Ignis who taunted Lora with her father's voice.

He speaks low enough that no one else can hear anything more than a murmur, "Loraphne, I told you once I'd enjoy seeing you bow.".

And Lora said she'd rather be dead. She meant it.

He leans even closer, his breath hot on her cheek as he whispers in her ear. "Soon, I will be the most powerful Sovereign that has ever reigned. I will be a god."

Hate erupts in her veins, as outside thunder rumbles,

rattling the windows above. The crowd's attention gnaws like teeth at her back, waiting for her to bow, for her to accept defeat graciously. That's what a good, honest hero would do. But the stone of the fossil tooth against her sternum draws her back to the conversation she had with Ayc last night. He caught her alone in the hallway of the inn, the last two to find their rooms.

He pulled the tooth from around his neck and held it out to her. She only frowned at it.

"Did you know that a leviathan was said to be the most fearsome creature that has ever existed?" he asked. "They were glorious, terrifying, and mighty, all at once."

"I've heard that," Lora said, preparing herself for a terrible punchline.

"They're wrong. A leviathan isn't the most fearsome creature that has ever lived on land or sea. *You* are."

Lora's tongue curled, ready to snap back at him out of habit. But he didn't say it like an insult. He said it like a compliment. Glorious, terrifying, mighty. Lora wondered if that was truly how he saw her. Because she liked the sound of it.

He stepped closer and took her hand, pressing the tooth into it. He folded her fingers around it. Her curled fist fit only over the end of it, while the point extended outward, like a small, curved dagger. He covered her thumb with his and brushed it against the tooth's tip, letting its sharpness scrape against her sensitive skin. "You're the villainess, Lora. Marcellus doesn't get to be the villain of this story, and he doesn't get to win."

He locked onto her eyes then, and she saw it there, something she'd never seen in his eyes. A little bit of wickedness. And she understood exactly what he meant.

He left her then, alone in the hallway with a leviathan's tooth and a choice. A choice a hero would never consider. A choice she made long before she stepped into the great hall today.

She will not bow, and neither will her people.

She yanks the cord at her neck until the fossil rises from her armor and the cord snaps. She tosses the tooth into the air to adjust her grip and catches it so it forms that same curved dagger in her hand. And then she drives the point straight into Marcellus's throat.

CHAPTER
THIRTY-FIVE

- LORA -

A shriek wails through the great hall as blood rains across Lora's face. Bronwen calls her name, drowned by Yris's roar of "Loraphne!" Lora ignores them all and digs the tooth deeper into Marcellus's neck. His gurgling silences as she hits something more vital. She rips the tooth back and more blood sprays as Marcellus crumples to the ground, his wide eyes staring at the ceiling above. Red pools on the dais beneath him and forms a river down the steps.

"Not a god, after all," Lora seethes through her teeth. "Just a pathetic man."

A dead man, now.

Screams and scrambling of feet sound behind her.

"She's killed the future Sovereign!"

"Bitch!"

"Traitor!"

"Villain!"

None of them are wrong.

Both Wylder and Sterling have stumbled away, as though afraid the divine will strike Lora down and they'll be in the crossfire. She looks beyond the victors, to her Five. Bronwen's hand presses over her mouth. Tavish's eyes are wide as he clutches Saga's leash. Xylie's hands flutter around her face. Peregrin gazes around the room with a grim seriousness, but Ayc looks steadily at Lora.

She knows she has crossed a line now, one they can't follow her over. She will face this on her own.

The chaos fades and turns to stunned silence. The crowd stares at her, and she can only imagine how she looks, her face painted in blood. Guards rush in from the front and side doors, weapons drawn. Lora recognizes many of them, including Irving. She hates that he must be a part of this, knowing he'll bear unnecessary guilt in his heart for it. He's only a few steps away when Yris holds up a hand. "Wait!"

The guards halt, looking toward their Sovereign, confused.

"What do you mean, wait?" bellows a familiar voice. Erech storms from the crowd, his face red with rage. "She has murdered the Sovereign! She deserves to die where she stands."

"*I* am Sovereign," Yris corrects, her voice cold and sharp as steel. "And as you can see, I'm very much alive."

"Her treachery cannot stand!" another Lux Aester says, stepping to Erech's side, hands balled into fists.

"If you won't deliver justice, then I will," Erech roars, stalking toward Lora.

The entire crowd shies back, gasping. Yris does nothing —doesn't signal the guards, doesn't order Erech to stop, and

530

doesn't even look at Lora. She can't bring herself to order Lora's death, but she won't intervene either.

Lora raises her chin. She knew, before she walked into this room, that by choosing this action, she is forfeiting her life. No one will come to her defense. Not any of the crowd. Not Yris's Five who are near the front. Not Wylder who sends Yris a frantic look. Not even Lora's grandmother whom she can't bring herself to locate in the crowd.

Lora will be punished for this. She can fight back, but she won't. If she does, the guards, like Irving, will intervene, and she won't risk harming them. She'll accept her punishment and her fate with dignity. The Everadyn people will condemn her. Her remains will be cast into a watery grave, not even worthy to bury on Everadyn soil. But she'll be content, knowing her friends and her people, are safe.

"I will tear you apart with my bare hands," Erech says. The second male follows on his heels. Both of their eyes gleam silver.

Lora catches movement in the corner of her eye: Peregrin has shifted their weight and taken a grasp of their cane; Bronwen lifts a hand, the air pulsing around her; Xylie reaches into her bag. Tavish gives a command to Saga, and the dog curls back his lips to show his teeth. And Ayc— her Ayc—smiles at her as he removes his leather bracelets.

She shakes her head at all of them, silently begging them not to act. They won't suffer for her crime. She will face this alone.

Peregrin and Xylie still their movements. Ayc leans to whisper something in Bronwen's ear. She jerks her head to look at him, her mouth parting. Lora will never know what caused the shock on her best friend's face.

Because Erech surges forward.

And Ayc—foolish, reckless, ridiculous Ayc—steps in his way.

- AYC -

All Ayc's life he has been unsure where he belongs, unsure what to do next, unsure sometimes even who to be—and he's always had far too few choices to be able to sort it out. But as he chooses to step between his villain and the Lux Aester fae, he feels it like a puzzle piece clicking together deep in his soul. He is exactly where he belongs.

"Ayc," Lora hisses behind him, but he doesn't take his eyes off the fae as they both pull themselves to a halt.

Erech's silver gaze sweeps over Ayc. Recognition plays at the edges of his lips as he smiles. "Get out of the way."

"No," Ayc says, smiling wider. "If you take one more step toward her, I'll—how did it go, Lora? Rip out your heart and shove it up your asses?"

"Ayc!" Lora barks. "Get back!"

The fae throw back their heads and laugh at him, a full, hearty laugh.

Ayc's eyes flutter closed, and he reaches deep, to that dam he has so carefully built within himself. That he has put up to hide all his truth and fear and rage. The wall he fought to keep up every single day when Yris ensnared him and when children tormented him and when Lora crawled beneath his skin and refused to leave. Now, he lets it crumble. It turns to dust deep in his soul. The power—*his* power—surges, gusting over his skin like a biting winter wind, so cold it burns.

Ayc lets his smile fall.

"And what are you going to do?" Erech's companion says, still laughing. "You're a weak, pathetic human."

When Ayc opens his eyes, the fae's laughter dies in his throat. Red consumes Ayc's vision, but this time Ayc doesn't try to hide it. This time, he *lets* it burn. The crowd utters a cry as they stumble back. Saga whines, as Bronwen swears, "Holy shit!"

And Ayc knows what they see.

His eyes are red.

His voice growls, deep and monstrous. "Who says I'm human?"

Someone in the crowd screams it, while someone else says it like a curse: "Drakr!"

Lora whispers, "Ayc."

He doesn't dare glance behind him. He doesn't want to watch that one flicker of affection he saw grow in her eyes extinguish. But he will bear her hatred, if it means saving her.

"I almost didn't believe it. Marcellus was right about you," Erech says, visibly shaking off his surprise. "It doesn't matter. You'll be dead soon enough!"

"Let's not be foolish," Ayc says, though it isn't his voice. It's the voice of the monster that lives within him.

But of course, the two fae are very, very foolish. They charge forward as one.

"Bronwen!" Ayc yells. "The lights!"

The sorcerer raises her hands, and every candle in the room snuffs out. The storm building outside has already blocked all the light from the windows. The world goes black. And Ayc doesn't just become invisible—he becomes *one* with the shadow.

And then there is nothing but screams.

By the time someone manages to relight the candles, the two faes' bodies lay at Ayc's feet. A sword drapes from his hand— the sword he ripped from Irving's grasp after disappearing. Red, shimmering blood drips down the metal and onto the floor. It trails down Ayc's cheeks, and as he looks to the crowd, he tries to appear more fierce and less like he wants to throw up. He tries to look like he doesn't want to scrub his blood-soaked skin until its raw.

"Who's next?" Ayc growls.

The crowd withdraws once more. *Monster,* they seem to whisper. Ayc already knows.

It's the one thing he always feared he'd become, the thing that his own mother must have feared too when she buckled the bracelets on his wrists when he was a tiny boy. But here he is, becoming that thing. Willingly. For *Lora.*

A laugh—familiar and cold—barks through the air. He fixes his red-tinged gaze on Yris, and she grins back at him like she's won some sort of prize. Another bolt of lightning illuminates the room, and he looks back to the crowd. As the thunder follows, he avoids his friends' faces, not wanting to know what expressions they wear. Especially Xylie, whose own parents were murdered by Drakr. Ayc's breath trembles past his lips. How will she ever speak to him again?

A hand touches his shoulder, light as a butterfly's wing as it flutters by. Ayc braces himself for the impact of Lora's hatred and disgust. But when he faces her, he doesn't find it. Lora's eyes shine a brilliant blue, and in that blue, he discovers something deep and unfathomable, something he can't begin to name.

She extends a hand, and as her fingertips brushes his blood-streaked cheek, he almost jerks away in surprise. Her touch feels like forgiveness. Like salvation. But her smile—the small upturn of her lips? That feels like acceptance. And that is a balm that reaches deep into his soul.

"I see you, Ayc," she says softly. "I see you."

He desires to do foolish things, like kiss her here in front of everyone. Especially because he knows they both will likely soon be slaughtered, for this treason that was his idea to begin with.

The crowd mutters amongst themselves, and Ayc's sharp hearing catches a word on Sterling's lips. "Her chronicler."

He looks to Lora's wrist. A laugh flies from his mouth. Lora jumps.

"Lora, look." He catches her arm gently and raises it to show her.

All seven stones are glowing.

THIRTY-SIX

- LORA -

A rainbow of glowing gems wraps around Lora's wrist, and beneath the bracelet, her forearm is no longer tattooed with the list of quests. She blinks at it, unable to believe the sight. "I— I don't understand."

"You upturned the hands of fate." Ayc's grin rises on his face, blood-stained just like her own, and that smile lights up the room. It shines brighter than the sun. "Marcellus was destined to be Sovereign, and you changed destiny itself. You've won!"

No, that can't be right. Lora didn't drive that tooth into Marcellus's neck to steal his claim to Sovereignty. She did it to spare her people from the fate of having him as their ruler. And yet, the chronicler's magic seems to recognize that the game was still ongoing.

The murmur of the crowd grows louder now, a dozen voices rising in bewilderment, in excitement, in disgust.

"But the Trials were over," someone yells from the

crowd, someone who is, unsurprisingly, dressed in Lux Aester blue. They don't come forward, hiding within the crowd. "She can't win through villainy."

From her place within the cluster of Yris's Five at the front of the crowd, Onanna steps forward. Silver eyes burn from the shadow of her hood, the only thing visible on her cloaked frame. "I have studied every article that discusses the Trials. The rules have been written for centuries. All victors must yield their claim on Sovereignty by recognizing the winner, before the Trials can officially close. Loraphne did not yield her claim. She did *not* bow. And she is now the only victor left who has completed all seven quests and demonstrated worthiness."

The crowd rumbles like the thunder that roils outside. The sound echoes in Lora's ears, but it cuts off as Wylder steps before Lora and flings himself down to his knees. "Loraphne, I recognize your worthiness as Sovereign."

Lora's breath catches. *This can't—*

Sterling kneels beside Wylder and repeats the words. The glow of Lora's chronicler shines even brighter, the light beaming in all directions, until all that have gathered can witness it.

Yris lifts her voice. "My dear Everadyn fae, I present your next Sovereign, my daughter, Loraphne."

For the first time, when Lora's mother gazes upon her, she smiles like she's proud. While many in the crowd remain silent, many more cheer, until it's loud enough to rattle the glass that bears the symbol of all seven clans. No one else moves toward Lora or offers a protest, perhaps because they see it's inevitable, or perhaps, because Ayc, a Drakr, stands at her elbow.

Lora still cannot bring herself to look at her

grandmother, who has witnessed her win through treachery, not worthiness. Peregrin and Xylie clap. Bronwen calls Lora's name, and Tavish repeats it with a long whistle, and soon her name is being chanted.

The shock fades into grim realization. Lora has done it. She has won the Trials and will reign as the next Sovereign of Everadyn. She has completed the destiny she was born for and carried on her family's legacy. But no joy fills her heart. Ice spreads along her skin, and she fights not to shiver or shake.

Sovereignty is mine.

It's only then she realizes that she never wanted it at all.

- AYC -

Something is wrong with Lora.

Ayc watches her as people cheer her name, and he notices the shift. It's not a flicker of emotion or a change in posture. She holds her head like she already wears a crown, and her entire demeanor is one of unbreakable stone. It's not something Ayc can see. But he *feels* it.

He sweeps forward and keeps his voice low, so even Wylder and Sterling, who stand closest, cannot hear. "I think now is the time you should wave goodbye and make a dramatic exit."

It unfreezes her. She waves and heads toward a door behind the dais, away from the crowd. The crowd continues to cheer as Ayc follows. The door slams behind them and muffles the sound. Her hands flutter at her side, trembling like the first stone before a landslide. Ayc's normal restraint fractures, and he instinctively lays a hand on her back.

"Come with me."

She doesn't pull away. In fact, as he guides her down the hall toward his kitchen, Lora lists toward his side, almost leaning against his shoulder. The hallways are empty, and they go unnoticed until they are beyond the safety of his kitchen door. It's dark within the kitchen, rain beating at his one window. He leaves Lora's side to turn on the lamp, which fills the space with a dim, orange glow.

He glances around the small kitchen, this place that has been both his prison and his home. A thin flutter of flour still dances in the air. It doesn't feel possible that it has only been a week since he left. So much has happened. He has died and come back and everything feels different.

He feels different. He's no longer the ideological hero who left here. He's let everyone see the darkness within him, the villain he feared he would become.

He stares at Irving's sword that he still holds, unsure what to do with it, before carelessly tossing it onto the counter. Ayc returns to Lora, who leans against the door. She stares blankly at the floor, her color ashen, like she's fading fast. He slips his hands into his pockets to keep from touching her again.

"I would ask you if you're all right," Ayc says gently, "but I know you're not. What is it?"

She's silent for so long, Ayc thinks she won't tell him. That despite everything, mountains of rubble still exist between them. But finally, she speaks, her voice scarcely above the volume of a hummingbird's wings. "I didn't think it would end this way. With me as Sovereign. I thought I would be executed come tomorrow."

"I thought I would die with you," Ayc replies, his voice just as quiet.

She draws in a soft breath and looks up at him, the way she looked at him at her grandmother's house. The way that makes his heart stand still and his whole world tip sideways. But mercifully, she glares down at the floor just as swiftly. "I swore I wouldn't rule like my mother, but I gained my Sovereignty through treachery. I cheated. Just like her."

"Lora, you were willing to sacrifice your life to save your people a terrible fate. I think that makes you worthy to lead them."

She scoffs. "So you don't think I'm a villain?"

Hero. Villain. Ayc thought he understood those two terms clearly, but now they blur together in his head. Perhaps, if there is a villain within Ayc, there is a hero within Lora. More than perhaps. He has seen it, and it is breathtaking. Sometimes, she is dark as night, and sometimes, she is bright as the sun. And he finds it beautiful —every part of her.

Perhaps, the line drawn between heroes and villains does not account for this: there's bad in all of us, so there must also be good. At the end of the day, perhaps which outweighs which matters little. The most important thing is what we use all the good and all the bad parts of ourselves to fight for. What we choose to save, and what we choose to destroy, and what we ruin ourselves for.

"If what you did is villainy, then well..." Ayc shrugs. "Maybe you're the villain we need."

He isn't sure it's the right thing to say, but she straightens, no longer leaning against the door. A little bit of confidence steels her expression. "Not everyone will accept my rule. The Lux Aester are powerful. They will attempt to overthrow me."

"They can try." Anger flares through him at the very idea anyone might touch her, and his vision flashes red once more. Lora presses her eyes closed, shielding against the sight. An invisible fist clenches around his chest. The blood on his face singes his skin; his wrists feel naked without his bracelets. He leaves Lora at the door, grabs a dishcloth from a nearby drawer, and wets it at the sink. He scrubs at his cheeks, his neck, his hands, the white cloth turning a rusty brown.

The shadows seem to creep forward from the corners, eating at the orange light.

Lora's feet fall soft on the stone as she approaches. "Thank you for doing what you did in there. It was foolish, but I'm grateful, nonetheless."

Ayc rinses the cloth in cool water, wrings it out, and offers it to Lora. "I suppose you hate me even more now."

She makes a small sound, almost a laugh, as she accepts the cloth. But instead of cleaning her own face, she uses it to sweep at a place on his chin, a spot he must have missed.

"I've tried hating you, Ayc," she says, and she's close enough the breath of her words brush his neck. "I'm quite bad at it."

His nerves rattle and burn at her nearness. He barely contains the tremor in his voice. "Even though I'm a monster?"

Lora rolls her eyes. "Don't be ridiculous. Drakr are people, not monsters. People who have chosen to do monstrous things, but people, nonetheless. And you? You're still a cinnamon roll. Good, through and through."

He draws a breath through his nose to steady himself. It

doesn't help, because the air smells like anise. Like flour and Xylie's last brew of potions and Lora's hair. He leans back against the sink to add a little distance and pulls his bracelets from his pockets. The icy pulse of his power, like cool shadow coats his skin, fades as the bracelet's fasten. The storm outside must shift, though the rhythm of the rain doesn't change, because the light in the kitchen grows brighter.

As Lora scrubs at Marcellus's blood on her face, Ayc feels her gaze trace over him, like the soft caress of her nails. The lines of his face, the curve of his ears, his decidedly human features. She is still standing far too close, close enough he wraps his hand around the edge of the sink to keep from reaching out. She parts her lips as though she might say something, but the door flies open and a cluster of bodies tumble inside—the rest of Lora's Five. They leave the door gaping as they all scramble in.

Lora tosses the rag into the sink and steps away from Ayc. He should feel relieved, but his nerves cry out even louder at the distance. He can't bear to have her close, but it's worse to have her far.

"By the divine, there you are!" Bronwen breaks away from the others and rushes toward Lora. She flings her arms around her. "You did it, Lora! You're Sovereign."

Lora's shoulders stiffen, but if Bronwen notices—and surely she does—she doesn't say anything. Instead, she pulls back to look at Ayc. They are all focused on him now—Peregrin leaning on their cane, Tavish with puckered cheeks, Saga with his head cocked, and Xylie with her arms clamped over her chest. Like she's furious.

A beat of silence passes. Ayc waits for it—the downfall,

the judgment, everything he knew would come if he ever showed his truth.

"That was a great line, by the way," Bronwen says, her wide grin never wavering. She lowers her voice, mocking Ayc's deep, monstrous growl. "'Who says I'm human?'"

Tavish's puckered cheeks release in a burst of laughter. "I thought it was a tremendous performance, truly."

Even Peregrin cracks a small smile. "I'm proud of you, boy."

Emotion threatens to strangle Ayc, but he looks at Xylie who is still fixated on her feet. "Xylie, you look angry."

Her hands snap in the air. *"Of course, I'm furious. I can't believe I didn't see it!"*

"Xylie, I-I'm sorry." He is, though being a Drakr isn't something he can fix. "I—"

She shoots him a look so sharp it cuts him off. *"Don't. Don't you dare be sorry for who you are. Because if you think I'm mad at you because you're a Drakr, you're more a fool than I've always thought you."*

Ayc blinks. "Then why are you mad at me?"

"Aren't you listening? I'm not mad at you. I'm mad at me." She stabs a finger into her own chest. *"I should have figured it out. It was so obvious and I just didn't see it. You wouldn't tell me how you did the disappearing trick, because it wasn't ever a fucking trick."*

Ayc throws his head back and laughs. Profound relief soars over him, lightening an invisible weight on his shoulders. All these years of hiding it from everyone but Peregrin, of fearing the hate and retribution, and these ridiculous Five act like this. Like it means nothing. Like it hasn't, at all, changed the way they see him.

"Stop laughing." Xylie closes the distance between them

and punches him in the arm. Even though she puts force behind it, it doesn't hurt. At all. It only makes him laugh harder.

"So I guess you lied about your father?" Bronwen asks when he reins himself in.

"Bronwen," Lora says beneath her breath, "mind your own business."

Bronwen winces. "Sorry. You don't have to answer that, Ayc. She's right. It's not my business."

But Ayc has been wound tight in secrets for so many years. It feels good to let them unravel, like he can finally, fully breathe. "I don't know who he was. I only know that he was Drakr, and little else. When I was little, I kept disappearing at night and scaring both myself and my mother. Eventually, I figured out the connection between what I could do in the shadows and the stories I knew of the Drakr. Still, my mother never really told me much."

That was generous. His mother told him *nothing*. Ayc was far too young when his mother died to realize the full implications of his birth. What must have happened to her. How she would have had every right to hate Ayc, to see him as a reminder of trauma. But she loved him almost too much. His father was a monster, and Ayc has always feared he is one, too.

But the Five in the room ease that fear.

"Bet you were good at hide and seek as a kid, though, huh?" Tavish says.

"Not really," Ayc says. "I couldn't control it when I was young. I would do it randomly all the time, until my mother gave me these." He lifts his wrists to show his bracelets.

Xylie grabs one of his forearms and leans close to study

the bracelet. She draws a finger over the metal and the faded bear carving. *"Tungsten,"* she signs.

"Yes, it's tungsten," Ayc says. "To shackle the monster within, I suppose." Bitterness sneaks into his tone, and he laughs to disguise it.

Lora snorts, and Bronwen says, "You're joking, right?"

Ayc frowns. "No."

"Ayc," Lora says, "you'd have to wrap an adult Drakr completely in tungsten chains to weaken them. Given, you only share half the blood. But you can go fully invisible in the smallest bit of shadow, which mean you've inherited a strong affinity for shadow."

He must be imagining the awe in Lora's voice. He knows enough about Drakr to realize that's what his gift is called. Shadow affinity. The way sorcerers have affinity for magic and can manipulate it, so Drakr have affinity to shadow. Not every Drakr possesses it–though most of those conscripted into the Drakr armies do–and not all of them possess it to the same degree. It was why the Drakr in the Forest of Elodie didn't turn invisible when they fought Lora and Ayc. Even with the rain, there was too much light. Some Drakr can only turn invisible in the total darkness of night. Ayc needs only a bit of the shadow to fade.

"What's your point?" Ayc asks.

"The point is I don't believe that little bit of tungsten weakens you at all," Lora explains. "Besides, when you injured your hands in Somnia Ignis you were able to heal. Xylie's potions are good. They aren't so good you should have healed that quickly. If the tungsten did anything, it would have, in theory, suppressed that ability, too."

"But," Ayc protests, "when I was a child, before I learned to control it, it prevented me from disappearing."

"Maybe, it did. But you're not a child anymore. Have you ever tried to go invisible with the bracelets still on?"

Ayc shakes his head.

"The only way your bracelets could suppress all your innate abilities is if they were enchanted with *very* powerful magic," Bronwen says. "Suppressing *some* of your innate abilities, *while* keeping your healing abilities intact, that would..." She trails off and shakes her head. "Divine, very, very few sorcerers could manage that."

"But if they were enchanted, you'd sense it, wouldn't you?" Lora asks.

"Unless the caster took great pains to hide it." Bronwen frowns down at the bracelets, reaching toward Ayc's left wrist before dropping her hand. "But an object like that would have cost as much as a palace."

"That's not possible," Ayc says. "My mom was a baker."

Her smile returns quickly. "Then no, it's not possible."

Ayc fiddles with a bracelet's buckle, undoing it and then doing it once more. He's not sure what to believe. The bracelets have felt like a dividing line—a barrier between the man and the monster. He's believed that it has protected him and those around him. He's seen red in his vision, in moments of anger and moments of passion, but no one else has seen. His power feels as distant as an echo deep within him, but perhaps, it's been his imagination all this time. Perhaps, it protected him, because he *needed* it to.

Ayc looks at Peregrin. They're a warrior. They would have known the limitations of tungsten.

"Why didn't you tell me?" Ayc asks.

Peregrin shrugs. "You were a boy afraid of his own shadow and the bracelets comforted you. What did you want me to say?"

"Perhaps, Peregrin, you might have told *me* the truth." The cold voice comes like a blizzard, freezing the room as Yris sweeps into the kitchen. Ayc tenses and Xylie slides behind him. Peregrin's jaw tightens, and Tavish looks like he's swallowed a lemon drop whole.

"Mother," Lora greets coolly, stepping forward to block Yris's approach.

Yris keeps her narrowed eyes fixed on Peregrin. "I always suspected you were protecting the boy. Little good that it did him."

Peregrin doesn't take the bait and instead, glares directly at Yris, an advert sign of defiance they never demonstrated before. Yris flexes her fingers, her red nails freshly sharpened, like she's considering her punishment.

Ayc bolts a step forward, past Lora, and snaps, "What do you want, Yris?"

She swings toward him. Ayc digs his heels into the floor against the desire to run. He reminds himself that she no longer holds any power over him and lifts his jaw.

"I always suspected you to be a liar, but I could never prove it," Yris says. "Tell me, did that man who lied for you ten years ago know you were a Drakr? If he did, why would he have ever saved you?"

"Perhaps because he was being kind," Ayc says. "Something you know little about."

Yris flicks a wrist. "It scarcely matters. You're under my control and will continue to be under Loraphne's. You will be a fantastic weapon. A slaughterer of our enemies."

"No." The one word tastes like buttercream on Ayc's tongue—rich and smooth.

"Excuse me!" she snarls.

Ayc grins. "I said *no.*"

"You will have no choice. I am *commanding* it."

Lora shifts, placing herself between Yris and Ayc once more. "He is no longer Bound to anyone. The Binding was Severed."

Ayc wishes he could draw or paint or even etch stone, because the look on Yris's face—her wide eyes and twisted lips—deserves to be preserved for all of prosperity to see.

"I purchased a Severing stone," Lora explains. "If he follows me, it will be willingly."

Rage contorts Yris's face, twisting the beautiful features into something grotesque. The only true monster Ayc knows. "You foolish girl," she growls through bared teeth.

Lora bares her teeth right back. "I am not a girl. I am *Sovereign*."

"Not until tomorrow."

Lora lifts her chin high, looking more regal and powerful than the woman before her. "Yes, tomorrow *I* will be Sovereign. And you will be *nothing*. Not Sovereign, and in case you thought you'd rule over me, you won't be my mother either. You will pack up your belongings, and you will leave. I do not care where you go, but it will not be here. This is *my* castle now."

Yris hides the break in her stone well, but Ayc sees the crack—the flicker of panic and defeat that are the cake to the icing of his own defiance.

"Careful, daughter," she warns, snapping her mask back into place. "With how you won, there are many people who won't accept your rule. They will take it from you."

"They can try," Lora repeats Ayc's earlier words, silver lightning crackling through her eyes. "Ayc," she adds, "this is your kitchen. Do you want Yris here?"

"No," Ayc replies. "I don't."

"Then, Yris," Lora commands, "*get out.*"

Yris shows her fangs for a long moment more. She looks to Bronwen, who wiggles her fingers in a mocking wave, and then to Peregrin who no longer fears meeting her gaze. Yris storms away. Tavish, who stands closest to the door, kicks it shut behind her.

When Lora faces Ayc again, her chin is still held high, and she is so beautiful his chest aches. The dim light settles over her hair like a golden crown, like she is already a queen.

And there is no one more worthy.

THIRTY-SEVEN

- LORA -

The door squeaks softly, despite Lora's attempt to open it silently. Her footfall on the stone makes no sound. Moonlight bathes Ayc's kitchen in a mixture of silver and shadow. The cabinets cast long, dark shapes across the floor, while flour dances like fairy dust in the moonlight. Lora glances around the kitchen, but she sees nothing. Whenever she snuck in here in the past, she was always so certain that Ayc was sleeping, but now she understands he could be hiding in the shadows.

In hindsight, Lora should have known that Ayc is Drakr. The way his invisibility works only in shadows should have made it obvious. And she knew something felt wrong about how quickly his hands healed. But Lora never imagined that sweet, silly Ayc would have such power, especially when he never inflicted harm back on the fae children who tormented him.

What did Peregrin say?

Do not mistake his kindness for weakness.

Indeed.

Still, she creeps to the ice box. She hasn't been able to sleep. The events of the day keep reeling over and over in her head. Whenever she shuts her eyes, she feels Marcellus's blood spraying her face and hears the cheering of the crowd, and she is unsure which disturbs her more. She attempted to read, but couldn't focus on a full paragraph, let alone an entire page. She worked at the loom in her room, but the pictures in her head failed to take shape. So, she did what she used to do as a teenager: she came to raid sweets from Ayc's kitchen.

She has just creaked the ice box's door open when a soft whisper of breath teases her ear. "Hello."

It is instinct that propels her. She spins and drives her forearm into his throat, shoving back until he meets with the wall. In the moonlight, Ayc's grin shines. They've been here, in this same position, many times before. Like always, he makes no attempt to break away from her. It is instinct, too, that dictates she not release him, wanting an excuse to keep her body close to his, if only for a moment.

"Good evening, thief," he says. "Have you heard the one about the baker who rarely got into arguments? He was a loafer, not a fighter."

It's one of the worst she's heard. She lets the irritation give her the strength to break her desire to be near him. She takes a step back and then another. "Fuck, I hate you."

He remains leaning on the wall. "Not as much as you're going to hate me when I tell you I have no chocolate pudding for you to steal. I emptied the fridge before we left. Thought I might be gone for months."

Lora bites back a sigh. "I thought that might be the case. I just... couldn't sleep."

"Chilling the pudding would take too long, but I can make you some hot chocolate to drink."

He slips around her, flips on a light, and grabs a pan from where it hangs on a rack above the counter.

"That... would be lovely. Thank you." She is unsure what to do next, so she stands awkwardly and rubs at her bare wrist and forearm, where the chronicler and the quests lay only hours before. Her chronicler—and she assumes all the others—has been returned to the royal treasury. But she still feels the weight of it, even now.

"Have a seat," Ayc says, gesturing to a stool by the counter.

She settles onto the wooden stool and continues to fidget with her hands—first setting them on her knees, then gripping the counter, before eventually laying them carefully folded together on top. She watches him work in silence, in the single dim light, the way she watched him work at her grandmother's house. Each step is confident as he gathers supplies from around his kitchen and every motion is fluid as he measures and whisks ingredients and adjusts the heat of the stove. He wears a soft smile on his lips. Smiles have always felt like effort for her, but he wears it like a habit, like he isn't even aware it's there.

He's beautiful. It's not the right word, but it's the only one she has. Her heart swells, the ridiculous, foolish thing that it is. But just as swiftly, it plummets as she remembers. It wasn't merely the events of today keeping her awake tonight. It's the conversation she needs to have with Ayc. Perhaps, it isn't fair to wait until the morning, to force him to make a decision with only minutes to spare.

Her tongue feels twisted in her mouth, as though demanding her silence, but she manages to get his name out, "Ayc."

"Hmm?" he asks, as he stirs a little more chocolate into the mixture.

"I asked you once why you stayed in Wyntra." His shoulders tense slightly, but she continues, "You wouldn't tell me, but now I know it was the Binding stone keeping you here. But you aren't Bound anymore."

He frowns down at the pan. His whisk rasps against the side, a soft sigh of metal against metal. "And?"

She returns his question with one of her own. "Have you ever thought of what you'd do, if you ever had the freedom to decide your own future?"

He reaches for a cabinet and selects two mugs. They land on the counter beside the stove with soft thuds that he uses to hide a tired sigh. "I've never allowed myself the luxury to hope."

"Hope should never be a luxury. Everyone deserves to have hope in something."

He pours the chocolate into the mugs and sets one on the counter before her. Steam curls from the drink, which is the perfect shade of brown.

"What are you trying to say, Lora?" he asks.

She picks up the mug and strangles the warmth between her hands. She wrestles with the words, then pries them from her mouth. "You're not stuck in Wyntra anymore. You don't have to stay if you don't desire it. You could go anywhere. Do anything. Open a bakery, or travel from festival to festival across all of Everadyn. You could go back to Aluina."

His eyes narrow down at the drink in his hand. "And what is left for me there?"

"I don't know."

"And do you still want to help them, now that you're Sovereign?"

"Of course I do!" she assures swiftly. "That doesn't change no matter what you choose. I'm only saying that you *do* have a choice. You said yes to being in my Five out of obligation. At my coronation, you'll be asked to give an oath of allegiance. I want you to consider if that's really what you want to do. Or if you would rather..." She almost chokes on the word, and she takes a quick swig of her chocolate, scalding her tongue, barely tasting it. "If you would rather leave."

He sucks in a breath through his teeth. "Do you *want* me to leave?"

No. No. She doesn't. Many times in the past, she wished she never met him, if only because it would quiet the chaos he causes within her. But now after everything, she wants him to stay. She wants to hear his ridiculous jokes until she wants to punch him, if only because it reminds her that she is not the cold, dead, unfeeling thing she was raised to be. If only because he makes her feel alive in ways no one else does.

But she cannot be selfish. Not with him.

"I want you to be happy, Ayc," she says softly.

"That's not what I asked."

"It's the only answer I have."

He scoffs and glares down at his cup. In the silence, she shifts in her chair. Her favorite sweater, which she knit out of the softest yarn she could find, feels uncharacteristically scratchy against her skin. Ayc's mug shatters the silence, landing on the counter with a clunk that scatters a few brown drops over the edge. Then he lays his arms on the counter and leans across, bringing himself closer to her. He studies her eyes, her cheeks, the shape of her mouth. She longs to hide from his gaze. And she longs to bask in it. How does he always turn her into a walking conundrum?

When he speaks again, he has a soft hum in his voice, something that reminds her of the way he growled earlier, but gentler. "When I was poisoned," he says. "I had some of the strangest dreams."

His eyes are blue, but she remembers the way they fired red earlier, when he said he'd defend her. She was forced to close her eyes to hide how her own vision flared silver. Not because she was angry, but because of the image that roared to life in her head: his eyes blazing red as he worked himself inside of her while she laid, spread out for him on this very counter. His rumbling voice has the same impact, and she looks pointedly down into her hot chocolate.

"Like what?" she asks.

"Like baby dragon's biting at my toes and Bronwen praying."

"Well, like she said, Bronwen does sometimes—" Lora begins, but Ayc isn't finished.

"And you kissed me."

Air disappears from her lungs. She keeps her gaze fixed downward, so he can't see the impact of remembering that kiss.

"Isn't that strange?" he muses. "In what world would you kiss me?"

In this one. In every one. She would kiss him right here, with her fingers tangled in his hair. She would kiss him in the morning, after waking up entwined in his arms. She would kiss him the next day and the next. She desires to be the only lips he tastes, the only body he fucks, the only one he dreams about. Her rebellious lips part like she might say it, but she bites down on it before the words can escape.

Lora once asked her mother why she never took a permanent lover, why Lora was the product of a single night with an artisan who came to play at a festival at Wyntra. Her answer was cutting and cruel, like most of her advice.

Because love strips you bare, Loraphne. No shield can protect you then.

And she was right. Whatever road Lora must walk, it'll be hazardous. She'll have to fight to keep her throne, even as she's tries to undo all the wrong her mother and grandfather did or ignored. There will be many daggers aimed at Lora's back. And perhaps that's why Lora hopes that Ayc will leave. Marcellus and Wren used Ayc against her. She revealed her weakness to them, and others will see it, too. As one of her Five, Ayc will forever be in danger. But as her *lover*?

Someone would take him from her, and she has felt the pain of his loss once. She cannot survive facing it again.

So she forces herself to say, "That is a very strange dream, indeed."

He stares at her, and though his eyes don't turn red, something burns there. He reaches toward her, and she nearly bolts to the door, but she's plastered onto the stool. His hand cups one of her cheeks, the shape of his palm matching her face perfectly. He drags his thumb over her broad bottom lip—slowly, ever so slowly—to wipe up the chocolate that has spilled there. Every muscle in her body melts at that touch. The fire that she sees in him burns in her own veins. And he's looking at her like he *knows*.

I am so completely fucked.

He places his thumb in his own mouth, sucking the chocolate off, and the action feels like a promise. A promise that stokes an ache within her core. A moan builds in her throat. She swallows it down.

"Maybe," he says, his breath teasing her lips, "we both had the same dream."

She cannot move. She can't even breathe. She thinks he's going to kiss her, and divine help her if he does, because she'll let him. She will let him take her apart, piece by piece, right on this counter.

But he pulls back, smiling like he's won something. "Good night, Lora. You should get some sleep. Long day ahead tomorrow."

Through some great feat of strength, she takes the mug and stumbles to her feet. She forces herself to regain some degree of composure, enough to say, "You'll think about what I said?"

His smile vanishes; the light flicks out in his eyes. He nods.

"Good."

She forces herself to leave, not looking back, though she's aware he marks her every move. As she walks down the hallway, she sips her chocolate—it tastes perfect—and doesn't cry, though she wants to. She tells herself he won't stay, and even if he does, he'll never be hers. She'll find a way to extinguish the fire between them, even if she's left in ashes.

She is Sovereign. She does not have the luxury of hope.

The cold water of the Bellum Sea freezes Ayc down to his very soul, but it doesn't numb the thoughts in his head. As he strokes through the waves, he plays the conversation with Lora over and over in his head. He's certain now that the kiss was real. It's tattooed to his mouth, to his skin, to the roots on his scalp where her fingers tugged. He knew it the moment his thumb connected with the fullness of her lips, and her eyes tinged with silver. It was real. She kissed him. He doesn't understand why, but perhaps some part of her feels *something* toward him.

But it matters little. She denied the kiss, so she must want to forget it happened. And greater still, she tried to send him away.

Tried? Or succeeded?

He tries to picture the paths set before him. If he chooses one path, he will leave in the morning and not come back. He'll take his savings, enough for a month or two of rent, and start a bakery in Silvae. He'd have to sleep on the floor of his shop before he could afford an apartment with a bed, but it'd be worth it to wake every morning, beholden to no one but the loyal customers who delight in his creations. Or perhaps, he follows the call he's heard every time he looks at the water he swims in and returns to Aluina, to the people he left behind. But what good could he actually do on his on?

If he chooses the other path, Ayc will stay and swear allegiance to Lora. He'll follow her into the unknown and serve her and her people. No doubt he would hate some of her decisions, and no doubt others, like her desire to help Aluina, would make him want to bow at her feet in reverence. Staying will mean that Lora will have power over him, though he trusts her with that power now... mostly. After all, she chose to set him free.

Is that what she's trying to do now? Set him free?

He dives deep into the water, pressing his eyes shut against the darkness, trying to tune out everything but the water rushing around him.

When his lungs ache to the point of bursting, he puts his feet beneath him and shoves upward, breaking the surface of the water. He's only chest deep, and he stumbles through the silt toward the shore. He stops as something moves on the beach. He squints through the droplets pouring into his eyes.

"A bit late for a swim!" Bronwen calls.

"A bit late to be spying!" he calls back.

"You flatter yourself. I'm doing blood rituals and catching moonbeams." She raises her arms above her head, waving them eerily.

He snorts.

She drops her arms and says more seriously, "I couldn't sleep."

"That seems to be contagious tonight," he mutters beneath his breath, then raises his voice to say, "Do you want to turn around so I can get out?"

She mocks a gasp. "Ayc, are you naked in there?"

"Yes."

She turns her back, and he returns to shore. A slight stiffness lingers in his muscles; it's not that pain that lived there before, but an echo of it. He wonders how long it will remain, but right now, it's tolerable. He shivers as he quickly dries off with the towel he left draped on a large piece of driftwood and then pulls on his clothes. Bronwen hums quietly to herself. She's dressed in a nightgown with her thick, green cloak pulled over it.

"All right, I'm decent," Ayc says.

"Don't be so harsh on yourself," Bronwen replies as she turns around. "You're more than decent. Perfectly adequate, at the very least."

Ayc chuckles, but the humor dies as he catches sight of Bronwen's face. Despite the lightness in her tone, red rims her eyelids and bits of loose hair cling to her damp cheeks. "You look like you've been crying. Are you all right?"

The smile tumbles from her face. "Not really. Ryker was killed."

Ayc sucks in a breath. "What happened?"

"Lahlis. Or whoever he sent to do his dirty work."

"Fuck." Ayc scrapes a hand over his face as he pictures Ryker with his golden hair and dimples. It's a tragedy that he's no longer in the world. Ayc's stomach twists with sympathy. For Bronwen and Lora and, yes, even for Wylder. Fuck the Drakr, and fuck Marcellus for making the deal that led to that. Ayc hopes eternal torment is real and that Marcellus's soul has found its way there.

"I didn't know," Bronwen continues. "Not until I ran into Wylder a couple hours ago. I suppose Lora knew, and I guess I can forgive her for not saying anything. She's had a lot on her mind since—" Her voice began strong, but it trembles and then breaks. A tear tumbles from her eye and careens down her face. "Fuck, I thought I was all out of tears."

Ayc wraps his arm around her shoulders and leads her toward the path back to Wyntra. "Can I make you some hot chocolate?" Perhaps, it's a weakness to fall back on that method, but sweet things do help to ease a troubled soul.

She sniffs and wipes at her tears with a knuckle. "Only if it has alcohol."

"Done," Ayc agrees. When they reach the cliff, they can no longer walk side by side. He lets her go ahead of him. "Do you want to talk about him?"

"No. Distract me with something else."

"All right. What did the lizard say to the crow?"

"Not like that, silly. Tell me something real."

Something real. Now there's a dangerous thought for someone who is accustomed to living his life surrounded by an abundance of secrets. When he offers nothing, Bronwen suggests, "I know. We could talk about that dragon's egg you have in your oven."

Ayc flinches. Earlier, Xylie assisted him in putting the dragon's egg in his smaller oven. They lit a very small fire, enough to keep the dragon slightly warm like the rocks in the cave. Ayc has no idea if the baby inside will make it, with being carried all the way through Everadyn, but Ayc and Xylie are certainly going to try. That is—if no one finds out and takes the egg from him.

"How did you know?" Ayc asks.

"Tavish looked suspicious, and he can't keep a secret from me."

Ayc cringes again. "Is he going to tell, Lora?"

"Oh no. He was terrified of what I'd do if he *didn't* tell me. But he's more terrified of what Lora would do if she *does* find out. It won't be pretty."

Ayc can imagine. Lora might make every threat she's ever hurled his way seem mild in comparison. But he can finally admit to himself that he *likes* to see her angry, to know he's gotten under her skin. So, he might die, but there's a good chance it'll be worth it.

"So, are you going to tell her?" Ayc asks.

Bronwen throws back her head and laughs. "Absolutely not. This is too much fun. But she will find out you know. It's only a matter of time."

"Will you keep her from murdering me?"

"I shall try my best."

"That's all I ask."

As they walk through the village, they talk in low whispers about nothing in particular and absolutely nothing serious. When they pass Peregrin's house, Ayc catches a glimpse of Irving, Zinnia, and Peregrin through a window, snuggled together on their couch, arms and legs draped casually around each other. Contagious lack of sleep, indeed. Ayc tells himself he'll visit Ember tomorrow, though he doesn't know how to explain why he won't be giving back the leviathan tooth. He retrieved it from where Lora dropped it in the great hall, but it wouldn't feel right handing the boy a murder weapon.

Briefly, he worries that Zinnia and Irving will no longer want Ayc to be around Ember, knowing Ayc is a Drakr. But then, he doubts Peregrin keeps secrets from them, and they've never once hesitated to let Ayc near the most precious thing in their life. Ayc is grateful for the tremendous faith, a testament to their belief in his goodness. He'll lean on it in days he himself forgets.

When they enter the castle, Bronwen and Ayc are laughing at something Ayc is certain is only funny because of their sleep deprivation. The laughter dies when they round the corner of the hallway toward his kitchen and see the unwelcome visitor lingering by Ayc's door. Yris strides toward them, head held high.

562

"Yris," he greets, feigning warmth into his voice, an old habit. "Shouldn't you be packing?"

"I wanted you and I to have one more chat. Privately."

Ayc rolls his eyes. He's in no mood for games. "Whatever you want to say, just say it."

Yris draws herself up. "Very well. I wanted to remind you that you're still not free. You're foolish if you think you are."

"Your curse was broken," Bronwen snaps. Her eyes flare silver in the dark. Power vibrates from her skin. A shadow shifts in the corner of Ayc's vision. A royal guard, hidden just out of sight. Yris is never truly alone.

Yris narrows her eyes but doesn't look at Bronwen. "That's not what I mean. Lora has always had power over you. Do you want to know why I suggested that you be one of her Five?

He locks his jaw and says nothing, but she continues anyway.

"I knew that the only thing that might bring the monster out of you would be protecting her. I saw it all those years ago on the banks of the Ever River when you pulled her from the water. Nothing I've done, or anyone else could do, has ever brought it out again. But *she* could. And she doesn't need a Binding stone to do it." She comes one more step closer and hisses the next words. "She'll always have power over you, because you *love* her."

Ayc snorts. A habit. An instinctual shield. He feels Bronwen studying him, waiting for his reaction. He ignores her and refuses to give anything else away.

"Deny it all you wish," Yris says. "But you've been in love with her since you were children. You know you can never have her, but you'll still worship the ground she walks upon."

"We're done here," Ayc snarls. He storms away, whipping his door open. It should feel freeing to have the power to walk away, but Yris's chortle robs him of the victory. She's dealt him one last blow, a revenge for ruining her plans. As soon as Bronwen enters the kitchen, he slams the door closed to cut off the noise.

"Hot chocolate?" Ayc asks, not glancing Bronwen's way. He doesn't want to see what's written on her face. He rushes back to the stove, pulling out the same ingredients he used for Lora earlier.

Bronwen settles onto one of the stools. The air thickens between them, heavy and laden with unasked questions and answers that have the power to shatter souls. Bronwen says nothing, not until he sets a mug before her. It's two-thirds chocolate and a third spiced rum from an old bottle he found in the corner cabinet. When he makes his own fresh mug of chocolate, he swaps the ratio. The rum blazes down his throat.

Bronwen takes a long sip before setting the mug down. "Remember when I said you looked at Lora like you didn't know whether to kill her or kill *for* her."

He gulps down another swig, knowing where this is going.

"I think you figured it out, Ayc."

"Is it so obvious?" He forces a laugh. "I clearly hate her."

Bronwen drums her fingernails against the side of the mug. "I think that's *partly* true."

He glares into the dark pool of chocolate in his mug. And maybe it's the rum currently warming his body, or maybe it's his poor impulse control getting the better of him again. Or maybe he wants to admit it. Just once.

He exhales and with the long breath comes truth. "I hate

that I've been in love with her since the moment she burst into my life and put her blade to my throat."

"Ah." Bronwen lifts her mug toward him in a salute. "There it is."

"I've loved her even when she was cruel to me. What does that say about me?"

Bronwen sets down the mug. "Maybe, that you were a boy afraid of his own shadow who needed to believe that people can have monsters inside them and still be worth loving."

Ayc fiddles with the clasp of a bracelet, still damp from his swim. He hasn't taken them off nor tried to go invisible with them on to test Lora's theory. He's not ready to be rid of shield they provide, even if it's a fictional one.

"Or more likely," Bronwen adds, "because you've always believed in the goodness she was conditioned to hide."

Ayc sags onto a wooden stool. That one sounds far more honest, but in the end, it doesn't matter why Ayc loved Lora before the Trials began, because now he sees her clearly. Now, he's seen her smile, and he's tasted her lips, and he's glimpsed the heart she hardly ever dares show anyone. Seeing her is like staring into the sun. Beautiful, but it hurts.

It's why he kept up walls for so long, convinced himself she was a villain long after he saw contradictory evidence. Because when walls come down between two enemies, there's only one way for it to end. In total, wretched ruin.

And that's probably why he should leave and never look back. Yris is not wrong. He has done things for Lora he swore he'd never do. He revealed his darkest secret and drew blood without regret or remorse. What else would he be willing to do to protect her, even as he knows she'll never love him back?

He should go. He should definitely leave. He tries to imagine a life outside Wyntra. Without Xylie or Peregrin and their family and Tempest. Without Tavish and Saga and Bronwen. Without Lora.

And he cannot imagine it.

"I suppose you figured out the novel of Lora and I," Ayc says, to get a reprieve from his own head.

Bronwen smiles, twirling a finger around the rim of her mug. "Part of it, but the ending is still unwritten. And I think it will be quite an adventure. I can't wait to read the rest."

And just like that, Ayc decides. Perhaps, because for once, the freedom to choose is *his*, and Lora is the one who gave it to him.

"You know what, Bronwen?" He chuckles. "Neither can I."

THIRTY-EIGHT

- LORA -

Lora's grandmother drapes her in golden leaves she spun herself. The thin lace, light as spiderweb, lays over Lora's arms and the green fabric of her dress. The tiny crystal beads woven within the leaves spark in the candlelight as Lora turns to the mirror to see the full effect.

She supposes she looks like a Totus Omni queen. She chose the green of the dress to represent the Elodie Forest and because its fabric is soft as velvet. The plain, modest piece is made divine by the gold overlay. Yris sent a hairdresser to attend to Lora's hair earlier that morning, and they drew her curls up and pinned it in some design at the back of her head. She looks regal, elegant, and she hardly recognizes herself.

But the golden leaves she adores. They are perfect, reminiscent of the tree-adorned flags that have replaced the Lux Aester banners throughout Wyntra.

"How did you manage to get this done so quickly?" Lora asks, looking at her grandmother's reflection in the mirror.

Hellevi flicks her wrist, like the answer should be obvious. "I began working on it as soon as you told me you intended to compete in the Trials."

Emotion creeps up in Lora's throat; the faith of her grandmother feels like something she doesn't deserve, not when she won in such a deceitful way.

As though sensing her thoughts, Hellevi settles worn hands on her shoulder and steers Lora to face her. "I am proud of you, my darling. Your father will be proud of you, too. I'm certain of it."

The emotion strangles her, and Lora forces herself to breathe through it until she regains control. Undoing her father's exile—and the ones who were exiled with him—was the first order she intended to give as Sovereign. But now, everything feels treacherous. She will have to tread carefully. But she *will* undo it and soon.

A soft knock sounds on her bedroom door. Bronwen sticks her head in, and Lora beckons her with a flick of the wrists. She enters with a bag slung over her shoulder, looking utterly radiant in a burgundy dress that fades to orange at the bottom, like tree leaves in autumn. Her hair has been freed from its braid and hangs down her shoulders in ringlets. Unlike Lora, whose skin feels like it might crawl off her bones, Bronwen looks perfectly at ease in her femininity.

"You look beautiful," Bronwen says as she stops on Lora's other side. "But you also look like you want to come out of your own skin. So let's make you look vicious as well."

She reaches into the bag and pulls out armor similar to what Lora wore as a graduate of Adamant, but more ornate, tipped and swirled in gold. Bronwen helps Lora put it on, careful not to snag the delicate threads of the lace. The leather crisscrosses her chest to protect her heart and ends in buckles around her stomach. Horns curve upward from her shoulder pads and spikes line the wrist cuffs. When Lora inspects herself in the mirror, the image is fierce; striking. Almost right, but not quite. This is how she'll have to face all the people who have flocked to Wyntra, far more than were already there, ready to see her crowned.

Her breath quickens, and panic rises like a volcano erupting within her, suffocating her lungs, clogging her throat. It's been a long time since she's felt like this, since her years training with Peregrin. She tries to breathe like they taught her, but she can't—

"Damn," scoffs a voice from the doorway. "Your hair is absolutely wretched."

Air soars back into her lungs, though she's quite sure her heart has flown out of her chest, flying across the distance between where she stands and where Ayc is leaning casually against the doorframe. She can see him in the mirror, grinning at her. Her heart suddenly reappears in her chest and pounds against her sternum.

Ayc is here, and he, too, is all dressed up, similar to how she's seen him for dozens of performances. His worn brown vest now covers a forest green shirt. He's pulled his hair back with a ribbon and lined his eyes with a smoky black that make his blue eyes stand out even brighter. His rings that he left at home during the Trials have returned to his hands, and his earrings gleam like they've been freshly polished. Handsome is too small a word. He looks devilish, unique and utterly himself.

Lora looks away from his reflection before Bronwen and

Hellevi notice that she's staring at him. "And what exactly is wrong with my hair?" she adds a bite to her tone, facing him.

He peels himself off the doorway and approaches her, and she wonders again how she missed that he wasn't fully human, with the way he glides across the floor. Has he been pretending this whole time or has she just been too afraid to really look at him? "It looks like how your mother does her hair. And I'm not swearing allegiance to your mother today. I'm swearing it to *you*."

He meets her eyes as he says those last words, and she inhales sharply. No doubt blemishes his voice. She told him to leave, and here he is, staying. Which must mean it's because he *wants* to stay.

"He's right, Lora," Hellevi agrees. "You haven't worn your hair back like that in years."

Quite suddenly, as though she needed permission to feel it, Lora becomes aware of the tension on her roots and way the pins scrape against her scalp. She doesn't understand why she even allowed the hairdresser to touch her, except she perhaps felt she needed to look more like a queen, different from herself. But now, she can't stand it. Her hands flutter towards her head.

"Would you like me to undo it?" Bronwen asks.

"Please, and hurry. We only have a few minutes left."

As Bronwen and Hellevi work together to remove the pin, Lora watches Ayc in the mirror. He stands, bouncing to whatever melody only he can hear, spinning in circles as he absorbs the details of her room. Unlike her room in Avia, this room is devoid of much more than the basics: a four-poster bed, a vanity, a wardrobe, this mirror. The only thing within it that Lora truly loves are her loom, her bookshelf, and the oversized chair by the window.

He wanders close to the bookshelf, squinting at the titles. When he reaches out a hand, Lora snaps, "If you touch my books, I'm going to require one of your fingers as payment."

He folds his hands behind his back and spins back around. "Wouldn't dream of it."

Hellevi catches Lora's eye in the mirror and smiles.

When Lora's thick curls flow down her back once more, they are frizzy from the administration of the hairdresser, but it's *her* hair. Then Bronwen wiggles her fingers over Lora's head. Her scalp tingles, as the frizz eases and her curls shine like they do after Lora's intensive biweekly care regiment. Bronwen doesn't often waste energy on such frivolous things, and magic can damage the health of hair if used too frequently, but it's nice for moments like these.

Ayc appears at her side and stretches out his hand. The two clips she always wears, the ones she left on her vanity, sit in his palm. She takes them and carefully places them on either side of her face. This time, when she glances at her reflection, something unhitches in her chest. She might not feel like someone who is prepared to place a crown upon her head, but she, at least, feels like she will be herself.

Ayc's gaze teases like a caress down her spine. She twists her head toward him. There's an emotion in his eyes, one as deep and riotous as the Bellum, and she can't define it. She hopes her own expression is as unreadable. One day, she'll look at him and not remember what it's like to kiss him, to be kissed *by* him like she's something worthy of worship. Someday, she'll stop wanting him, as she should. But today is certainly not that day.

"One more thing," Ayc says. He reaches into his pocket and brings out the leviathan tooth, still on its cord. When Lora nods, he moves behind her and slips it around her neck. It settles onto her armor, just above her heart. The end of the tooth is no longer sharp, but broken and jagged. Lora wonders if it is still in Marcellus's throat.

"To remind you," Ayc says, "of who you really are."

When she stands outside the great hall, alone except for the guards this time, she curls her hand around the tooth and reminds herself of just that. She is not a girl terrified of being everything her mother tried to make her to be.

She is Loraphne, her father's daughter, and she is the most fearsome creature on land or sea.

So she lifts her chin like she already wears a crown and thrusts the door open. She enters the great hall like a lightning strike. Like an unreckonable force. Like the villain her people need.

~ AYC ~

She looks fearsome and beautiful and like every mighty queen from every storybook. And as Ayc watches Lora storm up the aisle between the crowd that fills the great hall, he cannot help but admit, at least to himself, that he loves her. He loves her beauty and her viciousness, her ferocity and her kindness. He loves every vibrant shade that makes her up. His heart is a foolish, hopeless thing, but it has always been hers.

And in this moment, he lets himself love her. Soon, today will be over, and he'll lock all his feelings back inside the wall he's carefully constructed. He'll chain it up next to the vibrations of pain that still linger in his body. He'll go back to pretending, because that's the only way to survive.

Lora sweeps past the crowd who make no sound, only stare in reverence, or curiosity, or even a few in disdain. She doesn't glance over when she passes her Five who stand clustered together near the front. Xylie has joined them, half hidden behind Ayc, her hands covering her ears despite the dampeners she wears. The crowd is much larger than the one she tolerated for Marcellus's ceremony. Lora said she could swear allegiance in private and didn't have to partake in the ceremony, but Xylie wanted to be here. And so she is —squeezing Ayc's elbow so hard it hurts, but here, nonetheless.

Lora comes to a stop at the end of the aisle, looking up the steps to where a single throne stands, its gryphon wings forming the back, its talons gripping the floor. Yris looks stiff as she sits upon it. Her Five gather on either side of her, a motionless wall of support. Between daughter and mother rests a marble podium, bearing a single silver pillow.

Yris stands, her black dress fluttering around her, glistening like stars. A stillness envelops the crowd as she removes the golden circuit on her head. She lays it carefully on the pillow on the podium, and then, without a word, she turns and exits the stage, taking a designated place among the crowd. Her Five follow her. Only Lora stands before the crowd now. She climbs the steps, the leaves on the lace sparking in the light.

She lifts a hand to her mother's abandoned crown. When her fingers brush it, a pulse of power surges through the room, and the crown instantly changes. The gold thickens and bends into a central peak. Black, spiraling vines grow and wind around the gold, sprouting leaves as it climbs toward the center of the crown. Lora sets it upon her head, and it fits her perfectly.

The podium vanishes, allowing Lora to take the last few steps to the throne. She turns, but does not sit, letting her people look upon her. And what a sight she is to behold. Ayc is so busy staring at her that he misses whatever cue must have been given. The rest of her Five assemble before her on the stairs, and he rushes to join them. When they lower themselves to their knees, Ayc doesn't hesitate to join them. Even Saga lowers his head.

Ayc peeks through his lashes, just enough that he can see the emotion that shimmers in Lora's eyes. She blinks hard and clears her throat, and when she speaks, her voice is steady and clear.

"Do you swear to give allegiance to myself as Sovereign, to be my guides and my advisors, and most importantly, to always keep the good of the people of Everadyn at the forefronts of your mind?" Lora asks.

"It is my honor," Bronwen, Peregrin, and Tavish say. Ayc murmurs it after. He's so going to have words for them. Clearly, they practiced this.

Xylie signs her reply.

Saga barks.

Tavish hurries to shush Saga, but a laugh escapes Ayc's lips. A few scattered laughs echo from the crowd, disrupting the solemnity of the moment. Lora's lips tug up on one side before she presses them into an obedient line.

"Rise, my Five," she says, "and serve Everadyn well."

They stand, and Ayc follows the lead of the others as they move to stand at Lora's side, where the previous Five once stood. Xylie hides partially behind the throne, but her breath is still coming easily. Lora lowers herself onto the throne, sitting on the very edge, her back stiff.

Seven people disentangle from the crowd and approach Lora. Ayc recognizes them as the seven regents, the leaders of the Everadyn clans, each wearing the traditional garments of their clan. When they come before Lora, they form a line and bow at the waist. At least, all do, but one.

Amos, regent of Lux Aester, does not bow.

A murmur ripples through the crowd, as the other six send Amos sideways glances.

"I will not bow to the wicked queen," Amos hisses through his teeth.

Ayc stiffens, fighting against the desire to force the man upon his knees. He must not be the only one. Power ripples off Bronwen's skin, and Peregrin's hand flexes near one of the knives they wear across their chest. Ayc's own sword hangs at his hip. As the new Sovereign's Five, the rule of being unarmed in the great hall does not apply to them anymore.

But Lora doesn't tense, as though she anticipated this.

"The laws of the Trials are clear—" The Lycendi regent, an ancient alchemist by the name of Busara, begins.

Amos cuts her off. "She won through villainy!"

"Surely, you won't stand for this," Dedryk—the Noxumbra regent and Wylder's father—says, looking to Lora. "You cannot let him get away with defiance. You must demand loyalty."

"You cannot demand loyalty," Lora says, her voice nothing but calm. "Obedience and loyalty are not the same." She directs her attention to Amos. "I can see that I didn't win your loyalty. But I will *earn* it."

"You won't sit on the throne long enough!" Amos says.

"Is that a threat?" Bronwen snarls, blue light glowing around her fingertips.

Lora lifts her hand to hold Bronwen back and gives Amos a calculated smile. "Perhaps you should be more concerned about your own leadership. You have denied your people liberties that should be theirs by nature. My mother cared more for your friendship and your frequent donations to the royal treasury than for the rights of her own people. I do not share that same sentiment. Straighten out your lands, Amos. Or I'll replace you with someone who can."

The little bit of color that exists in his pale face vanishes. "You don't have that type of power."

"Don't I?" Lora leans back into her throne, crossing one leg over the other. The slit of her skirt parts, revealing an expanse of bare skin from her calf all the way to where she's strapped a dagger to her thigh. She looks as though she was born to sit upon that throne, and the fire in her dark eyes quietly dares anyone to take it from her. The little coil at the end of her lips states she might just enjoy it.

And fuck, if it isn't single-handedly the most alluring thing Ayc has ever seen. Ayc looks away and takes a breath to cool the heat that ripples through him.

But the way her voice purrs her next words only turns the heat to a boil. "Are you willing to bet on it?"

The Lux Aester regent stares at her and then the other six regents. They offer him no aid. Amos gives the smallest bow of his head toward Lora and then storms away. Ayc knows better than to believe this is over. No matter how confident Lora looks, Ayc knows she understands too well. She and her Five had to fight to put her on the throne, and they will have to fight to keep it. It doesn't matter.

The monster within Ayc is done hiding. He's ready for a fight.

The ceremony gives way to partying. There's a feast and dancing, and for once, Ayc is not serving, but an honored guest. The word of his true identity has spread throughout the entire crowd. He can tell when people shy away from him, as he always feared they would, but just as many blatantly flirt with him. Maybe, some people have a thing for monsters.

It doesn't really matter, because Ayc has found his people. The ones who see him and love him anyway.

Zinnia and Ember rush up to him after the ceremony, Ember reaching Ayc first and throwing his arms around him in a hug that takes Ayc's breath away. Ayc catches Peregrin's brief smile as they watch Ayc and Ember together. Tavish lets Ayc pull him through the hall and introduce him to a sweet-looking Sal Maris female, who immediately coos at Saga and sneaks the dog a treat. Only gibberish comes from Tavish's mouth, and Ayc interjects to rescue him, but it's progress.

Ayc fills a plate full of treats and takes them to where Xylie watches everything in the silent hallway, peering through a crack in the side entrance. She tries one and tells him they can't compare to the ones he makes.

Bronwen laughs, her pale hair flying, as Ayc spins her around the dance floor.

They are enough. More than he dared hope. He has them, and in some small way, he has Lora, too.

Throughout the day, Ayc keeps his eyes upon Lora. She

talks politely or poises regally on her new throne or more commonly tries to disappear into the shadows of the hall. Irving trails after her, one hand on his sword. He catches Ayc looking each time and flashes a smile that lets Ayc feel as though it's safe to look away, if only for a time. Irving won't let anything happen to her.

But eventually, Ayc seeks Lora, and she's nowhere to be found.

He finds Bronwen laughing with a gorgeous female with pink skin and a gown that looks like living flames. Bronwen brushes her hand down the fae's arm in a clear indication that neither will be going to bed alone. He stops at a distance, not wanting to interrupt, and waves a hand.

"Lora?" Ayc signs when he catches her eye.

"She went for a walk," Bronwen signs back. No concern registers on her face, and she immediately turns back to the fae.

He knows just where to find Lora.

She stands on the cliff overlooking the Bellum, Irving and a couple of other guards lingering several feet behind. They say nothing as Ayc slips past them to join her on the cliff's edge. The salty air whips at her hair and the gold overlay, but the crown she wears does not slip. She stares out at the gray waters, watching the gnashing waves that stay riotous until they meet the horizon. He knows past that horizon there's a land where he once lived, before a girl burst into his life and changed everything.

There are things that he regrets, blood that cannot be unspilled, pain that lingers as a ghost even now, his heart that's destined to never be whole, and entire people whose suffering he refuses to ignore any longer, now that he has power to do something. But overall, he doesn't regret that he's here now. With her.

"Villainess," he says softly as he comes to her side.

He must imagine the smile that tugs at her mouth at the nickname, but there isn't disdain when she says, "Cinnamon roll. I see you decided to stay."

"That I did."

She studies him in the dim light, the thick clouds above casting shadows on her face. He fears she might ask him why he decided to stay. He doesn't know what lies he'll tell her, or what lies he'll begin to tell himself once today is over and he must go back to pretending he doesn't love her.

"I'll probably make you regret it," she says instead.

He quirks a smile. "Without a doubt." He nods out to the horizon and dares to ask, "What do you think of when you stare out at the sea?"

She looks back to the Bellum. The crash and sighs of the waves fill the space between them. It's millimeters today, instead of miles. "Before, I've mostly thought about all the injustices in this world. I've stewed in guilt over the things that I've done that have empowered those injustices. I've wished for the power to change things."

"But today?"

"Today, I'm trying to decide where to start. There are so many hurts in this world that need healing."

He twists his body to face her. "You can't undo every injustice in a single sweep. You've got a few decades to work on it."

"No." She turns to face him fully. "No more waiting. People have waited long enough. We start tomorrow. The first meeting of the Five is at sunrise. Don't be late."

"Fantastic. I'll bring breakfast." He grins wickedly. "Any requests? I'll make you anything but cinnamon rolls."

"You can make whatever you would like, but it's a shame. I'm quite fond of cinnamon rolls." She smiles, full and unguarded, and he wonders if she knows it too is a weapon. Forget a knife to his throat. Her smile can bring him to his knees.

Wings beat the air above them, loud and swiftly approaching. Ayc and Lora lift their heads toward the sky. Ayc expects to see a gryphon rider or two out on a patrol or practicing maneuvers, but the clouds obscure them from sight. As the sound nears, a warning shudders through him. Something about the sound isn't right. It's too loud.

Too big.

The shape that rips through a cloud above the sea is brilliant red and massive.

"Dragon!" Lora calls.

She grabs his arm and yanks him into a run. Together, they race back from the cliff's edge, trying to get somewhere less exposed. The guards run the opposite direction, toward them, swords in their hands. Metal hisses as Lora draws the knife at her thigh, and Ayc fumbles for his own sword. The wind whips with an unnatural power. The sound of wings descends until it's so loud it nearly punctures his ears.

"Get down!" Irving yells.

Lora flings herself down, pulling Ayc with her. He manages to maneuver his body so that when they fall to the rocky ground, his body covers hers. Something sharp scraps over his back, slicing fabric but not skin, a moment before the earth shakes beneath them like it might split apart.

When Ayc lifts his head, the massive dragon has landed only feet away. Its scales are variants of red, from the deepest of crimson to blood red to a burnt orange. Its mighty wings lift above Ayc and Lora's head, blocking out the little remaining sunlight and casting them completely in shadow. It curls its long head the other direction to snap at the charging guards. When that doesn't halt them, it bellows a roar and unleashes a stream of fire that propels itself toward the guards.

"Irving!" Ayc screams.

The fae flings up his hands and a field of green, large enough to shield the three guards, bursts from his palms. The fire parts around them.

"Stay back!" Lora yells from beneath Ayc. She shoves upward. Ayc rises with her and draws his blade, the two of them standing side by side.

"Come down from there and speak with me!" she calls.

The dragon's wing shifts, and Ayc sees what Lora noticed. The dragon bears a rider.

The cloaked figure who sits at the base of the dragon's neck slides down the dragon's leg, which is as tall as a tree. They land with bent knees and gracefully pull themselves to their full height. Within the shadow of the hood, red eyes burn.

Ayc steps closer to Lora, who lifts her chin, looking like she's ready for a fight. No, like she's ready for *war*.

"I'm sorry I missed your coronation but allow me to offer congratulations now." Ayc recognizes the Drakr's voice immediately, but he wishes he didn't. "All hail, Loraphne, the wicked queen! May your reign be short."

A FINAL WORD FROM THE AUTHOR

Lux Aester is a real place. I've lived there. Maybe you have, too. Maybe, you've seen Marcellus standing at a church pulpit, leading the campfire at church camp, or staring back at you from the television set claiming to be a United States Congressman. Yeah, me too.

I started this book warning that this fantasy book wasn't an escape. The misogyny, homophobia, transphobia, and oppression seen within this book is far from fictional. As I write this, there are 356 active anti-transgender bills being considered in 42 states and the Supreme Court is deciding how close to death a woman must be before she can receive life-saving medical care while experiencing a pregnancy-related emergency. As horrific as Lux Aester may seem, it's very much based on the world we currently live in.

After reading a book where the characters fight against systemic oppression reflective of the real world, you have two choices. You can say "That was a fun read", close the book, and never think about it again. Or you can recognize that our world needs heroes too—or maybe villains, depending on whose lens you're looking through.

If you choose to follow in the footsteps of your favorite characters, here are some few things you can do.

- Educate yourself. This is always the first step. Stay informed about ongoing issues that women, LGBTQ+ and other marginalized communities face.
- Support charities and organizations such as The Trevor Project, which aims to support LGBTQ+ youth and battle against unfair legislation
- Contact your representatives. Their phone number and email is readily available online. Call or write to speak out against unfair legislation and demand equity and justice. I know it can often feel like screaming into the void. SCREAM, anyway.
- VOTE. Government should be BY the people and FOR the people. If the people we elected are not doing what we ask, FIRE THEM.
- Cultivate a character where your LGBTQ+ friends and family will find you to be a safe place. We so desperately need one.
- And lastly, remember to support and promote LGBTQ+ and other marginalized authors. Stories change the world, and their voices deserve to be heard.

Stay villainous, ya'll.
Chanté A. Campbell

Acknowledgments

Community is a beautiful word, isn't it? As I type this, my six-week-old infant asleep on my chest, I cannot help but be amazed by the journey I have been on over the last year as I wrote this book. I certainly could not have accomplished it if it were not for the community that surrounds me. I am so deeply grateful for them.

Firstly, thank you to my book community, particularly my Booktok community. You all inspire me, challenge me, and embrace me. If not for this community, I never would have heard the term cinnamon roll and finally find a name for the type of love interest I've always adored. More importantly, I wouldn't have had the courage to dress up and do the cosplay that resulted in this book. You are a place where I truly feel safe and supported.

Particularly thank you to all the readers who were there through the development of this book:

To my street team, thank you for supporting me when I decided to take a break on my other projects to write this silly little book.

To my alpha readers, Megan, Amanda, Jen, Audrey, and Stephanie, you all were my Five. Thank you for talking me out of my doubt spirals and for reassuring me that, yes actually, I can write spice. Thank you for giving me your valuable opinions whenever I hit another snag in the road. You all were with me every step of the way.

To my beta readers, thank you for your time and your valuable feedback. And mostly critically, thank you for falling in love with the story in its rough form and giving me hope others would, too. I am so grateful to Nero, for taking time out of your busy life to give me your perspective that was greatly needed in this story. To Rizing, for all the text messages demanding book two, literally right after you finished reading it. To Rikki, who caught so many logical issues and helped me resolve them. To Jaime, for offering me valuable feedback as someone who also knows the burden of chronic pain. To Janae, for giving me really critical feedback and also for leaving the BEST reaction comments (one even complete with picture!). To my fellow authors, Selys and Kay, for gifting this book your writer's eyes.

To Moss, my sensitivity reader: Thank you for helping to ensure this book is sensitive to the readers who may encounter it. The education you do for your clients and on your TikTok is so valuable. You have made me a better, kinder writer... and a better person.

To Kelsey, my copy editor, for looking this over. I was a little mad at you for making me tweak my ending, but you were right, of course!

And to all the proofreaders who read it (and reread it) to make sure it was as clean as possible. Thank you!

This book would not exist without each and every one of you.

Secondly, I would like to thank the part of my community that though, were not involved on the development of the book, supported me the entire way.

A huge thanks to my cinnamon roll, my husband Rob,

for always supporting my dreams. Thank you for sharing my obsessions with dinosaurs (the love of fossils certainly made it's way into this story in an unlikely way). And most importantly, thank you for always trying to make me laugh with your silly antics (even when I want to punch you). Ya'll, I have a *type*.

To my boys, for no more reason than you are the light of my life. This is the fourth book I've written and published, and you are still the best things I've ever made. But particularly to my youngest. Thanks for the morning sickness and severe fatigue. Being unable to get off the couch certainly gave me some writing time, haha. And no, neither of you will be reading this book until you're 18. Or never. I am also okay with never.

To my physical therapist, who helped me survive the chronic pain flare I had during the time I wrote this. In the five years I've been your patient, you've taught me a lot about surviving with chronic pain and having grace with my body. There should be more people in medicine like you.

To all the friends who support my writing enough to ask and encourage me, but more importantly, have taught me what it's like to have friends truly see you and love you anyway. Molly, Audj, and Elise, friends like you don't come around everyday. Thank you for seeing me.

And lastly, I want to thank **me**, for taking everything (my ADHD, my autism, my chronic pain, my trauma, my queerness, my hopes, my fears) and daring to create this story out of it. Whatever becomes of this book, I am proud of what I've written. And in the end, that's what matters most.

Anyone want to go get a cinnamon roll?

ABOUT THE AUTHOR

Chanté A. Campbell (pronouns she/they) calls home wherever the RV is parked. When not writing their next novel or working as a nurse practitioner, Campbell enjoys adventuring with her husband, two children, and two dogs. She believes the random side quests are the best part of life. *Cinnamon Rolls and Villainy* is their adult debut. Their previous young adult novels can be found under the penname C. A. Campbell.

https://linktr.ee/cacampbellwriter

Printed in Dunstable, United Kingdom

67478182R00343